CAPTAIN'S SHARE

ISBN-10: 1-940575-04-4
ISBN-13: 978-1-940575-04-9

First Printing: August, 2013
Second Printing: December, 2014

For more information or to leave a comment about this book,
please visit us on the web at:
www.solarclipper.com

Publishers Note:

To my grandfather, Owen Wallace.

I inherited his eyebrows
and his fascination with technology.

He worked for NASA before it was NASA
and was the first of us to reach for the stars.
He won't be the last.

The Golden Age of the Solar Clipper

Quarter Share
Half Share
Full Share
Double Share
Captains Share
Owners Share

South Coast
Cape Grace*

Tanyth Fairport Adventures

Ravenwood
Zypherias Call
The Hermit Of Lammas Wood

* Forthcoming

CAPTAIN'S SHARE

NATHAN LOWELL

Durandus

CHAPTER ONE
DIURNIA ORBITAL: 2371-AUGUST-22

It is a truth universally acknowledged that a single man in possession of good fortune must be in want of a wife. However, a man of good fortune, in the company of a wife, may find himself questioning that truth–or at least its universality. With those dark thoughts and dire portents I collected my kit, gathered my fortitude, and prepared to get underway once more.

"Ishmael," she said, with a wheedle in her voice, "when are you going to stop this gallivanting around the quadrant and actually get a real job and settle down?"

Every time she asked me that question, it was a fresh cut. Every time a synaptic overload put a lock on my brain which my mouth couldn't overcome. Just as well. All the things I thought of later were mostly negative and not terribly helpful.

"Jen..." I began, but there was nothing behind it. I only shook my head in silence.

"Jen, what?" she said. "You've got nothing to say?"

"You knew what I was when you married me." It was feeble but all I could bring together.

"Ishmael, dear..." She pushed it hard and I braced for it. "That was what? Seven stanyers ago? You're still doing the same job for the same company and you're never at home!"

She was right about the time, and the company. "I made it up to first mate. That's not like the same job I started with."

She made a little "pfft" noise with her lips. "You're still sailing off for months at a time. I get to see you a few days when you're here and then you're off again."

"It's my job, Jen. It's what I do." I could hear the defensive whine in my own voice, but I couldn't stop it.

She shifted gears on me, maybe smelling weakness, and turned hard. "So, why did you get married, huh? Just to have a cheap place to stay in port? Did you think we'd just go on like this? You going out there and flyin' around and me back here pullin' pints and sloppin' burgers?"

I looked around our little crew quarters. Station living arrangements ran a bit on the close side. Not as close as shipboard but certainly not as spacious as living planetside. "Well, I've told you repeatedly that living up here is entirely up to you. If you want to live below, then go ahead." I recognized this as a dodge, and she didn't even bother to block it.

"And do what? Find a job in a bar down there?"

"I don't know. What do you want to do?"

"Well, I'd like to live with my husband." She bit the words off.

My tablet bipped to remind me I needed to be aboard. I grabbed my kit bag and looked to where she sat behind the dinette table, arms crossed over her stomach and glower on her face. "See you in a few weeks."

The door didn't close fast enough behind me to block off her response. "Bastard."

Every time I got underway again it was the same. Every time it got ugly. Every time my brain locked down. And every time I knew she was right, but I had no answer.

Why *did* we get married?

The cold bite of dock air snapped me out of my funk and I started thinking about what had to happen by 1300 to get underway on schedule. Six stans. Should be enough time and gods knew I'd done it often enough over the stanyers.

Still, each time we pushed back, there was a chance we'd not dock again. Each time was new in a way that made everything else somehow less. Each time was both awful and awe-inspiring at once. I sighed and stepped smartly down the dock. First mates didn't linger. Even married ones.

Stepping aboard the *Tinker,* I felt the station and all the things associated with it slough away, as if the closing lock severed the ties. It was not that all the trials and tribulations of home port went away. They simply ceased to hold sway. I could do nothing about them while underway, and even though the ship was still docked, mentally, I had already sailed for Breakall.

I smiled to see Able Spacer Dagostino on the brow. "How you holding up on brow watch, Ms. Dagostino?"

"Welcome aboard, sar. Just fine. It's as boring as they said it would be, but at least I'm the one callin' the messengers." She gave me a broad grin.

It was a standing point of contention on the brow. Messengers of the watch thought the watch standers had it easy until they got promoted to the post themselves. They soon appreciated just how deadly dull sitting there for twelve stans at a time could be.

I chuckled a little under my breath, remembering my first brow watch. "Yes, well, just remember the little people on your meteoric rise to fame and power, Ms. Dagostino."

She laughed in reply. "Aye, sar, but I'm pretty sure meteors don't rise, sar. They fall. That's what makes them meteors and not asteroids."

"Makes you wonder where the phrase came from, doesn't it, Ms. Dagostino?"

"Yes, sar, it surely does, but I'll leave such idle speculation to my betters and superiors, sar." Her eyes danced with humor and I confess I felt a little stab of immodest pride in thinking that when I'd first joined the *Tinker's* crew over a decade before, that grin wouldn't have been there.

Of course, Dagostino herself wouldn't have been there. She couldn't have been more than twenty-five. That sobering thought punctured my small bubble of hubris and left me feeling old. I kicked myself mentally. Thirty-eight was not old, although sometimes I felt it. I wondered how old I'd feel at sixty-eight.

"Thank you for your kindness to your elders, Ms. Dagostino. I'll make a mark in your record on the plus column."

"Oh, thank you, sar," she said as she registered my current mass allotment.

The "plus column" was another standing joke among the crew. While the *Tinker* did have records on all the crew–the Confederated Planets Joint Committee on Trade required every ship to keep good records–there was no plus and minus tally. One serious "minus" aboard, and nobody's tally would mean much. Good behavior wasn't a luxury in the Deep Dark–it was a survival trait–and the unit of interest was the ship, not just an individual crew member.

I started down the passage to drop off my kit when she stopped me. "Captain's compliments, sar, and would you join her in the cabin when you've stowed your bag?"

I turned to look and she was looking at the brow's terminal. The skipper must have seen me check in and sent a summons. She was a stickler for form, our Fredi, and I loved her for it. "Of course, Ms. Dagostino. My regards to the captain and I'll be with her in three ticks."

"You do know you two could talk to each other directly on your tablets, don't you, sar?" she asked after hitting the acknowledge and reply button. She looked up at me with her cheeky grin restored.

"Why, Ms. Dagostino! You come up with the strangest ideas at times." I heard her chuckling as I rounded the corner at the end of the passageway and started toward the ladder up to officer country.

Of course, we knew, and we did. Often. But there were times that the captain wanted the crew to know that she and the first mate worked from a common understanding that grew from a frequent and widely noised about series of meetings. Frederica DeGrut was no slouch when it came to managing the ship. I only hoped I had half her skill and panache when it became my time to sit in the cabin.

It was the work of a moment to drop my kit into my locker and knock on the cabin's door frame, since Fredi had the door propped open. "Good morning, Captain."

She smiled up at me from her seat at the small conference table. "Hello, Ishmael. Come in, and close that door behind you, if you would?"

I didn't read too much into the request to close the door. After nearly ten stanyers of sailing with the woman, I'd learned more than a few things. This was one of them. I'd come to the conclusion that she did it randomly so that the crew couldn't jump to conclusions about the nature of the conversations occurring within. Sometimes they were serious. Sometimes Fredi just wanted to talk about the little nothings that were really the everythings aboard a solar clipper. She made it a habit to keep the door open when in the cabin alone, unless she was asleep or trying to write reports. She liked feeling the flow of the ship, she'd told me once. But that left the issue of when to close the door when something serious was happening, and how to do it without telegraphing it to the crew. Her solution was to randomly close the door when in conference. Or at least, so I imagined. I never did ask her about it.

She poured me a coffee from the carafe on the table as I took my accustomed seat on her right hand. I felt her looking at me in that intensely birdlike way she has. At nearly seventy, she was just reaching late middle age for spacers. She wore her gunmetal-colored hair cropped, like the rest of us. Her laugh-lines were more pronounced than I remembered from my first days aboard when she had been the chief cargo officer.

But she wasn't laughing.

I glanced at her over the rim of my cup while she studied me. She wasn't laughing but she wasn't angry either. She looked sad.

"So, why *did* you get married, Ishmael?" she asked, breaking the silence after almost a full tick.

She smiled, not unkindly, at my shocked look.

"Don't be so surprised." She patted my forearm. "I've known

you for ten stanyers, Ishmael. I've seen you grow from a startlingly precocious boot third to a terrifyingly competent first mate."

I wasn't comfortable with compliments. I started to demur but she stopped me with a "tsk" and a sharp pat on the arm. "Don't interrupt your captain. It's bad manners." She said it with a grin and a twinkle in her eye.

She settled back into her chair, cradling her cup in both hands just below her chin. "As I was saying. I've known you for ten stanyers and for the last five of those, you've been coming back to the ship like a whipped dog every time we're in home port."

She had me.

I leaned forward on the table and stared down into my cup. "That obvious?"

She wrinkled her nose a little and gave a little shake of her head. "Not obvious. You mask it well, but I recognize the signs."

The bitterness in that last statement took me by surprise a bit. "Voice of experience?" I asked.

She made a non-committal nod and shrug. "Something like that." She sipped her coffee and waited, her sharp eyes watching me over the rim of her mug.

"I don't know," I told her. It wasn't much of an answer but it was real.

She chuckled. "It seemed like the thing to do at the time..." she let the statement trickle off at the end.

"Yeah, well. At the time, it seemed like that was what grown-ups did. Got married, settled down, had kids. It seemed like it was something I was supposed to do. I'd known Jen for a couple of stanyers and we always hit it off like gang busters when I was in port."

"So you got married, but you didn't settle down," she prompted me after a half a tick.

"Well, I did, really."

"Really?" she asked with that snarky little lilt at the end.

"Well, it felt like it. I could have taken other jobs. Gone to other companies. And it's not like there aren't plenty of opportunities for–" I stopped cold, realizing where that statement was going.

"Advancement?" she suggested with a smirk.

"Yes, okay, advancement."

We both knew that wasn't what I was talking about, but she also knew I wasn't tom-catting around. Some officers might have had a lover in every port, but I wasn't one of them. Not that I wasn't tempted often enough. I just didn't.

We sipped for a few ticks but she wasn't done with me. "So, you think you've settled down, but Jen thinks you're still a spacer and you'll never settle down because what you mean by settle down and what she means by settle down aren't even in the same system."

All I could do was sigh and nod.

She gave a little sideways nod and a kindly smile. "So the question of why you got married isn't really important, is it?"

I gave my head a little shake. "No. It's not. The question is how am I gonna deal with it now?"

"Good." She said it a bit sadly and with a small sigh. "I was afraid I was going to have to explain it to you."

I realized that I'd known that for a long time. Admitting it didn't make it any easier. It might be the first step to solving the problem, but it still looked like a long road ahead.

She didn't let me stew on it, though. We both knew there would be plenty of time for stewing on the long voyage out to Breakall and back.

"Good," she said again, more forcefully. and her tone shifted to business. We started tracking through the thousand and one details that we needed to cover before the crew reported aboard and the ship pushed back from the orbital.

Chapter Two
Breakall System: 2371-September-24

The jump into Breakall wasn't exceptional. Ms. Behr hit the Burleson limit dead on and we slipped in without a hiccup. The ship secured from navigation stations just before the watch change at 0600 and first section took the duty. Since I was the OD for first section, that meant I got to settle in with a fresh cup of coffee while the messenger of the watch brought my breakfast tray from the galley.

It's funny how old habits die so hard. Almost eight stanyers since I'd been systems officer and I still reviewed incoming traffic logs when I was on watch. Being first mate had its own load to haul but part of that load involved making sure the ship stayed safe. In the Deep Dark extra eyes sometimes meant living to get to port.

That's how I happened to spot the HazNav notice in the incoming traffic queue. We got a fresh load of data at each jump, picking up a packet from wherever we'd been and trading it wherever we went, for updated news of the system. A few light-days out from the primary, the data on the buoy was relatively fresh and it would only get fresher as we moved inward. Usually, that incoming packet was nothing to beam home about. It held some limited price and cargo data, some news and sports scores. We had to have the sports scores. I suspected the betting pool in engineering berthing of tapping the feed directly but so long as the wagering was fair, there wasn't any reason for me to interfere.

That particular packet carried a high priority flag and that wasn't usual. Our current third, a competent and slightly crazy individual named Julianna Kazyanenko, scampered up the ladder to the bridge even before the packet finished its load up.

She grinned at me as she slipped into the systems' console. "You readin' my mail again, Ishmael?"

"That's 'Mr. Wang' to you when I'm on duty, Ms. Kazyanenko!" I tried to growl and look fierce.

"And who are you when you're ta home, then?" she shot back. She wasn't really paying attention to me. An excellent systems and comms officer, her focus was already deep in the machine.

Mark Clemming had the helm and he stared straight ahead. I could just see his face from where I sat. I looked across the bridge to where Kaz was ripping the data packet apart to extract the HazNav notice.

"So you *were* reading my mail." Her attention was still riveted on the message traffic. "It's not far from our track."

I'd already keyed the course plot into the big display above my own station and saw we'd be moving within a few thousand kilometers of the hazard. That was unusual enough that I sent a copy to the skipper and another to the astrogator.

HazNav–Hazard to Navigation–notices were not unusual. They were part of doing business in the Deep Dark. Sometimes things got a little cosmic out there and ships needed to know about the odd rock, extra stellar ejecta, or dropped baggage. Most things were just part of the equation–stuff you don't think about because the systems all deal with it routinely. Between the shielding created by the sails and the simple expedient of steering around the obstacle, most HazNav notices had advice about avoiding planets, missing moons, and generally not being stupid while navigating a cargo hauler.

That HazNav notice was different. The location and course of the hazard is coded in the header, but the specific nature of the hazard is usually buried in the comment notes. Kaz and I saw the comment at the same time.

She swore.

I bipped the captain.

This wasn't the normal stray rock or lost bag.

It was a ship.

The captain bounded up the ladder to the bridge and leaned down to read over my shoulder. I leaned back to give her a look at my screen.

"What do we have here, Mr. Wang?" She straightened and looked out the bridge window as if to try to see it, although we were still two or three days out.

"Haz Nav warning came through a few ticks ago, Captain. Ship is running ballistic, and apparently abandoned."

"We can't be the first ones through here. Any indication of who it is and how long she's been there?"

I looked to Kaz who shook her head. "Not much on the HazNav record, Captain. Originally reported by the *Billi Baddings*, a tractor out of Gamblin, four days ago. Derelict is the *Chernyakova*, a Barbell like us, out of Greenfield, but no notes on the circumstances of that report."

Fredi looked thoughtful, crossing her arms across her chest and pulling at her lower lip with her fingers as she stared off in the direction of the derelict. "Greenfield is a bit out of the way, don't you think, Ms. Kazyanenko?"

Kaz looked at the tank that held a three dimensional representation of the sector. A few clicks on her keyboard and the display zoomed back. She made a couple more clicks and a system pulsed. We all focused on the display.

"She could have been making the loop," Kaz said.

A string of systems looped around from Diurnia, out and down, and back and up–like a series of beads on an irregular string.

Fredi looked at it for a long moment. "That's an awfully long trip for a Barbell," she muttered.

The Unwin Barbell design hulls were common in the quadrant. They were basic 'one can' design bulk haulers. They had the advantage of a single cargo pod–the one can–that was completely isolated while underway. The container slipped in between the forward and after nacelles, where it locked against the spine. Once locked into place, the hull blocked the container's loading ports, located in either end. The contents were effectively sealed in until that can was delivered to the destination port and unmounted from the ship.

They also could not get underway *without* a can because the stresses on the bare spine would separate the navigational systems in the bow from the propulsion generators in the stern. The can itself provided stability to the backbone by locking the fore and aft nacelles tightly against itself. With no can, the ship amounted to two bricks on a straw.

"Ms. Kazyanenko, please plot a rendezvous course with the *Chernyakova*. See what that does to our transit time to Breakall Orbital, if you please?"

"Aye, aye, Captain. I'll have the breakdown for you in a couple of ticks."

"Thank you, Ms. Kazyanenko." The captain turned to me and asked, "Any ideas?"

"Anything I've got is speculation, Skipper."

"Yes, Mr. Wang. That's what I'd like to hear. Your speculations on what might be out there."

"The can is the weakness," I said with a shrug. "If she lost her can, there's not much else to do."

"Why didn't the *Baddings* tow her?"

"Maybe she was full up," I said. "Although an unloaded Barbell, wouldn't be that much of a load for a tractor like that."

"Unless she wasn't unloaded," the captain said.

"True, but if the can's still there, why abandon her?" I asked. "And why isn't the place swarming with operators looking to cash in on the salvage rights?"

Her idle smile turned a bit shark-like at that and a sharp little twinkle lit her eyes. "Maybe we just haven't arrived yet."

Chapter Three
Breakall System: 2371-September-27

It took us three days to close the gap on the derelict freighter. Kaz used the time to find out what there was to know about the ship and the crew. It wasn't much. The *Billi Baddings* had come across it drifting on a ballistic course, more or less stable, but without sails or keel extended. The *Baddings* had carried a full load and, judging from the rather terse statements from her captain, perhaps a bit more than they should have. Going alongside, or even doing much more than taking evasive action was beyond the tractor's capability. The reports were sparse, but while the can was still there, there was no sign of crew and no response to hailing.

We went to navigation stations just after 0800. We saw the hull in the distance. We were that close to it. Ms. Behr had done a bang up job of laying our track right along side theirs so we held station about five kilometers astern.

"How stable is her track, Ms. Behr?" the captain asked as we stood gazing out the armor glass.

"Track is stable as ballistic can make it. There's a slight wobble on her but she's not spinning, and you can see she's laying more or less steady. No pinwheel that I've been able to detect."

"Any response to hail, Ms. Kazyanenko?"

"No, Captain. Only automated signals and none of those are distress. Just ID beacons and proximity radars."

The captain frowned. "Then they have power." She turned to the engineering chief officer, Amela Menas, who was running her own scans from the engineering terminal at the side of the bridge. "Mel? Anything you can add to this puzzle before we commit any more resources to solving it."

"She's got power. I'm seeing one hot reactor in her engineering spaces. There should be at least one more, I'd have thought." Chief Menas was thinking out loud for all of us to hear. She didn't look up from her screens and her voice sounded as if she were far away. "No sails. No keel. Heat signatures look normal. Mostly."

"Mostly?" the captain asked.

"The can is a little warmer than I'd have expected. Not much and it might just be errors in the instruments. Might be something that's in it keeping it half a degree warmer."

We'd all seen that happen before as well. The cans got loaded at the cargo terminals. They normally carried only bulk items that wouldn't be damaged by the cold of the Deep Dark. The containers themselves consisted of little more than bare metal buckets with hatches on the ends. They were cans in a literal sense. But some cargoes didn't do well in that extreme cold so some cans had a little extra insulation in them and a low yield heater–just enough to keep a bit of warmth in the can. In the Deep Dark, refrigeration was seldom a problem. Warmth was.

"So, where's the crew?" the captain mused.

"Life rafts are still in their pods, Skipper," Ms. Behr said. "At least the doors are closed. If they left that way, the pods would be open."

That was the point where we all had the same, unsettling thought. I, for one, had been trying not to think it. If the crew hadn't left, then they'd still be aboard. If they were aboard and not answering the hail, then the prognosis was grave indeed.

The captain took a deep breath and let it out. "There's no help for it, I guess. We're gonna have to go over and knock on the door."

Chief Menas blew out a noisy breath, her eyes locked on her console's display. "I hoped it wouldn't come to this, but I think you're right, Captain. The ship's launch is prepped. Ulla's in the pilot seat running the checklist now. Who do you wanna send with her?"

The captain scanned the bridge, as if she hadn't already made up her mind. "Ishmael, sign me onto your watch. I relieve you. Get into a softsuit and run over there with her."

I expected that much. I had gotten my softsuit qualification when I made first mate. It meant I could put on the soft-fabric 'goin' outside for a walk' suit and be pretty confident that I'd be able to come back in alive. Going outside wasn't really something that we needed to do a lot as Deck officers. The Engineering crew had three ratings qualified on 'hardsuits'–more armored exoskeleton than suit–and they handled most of the outside work that needed doing.

Sending me in the softsuit meant she wanted me, probably literally, to knock on the door.

"Aye, aye, Captain. You have the watch." I typed the few commands needed to pass over the formal watch stander title to the captain and headed aft to Engineering.

Half a stan later, Ulla Nart eased the ship's launch off the lock downs and out of its little pocket hanger in the aft nacelle. The boat wasn't used much, but when we needed to go short distances in local space, it was indispensable. The regs classified it as safety equipment but it was a capable small craft.

"What do you think we'll find, Mr. Wang?" Ulla asked. She was focused on her flying and her brain was engaged there, but the stress of flying over to what we all thought was probably a huge tomb had her talking without thinking.

"I'm pretty sure we'll find an Unwin Barbell class cargo hauler, Ms. Nart," I said.

She snorted in amusement. "Judging from the looks," she nodded at the rapidly closing hull, "I think you may be right, sar."

We approached from the stern and passed along the port quarter. I looked out the starboard side of the boat and tried to get a look at the engines as we slipped past. It was too dark back there to see much. The ambient light from Breakall's primary didn't provide that much illumination and the hull was angled away. Black shadows provided little information.

"Easy does it, Ms. Nart," I said. "I'd like to get a good look at the ship's skin."

"Easy does it, aye, sar," she said. The huge hull seemed to scrape by just outside the armor glass. We didn't want to get close enough to leave paint or other valuable parts of our launch bruised onto the pitted surface.

I didn't really know what I was looking for. I was still trying to figure out how this thing could be happening at all. Twenty billion credits of freighter didn't just fly itself through the Deep Dark, and these vessels carried a lot of safeguards built into them. Why, then, was this great beast doing a good impression of a modern-day *Flying Dutchman*?

"Talk to me, Ishmael." The captain's voice came over my suit comm.

"Nothing to see here, Skipper. Hull is clear. No sign of puncture or fire damage. Mostly it's just the can's skin. Nothing stood out when we came by the stern. Nothing obvious on what I can see of the spine."

Ulla knew her flying business and we settled into a position with zero delta velocity relative to the hull and just outside the *Chernyakova's* port bridge wing. I layered on an optical magnifier and scanned the dark glass. I could just make out the flickering of bridge readouts and displays. I couldn't see well enough to know what they were showing, but the flicker and glow was bright enough to show in the shadowy emptiness of the bridge.

"The bridge lights are off, but the displays appear to be active, Captain. I can't see what they're displaying but they're on and displaying something."

"Any signs of alerts or a warnings?" Mel's voice sounded calm on the channel.

"Not that I can see. No red or white strobing lights. Nothing that looks like a flashing screen that I can see from this angle. Just looks like a quiet day on the bridge."

The captain added, "Except with no people?"

I looked closely, trying to see if there were any moving shadows, any silhouettes moving between me and the light sources inside the bridge. "Correct, Captain. No people."

"Ms. Nart?" the captain's voice came over the launch radio. "Maneuver onto the top of the bridge and see if you can engage a locking clamp, if you would?"

"Aye, aye, Captain." Ulla bit her lip and moved us ever so gently up and over the bridge. The ship's wobble was apparent from this range. We couldn't get too close to it without running the risk of a bump.

The locking clamp was a sort of magnet that held the launch down to a deck. The bridge roof wasn't one of the approved strong points but if Ulla could get the magnet locked down, we could reel ourselves onto the top of the bridge and ride the wobbling hull.

Ulla used a joystick controller to maneuver the locking clamp closer to the ship but we weren't quite close enough to engage the bridge roof. She looked at me and gave a dry swallow. "We'll need to be closer, sar. Please check your belt. This could get bumpy."

With one hand holding the clamp's joy stick, she nudged thrusters with the other and we slipped another couple of meters closer to the wobbling freighter. It was nerve-wracking, drifting slowly, slowly, slowly down toward the behemoth under us, not really knowing if the hull would suddenly take a bad jink and slam up under our feet.

Without warning the launch dropped a solid two meters very fast, and I could almost hear the "chunk" sound as the locking clamp engaged . Suddenly we were riding a bobbing, weaving deck that almost seemed to have a life of its own.

Nart retracted the cable, which had the effect of pulling us down to the hull, and with a delicate touch, she fired off two more clamps from the middle and stern of the launch. It didn't take long before we were nailed down and riding on the back of the dinosaur. I wasn't sure I could stand up with all the motion on the ship, but after a few steps, it became almost second nature.

I headed for the launch's little airlock aft. "We're locked down, Captain," I said on my suit comm. "I'm heading down to knock on the door."

The helmet sealed around my ears and left me breathing too close to my face but breathing was the point, so I didn't complain. A positive suit pressure test proved I had no open gaps in my gear and I started the small personnel lock through its cycle.

No matter how many times I cycled through a vacuum backed airlock, the effect of having the world go from normal to silent was always a bit disturbing. I could hear my body and the radio, and even the small machinery that made up the integrated life support system of the softsuit, but outside went from background noise to nothing. The outer door popped open. I felt the small click through the soles of my boots, but I didn't hear a thing.

Protocol called for me to clip a safety line to the D-ring mounted just outside the airlock. If something happened, Nart could reel me in. I stepped out and pushed myself down to the weaving deck before shuffling to the back of the bridge. I got down on my belly and hoped that the bobbing and weaving hull wouldn't throw me off. I leaned down over the edge and took my first direct look into the back of the bridge, upside down and all. I lay there for a few ticks, letting my eyes adjust to the light levels inside and watching for shadows.

One screen on the bridge was solid red. It took me a moment from my upside down perspective to see which one it was–Environmental. As my eyes adjusted to the view, I saw shapes–one on the deck near the OD's station. Another at the helm station. They weren't moving. Judging from the wet looking outline gleaming around the shape on the deck, they weren't going to.

"Captain, I don't think they're going to be opening the door for us."

I heard her sigh. "Thank you, Mr. Wang. Grab some images and get back here. We'll file a report."

Chapter Four
Breakall System: 2371-September-28

"Very well, ladies and gentleman," the captain said, "what we know is sparse. What we have is a tragedy. We don't know what kind of catastrophic failure they've had and we'll need to be careful going in. For the record," and she nodded to the log recorder on the table in front of us, "I have filed a formal salvage claim against the derelict vessel *Chernyakova* now lying three kilometers off our starboard bow. That claim has been acknowledged pending CPJCT validation, when and if we reach Breakall orbital. The authorities have been notified as to the condition of the ship. They already have a packet en-route with a forensics team. It won't be here for another ten days, but we have been granted clearance to enter the hull pursuant to our claim of salvage."

She paused then and looked around at us. There was a strong sense of 'it-could-have-been-us' around the table. The simple fact that the ship across the way was a Barbell, just like the *Tinker*, re-enforced that feeling. Having been through one near calamitous environmental failure underway myself, I was only too aware of how fragile the ships really were. Around the universe, clippers sailed trillions of kilometers every day, and while the safety record for the big ships was actually better than planet-side pedestrian travel, periodically one got lost or destroyed close enough to you that it mattered.

"Ms. Kazyanenko reports that there has been no response to hail, no distress call, and no sign of electronic emission since we've been here over the last twenty-four standard hours. Mr. Wang's physical exploration of the bridge through the glass revealed no signs of life. The ship has been designated as abandoned under the Joint Committee rules, pending discovery of any living person aboard."

She paused again to let that sink in. There was a possibility that somebody might be aboard, but too injured to get to the bridge. If that person were a member of the crew, then the ship's status would depend on a Joint Committee hearing and our salvage claim went up for grabs. We stood to make a lot of money if we actually managed to pull off the salvage. We might lose a lot of money by delaying our cargo delivery at Breakall.

Fredi took a deep breath and let it out slowly. "Our options are to sail on, to stand by and await the authorities, or to try to board the vessel and consummate the salvage claim."

We all knew that there might be somebody aboard over there who needed help. We also knew that the twenty-four stans we'd been sitting off their port quarter represented one standard day of pain and suffering to anybody who might be still there. CPJCT regulations required us to wait that long before we could attempt to break into the ship on our own. We were rolling the dice with other people's lives, but the Joint Committee had to protect a variety of interests and, in the light of the evidence, we had no probable cause for suspecting any ongoing emergency condition.

"Is your boarding team ready, Chief Engineer?" Fredi turned to look Mel in the eye.

"Aye, Captain. Hardsuits and tool kits. Let the record show that I have assigned Spec One Power Sondra Strauss and Machinist Christopher Marks to attempt to key the emergency lock on the after nacelle."

"Thank you, Chief Engineer." She turned to me. "Mr. Wang, I formally charge you with command of the salvage team in the name of Diurnia Salvage and Transport under the authority granted me by virtue of being captain of this vessel, and the long-standing rules and regulations of deep space salvage as outlined in the Confederated Planets Joint Committee on Trade, Title Twelve, Section Seven. Do you understand your rights and responsibilities under that charge?"

"I do, Captain."

"And do you agree to accept this charge?"

"I do, Captain."

"Very well, Mr. Wang. Please state for the record your intentions."

"As soon as is practically and legally feasible, I will convene a team consisting of the engineering crewmen previously named by Chief Engineer Menas along with Able Spacer Martin Udan and Spacer Apprentice James Belnus. We will use the ship's launch to navigate to the emergency access lock in the engineering section of the *Chernyakova*. Assuming that the engineering team is successful in gaining access to the ship, my team will establish operational control of the vessel, stabilize its attitude and attempt to restore steerage way using ship's engines, navigational thrusters and any other appropriate ship's systems that might be available. We intend to render aid and assistance to any individuals found aboard, or failing to locate any living members of the crew, to consummate a good-faith claim of salvage in the name of Diurnia Salvage and Transport in as much as we are able to ascertain our legal standing with the information and understanding we currently possess."

I rattled it off pretty smoothly. It sounded like I knew what I was doing, but the truth was that Mel, Fredi, and I had banged the whole thing out over dinner in the wardroom the previous evening. I actually read the points off my tablet to make sure I had all the correct legal bandiflage needed to cover our collective stern quarters from any charges of breaking and entering or piracy in deep space by trying to take over a ship that, technically, wasn't ours to mess with.

"Thank you, Mr. Wang. You have my authority as captain to carry out your mission as outlined and ratified by this board consisting of the senior officers present in the area with names and ranks appended to the log record. This meeting is adjourned."

She reached out and clicked the recorder off before looking around the table. "Now, we wait."

Chapter Five
Breakall System: 2371-September-28

The launch felt a bit crowded with the six of us. The two engineering crew just locked their hardsuits to the decking along the center aisle. I was back in the softsuit but Udan and Belnus wore only emergency ship suits with extra air packs. The plan was for the engineers to cross first and establish a line connection. They wouldn't open the lock until I was there as senior officer. The access would then technically be under my direct supervision and responsibility, thereby serving the legal niceties. It seemed an awkward dance, but with that much money–to say nothing of the legal liabilities should things go wonky on us–everybody followed the forms down to the letter.

Ulla remained quiet on the trip over. With the extra hardsuits and tools aboard, the launch probably handled about as nimbly as a brick in ice water and she proceeded with all due caution. It only took a few ticks to take up station directly astern of the *Chernyakova* and slightly above the huge, open mouths of her main engines. We didn't want to be in line with those, even given the remote chance of their firing.

She had enough of an angle to shine an arc-light onto the hatch area. We were able to see the ship's wobble as the spot stayed steady while the outline of the door wove a lopsided figure eight in the light.

"Ms. Strauss, Mr. Marks, you are cleared to debark and establish the line. I'll follow you over on your signal."

They said, "Aye, aye, sar," almost in unison and then lumbered aft to the lock and had to cycle it twice to get both of them out.

"Hold the fort, Ulla," I told her with a smile I didn't really feel.

She smiled back and nodded once in agreement.

I cycled the lock and ran the suit check while I waited for it to allow me to enter. I could see Strauss and Marks using their suit thrusters to jet over to the stern of the ship, trailing safety lines just like in the exercises. By the time I'd cleared the lock and stuck my head out into the silence, they'd already clipped a line to the D-ring outside the hatch and I had a clear road from the launch to the hull.

I heard Ms. Strauss's voice on the common working channel. "We're secure on this end, sar."

"On my way, Ms. Strauss."

I deliberately and carefully clipped my own link to the safety line, securing a second line to the launch, just in case. The softsuit didn't have any maneuvering jets but hand-over-hand along the line worked just fine in zero gee.

"We are at the lock, Captain," I said on the common working channel.

"Proceed, Mr. Wang." Fredi's voice sounded calm and cool on the radio.

I turned to Marks and nodded my head inside the helmet. He smiled back and turned to the keypad next to the air lock. He had just started to attach his break-in tool to the locking mechanism when Strauss held up her hand to get his attention.

I could see the puzzled look on his face through his helmet as she made a little shooing motion. He backed off a bit to give her room.

She reached over and tapped a series of nine keys on the keypad.

The tattletale over the lock turned amber to indicate that the lock was cycling.

Strauss smiled and I heard her voice on the working channel. "Let the record show that the emergency access hatch responded to the default access code. We didn't need to crack it."

"Good thinking, Ms. Strauss," the captain said.

We had already determined that the lock would only hold two of us by experimenting back on the *Tinker*. As the two senior staff, Strauss and I got first look so we slipped into the lock when the outer door finally admitted us. Strauss punched the button that would cycle us into the ship.

The inner door opened onto the *Chernyakova's* hanger deck. Their launch rested on its skids, locked down securely and ruling out the idea that the crew might have abandoned ship that way. We shuffled out of the lock and I punched the cycle button while Strauss limbered up her atmosphere sniffer.

"We're inside, Captain. The launch is here. No signs of trouble." I hoped I didn't sound as spooked as I felt. "The lights are on but there doesn't seem to be anybody home."

"Thank you, Mr. Wang."

"Mr. Udan, Mr. Belnus, if you'd join us, we'll begin our search."

They responded on the working channel and I turned my attention to the hangar.

Strauss held her sniffer up so I could see the readings. The carbon dioxide was low, but hydrogen sulphide and methane were elevated. Apparently, the scrubbers worked but I was pretty sure I didn't want to smell the air. We did a quick survey of the hangar while we waited for the rest of the party to join us.

Ms. Strauss used her local speakers to talk to me. "Could use a bit of a tidy, don't you think, sar?"

Odd bits of trash and cast-off equipment littered the hanger and the deck itself was in need of a good swabbing. I shined my portable light back into the corners and looked under the belly of the launch.

I agreed with her. "I wouldn't want to try to fly that out of here with all this flammable material in here."

"Given how little of it is tied down, I suspect there's no danger of fire." Ms. Strauss said. "I bet as soon as you opened the big lock door, most of it would be swept out by the first blast."

I measured the door and the space with my eyes. "Been a while since they've used this, Ms. Strauss?"

"Looks that way, sar."

The lock popped open behind us. Mr. Udan and Mr. Belnus stepped onto the hanger deck in their softsuits. I saw them looking around uneasily. I knew the feeling.

In a couple of more ticks, the lock cycled again allowing Mr. Marks aboard.

"Salvage party now on the hangar deck, Captain. We are commencing our sweep."

"Carry on, Mr. Wang."

What followed was a nightmare. We found the crew. Most of them were where one might expect to find crew. Or at least where they'd have fallen. After the first few swollen corpses, we learned not to look too closely. There was nothing we could do for them. Even cleanup needed to wait until the forensics team arrived.

In the meantime, we did what we could to regain stability in the ship. It was a challenge. The ship looked like it hadn't been cleaned in a stanyer. The watch standing consoles were smeared with dirt and grease in the engineering spaces. There were empty and near empty coffee cups, mess trays, and more odd bits of cloth and clothing than I had ever seen aboard a ship.

We used standby consoles and the emergency bridge connections in Engineering to stabilize the ship and begin a preliminary investigation. We needed to know what killed them before we could take off our suits and the clock was ticking. I led Mr. Udan and Mr. Belnus forward to survey the bridge while Ms. Strauss and Mr. Marks started up the extra consoles in engineering and began looking at the ship's physical status.

The trip through the spine was difficult. I tried not to look too closely at what I had to walk around on the way. Hanging wires, broken ductwork, and the swollen body I had to step over didn't make it easy to ignore my surroundings.

When we got to the bridge, I fired up an extra console at the forward end. We used that to establish a control link to engineering. It gave us a look at ship's status and provided access to the logs and autopilot. In a matter of half a dozen ticks, automated station keeping jets damped down the bobbing and yawing so we didn't have to worry quite as much about losing balance and falling on or in something unfortunate.

I sent Mr. Belnus to survey below decks and put Mr. Udan on bridge watch. While we were on ballistic trajectory–and while a corpse occupied the helm–there wasn't much we could do except keep an eye open.

Ms. Strauss called on the working channel. "I think I found it, Mr. Wang. Scroll back in the gas mixture logs, sar."

I pulled up the environmental logs and started scrolling back. The levels of methane and other gaseous by products of decomposing bodies showed clearly but I scrolled back almost to the point where the ship had gotten underway.

I saw the reading on the screen but I couldn't believe it. "Carbon monoxide?"

"That's what it looks like, sar. It's gone now, but it's in the record."

I traced back more and followed the history forward. Shortly after getting underway, carbon monoxide spiked in the ship's atmosphere. The levels were in the fatal range and the physical evidence around us reinforced the record.

"Why didn't any of the alarms go off, sar?"

My fingers tapped the keys awkwardly in the heavy gloves but I persevered and brought up the alarm status. They were all red. "Sar? The environmental alarms are all shut off."

"I see that, Ms. Strauss."

Mr. Udan watched over my shoulder and saw the list. "How is that even possible, sar?"

"I don't know, Mr. Udan. It's like the sensor control unit is gone. The sensors are there. The system is recording, but the alarm circuits are not active." I thought about it for half a tick.

"That's a general systems module. See if you can find what caused the spike in carbon monoxide, Ms. Strauss. I'll go check the systems closet."

"Aye, aye, sar." Her voice sounded distracted over the radio. "Maybe I can find the lead sensor in the data stream."

The data closet on Barbells was tucked under the bridge ladder. I left Mr. Udan on lookout and made my way down. It was the twin to the one on the *Tinker* and it took me only a moment to find the correct cabinet. When I pulled out the drawer, the gap in components was obvious. The slot that should have held the subsystem for managing alarm routings was empty. In its place was the red maintenance card required whenever a component was pulled for maintenance. Scrawled on the face was a date–July 21, 2371–and some initials. They'd been flying without alarms for almost two months. The sensors all worked. The systems recorded the readings, but when the readings reached critical stages, the interface that should trigger the ship's alarm system wasn't there to respond to the signal.

It was an appalling breach of safety protocols.

On a hunch I went down the passage to the spares closet and pulled open the door. It wasn't completely empty, but very nearly so. On the *Tinker* we had a spare for every single component in the data closet, along with some spare racks and odd bits. I had never tried to do it, but when I'd been systems officer, I'd made sure we had all the parts we needed to rebuild the closet from the bulkheads out in case of emergency.

The nearly empty closet in front of me was frightening.

I opened the general communications channel and called to Ms. Strauss. "Find the source yet, Ms. Strauss?"

"Yes, sar. A smoldering burn in a pile of castoffs in a corner of the engine room. Looks like an electrical spark from a broken lamp. The timing is consistent with kicker burn on their push out of Breakall."

"Check the fire detection systems, please?"

"Doing it now, sar." There was a pause. "Yes, they detected the smoke, but the heat signature was below threshold."

"Any indication of how long it burned, Ms. Strauss?"

"Looks like about three days, sar. Fire system reset then and that's consistent with the peak carbon monoxide readings." There was another pause. "Their systems detected it. Why didn't they respond?"

"There were no alarms."

"Yes, sar, but the watch standers should have seen the readings."

"Which watch standers, Ms. Strauss?"

"Environmental and engineering both registered it on the logs, sar."

"How long between the time the fire started and the carbon monoxide reached critical levels, Ms. Strauss?"

I waited for her to check the logs. "Looks like about eight or nine stans, sar."

"Check the watch logs. They had to have had a change in duty during that time. Did they note anything?" I headed up to the bridge and crossed to where Mr. Udan had the extra console running. He had heard the exchange on the working channel, of course, and stepped back so I could access the terminal.

"Looks like the first signs showed up just before they secured from navigation stations, sar. The readings were elevated but there's no note in the logs."

I scrolled back in the OD logs and found the bridge records. "None up here, either, Ms. Strauss. Was there anything at the watch change?" I scrolled forward and saw only routine entries.

"Found it, sar. 'Elevated CO noted. Sensors flagged for malfunction.'"

I shook my head to myself. "There's nothing in the bridge logs. If they notified the bridge, it didn't get noted."

The circuit got quiet. I don't know what the others were thinking but I was imagining what must have followed. Around the ship, crew would have started falling into a final sleep as the carbon-monoxide gas built up in their bodies. Some of them probably had headaches. They might have noticed some blurry vision. Given the number of people we'd found in their bunks, only the few watch standers might have been in a position to make a difference. Environmental and Engineering watch standers would have been the first to succumb as the heavy gas pooled in the stern nacelle. It wouldn't have taken long for the environmental systems to pump the forward section full of deadly gas as well. I wondered if the body in the ship's spine might have been the messenger sent aft to find out why nobody back there was responding.

I shook off the images and fired up the command circuit. I needed to let Fredi know what I'd found. I stood at the front of the bridge facing forward.

The coldness of the Deep Dark seemed clean.

Chapter Six
Breakall System: 2371-October-02

The forensics team asked us to chill the ship down to just above freezing to "help preserve the evidence." Enough time had elapsed that the "evidence" was pretty far beyond "preserving" so we lived in our suits when aboard. We also used the thrusters to turn the ship. While we were still on a ballistic trajectory, the course curved inward and toward the investigative team racing out to meet us.

Four days after turning the ship, we rendezvoused. Their ship was a fast packet in the twenty metric kiloton range and they boarded by the simple expedient of docking with us nose-to-nose. That allowed us to use the main locks on both ships and walk between them. I was at the brow to meet the team when we cycled the locks. Both ships had breathable air, but we didn't want to contaminate theirs with what we knew ours must smell like.

When the lock opened a team of six professional looking individuals wearing black softsuits stepped out. The suits had the Confederated Planets logo on the breast and the letters TIC across the back

I was impressed. The Trade Investigation Commission was the big dog in the enforcement arm. More often than not it was the TIC that sent in the marines. They looked like salvation to me. These folks did not mess about, brooked no hanky-panky, and knew their business–and everybody else's–inside and out.

The leader of the TIC Team waited patiently for me to track onto his face. "You are Acting-Captain Ishmael Wang?"

"I am."

"I'm Field Agent James Waters representing the CPJCT Investigatory Commission. We request permission to come aboard to offer aid and assistance to you and your crew under the terms of the Emergency Relief Clause of Title Twelve and also to begin securing available evidence pursuant to our investigation of the death of the crew. We further stipulate that we recognize that you and your crew are operating in good faith to safeguard the vessel and that evidence to the best of your abilities–pending any evidence to the contrary which we may uncover–and that you have successfully consummated a claim of salvage against this vessel, its cargo, and relevant appurtenances pending adjudication by the appropriate legal authorities."

Obviously this guy practiced the speech. I couldn't imagine that he did it often enough that he'd be able to just rattle it off like that.

"Permission granted, Agent Waters. Welcome aboard and I'm glad to have you."

"Thank you, Mr. Wang. We'll begin with a survey of the ship, dump out the computer data cores, and begin retrieval of the remains. This is likely to be uncomfortable and unpleasant. If you'd like to send your people over to the *Pertwee*, you're welcome to use our facilities."

"Thanks. We've been shuttling crew between here and the *Tinker*, but it's still been a long and trying few days."

He nodded before giving a hand signal and the whole, black-suited lot of them tromped into the ship.

It took them a surprisingly short time to clean up the bodies. One of the *Pertwee*'s holds was turned into a morgue and their team included two coroners. Within a day, they'd removed the bodies, copied the computer cores, taken photographs of much of the ship, and even cleaned up a lot of the more unfortunate by-products. We all gave depositions about what we'd found and walked a team of examiners through our boarding process–explaining what we'd touched, where we'd looked, and what we'd found.

When it was over Agent Waters invited me to the *Pertwee* and we shared a cup of coffee on their mess deck. It felt good to peel back the softsuit a bit and breath real air. I'd had a few hours out of the suit back on the *Tinker* over the previous couple of days but I was feeling a bit worse for wear and had some 'suit chafe' in places it didn't bear to think too long about.

"You've done well, Mr. Wang. Are you going to be able to take the ship in from here?"

"I think so. The *Tinker* has a crate of spares for us. We know what mistakes the previous crew made. We won't be making them."

"We cleaned up what we could, but that's not going to be a pleasant ship to ride in," he said with a rueful smile.

I sighed. "Yes, I'm sure. Is there anything you need us to safeguard?"

He shook his head. "We took samples and swabs of everything. This really looks like a simple case of carelessness. Everything on this ship is held together with baling wire and spit. Even their food stores are barely up to regulation."

"We noted that, too. There's plenty to get the few of us back to Breakall, but I wouldn't have wanted to be heading out into the Deep Dark with so little food."

Agent Waters snorted. "Or spares, or tankage, or anything else."

"Were they that broke?" I asked.

He shrugged. "If I knew, I wouldn't be able to tell you, but it looks like a shoestring operation that just ran out of string."

We sat there for a moment and then he stood. "Well, Mr. Wang, I'll let you get back to your ship. I need to follow up with the investigative staff." He grimaced. "If it's any consolation to you, I'll be filling out reports all the way back."

I grinned and stood up myself. "I'd almost be willing to trade you, Agent Waters. This is going to be a long three weeks."

I pulled my suit back around me and buttoned it up.

Agent Waters looked at me strangely. "The air is breathable in there."

"Yes, but we're going to change out the air and reload it to try to purge some of the smell."

"Good luck with that. It'll help some, and I'd recommend you keep the ambient temperature way down. It'll help control the smell."

I nodded my thanks and headed back to the locks. It took only a couple of ticks to cycle through to the *Chernyakova*. We released the latches and the *Pertwee* used her maneuvering thrusters to pull back and fall off to starboard. We set about clearing as much of the smell as we could.

Fredi sent over a replacement circuit board so we were able to get alarms back online. With just the five of us as a skeleton crew, we were going to be relying on automated systems a good deal. We vented the tainted air and refilled the ship with a clean mixture that was clear of methane and the other gaseous byproducts of decomposition. We used the depressurization process to test the alarm circuits. They triggered correctly when the hull pressure dropped. They also put up a proximity alarm because we were sailing so close to the *Tinker*.

I was on the bridge with Mr. Belnus and Mr. Marks when the hull pressure stabilized. We looked at each other, nobody wanting to be the first to take off the helmet and breath ship's air. As ranking officer, I did the only thing I could do and pulled the seal on my suit. The cold ship air rushed in carrying a whiffy carrion odor that I won't try to describe. It wasn't enough to make me retch, but I had to swallow a couple of times.

Mr. Belnus and Mr. Marks followed my lead. They both made faces but kept control.

"Let's get some cleaning gear up here and scrub down the bridge with something strong and chemical smelling, gentlemen." I blinked my eyes against the odor. "And maybe we should do that first."

Mr. Belnus headed for the cleaning locker below decks and returned shortly with sponges and buckets of hot water with a resinous smelling soap so strong that it pinched the lining of my nose. We all leaned close to the buckets and took lungs full of the moist air. It helped a little. After a fast hour's washdown of the bridge, the smell wasn't entirely gone, but the resin soap gave it a run for its money.

I left the deck ratings to finish putting away the cleaning gear, and made my way aft to check on engineering. By the time I got there, the odor didn't bother me so much. Perhaps the proximity to the scrubbers made a difference, or perhaps my nose got numbed to the stimulation.

I found Strauss and Marks working in the engineroom.

"This place is filthy, sar."

I looked around and had to agree. "The bridge was a little better but obviously they didn't place much value in cleanliness, Ms. Strauss."

Mr. Marks sighed. "It was worth their lives, sar. Too bad they valued that so little."

That was a sobering thought. Like we needed any more somber thoughts. He had the right of it. If the pile of rubbish hadn't been there, it couldn't have caught fire. Of course, if they hadn't shorted themselves on the spares, the ship would have alerted them to their danger. Looking around once more, I grabbed a sweep and started to help clear the trash and other detritus.

It took us a couple of stans to get the ship clean enough to start up the sail and keel generators to get underway. The ship responded well enough and the *Tinker* led us into the gravity well acting as escort and warning. We operated with a skeleton crew, and while the Emergency Relief clauses of Title Twelve allowed for it–better to have some crew than none–we were unable to keep up the normal watch rotation required for a vessel of the *Chernyakova's* class.

The watch stander merry-go-round went at a blinding pace as we traded watch-and-watch around the clock. Ms. Strauss and Mr. Marks handled engineering while Mr. Udan and Mr. Belnus traded off on the bridge. Every twelve stans I'd relieve one or the other to give each pair a chance to sleep a little bit.

Meals were catch-as-catch-can. I usually tried to have something warm and pungent on the stove as often as I could. The general lack of cleanliness extended to the mess deck and galley, making even that an extended chore.

We found enough unstained mattresses to outfit five bunks in Deck berthing and piled all the stained and damaged ones in Engineering. It was a small help but over time even the smallest improvements added up.

After a couple of days of having to clean everything we wanted to use, we had cleared enough of the mess that we could at least function without having to undo the neglect of the late crew. By then we were all so tired–and so used to the smell–we didn't notice it any more, but I knew it would stay with me for a long, long time.

CHAPTER SEVEN
BREAKALL ORBITAL: 2371-OCTOBER-31

I had expected that once we docked, it would be a simple matter of shutting down the ship and turning it over to the authorities for disposition. In hindsight that was a silly assumption on my part. Docking went smoothly and the shore ties allowed us to secure most of the power and propulsion systems but a ship like the *Chernyakova* is never unattended. Until we could arrange for a caretaker service, we were caught doing it ourselves.

Then there was the small matter of the ongoing investigation.

The TIC people were professional and they were thorough. They were also adamant that we should remain with the ship until they'd gone through the entire vessel one more time. I walked Agent Waters and his team through the ship again, showing them what areas we'd cleaned up and which we hadn't. The contrasts were striking.

I escorted them back off the ship and he stopped me at the lock. "Mr. Wang, we recognize that your part in this is to claim the prize money for your company and that you have no connection to whatever else is going on here. Nothing that you've done or said changes that and it will be in my official report. It may take us a couple of days to get this cleared up, but it will be cleared up."

I left him there conferring with a group of black-suited agents while I headed for Deck berthing and a bunk. Fredi had loaned me a few more hands so we had enough people to watch the lock and keep the coffee pot full. The ship had no operational mission, and my sole purpose aboard was to safeguard the salvage claim until the authorities let us turn it over to caretaker services.

In the meantime, I had about three weeks worth of sleep to catch up on.

After the long, grinding run in from the Burleson limit, the three days in Breakall seemed almost idyllic. True, none of us could leave the ship. At least not for long. TIC did let us go out to dinner—accompanied by a discreet field agent. The *Tinker* ran short-handed, but they picked up a couple of locals and the skipper filled in as OD, so it wasn't too desperate. I just hoped that we'd see the prize money from the effort relatively quickly and that it would have been worth it.

On the morning of November 7th, the TIC had gleaned what they needed from the ship and I signed the papers that relinquished the ship to the company lawyers. I had no idea whether the *Chernyakova* would go to the breaker's yard or would be put up for sale. The insurance companies in at least three systems were already screaming bloody murder, and given what I'd seen staining the decking, they had the right of it.

After the last affidavit had been signed, witnessed, notarized, blessed, and paid for, the five of us remaining from the prize crew were finally free to walk about the dock. Of course, the first thing we did was shoulder our kits and head back to the *Tinker*.

Walking through the lock again was like coming home. As much fun as it was to have the whole ship to ourselves, the *Chernyakova* never seemed like much more than a hull to me. We spent a lot of time on her, but ultimately, I didn't really have anything personally invested in her, except survival. The *Tinker* was home, and I was ready to go home. I wanted to try to wash off some of the odor that still lingered. I wondered if I'd ever feel clean again.

As I stood there feeling the warm glow, Ulla Nart welcomed me aboard. "The captain's compliments, sar, and she asked if you'd report to the cabin at your earliest convenience."

"Thank you, Ms. Nart. That was her message? 'Earliest convenience?'"

"Yes, sar."

"If you'd let the captain know that I'm on my way?"

I didn't stop for acknowledgment. It wasn't unusual for the captain to summon me upon my return and I had hoped to spend some decompression time with her. In Officer Speak, 'Earliest Convenience' was a special phrase. Like most polite contrivances, it didn't mean what it said. I hustled my buns to officer country and was knocking on the cabin's door frame in less than half a tick.

"Ishmael Wang reporting as requested, Captain."

"Come in, Mr. Wang. You can leave the door open. You're leaving again." She held out her tablet and used it to send a document to me.

I dropped my duffel on the deck to free a hand so I could look at it. It was an invitation to sit for Captain and I was due at the

CPJCT offices on Breakall in less than a stan. "Captain?"

"Talk later, foolish man. I was beginning to think those TIC people weren't going to let you go in time. You need a decent shower, a good shave, a pressed set of khakis, and your ID. You need to be there in 30 ticks. Go." She snapped the orders with her usual efficiency of communication and a gentle smile.

I went.

In spacer terms, half a stan is twenty ticks more than you need to shower, shave, and skin into a fresh uniform. Eleven ticks after leaving the cabin, I was leaving the ship again and walking deliberately–not running–to the lift. The CPJCT offices were on the oh-one deck opposite the lift. They owned the station but kept a low profile with a discreet presence and a modest sign. Unless you needed them, you'd never see them.

I skidded into the lift and stood outside the office door with time to spare. I checked my uniform in the reflection of the glass and smoothed a bit of wet hair. I had no idea how the invitation had been wangled but it had been. I didn't even think about whether or not I wanted to sit for the exam. Unlike the Mate's exam, the Captain's exam was by invitation only.

You could sit for Mate once you had the requisite time in grade and thought that you knew your stuff. You only needed to attend one of the periodic exam sessions and take the test. They were often proforma events, not too fraught with formality. You paid the fee, you took the test, they gave you the ticket–or not.

The Captain's exam was different. There was a minimum time in grade, of course, but captains were not part of the normal test rotation. The Captain's exam occurred whenever somebody was invited.

There were forms and fees that needed to be filled out and paid, and I suspected the not-so-frail hand of Frederica DeGrut held the spoon that stirred that particular pot. The CPJCT then convened a panel of not fewer than three 'Licensed Captains in Good Standing.' I understood that most captains deemed it an honor to be selected for a board but it took a fair amount of valuable time away from their normal duties to pass judgment on the invited first mate.

Before I could face the panel, I had to pass the written test covering law, navigation, accounting, engineering, and more. It was all in there–over a decade's worth of experience and expertise–distilled down to a few hours of test taking. A smiling, smartly dressed clerk showed me to the testing room, had me verify my identity against that on record, and waved me to my seat.

"This first exam is three stans, Mr. Wang. At the end of that time, or when you finish, there is an intermission of one stan where you may get something to eat, refresh yourself, or otherwise make ready for a similar period to follow. Upon completion of the second half, you will be finished for the day. Your results will be transmitted to the Board of Captains. After review of the record, they may or may not summon you to an Examination within one standard day. Do you understand the process, Mr. Wang?"

"I do."

"Do you grant permission for the Confederated Planets Joint Committee on Trade, represented by the designated Examination staff on Breakall Orbital, to release your confidential records to the Board of Captains for the purposes of determining your suitability to achieve the rank of Captain in Good Standing?"

"I do."

"Thank you, Mr. Wang, and good luck."

The testing screen in front of me lit up. I never heard the door close behind me when the clerk left the room.

A little more than two and half stans later, the screen went dark. I smiled to myself remembering other tests and the feeling of surfacing from a deep pool. I sat back in the chair and scrubbed my eyes with my fingers. It felt good.

The door opened behind me and the same clerk ushered me out. "There are a couple of nice restaurants just below us on the oh-two deck, Mr. Wang. If you'd like to go stretch your legs, grab a bite."

I thanked him and headed off for a light meal. I happened to have been on Breakall once or twice in the last few stanyers and I knew where I could find a plate of bacon and eggs with my name on it. Cholesterol and fat have a place in one's diet. My body let me know that I could no longer ignore the amount of said dietary delights I could consume, but after the previous few weeks, I felt I'd earned a bit of leeway.

Lunch didn't take long, and at the appointed time, I dived deep into the exam pool once more. Second half, same as the first. I have no idea what was in either of them—only that the questions spooled out in front of me and my answers disappeared into the machine. When it went dark again, I knew it was over and I felt done in.

The friendly clerk fetched me from the cubicle and showed me to the door. "That concludes the written exam, Mr. Wang. The results and your records will be transmitted to the designated Board of Captains and they may, at their discretion, summon you to an Examination. They are bound to make that summons and convene the Examination within the next twenty-four standard hours. Do you understand, Mr. Wang?"

"I do."

"Then good luck, Mr. Wang."

I headed back to the ship. I didn't know if I had passed or not. The written exam was a fig-leaf offered to potential captains. They wouldn't tell me if I passed or not in order to save face should the Board of Captains determine that my record wasn't sufficient to warrant promotion. I could at least tell myself that I flunked the written portion.

The captain's traditional summons was waiting for me when I got back to the ship. As tired as I was, it felt good to spend a quiet evening aboard in the company of my friends.

The Summons to Examination came just after 0800. The *Tinker* was still trying to settle into a watch rotation that had been all but destroyed by the disruptions of the previous weeks. Watch standers are resilient but, in the face of too much change, the watch standing merry-go-round has a tendency to wobble. I was due for the overnight OD watch starting at 1800. I was pretty sure I'd be back in time. I only hoped I'd be able to stay awake for the whole thing. In the meantime, there was this small matter of the Summons.

"Dress for this one," Fredi had advised. "Wear the full kit."

"You think it'll impress 'em?"

"Not as much as *not* dressing up would." She grinned. "That kind of impression you don't want to make."

"Good point. Have you been tapped to sit on any Boards, Captain?"

She just smiled. "I'm sworn to secrecy. Part of the deal."

"What do you think my chances are?"

She looked me up and down. "I'm biased, but I think you'd make a fine captain." She looked me in the eye with a wicked grin and twinkle combination before adding. "Someday."

"Someday?" I almost choked. She could still surprise me.

"Keeping you humble, Mr. Wang." She turned serious. "It's yours to lose, I think. Be yourself. Don't let them lead you down any roads you don't want to go."

"Thanks, Captain."

"If I didn't think you could do it, I wouldn't have put you up."

"Wow, they acted fast."

"Not really." She made an apologetic face. "I put you up in the

Spring. They're just getting around to it now."

For some reason, that made me feel better. I was still tense. Making captain was one of the Big Deals in a spacer's life. Not everyone wanted it. Not everyone who wanted it, got it. At thirty-eight, I wasn't the youngest candidate, but I was still on the low edge of the curve. If this board passed me over, I could be renominated in a few months.

"Scoot. They'll expect you to be early."

I scooted.

The Summons was to the same office that I'd taken the test in the day before. The same clerk welcomed me with a smile and ushered me down the passage to a small waiting room in the back. The space was done up nicely–formal without feeling stuffy, comfortable without looking lived in.

He showed me to a chair just outside the conference room door. "The Board will convene shortly, Mr. Wang. Please wait here until they call you in."

Over the stanyers in the Deep Dark waiting was one thing I'd gotten much better at. I'd learned how to drop into a kind of trance while waiting. It wasn't like I could check out completely, but waiting became a kind of Zen. I'd learned to be in the moment so that the moment could move me along. Anticipating when the waiting might end made me more aware of the slow and awful passage of time.

The door to the conference room opened and Field Agent Waters stepped out. I almost didn't recognize him without the black TIC jump suit. He wore dress khakis with gold captain's stars. "Nice to see you again, Mr. Wang."

"Nice to see you, too, Captain Waters."

"Please come in and meet the board." He held the door open for me and closed it after us.

The man and woman inside wore dress khakis as well and were refilling coffee mugs from a carafe on the side board. They looked up as the door closed, and both of them gave me a frankly appraising look. It wasn't hostile or even confrontational. More like a "so, this is the man behind the file" look.

"Captain Susan Zee of the *Astrolabe*, First Mate Ishmael Wang from the *William Tinker*." Waters did the honors and Captain Zee extended her hand.

"Nice to meet you, Mr. Wang." Her voice was a rich alto and her hand was smooth and strong.

"I hope my file wasn't too boring, Captain."

"Boring. No. Not the word I'd have used." Her face had a friendly smile but I felt that she kept a bit in reserve.

"Long is the word I'd have used," the man standing beside her said and held out his hand.

"Captain Brandon Gamblin of the clipper *Chthulu*, may I present First Mate Ishmael Wang."

"Captain Gamblin."

"Your jacket is rather extensive, Ishmael. You've done a lot." His collar showed the silver star of senior captain and he had the steady look of a man who'd been around. I'd seen the look before.

I grabbed a mug of coffee so I'd have something to do with my hands, and we settled around the conference table. Nobody sat at the head of the table, but they sat on one side and I sat on the other.

Captain Zee started with, "So, tell us, Ishmael, why did you decide to sign onto the *Lois McKendrick*?"

We started precisely at 0900 and I don't remember much about the next six stans. I do remember that at 1200 an orderly opened the door, wheeled in a cart-based buffet and we continued to talk over lunch. The conversation never felt forced or hostile. At times it was jocular and others serious. It was always focused on me. What did I do? Why did I do it? What was I thinking? Do I think I was right? What might I have done differently?

Walking out of the office at 1500, my dress uniform felt damp across the small of my back, and I was exhausted, but also jubilant. They'd gotten me to remember things I'd forgotten–some good, some not–but really all things that were part of me, things that contributed to making me whatever I was.

Pass or fail, it had been a great conversation. I only wish I'd learned more about them.

CHAPTER NINE
DIURNIA ORBITAL: 2372-JANUARY-08

The return to Diurnia was uneventful and the return to normal operations a relief. The watch stander merry-go-round lost its wobble and regained its smooth, machine-like precision as we followed the long trail back from Breakall and the old grooves re-asserted themselves. As we secured the ship in its dock, I could almost feel it shifting gears to the more relaxed cycle of port duty.

Being in port was no less a merry-go-round, but the off-duty portions provided opportunities to get off the horse and stretch one's metaphorical legs in ways that being underway couldn't. This change could be both good and bad. I found myself contemplating my delayed return to what my wife would deem "real life." If I was going to be honest with myself, I had to admit she had a point about my being a spacer. Not for the first time, I wondered just how fair this situation was to either of us.

"Secure from navigation detail, Ms. D'Heng." Fredi's voice cut across my reverie and returned me to the immediate needs of the ship. She waited for Charlotte to finish making the announcement before she turned to me. "You may declare liberty at your discretion, Mr. Wang. I believe first section has the watch."

"Aye, aye, Captain. Please make the announcement, Ms. D'Heng."

Charlotte finished the announcements and the bridge crew began turning their terminals to standby, standing up, stretching and flexing after sitting in the same place for the better part of four stans.

"Excellent work, everybody. Enjoy your liberty." Fredi's voice was clear above the rising murmur of the bridge crew preparing to leave. She turned to me with her bright smile. "If you'd join me in the cabin when you're free here, Ishmael?"

"Of course, Captain."

With a final nod she headed down the ladder, uncorking the bottle and letting the rest of the crew exit the bridge in good–if rapid–order.

I took a moment to drop a note to Jen before heading down. My traditional message on return was a brief "Honey? I'm home." It was a kind of joke between us. I added, "Sorry, I'm late. The rush hour traffic was murder."

It wasn't the first time I'd used that phrase, although I had to explain it to her the first time I did. Apparently "rush hour" was an unknown concept on Diurnia. Population densities and worker distributions did not contribute to a mass daily migration of labor during relatively short periods of the work day. It was equally foreign on the Orbitals and out in the Deep Dark. We'd had rush hours on Neris and Port Newmar. My traditional spousal greeting upon return was actually something my mother used to say when she'd come back from teaching and announce to our small apartment at large, "Honey? I'm home."

I hadn't thought of her for months. Twenty stanyers later, thinking of her and her death could still catch me like a punch in the gut sometimes. I stood there on the darkened bridge and looked through the armor glass to port and starboard–admiring the bright livery of the ships nuzzled up to the locks. I wondered what she'd have thought of it all.

I wasn't in any hurry to leave the bridge. I had the first watch and wouldn't be able to get off the ship before 1800. We docked just before 1000 so I had plenty of time to get stuff picked up. I'd also have all evening and the next day to make it up to Jen. It was good to be back on the *Tinker*, and good to be docked. It was an odd feeling. Twenty stanyers since I'd first signed on and I still looked forward to each trip. I remembered wondering if I'd like it well enough to do it as a career when I first started out. It was a legitimate concern, but from the bridge of the *Tinker* looking aft down the spine and back across two decades, it felt like the right decision.

With a sudden pang, I wondered if marrying Jen had been.

I gave myself a shake and headed down the ladder for the cabin. Fredi looked up as I stood in the threshold. "Thank you for coming, Ishmael."

"My pleasure, Captain."

It was true. We'd grown close over the stanyers since she'd taken on the mantle of captain. I'd worked my way up through the officer ranks right here on this ship under her amazingly insightful mentorship. She had the greatest of skill in knowing when to kick my butt and when to pat my back. I remembered a few times when she had done both. The thought made me grin.

She sat at her desk, lounging comfortably in the chair. Many of her mannerisms were birdlike and quick–the way she cocked her head to look at something, or to think about what she saw. She had a kind of "look with the left eye, look with the right" motion. When she sat, though, she didn't perch. In that she was more catlike. Occupying a chair like it was built for her and her alone and she would make herself comfortable in it, thank you very much.

I wasn't the only one feeling thoughtful by the look of it. Fredi had a kind of speculative, far away look in her eye and held the owl whelkie I'd given her so many stanyers before in one hand.

"Have a seat, Ishmael." She nodded at the chair.

I sat but I was beginning to get a little concerned. This was not like her. We often had little chats about all kinds of things, especially after a voyage. I'd never known her to look so wistful.

"What's going on, Fredi?"

She sighed and looked me directly in the eye. "I'm retiring, Ishmael."

"Retiring? As in leaving the *Tinker*?"

She half closed her eyes and gave a little sideways shrug. "Those two things are more or less related, yes. I suspect the company would object if I stopped working for them and still lived aboard."

"But why?"

She gave a small chuckle. "Because it's time, my friend. I was ready to retire more than a decade ago. Even before we won the ship back from Burnside. I've been putting it off until I thought the time was right."

"And the time is right now?"

She gave a small but emphatic nod. "It is indeed." She took a medium-sized envelope from the top drawer of her desk. The color, shape, and weight screamed 'official.' She tossed it onto my side of the desk "Congratulations."

The envelope was from the CPJCT, if the printed cover was any indication, and it was addressed to me.

"An envelope?"

Fredi grinned. "In some ways they're old fashioned." She pointed to a framed certificate above her desk. "They do have the electronic records, of course, but they send a paper one, duly signed and sealed."

I opened the envelope and pulled a Master's License from it. It was heavy. The paper wasn't really paper but some kind of flexible plastic. It looked like paper and it made me eligible to be captain on any space going vessel up to and including five hundred metric kilotons, pursuant to appropriate certifications and endorsements.

I stared at it for several long heartbeats–reading and re-reading, running my fingers across the surface. The letters felt slightly textured, actually embossed onto the surface.

Fredi sat there the whole time, watching me and smiling.

Something in the way she sat there, something in her face, told me that she wasn't finished. "Thank you. How did you know what it was?"

"Lucky guess, and they don't send the rejections in physical envelopes. This was waiting for us when we docked but I had a tweet from a little bird before we left Breakall. You did a great job out there, Ishmael."

I warmed at her praise.

"Change of command will happen at noon. Mr. Maloney will be here to do the honors."

My mind raced as I considered the implications of the Master's License in my hand and the opening in the Diurnia Salvage and Transport's roster of captains.

"Ishmael?"

I looked up.

"You're not going to be offered the *Tinker*." She said it gently like she was breaking bad news.

"Of course not, Fredi. This too nice a berth for a junior captain, but Maloney must have offered it to one of the other skippers in the fleet and maybe I'll get the one they're leaving."

She snorted a short laugh. "I should have known. You were always the practical one." She paused as something occurred to her. "Mostly."

"Do you think he'll offer me the empty slot?"

"I recommended that he give you this one, to tell you the truth. Plum job or not, you've earned it and having you step up provides some continuity in the command structure."

I considered this bit of news and shook my head. "Geoff Maloney is too practical for that. No matter what he thinks of you or me, he's got twelve other Captains to manage."

"Almost his exact words."

"Is he going to offer me the open slot?"

She caught my eyes in hers. "Yes, but you're not obligated to take it."

"Not take it?" That comment surprised me. "Why would I not take it?"

"Not all promotions are a step up."

"What? You think tractor captain isn't as good a job as first mate on a Barbell?"

She barked another short laugh. "You always tickle me with your ability to analyze these problems." She looked down at the whelkie in her fingers. "No, skippering a tractor is a great first berth for a new captain. They get lots of hands-on skippering practice, not a lot of freight at risk at any given time, and a small crew to aggravate–should it come to that." She looked up at me again. "But you know from hard won personal experience that some berths are more challenging than others."

That was the first lesson I learned on the *Tinker* and Fredi knew it well. I knew what was coming next. "*Agamemnon.*" It wasn't a question.

Her eyebrows gave a little bob in acknowledgment and she confirmed it. "*Agamemnon.*"

I took a deep breath and looked down at the fresh Master's License still cupped in my hands. "Did he say why?" I asked without looking up.

"No, but I can guess. Delman's been skipper there for the last six stanyers. He's been a good corporate soldier and taken what Maloney has thrown his way."

"None of the more senior captains wanted to move up?"

She ticked them off on her fingers. "From the tankers, only Sylvia Franklin is senior to Delman and those Manchester tankers are too comfy compared to this." She waved a hand in the air, indicating the sumptuous captains quarters. "Besides, the tankers have small crews without being shorthanded, she's got a good relationship with her first mate, and they're making out like bandits on the triangle trade between Diurnia, Welliver, and Jett."

She made good points. The Manchester ships were nice to sail in and the tanker trade in lox, liquid nitrogen, and salt water made that crew so rich, they joked about buying out Maloney and going solo.

At least, I think it was a joke.

"Yeah, okay. What about Steve Baxter on the *Perseus*?"

"He won't leave *Perseus* without Jimmy March and Mel's not stepping down just yet, so there's no slot here for Jimmy as chief engineering officer."

"And everybody else is junior to Delman?"

"Yeah, *Theseus*, *Hector*, and *Ajax* all turned over in the last four stanyers. Tractor captains don't usually stay tractor captains for long. A fact you should remember." She gazed at me with lowered brows and a serious expression. "You should also remember that they turn over regularly, and that both Avery and Smertz are not that far from retiring themselves. You could do worse than to stay here under Delman and try for one of those slots when the time comes."

I thought about that for a few heartbeats. "True, but Maloney will have to give the *Ellis* to somebody with a lot higher profile than me. That's practically his private yacht. Skipper there is a pure prestige job and the shares have to be miserable."

She laughed again at that. "My friend, you have a higher profile than Avery ever thought of. Geoff Maloney owes you for what you've done here and he knows it. He'll owe you a lot more if the salvage hearings ever get around to granting our claim. You'd be surprised by the size of those shares, I think."

I thought about it for just two heartbeats. "No, I'm not a taxi driver. I don't think he'd offer it to me and I'm not sure I'd take it if he did. And Smertz has the *City of Granby*. I'd be in the same position then as now. First mate on a Barbell looking to move up won't be offered command of a tanker while there are senior captains who might take it. It'll be the same game of musical chairs but with different ships."

"True, but maybe it wouldn't be the *Agamemnon*."

She made a good point with that.

She pressed on. "What will Jen say?"

"About my being captain?"

"Yes."

I lowered my chin to my chest and closed my eyes. I could imagine only too well what Jen would say.

"She wants me to give up being a spacer and settle down."

"I know. What would you do?"

I took a deep breath and looked up again. "I don't know. Maybe be a cargo broker. I know the biz and I know a few people. Carmichael and Farnam are always looking for people."

"Ever wonder why?"

I gave a little shrug. "No. I know why."

She didn't push it, a gesture for which I was heartily grateful. "Well, Mr. Maloney will be here around 1130. Delman will be with him. Change of command will be at noon." She looked up at the chrono. "You got about a stan to think about things before it all starts hitting the fan. Why don't you go pack?"

I blinked. "Pack?"

She nodded sadly. "I really do think that staying here might be a better choice for you, Ishmael, but I'm betting you're not going to be able to resist putting that ticket to work."

"Is that a bad thing?"

She thought about it for a long moment. "No. But it's the *Agamemnon*."

"True." I grinned with the dark humor of it. "Maybe he sees it as another rescue mission."

"Oh, you mean like putting you on the *Billy* right out of school?" She snorted. "Maybe. But I don't think so."

"You're right. I better go pack."

I stood up and headed for the passageway.

"At least sleep on it."

I stopped at the door. "I will. Maybe things will look different in the morning."

She snorted as I left the cabin. She didn't believe it for a second and I'd already made up my mind.

CHAPTER TEN
DIURNIA ORBITAL: 2372-JANUARY-08

At 1130, the brow watch bipped me to let me know we had guests at the lock and I went down to meet them. The three of them stood just inside the lock–Maloney in the lead, Delman in the middle, and Kurt bringing up the rear. I never really understood why Maloney felt he needed a bodyguard, but I respected Kurt. We'd met several times since I'd been with the company. He was a good and honorable man, and if Geoff Maloney thought he needed a bodyguard, then who was I to say.

"Welcome aboard, gentlemen. The captain is expecting you."

Clemming had the brow watch and nodded discreetly when I glanced in his direction. He'd notified the captain already.

We trooped up to the cabin and exchanged the appropriate pleasantries for a few ticks before Maloney turned to me. "Mr. Wang, why don't we leave them to talk captain talk for a bit."

Fredi winked at me as Maloney turned and left without waiting. I followed him out and Kurt trailed behind. We headed to the wardroom and settled into chairs at the foot of the table. Kurt stood just inside the wardroom door.

"Fredi told you my plan?" Maloney wasn't much on preamble. He could small-talk with the best but when it came to business, he was all business.

"Not in detail, sir, no. She's stepping down. Delman's stepping up. You're thinking of putting me in his empty slot on *Agamemnon*. If there's a plan beyond that, she hasn't shared it."

Maloney sat back in his chair and his right hand slapped the table top softly. "That's my plan. No hidden agendas. Simple assignments of the people I've got in the slots that are available."

"Who are you thinking of putting in as first mate here?"

"Behr's ready to move up. It'll be up to Phil. I'd have to find a second to replace her. Kazyanenko can't yet. She needs another year in grade before she can sit for the ticket. I'll put it out to the fleet first. See if anybody wants to step up before I open it to the Union. There are a couple of thirds who're eligible to move up, but whether they want to move or not..." Maloney shrugged.

"And if I decide to stay here?"

"You could do worse." He grinned humorlessly. "I know what the *Agamemnon* is, Mr. Wang, and it's not an easy berth. Phil Delman has held it for a long time, and he's paid his dues. In all honesty, I probably owe you better, but this is what I've got and I'm giving you first refusal on it. Nothing up my sleeve. No agendas other than she needs a skipper. If you decide to stay here, I open it to a Union posting–no harm, no foul."

"Salary and contract?"

"Standard contract. You've seen them before, but I'll give you a seniority bonus for service here. You've done well by me, Mr. Wang, and I see no reason to start you at the bottom rung. How does base plus ten sound?"

I let that sit for a heartbeat before offering a counter. "Plus twenty."

"Plus fifteen, and I'll repaint the cabin."

"What color?"

"Your choice."

"Can I sleep on it?"

"I'd expect you to. Big decision like paint color shouldn't be rushed."

Kurt grinned at me over Maloney's head.

It was a good offer and I nodded. "Okay, I'll sleep on it. Talk it over with my wife, and I'll send you my decision in the morning."

Maloney slapped the table once more. "Done." He held out his hand and we shook on the agreement. "Now, let's go get Phil and Fredi swapped around." He rose, Kurt held the door for him, and we all trooped back to the cabin to gather the two captains before heading up to the bridge.

Kazyanenko was already up there and her eyes widened to see us all come up the ladder. She didn't say anything, but stood at her station, eyes flipping from Fredi to me to Delman to Maloney and back. I found it interesting that Kurt disappeared from her consideration. He stood at the top of the ladder, out of the way while Fredi went to the ship's announcer at the back of the bridge and, with a nod from Maloney, keyed it open.

"Attention all hands. This is the captain speaking. As of 1200 hours today I will be retiring as captain of the *William Tinker*.

Thank you all for your tireless efforts and exemplary duty. I'm proud to have been your captain. In a few ticks, Mr. Geoff Maloney will recognize the change of command by appointing Captain Philip Delman in my place. At that time all security logs, records, and access will pass to his control. Please grant him the same dedication and respect which you have always given me in unstinting measure. Thank you, everyone. That is all."

Chief Menas joined us on the bridge and her eyes were shining a bit. I knew this couldn't have been a surprise to her, but I hadn't had a chance to talk to her about it. She walked over to stand beside me but before we could do more than nod, Maloney spoke.

"As of 1200 hours on this date of 2372 January 8th, with you as witnesses and with the authority as the owner of this vessel, I hereby relieve Captain Frederica Victoria DeGrut from her duty as captain of this vessel and appoint in her place Captain in Good Standing Philip Robert Delman to carry on command and operation of the *Solar Clipper William Tinker* pursuant with the rules and regulations set forth under the Confederated Planets Joint Committee on Trade and in accordance with the terms of their respective contracts." He turned to Fredi with a smile and a handshake. "I take this step at the request of Captain DeGrut and offer my heartfelt thanks and support for all she has done for the company, the ship, her crew, and for me."

Fredi shook the offered hand and nodded but didn't say anything.

Maloney turned to Delman and offered the same hand. "Congratulations, Captain Delman. I'm confident that you'll continue your exemplary service in command of the *William Tinker.*"

Delman took the hand and then offered his to Fredi.

Then the mob that had gathered behind me while I was watching the change over exploded onto the bridge. I'd gotten used to thinking of the bridge as relatively spacious but with an extra fifteen crew up there I began to fear for the structural integrity of the vessel. Everybody seemed to be laughing and talking and crying at once. Everybody but Kurt, who'd managed to create a security buffer in front of his boss, and Captain Delman who stood blockaded in the corner and looked a bit ignored, if the truth were told.

I stepped around Kurt, who smiled and winked at me without taking his eye off the boiling and joyous throng, and held out a hand. "Congratulations, Captain Delman. I'm Ishmael Wang, First Mate."

He smiled then, and it seemed an honest enough one. "Ah, Mr. Wang. Congratulations on getting your Master's License. A milestone, to be sure."

"Thank you, sar. I owe a lot of it to that woman over there." I nodded in Fredi's direction.

"She is an amazing inspiration." He didn't offer more.

"She is. Will you be aboard this afternoon, sar?"

"I will, Mr. Wang. Now that the change of command is official, I'll have my grav trunks brought over from the *Agamemnon* and stowed in the forward locker. I told Fredi to take her time, but she claims to be mostly packed and expects to be off the ship by 1400. Right now, though, I think I'll slip out and grab some lunch while things settle here. There'll be plenty of time to get acquainted as we go, I think."

"Maybe not."

My quiet comment made his head turn slightly as he regarded me from the corner of his eye.

"Any insights you can share about the *Agamemnon* and her crew before I go off duty at 1800 would be much appreciated, Captain."

Understanding surfaced. "I suspected as much. Why don't you and I plan on a nice cuppa tea around 1500 in the cabin?"

"Thank you, sar. I'll look forward to it."

Kurt stepped a little bit to the side and Captain Delman slipped out of the protected corner and down the ladder.

"Thank you, ladies and gentlemen." Maloney didn't have to raise his voice much because as soon as he spoke, a hush spread across the space. "Unfortunately, I've got a meeting with the Committee at 1300 and they get testy when I'm late."

He turned to Fredi once more and spoke more softly. "Best wishes, Fredi. I know this wasn't an easy decision for you. Please, if you decide to come out of retirement, let me know. I'll find something suitable for you."

She smiled graciously in return. "Thank you, Geoff. I"ll keep that in mind."

Maloney nodded to the crew and Kurt cleared a path to the ladder. I accompanied them to the lock to see them off properly. None of us spoke until we got to the lock.

"I'll expect to hear tomorrow morning." Maloney spoke quietly. "You're under no obligation to take it and, in a lot of ways, I'd understand and appreciate if you wanted to stay here. Either way you decide is okay with me, Mr. Wang."

"Thank you, Mr. Maloney. I appreciate that. I'll send word first thing in the morning."

"Very good, Mr. Wang. Now, I really must be off."

Kurt led the way out of the lock and they hurried off to keep their appointments.

Clemming looked at me with one raised eyebrow as I turned

back to enter the ship.

"Something I can do for you, Mr. Clemming?"

He grinned. "Yes, sar. If you could send Belnus out. I'd like to get lunch."

"I'll do that, Mr. Clemming."

He looked down at the desk and then raised his eyes to peer out under this brows. "Will you take the *Agamemnon*, sar?"

I marveled at the reach and power of scuttlebutt. "I don't know yet, Mr. Clemming. I'm going to sleep on it overnight."

"Yes, sar. Of course, sar."

I headed into the ship and behind me, he added a final shot. "Good luck with that, sar."

I chuckled, wondering if he meant the sleeping, the decision, or the *Agamemnon*.

I stopped at the closet that we euphemistically called the ship's office to check on the OD logs, before heading up to the mess deck for lunch. It had been long standing tradition aboard for in-port watch standers to eat on the mess deck, officers included. That saved the mess crew from having to set up the wardroom for what was often a single person.

Mel and Marcus held down a table in the corner. I joined them with a full tray and a fresh cup of coffee, after reminding Belnus that Clemming was waiting .

I decided to beat them to the punch. "So? How long have you known that Fredi was retiring?"

Mel looked sideways at the cargo chief before answering. "She's wanted to retire for stanyers. She's just been waiting for you to pass the exam."

"Congratulations on that, by the way." Marcus toasted me with his coffee mug.

Mel smiled and lifted her own mug. "Yes, congrats. It's been a busy day. Anyway, we talked about it while you were over on the *Chernyakova*. She put your name in months ago. I think she was beginning to think they wouldn't ever get around to it."

"Well, I haven't been the easiest person to catch up with." I dug into the chicken casserole. Chief Vorhees had certainly improved his cooking over the stanyers. I was surprised he hadn't moved up and on, but he seemed happy enough where he was.

"Are you kidding?" Mel snorted. "I've seen them pull firsts out of the lock on docking to sit. If they'd wanted you, they'd have found you."

The chicken was good. It was easy to overcook chicken when making it in bulk to feed a group, but John managed to keep it moist and tasty.

Marcus leaned in. "Are you going to take it?"

I looked at him over my cup. "I'm sleeping on it overnight."

"You're gonna take it." He didn't ask this time.

Mel put a hand on his arm. "Down, boy." She said it with a smile.

"This isn't something I can commit to without at least talking it over with Jen."

Mel looked at me with a bit of a sour look. "Good luck with that."

I shrugged with my eyebrows and savored the coffee.

There wasn't much more to say and the lunch mess was nearing its end so we bussed and bustled then I headed back to my stateroom to get my kit together. When I got there, I realized that I had already made up my mind. Or rather, I admitted that I'd made up my mind. I stood there in my room, locker open, and felt bad for what was about to come.

"Some things are worth doing." I told myself that out loud as I started stripping ten stanyers of accumulated living off the desk, out of the drawers, and down from the bulkheads. It all went into the grav trunk. I tossed a pair of dress khakis and a shipsuit into the kit bag and zipped it up.

I looked up at the chrono on the wall and realized that it was almost 1400. I'd packed my whole life in less than half a stan. Thinking ahead to the evening, I winced at the oversight.

A soft tap came from the door and I stepped back from the grav trunk so I could open it.

Fredi stood there–already in civvies and looking calm and relaxed. Her eyes flicked into the stateroom and back to mine. "I thought you were gonna sleep on it."

I shrugged. "I figured that I should be ready in case I decide to take it."

She smiled knowingly. "Uh huh." She then opened her arms and gathered me into a hug. She felt frail and small. Probably because she was frail and small, but she hugged fiercely and with abandon. When she let me go, she looked up into my face and I realized for the first time just how short she was. I'm not a tall guy, but as long as I'd known her I always thought of her as taller than me, probably because I always looked up to her. Stepping back from the hug, her bright, birdlike eyes gleaming in the light from the overhead, I realized how much stature has to do with perception.

She held out her hand. "Here. You'll need some and I'd be honored if you'd wear these"

The golden stars of captain gleamed in her palm.

"Those are yours!" I blurted it before I thought.

"Actually, they were my father's. He gave them to me when he retired. I carried them for stanyers before I was able to wear them. They should stay out here in the Deep Dark. He'd have liked that."

She caught me by surprise and I couldn't speak.

She glanced into my compartment once more but didn't say anything. Down the passage Apones maneuvered her grav trunks out of the cabin and she turned at the movement. "God speed, Captain Wang. And safe voyage." She smiled up at me one last time and some whim or other darted across her face. She reached up and pulled my face down to hers and kissed me on the forehead.

Then she was gone–just flitted off down the passage, a hawk in sparrow's feathers–looking almost grandmotherly with her gray hair already growing out of the 'spacer crop' and into something less formal. Apones ducked his head in my direction once but said nothing before turning to scurry after her with the grav trunks in tow.

Around 1430 I went down to the galley and found John Vorhees lining up the evening meal. He was a methodical sort and liked to make sure he had all the stores he needed before he began the the cooking. It worked well for him and he'd trained his messmates to handle a lot of the routine work with minimal supervision.

"Congratulations, Mr. Wang." He said it as soon as I stepped into the galley.

"Thank you, Mr. Vorhees."

"Will you take it, sar?"

"I'm going to sleep on it. See what my wife has to say, I think."

"Yes, sar. Of course, sar." He grinned.

I could sense I had a bit of an issue with credibility.

"Is there something I can help you with, sar?"

"Yes, John. It seems the new skipper is a tea drinker..."

"Oh, yes, sar. I know. Mr. Wyatt from the *Agamemnon* sent over a few of his favorites and I've put a kettle on the stove. If it catches on, we'll reconfigure the hot water tap out at the urns."

"Think it will?"

Vorhees shrugged. "I like a cuppa now and again myself, sar. Some of the other crew may find it to their liking."

"Would you send Mr. Veck up to the cabin with the appropriate fixings around 1500, Mr. Vorhees?"

"Already on it, sar." He nodded to a tray with two cups, an open tea pot, and a small plate of what looked like sugar cookies.

"Very handsome, Mr. Vorhees. Very handsome, indeed."

"You taught me well, sar." He was serious.

"Carry on, Mr. Vorhees."

"Aye, sar."

I started back out to the mess deck but stopped in the door. "Wyatt sent over tea? From the *Agamemnon*?"

"Oh, yes, sar."

"Out of the goodness of his heart? Or did he want something in trade?"

"Oh, well, sar. It wasn't like that at all, sar."

"What was it like then, Mr. Vorhees?"

"Once the announcement was made and formal and all, I sent Veck over to the *Agamemnon* to see what the captain liked in terms of food and such, sar. I wanted to make the new guy feel welcome, you understand, sar."

I tried to stifle a grin. "Go on, Mr. Vorhees."

"Mr. Wyatt is their cargo man and does most of the cooking because he knows stores and buying and selling. Sar."

"Yes, it's a small crew, Mr. Vorhees. I suspect there's a certain amount of doubling up required."

"Indeed, sar, indeed."

"Go on, Mr. Vorhees. You sent Veck over to find out what the skipper likes?"

"Oh, yes, sar. Mr. Wyatt was quite helpful and gave Veck a nice list of recipes that the new captain favors, and even sent over a few boxes of tea in return." Vorhees winced.

"In return, Mr. Vorhees.? In return for what?"

"Well, Veck might have had a bucket of Sarabanda Dark with him when he went over, sar."

"Might have had a bucket?"

"Yes, sar." He paused for a couple of heartbeats. "Or two."

"You sent two buckets of my favorite coffee to the *Agamemnon*–just to be neighborly–while you found out what the new skipper liked to eat and drink?"

"Exactly, sar. Neighborly. I couldn't have said it better myself, sar."

"You didn't send a list of my favorite meals over as well, did you?"

"Oh, no, sar. That would be impertinent."

"Thank the gods for that."

"They don't have a cook who could make them, so what would be the point, sar?"

"You raise a valid point, John, and one I wouldn't have considered."

"Thank you, sar." He smiled at me. At me. Not at the first mate. At me. "You taught me well, sar. Safe voyage and thank you."

"Thank you, John. Safe voyage."

I managed not to bump into the door frame leaving the galley. I was touched beyond measure by the gesture.

I went out to the lock to check on Clemming and found Belnus holding down the chair. "All quiet, Mr. Belnus?"

"So far, sar. It's early yet and the first ones off on liberty haven't really had a chance to get into much trouble yet. The rest haven't had a chance to go."

I chuckled. "The only real entertainment on brow watch is watching them stumble home."

"So true, sar."

The chrono over the lock read 1445. "Is Captain Delman aboard?"

"Yes, sar. He came through just a few ticks ago, while I was relieving Clemming."

"Is he wandering around loose?" I must have sounded alarmed.

"Oh, no, sar. Clemming took him up to the cabin."

"Very well, Mr. Belnus. Carry on."

"Aye, sar. Commencing to carry on." He chuckled and settled down to the watch station and pulled up what looked like the ship handler course.

I headed up to the cabin and knocked on the door. I knew it wasn't going to be Fredi's voice. I knew Philip Delman would respond, but it still took me aback just a bit to actually hear the baritone, "Come."

I slipped in and closed the door behind me. "It feels almost fatuous to say 'congratulations' or 'welcome aboard' under the circumstance, Captain, but congratulations and welcome aboard."

I found him standing in the middle of the cabin. An open grav trunk all but blocked the door to the sleeping quarters and he'd put a single picture on the desk. All I saw was the back. He chuckled sympathetically. "Yes, thanks. I know what you mean." He scanned the cabin in a slow turn. "I'm just trying to figure out what color."

"What color, Captain?"

He held out his hand. "We're either going to be working together for the next while or you'll be going over to my old berth to figure out what color to paint that cabin. Whichever way it works out, call me Phil." He smiled.

I shook his hand. "Ishmael, then, Phil. Tea should be right along. "

The knock on the door came right on cue. Phil replied with, "Come."

The door swung open and Vecks walked in doing a credible job managing the two-handed tray I'd seen in the galley. "Mr. Vorhees' compliments, Captain, and a fresh pot of Lapsang."

"Captain, this is Mess Attendant Neil Vecks. He assists Mr.

Vorhees in the galley."

"Thank you, Mr. Wang. You may put that right on the table here, Mr. Vecks. And thank Mr. Vorhees for me."

Vecks slipped the tray onto the boardroom table. "Aye, aye, Captain. Is there anything else I can do for you, Captain?"

The captain actually stopped to think about it for a moment before shaking his head, "No, thank you, Mr. Vecks."

Vecks grinned, nodded his head once, and slipped out, closing the door behind him.

We turned to the tea. It did make a nice break from coffee. I wasn't much of a tea drinker but the smoky, resiny flavor of the Lapsang was one I recognized from long ago and far away.

We settled back into the chairs and Phil opened the conversation. "So? What do you want to know, Ishmael?"

"Anything you think I should know that will help me decide to take the *Agamemnon* or not."

"Well, I assume you mean the reputation the ship has?"

I gave a sideways kind of nod. "It's got a bit of odor among the crews."

He sipped his tea and thought for a moment. "The ship has had its problems. As crews go, well, let's just say it's small. I've been their captain for going on six stanyers, and the only constant has been the first mate. She was there when I joined the crew and I suspect she'll be there when you leave."

"That's a long time in grade. She hasn't been invited to sit for Captain?"

"She has, actually. Twice that I know of."

"Anything you can share?"

He stared into his mug for a moment. "I never heard anything from the panels. I have my suspicions but I'll let you draw your own conclusions after you've met her. Next time we're in port together, look me up, buy me a beer and we can talk."

"Fair enough. You sound like you think I'm going to take it."

"I do."

"Should I?"

"I'd be lying if I said yes. But I'd probably be lying if I said no. Truth is, Ishmael, I haven't a clue what you should do. I'd be pleased if you'd stay on here and help me get settled with my new crew. You've been aboard here longer than I was on the *Agamemnon*. You probably know more about this ship and crew than Fredi does."

I shook my head. "No, I doubt that."

"Regardless, I don't know what you should do and I don't know what you need to know to help decide. I'll spare you the embarrassment of having to tell me that my old ship is known as the worst ship in the DST fleet. At least some of that is my fault, because as you likely already know, it's always the captain's fault."

"True, but your first mate has rather a sharp reputation on the docks and your crew, for all its small size, gets in as much hot water with the authorities as any two other ships in the fleet."

He sighed. "Yes. Sad but true. As I said, I'll leave you to draw your own conclusions regarding the first mate. She has a sharp reputation as you put it, and I won't argue that it's not deserved. Maybe you'll have a different experience, so I'll not color it any more than your own preconceptions already have. As for the crew..."

He sighed and sipped his tea.

"When you put the three biggest troublemakers in the fleet into the same hull, I'm not sure what you should expect except that they'll get worse."

"Put 'em ashore?"

"Ah, they're just clever enough not to step over the line. They're maddening in that regard. They're barely competent to stand watch. The first mate mostly deals with them, dragging them in for masts every few weeks. The second mate is in charge of bailing them out of the local brig when needed. My preference would have been to toss the lot of them onto the nearest dock and leave."

"Why didn't you?"

"I tried. They're never bad enough to fire without a Union grievance being filed. The legal boffins assured me that the grievance would likely be upheld. I don't see it myself, but the legal group is a conservative lot and putting up with the shenanigans is easier than defending a grievance."

"Easy for them. They're not out in the Deep Dark, locked in tin can with them."

He toasted me with his mug. "You understand very well."

"What's their rationale?"

"Prejudicial circumstances."

"Say what?"

"That's the legal term. 'Invalid termination due to prejudicial circumstances.'"

"What does that mean?"

"It means they think we don't like them."

"But you *don't* like them. They're troublemakers."

"And that, my dear Ishmael, is exactly the problem. They've got us dead on. We don't like them. And they know we don't like them. And they continue to make sure that we continue not to like them."

I groaned. "And so long as it goes on, you can't fire them,

because it's not grounds for firing them. And you can't defend against a charge of prejudicial circumstances even if you had a valid reason."

"Exactly right. Welcome to my nightmare. Are you certain you want to take it on?" He smiled sardonically.

"Actually, I was never certain I wanted to take it on. I have. . . some personal issues coloring my decision as well."

He glanced at my wedding band. "Wife not happy with your becoming a captain?"

"Actually, she doesn't know yet. I just found out this morning."

"You've had a busy day, Ishmael."

"So have you, Philip." I took a deep breath and decided to take a chance. "No, she's not happy with my being a spacer. Period."

"Really? What's the problem?"

"She's station staff here. She thought once we got married, I'd settle down. I thought I had settled down by staying with the *Tinker* all this time. Milk runs and home for a long weekend every other month."

"You married a stationer?"

"Yes."

"How long have you been married?"

"Seven stanyers."

"Kids?"

I shook my head.

He stared at me for a long moment. "Ishmael, you're a spacer. At the risk of putting our professional relationship at risk, I have to ask. What were you thinking?"

I took a deep breath and blew it out before answering. "Well, I'm not a spacer."

He barked a laugh. "You're dressed like a spacer. You ship out on a ship. You've been to the academy on Port Newmar. You've sat for bloody captain and made it on the first go. Ishmael, my lad, I hate to be the one to tell you. You most definitely are a spacer."

I laughed. "Okay, you've got me there. What I mean is that I wasn't born to it. My mother was an ancient lit professor at a university over in Dunsany Roads. When she died, the company there wanted to deport me, but I signed on a freighter instead. That was twenty stanyers ago now, and I know a lot more about being a spacer than I did then, but I didn't grow up a spacer."

"Still, you married the station?"

"I was young. You have to understand that to groundlings, getting married is growing up. If you're not married, you're not grown up. It's how I was raised. Grow up, get married, get a job, have a life."

"Then what?"

"Die, I guess."

Philip snorted. "Well, life has long been recognized as a terminal condition. You were hot to grow up and so you married this stationer and she's been somewhat less than accepting of your life choices for the last seven stanyers?"

"A fair summary."

He lifted his mug in toast again. "In that case, Ishmael my lad, you're not going to have any problems with *Agamemnon*. If you can manage that situation, nothing about my lads and ladies over there should faze you."

"I'm not sure I am managing it." I don't know why I admitted it. Something in his glib response.

He turned to face me directly then. He spoke softly but quickly. If his responses were glib and flip before, nothing that he said next carried the least bit of humor. "Then you're smarter than you seem and you seem pretty smart to me. My opinion is that you're probably not managing it except through massive application of avoidance behavior and that's gonna bite you in the ass eventually. That experience will serve you in good stead if you decide to take the *Agamemnon*. I know because that's exactly what I've been doing for the last five stanyers. It's not pretty. It's not clean. It makes you feel more than a little soiled about the soul at times, but it'll get you through when the alternatives don't come or are less palatable. I can only imagine you've faced that situation once or twice already when dealing with your more personal problems at home. I can't advise you on this, Ishmael my lad. My only answer was to get the hell out and here I am. I'm not proud, and I'm not sure, but I'm by the gods now captain of this ship and I can maybe, just maybe, begin to turn my own life around."

His delivery left me breathless and rang in my head like truth in the night. He'd shown me a side that I hadn't expected, although I should have, and in doing so he held up a mirror. I didn't like what I saw in it and I put my face into my mug of tea to escape the view.

When I surfaced again, I looked over. He was spinning his mug on the table in front of him, facing it but staring into the middle distance.

"Thank you, Captain." I meant it.

He chuckled uneasily. "I'm not usually so forward on the first date, Ishmael."

I snorted back a laugh of my own. "I appreciate the candor, and I'm sorry I'm not going to be here to work with you. I think you'd be a hell of a skipper to work for."

He looked over at me then. Some of his earlier good humor had resurfaced. "I'm sorry, too, Ishmael. You'd be a good man to have as first mate. So? How's this second who's moving into your stateroom?"

"Vonda Behr."

He interrupted me. "A woman?"

"Yeah. Very competent. Terrific astrogator. Has the crew eating out of her hand."

He looked skeptical.

"You have a problem with women officers? I thought you liked Fredi?" I was a little confused by his attitude.

He took a deep breath and let it out. "Sorry. When you meet Gwen, you'll understand. I'm just feeling a little gun-shy at the moment."

I shook my head. "Vonda is good people. Fredi wouldn't have it any other way."

"I can accept that." He grinned a little sheepishly. "I do have my own small crosses to bear, you see."

"For what it's worth, Skipper? I think you're gonna do fine."

He smiled at me. I was surprised by how much I appreciated it. "Thanks, Ishmael. I think you will, too."

The conversation petered out. After that, there didn't seem to be a lot to say.

Eventually he spoke. "So what color are you gonna pick, Ishmael?"

"Color?"

"For the cabin on the *Agamemnon*."

"I think, a pale green. Something with a bit of yellow in it. You?"

"Blue. Pale blue on those three bulkheads and a rich navy accent wall over there."

I looked around, trying to envision it. "That should be nice."

He looked up. "Yeah. I think blue."

"He does that to every captain? The paint the cabin thing?"

"I don't know. Actually, when we were negotiating for me to take the *Agamemnon*, I think I suggested it to him. We were dickering over percentages and he was at a point where he wasn't gonna budge and I wanted the last chip on the table. So I agreed to whatever the offer was, but he had to paint the cabin. He took it."

I snickered. "What color did you pick?"

"White."

"Why white?"

"I thought it would make it look bigger."

"Did it?"

He shrugged. "I don't know. I never saw it before it was painted."

"What color is it now?"

He smirked. "Still white. It's due for a fresh coat, but damned if I'd pay for it."

CHAPTER TWELVE
DIURNIA ORBITAL: 2372-JANUARY-08

Kazyanenko relieved me sharply at 1745 and I took her up to meet the captain. They hit it off well, he was already relaxing a little and his jovial manner matched well with Kaz's irreverent streak. I excused myself and grabbed my kit from my stateroom. By 1800 I was heading down the passage on the oh-seven deck where station crew had quarters.

Whatever other issues we had, and for all that my leave takings were often cold, I had to admit that my homecomings were always hot. I walked into the apartment to find the small kitchen table set for a candle light dinner for two. Something smelled wonderful, but nothing was served. It looked like a prepared stage, but the actors had not yet arrived.

I walked through into the bedroom. She was there and my heart caught in my throat. She had a way of looking at me that stopped me. Just froze me in my tracks. It wasn't a pose or a particular facial expression. It was more like what command presence is when done right. Only it was more like command presence in reverse. And in spades. It was more than "I love you" and greater than "I want you" and I have no idea how she did it or where it came from because when ever she used that particular look, I stopped thinking.

My welcome was brutally satisfying, totally exhausting, and short. Less than half a stan later we lay tumbled together in what had been a reasonably well-made bed but had degenerated into a pile of linens draped in a loose array I could relate to on a personal level. The operative words being "draped" and "loose."

She lay across my chest, not quite purring. Her flesh, pink and warm from the exertion, stuck to me as she made small shifts in her weight.

"Oh, hi, hon. Welcome home." Her voice had a husky quality to it that had gotten more pronounced as we got older. Or maybe it was my ears.

"Thanks. Miss me?"

"Oh, a bit." She sat up, totally unconscious of her nakedness and sat cross legged beside me. "So, you found a ship?"

"Yes. It was pretty grim in places. And exhausting."

"You seem pretty well rested." She patted my thigh playfully.

"I had a chance to sleep again on the way back."

"Dinner's keeping warm. You hungry?"

"Yes, it's been a long time since lunch and a busy day at that."

"When do you have to go back?"

"We need to talk about that. Let's get some dinner and I'll tell you about the *Tinker's* new captain."

She started crawling for the edge of the bed and I took my time watching her crawl. Seven stanyers and she could still make me forget to swallow. "You'll need to pull those eyeballs back and find some pants if you're going to eat." She said it with a giggle as she stood up and pulled on a cotton shift. It fell only to the top of her thighs and I wasn't sure if it was a nighty, a dress, or just a tee-shirt.

I didn't really care at that moment.

She went to the kitchen and I pulled on a pair of jeans, threw on a tee shirt, and followed. By the time I got there she had dinner out of the oven and onto plates. A meaty stew with lots of root vegetables in a broth so thick a spoon would stand in it. She had a pretty fair hand in the kitchen and this simple meal with a crusty loaf and a glass of wine was probably one of my favorite meals of all time.

The warm afterglow didn't hurt either. She looked good tousled.

We got about half way through the dinner demolition before either of us spoke. "New captain on the *Tinker*? What happened to Fredi?"

"She retired."

"That was sudden."

"Apparently she'd been thinking about it for a long time. Just decided it was time. The company moved another skipper over to take her slot."

"Who'd they move?"

"Delman off the *Agamemnon*."

"Oh, wow. That must have come as a surprise?"

"He was due for rotation and none of the skippers who were senior to him wanted to move."

"Who will they get to take the *Agamemnon?*"

"That's what we need to talk about." Dread curled heavy fingers around my gut and squeezed.

"What? You're not being transferred to that tub are you?" Her knowledge of the ships and crews never ceased to amaze me, but then, she worked in one of the bars that catered to that clientèle. She probably knew more about the *Agamemnon* than Philip Delman.

"Not if I don't want to. They offered the ship to me. I have first refusal."

She looked confused. "How can they do that? You're not a captain."

I didn't answer right away.

"Ishmael? You're not a captain. Are you?"

I nodded staring at my food.

"You're a captain?"

I looked at her trying to decide what kind of mood she was in. "Yes. I'm a captain."

"When did this happen?" She stared at me in wide-eyed amazement. I couldn't tell if it was happy amazement or despairing amazement.

"Well, I got the news this morning after we docked, but I sat for the exam while we were tied up in Breakall dealing with the TIC people."

"TIC? You were working with the TIC?"

"Well, yeah. The crew on the ship we found. They were all dead. It was horrible. We lost a few days heading into Breakall and another five or six there. That's why we're a couple weeks late getting back."

"The company sent a message around to dependents to let us know you were going to be late because of the incident, but I didn't realize it was so serious."

"It was one for the books. I hope I'll ever see anything like that again."

She paused before asking for confirmation one more time. "But you're a captain?"

I nodded. "I sat for it in Breakall, and by the time we got back, the license was waiting for me at the dock. I talked to Maloney this morning before the change of command and he offered me the *Agamemnon,* if I wanted it."

"What'd he give you? Standard plus bonus?"

She really did shock me sometimes. "Yeah. Fifteen."

She gave a low whistle. "And what color have you decided?"

I must have been gawking. I wasn't speaking–that much I'm

sure of.

"Don't look so surprised. That's been Maloney's closer for–sheesh–at least three or four stanyers now."

"I don't get out much."

She giggled. "True. And you don't have to listen to them argue about this or that shade of blue or green. Gods, you'd think they were trying to match their gowns at a wedding or something."

I laughed at the image. And at the response that I was so clearly not expecting to get.

"So, you think I should take it?"

"Ishmael, my dear, stupid husband, whether I think you should or not is really not the issue. You're going to take it. You've been working for this as long as I've known you." She paused to chase a bit of stew around her bowl with a crust of bread. "I'd much rather see you take it and be captain than to see you continue to be first mate anywhere. You're still going to be gone, but at least you'll get paid better and you'll be doing something that's actually worthy of your skills and talents."

I considered asking where she'd put my wife, but I decided that flip and glib were two places I should avoid in the short term. "I'm...surprised you feel this way."

She popped the last of the bread into her mouth and washed it down with a swallow of wine. "Don't be. I had a lot of time to think while you were out there. It won't be long and I'm going to be 40. That's a milestone for women, in case you hadn't gathered, and I've decided that I'm in charge of my happiness. I intend to pursue it."

"What will you do?"

She shrugged. "I really don't know. I've been getting used to the idea over the last week or two and thinking how silly it was for me to be upset by you going away. I'm a big girl. I can deal with it." A sly smile crept across her face. "And when you're here, my dear, you are very much here." She waggled her eyebrows at me.

She caught me unaware and I barked a laugh.

"I've been talking to some of the other girls at work. They have husbands around all the time, and you know what? Half of them wish they'd ship out. Seems like there's a lesson there."

"Well, I've gotta say, you've caught me completely flat-footed, hon. I never expected this."

She shrugged a shoulder and the cotton fabric slipped across her skin. "I wasn't really thinking it through. I'm sorry for being such a pain."

"It's all right." I was in shock. My brain had not engaged but my mouth was definitely moving. It was not all right, but I was reminded again just how much I loved her. I could forgive her for the past if it meant we could move on.

"Besides, I'm gonna be a captain's wife. I can visit you aboard when you're in port." She waggled her eyebrows again. "I never did it in a space ship before."

I laughed outright. "You know what? Neither have I?"

It was her turn to look surprised. "Never?"

I shook my head. "Never. There was never an opportunity while I was single and never a temptation after."

"Aww. You're so sweet." She started clearing away the dishes. "Never?"

I shook my head. "Never." I got up and helped her clear away. When we were done, I gathered her in my arms and leaned back against the counter, holding her and rocking.

"So, when do you have to go back?"

"I need to tell Maloney in the morning around 0800. He'll probably want me to take command immediately."

She nodded against my chest. "Do you know when you'll be getting underway?"

"No, but he needs to paint the cabin, and I don't know what their sailing schedule is yet."

"Won't take him long. I bet he has it painted by noon. What color will you tell him?"

"I was thinking green, a pale green. Something with a little yellow to it."

She laughed. "Ishmael Wang, color expert."

"Why? What color should I paint it?"

Her answer was instantaneous. "Yellow."

"Yellow? Why yellow?"

"Not bright yellow, ya lug. Something pale and pastel. Light enough to make the walls push out a little bit and with just a hint of color to remind you that the Deep Dark isn't the only thing out there."

"Pastel yellow? Isn't that a little...I hesitate to use the term but...girly?"

She pulled her head back so she could look up at me. "Dear? You were the one who was just telling me pale green with just a touch of yellow. You forfeited your right to claim that yellow is girly."

I laughed. "Yellow."

"Your call. But if it's ugly, I won't visit you." She grinned and grabbed my hand. "Now shut up and come with me. I have a little chore for you to do."

She led me back to the bedroom where she nonchalantly pulled all the loose covers off the bed and threw them onto the floor and stripped the tee shirt off to add to the pile. She crawled onto the mattress and looked over her shoulder at me to give me that look. "You gonna stand there or are you gonna come give me a hand?"

CHAPTER THIRTEEN
DIURNIA ORBITAL: 2372-JANUARY-09

Jen needed to sleep in. She had the afternoon and evening shift at The Miller Moth. I woke at 0530 and couldn't get back to sleep. I smiled to myself, slipped out of bed and into the shower to sluice off some of the evidence of the previous evening's festivities. I had a feeling the silly grin wouldn't wash off and I didn't try.

It was a matter of a few ticks to do the needful. When I padded back to the bedroom, Jen made a sleepy kind of mumble of inquiry.

"It's 0530. I'm going to get breakfast before heading over to the ship. Sleep."

"Okay." She said that quite clearly and was snoring delicately by the time I'd put on my khakis.

One of my favorite places to eat on Diurnia Orbital was a diner on the oh-two deck called Over Easy. They served breakfast around the clock, the eggs were fresh, the coffee rich, and the bacon was done just right. It would be unfair to use the phrase 'greasy spoon' to describe the place because it was nothing if not immaculate, but it had a slightly worn, not quite perfect appearance to it–like your favorite pair of jeans, the ones that had a hole in the pocket and a bleach stain down the left leg. They didn't really look great, but they just fit. That was Over Easy and I ate there at least once every time I was on the orbital.

I slipped through the door just after 0600 and the place crawled with people. For a breakfast joint, this was peak time, and Over Easy had a large and dedicated following of cargo agents, tug jockeys, can loaders, and office workers. I spied an open stool at the counter and slipped onto it with a nod to the kid behind the counter. His tag said "Phil" and the coffee pot in his hand looked good. I nodded once and he poured.

"Ya know what ya want?" He had a friendly smile, and a slash of freckles across his face. Over Easy was one of the few places on the orbital where women were never on the service staff. I'd never asked about it, but it struck me anew every time I came in.

"Three eggs, over easy, wheat toast, four rashers, and a pile of Frank's finest."

He nodded, scribbled something on a pad and clipped it to the metal ring hanging in the pass thru to the kitchen. When he finished, he turned back to me, topped off the one sip I'd gotten from the mug and moved on down the line–topping up, clearing off, and wiping down as he went.

From my angle at the end, I couldn't see into the kitchen, but I could hear the cook rattling about back there and the hiss and sizzle of a hot metal grill. The sound had a magic all its own and added an understorey to the morning hubbub in the café. I sipped the coffee and scanned the crowd. The waiters circulated fluidly among the tables and patrons. The women in the crowd, mostly sitting in the booths and at the tables, obviously enjoyed the view as the waiters moved among them. For the first time in all the stanyers I'd been eating there, I noticed that there were a lot of women. Maybe there was method in the madness after all.

A plate landed on the counter in front of me at the same time I heard the familiar "Thanks, Frank" from Phil. I turned to admire the masterpiece.

For me, any day that starts–or finishes for that matter–with a plate of bacon and eggs is a good one. It's a taste from my childhood and one I never tire of. I've had many bad plates and more good ones, but Frank's were something special. I don't know if it was something he did to the eggs, the pepper he put on the bacon, or what, but I never found another place that served up bacon and eggs that reminded me of home so strongly.

I only discovered the potatoes after a dozen trips to the counter. The guy next to me that day got a plate that had a mound of slightly toasted, heavily spiced, and onion-laced potatoes instead of the normal hash browns or home fries. Looking at them made me drool. He told me they were called "Frank's Finest" and you had to order them special or you only got potatoes.

I'd been ordering them ever since and only wished I knew the recipe. I suspected that even knowing it, wouldn't have helped much. Without the hot grill, the mixture of drippings, and Frank's touch with a spatula, any recipe would be forever incomplete.

I savored the meal giving each scrumptious morsel the attention it deserved and lingering over my coffee–for about four ticks. And then I was down to bare plate, empty mug and the faint sense that

I wanted to go around one more time. I signaled Phil, he brought me the tab, and I headed up to the *Tinker*.

When I walked thru the lock, Pinkus was on the brow and looked up with surprise. "Mr. Wang! I didn't expect to see you on your day off."

"Good morning, Mr. Pinkus. I just needed to pick up a few things."

He eyed the chrono over the lock. "Yes, sar. And congratulations, sar. We'll miss you."

"Miss me, Mr. Pinkus?"

"Yes, sar. You're going to take over the *Agamemnon*, aren't you, sar?"

"I haven't actually accepted that post yet, Mr. Pinkus."

"Oh, I know, sar, but you will. And we'll miss you."

"Thank you, Mr. Pinkus. I'm glad I can be such an island of certainty in this universe of chaos."

"We appreciate it, sar."

"Is Ms. Behr in the office?"

"Actually I believe she's on the bridge, sar. Astrogation updates."

"Thank you, Mr. Pinkus."

I headed into the ship as he said, "You're welcome, sar. And, sar?"

I stopped and turned back to him. "Yes, Mr. Pinkus?"

"Could you hold off until 0730 to tell the skipper?"

"0730, Mr. Pinkus?"

"Yes, sar. I've got 0730 in the pool. There's a hundred credits riding on it."

"I'll see what I can do, Mr. Pinkus."

"Thank you, sar. You're an officer and a gentleman, sar."

I glanced down at my uniform. "Yes. Well. Carry on, Mr. Pinkus."

I found Vonda on the bridge as Pinkus had said. She smiled at me and then looked at the chrono. "You're up early."

"Yeah, I had a few things on my mind."

She snorted. "I dare say. Congrats on making captain, Ishmael. It's been a pleasure serving with you."

"You sound like you think I'm leaving."

She looked startled. "Aren't you? I thought you were taking the *Agamemnon*."

"What makes you think that?"

"It's all over the ship! You even packed up your stateroom."

"Who said that?"

"Oh, well." She looked a little sheepish. "I looked in last night."

"Fire watch?"

"No, I was measuring it for drapes."

"Drapes?"

"Sorry, private joke. I was looking to see how much different it was than mine. Getting a feel for it before...um..."

"Before you move in?"

She shrugged. "Well. Yeah."

"And your assessment?"

"It's not as big as I thought it would be."

"You sound surprised. Surely, you've seen the inside of my stateroom before."

"Well yeah, of course, but never looking at it like I'm gonna live in it. Besides your stuff has always been there."

"Good point." I changed the subject. "So, have you met the new captain?"

"Oh, yeah. He was on the mess deck at breakfast. We had a good gab. He's not quite what I expected."

"Yeah, me either." I paused before continuing. "Do you think I should take it?"

"The *Agamemnon*? Why wouldn't you?"

"Because it's the *Agamemnon*."

"Ishmael? If it were any other ship? Any other tractor for that matter, would you be asking this?"

"No."

"Then why are you asking it about the *Agamemnon*? Because of its reputation on the docks?"

I shrugged. "Yeah, I guess."

She snorted. "You fixed up *Billy*. Took her from the *Stinker* to *Sweet William* and you were barely out of Academy. You're gonna have trouble with three punks and a first bitch? I don't think so."

"Would you take it?"

"Man, I'd have already taken it. I'd be over there right now rousting them out, kicking butt, taking names, and calling the cat rude names."

"They have a cat?"

She looked at me with a certain degree of exasperation before she realized I was kidding her.

I asked her the question I needed answered. "You gonna be able to work with him?"

She knew who I meant and paused a moment before answering. "I think so. He's not Fredi and I'm kinda spoiled, but he's got a good sense of humor and he's been around the dock enough times to know where the lock handles are."

I held out my hand. "Safe voyage, Vonda. It's been an honor."

She smiled at me, and took the hand. "Safe voyage ... Captain."

"Well, not captain yet. But thanks."

I headed down over the ladder but not before I saw her check the chrono again.

"What time did you have, Vonda?"

"What time?"

"Yeah. What time?"

"0600. I know you're an early riser."

"Sorry about that."

She shrugged. "Pinkus got the prime slot. That's the time I'd have picked."

I glanced at the chrono. "Who has 7:15?"

She smirked. "Captain Delman."

I laughed all the way to the mess deck. I didn't really need a cup of coffee but it was good to see the crew, such as it was, on an early morning after the first night in port. I lingered over the mug before slotting it into the rack for cleaning.

At precisely 0730, I knocked on the captain's door. From inside I heard a baritone voice say, "Damn."

Chapter Fourteen
Diurnia Orbital: 2372-January-09

When I finished with Captain Delman, I flashed a formal acceptance message to DST's main office on the orbital. I keyed my stateroom door one last time, made a final sweep through to make sure I hadn't left anything embarrassing under the bunk or in the head. Satisfied that I'd grabbed it all, I locked the grav trunk and fired up the lifters. It moved easily, but it massed a lot. I'd learned over the stanyers to tug gently, move carefully, and keep my toes out from under it in case I needed to cut the grav to keep from squashing myself or an innocent bystander.

With some level of aplomb I managed to back it out of the stateroom and into the passageway without adding any noticeable additional defects to the paint job on the door frame. Vonda would probably paint it anyway. It wasn't even 0800 and nobody was about, but that was just as well. When I got to the brow, I found the captain waiting there with Vonda and Pinkus. The captain and Vonda took care of a small but meaningful administrative detail by officially checking me off the ship, clearing my key codes, and giving me two data cubes. One held the ship's copy of my official record, and the other contained a copy of my personal data space on the ship's system. My records would not be purged, of course, because that would remove all my watch standing records and associated reports. My record would be marked as inactive on the ship and frozen at its final state.

There wasn't much more to say, but "Safe voyage" and everybody said it. I turned to slide the grav trunk out the lock and I heard the captain say, "0730, on the nose. Congrats, Pinkus," as the lock closed behind me.

I set off down the docks heading for number twenty-eight and the *Agamemnon*. I got about halfway there before my tablet relayed a message from Geoff Maloney asking me to meet him at the ship at 0830. I changed course and headed for the lift. I had time to do some shopping before reporting to my nightmare.

While I waited for the lift to arrive, I dropped the grav trunk to the deck and popped the top for a tick. I'd stashed Fredi's stars just inside the lid and I swapped out my first mate's flashes for the well used gold stars of captain. With Maloney's reply, it was official.

I was a clipper ship captain.

I secured the trunk lid and lifted it on its field once more just as the lift's double doors whooshed opened. I stood aside while several crew trooped out. Smiling to myself I strode confidently in my most captainly manner into the lift and was promptly smashed against the car's back wall by the free floating mass of my grav trunk floating along behind.

Luckily nothing serious got injured. My pride and vanity–apparently needing a bit of adjustment–did not fall into the category of "serious" things and I maneuvered out from behind the trunk before dropping it to the deck and punching the keys for the oh-one deck.

Shopping took a little longer than expected, but I completed my tasks without further injury to my self or my esteem and reported to the lock at precisely 0825. I stood directly in the path of the video pickup on the lock but nobody bothered to open up to find out what I wanted. To be fair, I didn't ring the bell either.

A tick before 0830, Geoff Maloney with Kurt in tow came up the docks. They both smiled at me and Kurt pressed the call-button. We waited for the lock to open.

When nothing happened after a solid tick, Kurt mashed the call-button again.

We waited some more.

I turned to Mr. Maloney. "Maybe nobody's home."

He looked a bit peeved. "They're expecting us. Or should be. I sent a message to the acting captain that we were on our way."

"Who's acting captain?"

"Chief engineer. Greta Gerheart."

"Did you send it to her, or to the ship?"

"Ship, of course."

I considered for a moment. "She hasn't received the message yet."

He glowered. "Either that or she's just ignoring it."

I shook my head. "No, if you sent it to the ship, it'll wait in the communications queue until the comms officer grabs it and routes it. The larger question is why hasn't the brow watch answered the call button?"

"Probably because the worthless git has fallen asleep on watch again and hasn't heard it ringing." The voice came from behind us and it echoed off down the docks. Maloney and I turned to see who had spoken. Kurt had already turned and was in threat assessment mode.

The woman wore undress khaki's with first mate flashes on the collar. She spoke with the deep, almost gravelly voice of a heavy worlder. She was built solidly, low to the ground, and not unattractive in a burly, fireplug kind of way. Her scalp under the officer's cap was shaved and oiled–a style which did nothing to soften her angular features and square shoulders.

Geoff Maloney spoke while I was still assessing. "Ah, Ms. Thomas. Good. May I introduce Captain Ishmael Wang. He'll be taking Captain Delman's place as soon as we can get him logged into the ship."

Her gaze was frankly appraising as she gave me the once over. "I figured."

I smiled and held out my hand. "Thank you, Ms. Thomas. I look forward to working with you."

A sly look crossed her face as she gripped my hand. She squeezed. I smiled. I didn't squeeze back. I just held while she tried to work her mind around the fact that nothing was happening. She abruptly let go and stepped back, pulling out her tablet. She covered her imbalance by keying the lock. It popped open, rising slowly on its hinges.

Kurt gave me a wink and a nod and even Maloney looked impressed. We followed the first mate through the lock and onto the ship. She stopped with her fists balled onto ample hips and stared in head-shaking amazement at a rather slovenly able spacer sprawled across the top of the watch stander's small desk. It seemed impossible that anybody could find body balance on the short and narrow surface, but he gave every appearance of being asleep. We stood there looking at him but it was Kurt who alerted me to the stool behind the desk. It spun slowly on its swivel.

Ms. Thomas looked like she was about to let loose, but I forestalled her with a raised hand and crossed to the desk.

I leaned down and spoke softly but clearly, almost in his left ear. "Very cute, spacer, and I'll give you credit for your skill in balancing, but if you're done with the dead spacer act, I really need to have access to that terminal under your butt."

He bolted like he'd been stabbed, lost his balance, and fell onto the metal deck. I winced as he cracked an elbow on the way down.

"Thank you, Mr. . . . ?"

He looked up at me from the deck, his eyes having to roll up almost to his forehead to see me where I stood near his head.

"Schubert, sar. Wendell."

"Nice to meet you, Mr. Schubert. You know how to make a first impression rightly enough. Perhaps while I'm here we can work on making it a *good* first impression instead of this one, eh?"

Ms. Thomas inhaled and was about to unload, but I caught her eye and gave her a little shake of the head. She saw it. Her eyes narrowed in response.

And she unloaded anyway.

She proceeded with a rather credible and sharply focused verbal flensing that included commentary on parentage, unlikely applications of bodily parts, and ended with imprecations of toxic levels of insectile infestation of certain body cavities. Even Kurt looked impressed.

The only one who didn't look impressed was Mr. Schubert.

When she was through, I turned to Geoff Maloney. "Yes. This will do nicely," I said. I reached into my pocket, pulled out two paint chips, and handed them to him. "Lighter color on the flat walls. Darker color on the curves. Any chance you could have that done before noon?"

"I'll see what I can do, Mr. Wang."

"Thank you, sir, I'd appreciate it. And now? If we could get me signed in? I think I've got some work to do."

By 0900 the deal was done. My tablet was locked to the ship net, and my codes and keys had been verified as captain of the *Agamemnon*. I showed Mr. Maloney and Kurt to the lock and stood with them outside.

"Well, your first moments as captain will be burned into your memory, I should think." Maloney flashed me a sardonic smile.

"And the deck in there, if I'm any judge." I smiled back and held out my hand. "Thanks. I was leery about this before but, I have to say, I'm looking forward to working with these people."

Maloney looked at me sharply to see if I was kidding. "Really? After that little stunt?"

I looked over my shoulder. "Yes, sir. Actually because of that little stunt. If the rest of the crew is anything like the ones I've met so far, this should be a lot of fun."

"Fun?" Maloney was chuckling in incredulity. "You have a strange idea of fun."

I shrugged. "That spacer has nerve, creativity, and a wicked sense of humor. Properly focused, he could be something really impressive."

"He?" Maloney looked confused. "Don't you mean she?"

"Oh, Thomas? No, I mean Schubert. Thomas has other problems. I don't know if we can help her or not, but I have some ideas."

Maloney was dumbfounded. "You got all that from a derelict spacer and steam whistle?"

"I might be right. I might be wrong. The worst that can happen is that the *Agamemnon* is the worst ship in the fleet." I paused for just a heartbeat. "Oh, yeah. It's already the worst ship in the fleet." I shrugged.

Kurt turned to scan the docks for threats and I could see his mouth twitching back a grin.

Maloney shook his head and chuckled a little. "I've seen some cocky skippers in my day, Ishmael, but I've either made the best decision of my life or the worst. Anything else?"

"Yeah. Why did you name it *Agamemnon*?"

"Why not? He was a hero of the Trojan war. King of ancient Greece."

"Actually, Mycene or Argos depending on what language you're reading it in and he offended pretty much every god going. He stole another man's woman, got his men lost in transit, and in the end, when he finally made his way home, he was killed by his own wife and her boyfriend. Not what you'd call a stellar example to hold up."

Maloney was staring at me, his head cocked just slightly.

"Oh, and one more thing?"

"Yes, Mr. Wang?"

"Paint. Please don't forget the paint. I've got a lot of work to do here and the sooner I get at it, the better we'll all like it."

"Kurt, would you call the office. Get these chips to Jameson and see to it that the cabin is painted immediately?"

"Of course, sir." Kurt took the chips, and tapped the surface of a discreet ear piece in his right ear.

"Thank you, Mr. Maloney."

"I think you're welcome, Ishmael. Safe voyage."

"Thank you, sir." I turned and walked into the ship, punching the lock closed as I passed through the far side.

Back aboard, I found Mr. Schubert at the watch desk looking not very repentant, and trying to appear not very interested in the new captain.

I looked down the passageway into the ship and saw no one in sight, so I turned back to the watch desk.

"Did you wish to make a statement, Mr. Schubert?"

"A statement?"

"That should be, 'A statement, sar,' Mr. Schubert, or perhaps 'Sar? I'm not sure what you mean,' or even 'Excuse me, sar?' Any of those would indicate your lack of understanding for the request, Mr. Schubert. The operative point I wish to make, however, is that the honorific 'sar' should be included whenever addressing an officer in an official capacity when not specifically using name or title."

I took a breath to let him catch up.

"Do I make myself clear, Mr. Schubert?"

"Not exactly. No."

"'Not exactly, No..' what, Mr. Schubert?"

"Huh?"

"Let me put it in words you might understand, Mr. Schubert. When you address me, you address me as Captain, Captain Wang, or sar. Repeat after me, Mr. Schubert. 'Yes, sar'"

"Yes, sar."

"Yes, Captain," I said.

"Yes, Captain."

"Aye, bloody aye, Captain Wang, sar."

"Aye, bloody aye, Captain Wang, sar."

"Very good, Mr. Schubert. And the next time you choose to

play the fool with me, Mr. Schubert, we'll be addressing you as Spacer Apprentice Schubert. Do you understand me, Mr. Schubert?"

"Yes, sar. Perfectly, sar."

"Thank you, Mr. Schubert. Carry on."

I turned to activate my grav pallet as Schubert said, "Aye aye."

I didn't turn back to him, but froze in place and cocked an ear. "Sar."

I headed into the ship and found the ladder up just where I'd have expected it to be, just around the corner from the lock. The grav trunk followed right along up the ladder behind me and I found myself in officer country. According to the schematic on my tablet, the cabin was on the forward end of the hull and held pride of place across the bow of the ship and just above the main lock. I wondered what that would do to my sleeping, having the cabin above the lock. Then I remembered the crew only had eight members—about the same size as a single watch section on the *Lois*. With that perspective, I suspected I might be grateful to be able to hear when my boys and girls came home in the night.

As usual, what I expected completely failed to match what I found. I'd heard the Damiens were small and uncomfortable, but I was used to the Unwin Barbells and their extremely low overheads. Both ships were twenty meters tall from top to bottom, but the Barbells had six decks in that distance while the Damiens had only four. That made for considerably more overhead room, even in officer country. The main deck felt almost like a ballroom. There were other considerations but the fact that the crew was pared down to the minimum necessary to stand a three-watch rotation meant that all the space, storage, and logistical requirements were pared down almost geometrically. The tractor carried only about half as much cargo as the barbell, but needed less than a third of the crew. Granted, they were mostly officers, but still. The economics of this design seemed wildly under appreciated, and I was pondering that when I stepped into the cabin.

I don't know what I really expected. The schematic showed the cabin carved out of a crescent of the curved bow by a single straight bulkhead. What the schematic didn't show was the port. I stepped into the cabin and looked straight out to the skin of the orbital. The view was shocking. I walked deeper into the cabin and almost up to the armor glass. A low bench ran around the curve of bulkhead under the armor glass with a few tatty-looking throw pillows on it. The armor glass itself was a full meter and a half tall, curved back following the smooth arc of the hull, and ran about five meters across the bow right above the lock. There couldn't have been more than two meters between the outside of the cabin's armor glass and the skin of the orbital. I was close enough to see pits and scratches in the surface of the outside of the lock. I wondered what the view would be like out in the Deep Dark.

I had to shake myself to break the spell of the port. I looked left and right. The cabin wasn't large in terms of floor space, but it had all the fixtures I thought a cabin should have, including a small conference table, a desk, several repeater screens, a separate sleeping room with its own head and two grav trunk lockdowns–one in the sleeping room and one on the other side of the cabin, tucked under a bump in the outer bulkhead that probably held a shield generator node.

Compared to the staterooms I'd been living in, it was practically a palace.

I slipped my grav trunk into the secondary lockdown to get it out of the way and pondered my next step. A loud voice in the passage outside reminded me.

I opened the door, stepped out of the cabin, and looked down the ladder. Ms. Thomas stood below, talking to somebody out of sight farther down the passageway. "Ms. Thomas, if you have a moment, would you join me in the cabin?"

"I'm kinda busy at the moment, Captain."

I blinked and looked down at her.

She turned back to the conversation already in progress and resumed her discussion of what sounded like the menu for the noon meal. I realized I needed to get a better feel for the state of the ship, so I dropped down the ladder for a closer look at what could be important enough to ignore a summons to the cabin.

A weedy looking officer wearing cargo pips on his collar stood at the open passage into what looked like a combination galley and mess deck. He seemed slightly taken aback to be confronted so summarily, but I smiled and held out a hand. "You must be Mr. Wyatt. I'm the new guy."

He took my hand in a half hearted shake and blinked rapidly several times. "Yes, hullo." His eyes finally flickered to the stars on my collar and back to my face. "Captain."

"Ishmael Wang, off the *William Tinker*."

"Yes, Captain. I've some of your coffee here. The messman was quite insistent that I take them. The buckets."

"Oh, I hope he wasn't an inconvenience."

"Oh, no, Captain. Quite polite. Just determined."

"My apologies for the zeal of my former crew. They were anxious to get off on the best foot possible with Captain Delman as well."

He nodded absently, looking slightly lost, back and forth between the first mate and me.

Ms. Thomas gave me a rather sharp look as if in rebuke for interrupting her conversation, and continued her talk with Wyatt. "I was really hoping we could get some of those sausages from Maurice for lunch. Are you certain you tried, Avery?"

"Yes, Gwen, I did. Maurice sold out yesterday. You know he only makes a few at a time. They're very popular."

"How are we coming on the resupply of the larder? We'll need enough to get us through to Jett."

I wasn't sure if I needed to interrupt this cafe klatsch or not. On the one hand, a discussion of one crewman's preference on the lunch menu was hardly worth my time, on the other a discussion of having sufficient ships stores to make the next port perhaps should be. Avery Wyatt was supposed to be good with stores. Looking at him, I wondered if he could find a noodle in a pasta factory.

The two of them ran down after only a few more ticks and Wyatt walked back into the galley, while Thomas headed toward the brow.

"Ms. Thomas? The cabin, if you please."

"I was just going to check on Schubert, Captain."

"I appreciate that, Ms. Thomas, but please, join me in the cabin. Now. Mr. Schubert can wait, unless you're aware of some emergency that has not been made public in the ship...?"

"Oh, no, Captain. I was just going to check to make sure he hasn't gone back to sleep."

"He wasn't asleep before, Ms. Thomas. The cabin, if you please."

I started up the ladder and was halfway up before I realized that Ms. Thomas wasn't behind me.

"Ms. Thomas?"

She looked up at me, then out to the brow and then actually paused. I presumed she paused to decide which direction to go.

"The cabin, Ms. Thomas. It's this way."

She flushed with a scowl, turned toward the foot of the ladder and started up. I continued on into the cabin and she came after me.

"Please, close the door, Ms. Thomas."

"I don't think that's wise, Captain."

"Why is that, Ms. Thomas."

"Because it would be unseemly for a male and female to be closeted without chaperone, Captain."

"And is my virtue at risk, Ms. Thomas? Do you have designs upon me already?"

She flushed again. "No! Certainly not, Captain, that's preposterous."

"Then please accept my heartfelt assurances that I never screw with crew and that your virtue is safe from me, Ms. Thomas. Have I made that clear?"

"Well, yes, Captain but–"

"Ms. Thomas, shut up."

"What?"

"I said shut up."

For a wonder, she did.

"Close the cabin door, Ms. Thomas. I'm not in the habit of discussing personnel matters in the open passageway."

"But–"

"Ms. Thomas. I gave you an order. I suggest you follow it."

She turned and closed the cabin door.

"Thank you, Ms. Thomas."

I took a seat behind the desk. She started to sit across from me.

"You will stand at attention, Ms. Thomas. I need to make some things clear to you before we go any further."

"But –"

I looked at her. I didn't say anything. She subsided, but she was not braced at attention.

"Are you not familiar with the form of 'attention' Ms. Thomas? I can get Mr. Schubert up to demonstrate it for you, if you wish."

"No, Captain. That won't be necessary." She glowered, but she braced.

"Thank you, Ms. Thomas." I sat there and looked at her for several long ticks. To her credit, only her eyes moved and just ever so slightly. She didn't actually break her gaze from the point just across the cabin.

"Now, let's get some things clear, Ms. Thomas. I am your boss. When I ask you nicely to do something, please consider that a direct, immediate, and imperative order. When you receive such an order, I expect you to carry it out immediately, without discussion, and without question unless the order is unclear, or unless you believe the order is illegal, or unless you believe the order puts the ship or her crew in danger. Do I make myself clear, Ms. Thomas?"

"Yes, Captain."

"Good. Sometimes those orders will not be verbal. For example, this morning on the lock–"

"Oh, I'm sorry about that, Captain, Schub–"

"Shut up, Ms. Thomas. The ship is not in danger, no crew is at risk. You are at attention. You are talking when you should be listening."

She stood silently.

"Thank you, Ms. Thomas. As I was saying before I was so

rudely interrupted, this morning on the lock I gave you one of these non-verbal orders. I saw you see me shake my head. That head shake was to tell you not to berate Mr. Schubert in front of the owner of the line. I had a very good reason for that order, Ms. Thomas. I saw you when you decided to ignore that order and berate Mr. Schubert anyway. Do you have any explanation of why you did that, Ms. Thomas?"

"Sar, Schubert is a miscreant and a troublemaker. He goes out of his way to cause problems on the ship. He regularly falls asleep on watch. He is repeatedly derelict in his duty. He needed to be reprimanded, Captain."

"Thank you, Ms. Thomas. I appreciate your input on this matter. What was the purpose of this reprimand?"

"To teach him a lesson, Captain. He cannot skylark and not have there be consequences."

"And what consequences would those be, Ms. Thomas?"

For the first time she seemed confused. "I don't understand the question, Captain."

"What consequences did your reprimand visit upon Able Spacer Schubert?"

She blinked several times before answering. "Well, the reprimand itself, Captain."

"You're referring to the actual tongue-lashing?"

"Well, yes, sar. That had to have been unpleasant, Captain." She seemed quite proud of herself.

"Well, let me commend you on your creativity, choice of imagery, and actual language usage, Ms. Thomas, and I do freely admit it was unpleasant."

"Thank you, Captain."

"You miss my point, Ms. Thomas. It was unpleasant for every one *except* Mr. Schubert—and possibly you. Let me assure you that I found it exceptionally unpleasant and that Mr. Maloney found it a good representation of why this ship is considered the worst in the fleet."

She stood there silently. Her mouth tried to open but she never found the handle.

"Because you were unaware of my petty insistence that my orders be followed, I will grant you a pass on the incident on the lock. Further because you and I had not yet had this little discussion to establish the ground rules on our professional relationship, I will ignore the three flagrant cases of insubordination you were guilty of in the passageway below. And since this is a friendly discussion of the way we will be working together, I'll overlook all the times I have had to repeat simple orders here in the cabin before you were willing to actually follow them. When this discussion is over, that amnesty will be at an end. You are my first mate, the good right hand of any captain, and I need to know that my right hand will do what I expect. When I need it to clench, I expect it to clench. When I need it to open, it must open. When I need it to hold, by the gods it will hold. Do I make myself clear, Ms. Thomas?"

"Yes, Captain."

"And are you willing to do it, Ms. Thomas? Are you willing to be my good right hand?"

"Yes, Captain."

"If you think I am making unreasonable or unreasoned demands upon you, I want you to tell me now, Ms. Thomas."

"No, Captain, I do not think you're making unreasonable demands."

"And are you able to do it, Ms. Thomas?"

I gave her a lot of credit at that point because she didn't just sound off. She tried a couple of times before she found an answer. "Captain, I don't know. I think so and I think I'd like to try my best to do it."

"I think so, too, Ms. Thomas. And I believe you can do it."

"Thank you, Captain."

"Okay, now that we've had our little talk, why don't you go prop that door open and have a seat. We have a lot of work to do in a short time and we best get at it. The painters will be here shortly and I'll want a tour of the ship while they're busy in here."

Once I got her attention, Ms. Thomas demonstrated a thorough knowledge of the ship and her systems. The ship itself wasn't terribly complicated. The hull was a basic egg shape, twenty meters in diameter and slightly elongated on its axis of travel. The aft end was chopped off square and that's where we linked up with our cargo containers–up to three of them at a time. The bow held a standard ten-meter universal docking ring just like every other clipper in the universe. We had sail and keel, some small maneuvering thrusters, a burleson drive, and enough fusactors to drive it all for a few stanyers. While the painters worked on the cabin, we crawled from keel to bridge and Ms. Thomas gave me the run down on each system.

At 1200 we adjourned to the eat-in galley. The compact space held two rather utilitarian four-seat table units bolted to the deck and a serviceable looking galley with range top, two ovens, grill, chiller, and the requisite sinks and storage. Just looking at it, I thought maybe the galley would be sufficient to feed two or three times the crew we were rated for. I looked at the coffee mess and was pleased to see that it was small, but commercial grade, with a pair of thermal carafes and a spigot for boiling water.

The crew who were aboard and awake joined us for lunch. I counted noses and realized that it was most of the crew. The enormity of what I'd done sank in as all five of us settled down to lunch. I was a bit taken aback to see Wyatt had opened a can of soup and put out a loaf of bread alongside some sad-looking cold cuts. Judging from the crew response, it appeared to be a normal lunch mess. I sighed and made a note on my tablet. Wyatt might know stores and how to purchase, but it didn't look like he knew how to eat at all.

The newcomer to the lunch party was a cute young woman who looked to be maybe thirty with nicely cropped sandy brown hair, a peaches and cream complexion, and the collar pips of chief engineer. It seemed that Gretchen Gerheart was not what I expected, either. She smiled pleasantly when introduced and apologized for not being awake when I'd come aboard.

"I'm sorry for not being here when you arrived, Captain. I got the messages when I woke but I had the overnight watch and racked out before the messages came in."

She seemed pleasant and competent enough. The engineering spaces that I'd toured seemed clean and well maintained. I wondered, idly, what she'd done to warrant assignment to the *Agamemnon*.

Mr. Schubert grabbed a sandwich, a cup of soup, and a drink and returned to the brow. I had to admit, the ship was set up very nicely for short-handed operation. With the mess deck just inside the lock, the call buzzer would be clearly audible from the galley–and probably anywhere else on the ship.

Crew berthing lay across the corridor and the three ratings shared a rather spacious single room where the bunks rose in a single line up the bulkhead. The high clearance made the three-up arrangement of sleeping quarters actually more spacious than those I'd used on the *Lois* and which the crew of the *Tinker* were used to. Hanging all three bunks on a single wall left a relatively large floor area and room for much larger gear lockers than normal. Aft of crew quarters there was even a small workout room with a single treadmill, a weight machine, and a stationary bike. I began to wonder where the stories about tractors being cramped came from.

The foreman of the paint crew showed up at the door to the galley before I could really get a handle on either Wyatt or Gerheart, but on the surface they seemed personable and used to Ms. Thomas' volume.

"'Scuse me, folks, but if the captain would care to see if there's any place we missed?"

I grabbed a swig of soup and rose to follow him up to the cabin. They'd done a very nice job on the painting and the yellow color worked nicely to brighten the space without being overpowering. I'd picked a pair of low saturation yellows and liked the way the two tones played.

"Excellent, Mr. Jameson. My compliments to you and your crew for excellent work on short notice."

He beamed. "Our pleasure, Captain. We'll be out of here in a few ticks. The paint should be mostly dry in a stan. You'll be able to work in here then, but I'd refrain from hanging pictures or anything for at least two."

"So noted. Thank you, Mr. Jameson."

He nodded and signaled his paint gang. I got out of their way and headed back down to the galley.

When I got there, my soup was cold and the bread on my sandwich already drying out. I ate anyway. It hadn't been much of a meal to begin with, and I had bigger fish to fry.

I turned to the chief engineer. "What's our status in Engineering, Ms. Gerheart?"

"Status, Captain?"

"Fuels, spare parts, environmental controls...? Are we ready to get underway?"

"Oh, I think so, Captain." She smiled and shrugged. "The fusactors are fueled and ready. Maneuvering mass is topped off. We've got 80% in the tanks and they should be topped by the end of the watch. We've got enough air filters for a year and full spares."

She delivered the report in a kind of whispery, sing-song soprano into her soup mug. It made it hard to hear her and harder still to take her report as credible. I had no reason to doubt her, but made a mental note to double check her report.

"Thank you, Chief. Are there any equipment outages, maintenance issues?"

"No, Captain. The scrubbers are up to snuff. Number one is due in two days, number two in nine. Gray and dark water processing is clear. Particulates and gasses are within parameter. All equipment is operating nominally, and within service lifetime ratings."

She never looked up once or raised her voice beyond the singsong. I began to appreciate why she might be aboard.

"That sounds good, Ms. Gerheart. Thanks. Mr. Wyatt? Stores?"

"Stores, Captain?"

"Yes, Mr. Wyatt. Stores. You know? Food supplies, operational materials?"

"Oh, yes, Captain. We've got a full pantry and I think operational stores are up to regulation levels."

"You're the designated supply officer, Mr. Wyatt?"

He looked confused. "I'm not sure we have one, Captain. I just order what the captain tells me to."

"Ms. Thomas? Is there no supply officer in our little chain of command?"

"Sorry, Captain. Not that I know of. Captain Delman kept track of that. Avery here just ordered whatever the skipper said."

I began to see a pattern. "Training officer?"

They looked at each other before Ms. Thomas responded. "No, Captain."

"Morale officer?"

Ms. Gerheart giggled, but Ms. Thomas said, "No, Captain."

I sipped the cold soup and digested what I'd learned a bit before speaking.

"Who's the OD right now?"

Ms. Thomas spoke up. "I am, Captain."

"You're first watch?"

"Yes, Captain."

"Where are we in the rotation?"

"First is on until 1800, then second, and third section has it tomorrow morning at 0600."

"So you're running a straight three watch rotation?"

"Yes, Captain."

"I assume the second mate has the second watch?"

"Yes, Captain."

I turned to Chief Gerheart. "You were on last night. You have third watch? Is that normal?"

She looked up, rather uneasily. "Actually no, I was on because Mr. Maloney made me acting captain." She shrugged apologetically.

"Makes sense. Thank you. I'll take that watch tomorrow. Please concentrate on making sure the ship is ready for departure."

"Are we getting underway, Captain?" Chief Gerheart seemed surprised by the notion.

"We don't make any money tied up at the dock, Ms. Gerheart."

"Well, yes, but I thought you'd need more time to get used to the ship."

"Oh, I think I'll have a lot of time to get used to the ship while we're underway. What's our next port of call, Mr. Wyatt?"

"Captain?"

"Where are we going next, Mr. Wyatt?"

"I'm sure I don't know, Captain."

"You don't have a cargo?"

He seemed almost bewildered by the question. "I haven't been given one yet, no."

"Given one?"

"Well, of course. I get cargo assignments from the office."

"You wait for them to give you a cargo assignment?"

"How else, Captain?"

"You are aware that this is a free-trade port? Cargoes are available all the time here."

"Oh, of course, Captain."

"But you wait for DST to tell you which ones to take?"

"Yes, Captain. How else would I know which ones might be profitable?"

"Thank you, Mr. Wyatt. Let me get back to you on that."

"Of course, Captain."

I took a deep breath and pushed the remains of my lunch away. I had lost my appetite suddenly.

"Okay, people. I need to plug into the ship's systems for a time this afternoon, then I plan to spend the evening with my wife. I'll be back aboard in time to relieve second watch in the morning. Today's the eighth. Plan on getting underway no later than the eleventh."

Ms. Thomas perked up. "Where are we going, Captain?"

"I'll get back to you on that. I need to check a few things first."

"Can you do that, Captain?"

"Do what, Ms. Thomas?"

"Just decide to leave without knowing where?"

I considered the overhead and laid a finger on my cheek in a studied pose of consideration. "Yes. Actually I think I can. What I need from each of you, and Mr. Pall when I catch up with him, is the assurance that the ship is ready to get underway." I didn't want to alarm them, so I didn't hold out for assurances that we wouldn't all die before we arrived. I was beginning to think they doubted their mortality, collectively and individually.

They looked around at each other again, looking faintly impressed. I decided I needed to have a little chat with my new friend Philip Delman.

That would have to wait until I cracked open the ship's systems and had a good look about in the belly of the beast.

Chapter Seventeen
Diurnia Orbital: 2372-January-09

Around 1330 I settled into the watch station on the bridge. The ship only had four stations–helm, watch, systems, and engineering. There wasn't enough to the ship–or crew for that matter–to require more. Before I dug in, I fired off an intership message to Delman on the *Tinker* with an invitation to dinner at Jimmy's up on deck eight, my treat. They had good fish, better steaks, and the freshest greens on the orbital. They also weren't cheap, but it was petty cash compared to the value of the information I needed from Captain Delman.

The watch terminal wasn't configured to swap divisional displays, so I pulled a page from my old skill set and patched it so I could. In reality, that only meant taking out the block that somebody else had put in. There was no good reason for that capability to be blocked on the bridge. All the displays were visible from the captain's chair. I looked over to it and realized that the chair didn't have any displays of its own. It made a certain sense.

I scanned the personnel records first and didn't find anything I hadn't expected. Only the ratings had any serious black marks and the officers were all running in the "marginal" to "average" in their performance ratings.

Engineering status reports and logs confirmed what Chief Gerheart had said over lunch. Even her assessment of tankage was right on the money. I didn't see a single thing in that whole division that looked out of place, beyond parameter, or otherwise blemished. I wondered why she only got middling ratings.

I pulled up the ship's stores and ran through the spare parts and comestibles. It looked okay and I was about to flip the display over to check the astrogation updates, when something odd caught my eye. We had food enough. Head count, calorie availability, and durations were all consistent. I looked again and realized it was all the same food. According to the inventory, the pantry was stocked with about six or seven variations on the same sets of canned goods. The freezer inventory held luncheon meat, and what looked like a bunker load that was almost at its expiration date.

I ran a quick cross reference against procurement and realized that the freezers were full of stuff that had never been used. All but a few dozen kilograms of goods from the original procurements were still in the freezers. While I was there, I checked to see what else the ship had purchased. Standard rates on docking fees, fuel, water, consumable supplies and replacement gasses were in order. On a quick eyeball inspection the system records looked correct. A physical inventory of the freezers and pantries was definitely in order, but if the condition of the stores was anything like the inventory indicated, we had some serious issues.

I pulled up the ship net and sent a message to Wyatt's tablet. "Please join me on the bridge at your earliest convenience."

While I waited, I decided to check the ship's manifest record as well. I wasn't sure what I'd find, but since I was going to have the cargo chief for a little face time, it seemed a logical thing to do. The record was highly underwhelming with the median port stay being six days, and the average just over seven. The manifests all ran toward the commonest cargoes, nothing very high value and no priorities. A tractor like the *Agamemnon* could make half again as much on a voyage by taking a high priority, high value cargo like pharmaceuticals or electronics spares. As such, those cargoes were very popular and much in demand. It took a sharp cargo man to grab them up because everybody watched for them. The *Agamemnon* carried low value, low priority cargo that probably should have gone in a mixed freight container on a larger ship.

My tablet bipped and I opened the inbox to find that Philip Delman had accepted my dinner offer. The time stamp made me look at the chronometer on the screen and realize that my cargo chief had not yet reported to the bridge.

I sighed. "It's no wonder the ratings are always in trouble." I muttered it under my breath and I hoped nobody was there to hear it.

I found Wyatt in the galley pushing a broom around.

"Mr. Wyatt, did you receive my message?"

"Message, Captain?"

"Apparently not. Is your tablet malfunctioning?"

He looked surprised. "I don't think so, Captain. Why?"

I was beginning to understand a great deal more about why the

Agamemnon was the worst ship in the fleet, and it had nothing to do with the ratings.

"Because I sent you a message, Mr. Wyatt. That message should have resulted in your tablet alerting you so you would have known that a message had been delivered to you."

He smiled. "Oh, in that case, let me check." He stowed the broom and headed out of the galley.

Intrigued. I followed him out, up to officers country and into his stateroom where he opened his grav trunk and took out the tablet, still bipping for attention. He held it up for me to see. "No, Captain. Not malfunctioning."

"Can you tell me why your tablet is stowed in your grav trunk, Mr. Wyatt?"

"Safe keeping of course. I'm terribly clumsy, Captain. I've dropped a couple and broken them already. I keep this one here in my grav trunk to keep it safe."

"I see."

He started to put the tablet, still bipping, back into the grav trunk.

"Mr. Wyatt, you have a message. Don't you think you should read it?"

"I assumed you'd tell me since you were already here, Captain." He said it so reasonably.

"What if mine was not the only message, Mr. Wyatt?"

He shrugged in acknowledgment. "Excellent point, Captain." He lifted it up and tapped the key to bring up the display. "Oh, I see. Do you still want me to join you on the bridge, Captain?" He started to put the tablet back in the trunk.

"You did go to the academy, didn't you, Mr. Wyatt?"

"Of course, Captain."

"Where were you before you came here as chief?"

"I did most of my time with Saltzman Shipping. Worked on almost every one of their Leviathans at one point or another. Finally worked up to chief, but they had no openings. So, I wound up here."

"How long have you been with DST, Mr. Wyatt?"

"Two stanyers next April."

"Your last performance review wasn't great. Did Captain Delman talk to you about that?"

"Oh, yes, Captain. We had a nice discussion about initiative and entrepreneurial spirit."

"I can see that conversation had a large effect on your outlooks and attitudes, Mr. Wyatt."

"It did, Captain. I'm always on the look out for new opportunities. I haven't found any yet, but I'm always looking."

"Mr. Wyatt. Please keep your tablet near you at all times. You don't need to have it in the holster, but when I send you a message, I really need to know that you're likely to read it."

He frowned. "Captain Delman used to just page me on the announcer."

"Somewhat inconsiderate of watch standers isn't it, Mr. Wyatt?"

"I suppose so, Captain. I never really thought of it."

"Think of it, Mr. Wyatt."

"Now, Captain?"

"Mr. Wyatt, please forgive this question. Are you on drugs? Intoxicated? Anything like that?"

He didn't seem offended by the question, although he did appear surprised. "Why, no, Captain, why do you ask?"

"What was your graduation rank at the academy, Mr. Wyatt?"

"Well, you know the old joke, Captain? What do they call the officer who graduates last in his class?"

I supplied the answer with growing dread. "Sar."

He beamed. "So you've heard it."

"Were you always planning to be Cargo?"

"No, I was originally Deck."

"What happened, Mr. Wyatt?"

"My second year advisor told me that if I wanted to stay in the Academy I needed to change to Cargo."

"Was any reason given?"

"My grades were low and the evaluations were marginal."

"Any idea why that might have been, Mr. Wyatt?"

"Well, the work was rather boring and the instructors thought I was simple in the head."

"Are you?"

"Simple in the head? I don't think so, Captain, but I probably wouldn't know because I have no benchmarks for comparison."

"Do you know the freezers are full of food that's about to expire?"

"Yes, Captain. We've never used any of it, and Captain Delman never gave me any instructions on disposal. According to regulations we are required to have all that food in the freezer, but I'm not sure why since we've never used any of it in the time I've been aboard."

"You've been handling the mess chores the whole time you've been aboard?"

"No, Captain. It's only been since my last performance review really. Up to then, meals were rather catch as catch can. After the talk about initiative and entrepreneurial spirit, I determined that I would do that to demonstrate. Now I handle stores and fix meals."

"The pantry is full of canned goods, the freezers are full of food you don't use. Are all the meals about like what I saw at lunch today?"

"Oh, no, Captain. That was just in-port lunch."

"And underway it's different?"

"Of course."

I almost relaxed.

Then he added, "Underway, I'd open two cans of soup."

"I should have seen that coming," I said and scrubbed my face with my hands. "Are the inventories correct, Mr. Wyatt? The systems and the lockers actually match?"

"Oh, yes, Captain. I inventory them every trip. There's not much else for a cargo chief to do. Between you and me it seems rather a waste, but the regulations say I need to be here."

I was beginning to get a suspicion about Mr. Wyatt. It was unsettling, but less unnerving than surface appearance. "Tell me, Mr. Wyatt. How exactly do you get cargoes for the ship?"

"Well, after we've been in port a couple of days, I call the local DST affiliate and ask for dispatch. I tell them who I am and they give me a manifest. We get the cargo and go where it needs to be delivered."

"Avery—may I call you Avery?"

"Sure, Captain. That's my name."

"Avery, I'm gonna suggest something. Are you doing anything this afternoon?"

"Sweeping the galley, Captain."

"I want you to plan menus."

"What kind of menus, Captain?"

"Our menus. Sit down with a calendar, and for every day, put down everything you'd serve for every meal. Breakfast, lunch, dinner, and a midnight snack."

"That sounds easy enough, Captain."

"Well, I'm going to make it a little more difficult. You can't have the same meal in any two week period."

He blinked owlishly. "Two weeks? How many days worth of menu do you want me to do?"

"Well, how long does it take the *Agamemnon* to go from here to, say, Welliver?"

"I have no idea, Captain. Weeks. Maybe eight weeks."

I took a deep breath and tried to stay focused in the face of diffusion. "Okay, I want you to do menus for sixty days. Every day. Three meals plus the midnight snack and you can't serve the same meal twice in a fourteen day period." He nodded as if he really understood what I was saying. I needed to add one more caveat. "You can't serve the same meal more than three times in the sixty days."

"What do you mean by 'midnight snack,' Captain?"

"That's just something that the midwatch can grab when they wake up to go on watch. It doesn't have to be a sit down meal. It could be just some fruit, or a sandwich, or even soup that could be heated quickly in the microwave."

"Any other restrictions on the meals?"

"Try to keep caloric distribution even across the three meals. I want to see traditional breakfast foods in the morning, I'd like to see a full, three course meal at noon and evening–that means soup or salad, a main entree with two side dishes, and dessert."

"I know what a three course meal is, Captain."

"Sorry. I'm just thinking out loud here, Avery. I wasn't sure what I meant myself, so I was just saying it to see if I knew."

"Okay. How soon do you want these? And do the meals need to be something I can cook? Or just anything that sounds good?"

"Let's start with anything that sounds good, and I'd like the whole list by morning."

"Tomorrow morning, Captain?"

"Yes, Avery. I'd like to review the menu list when I take over the watch at 0600."

"Aye, aye, Captain."

"Do you think you can to that?"

"By morning, Captain? Of course. I could probably have it done in a stan."

"Really?"

His look of confidence started fading. "I don't know, Captain, but yes, I think so."

"Well, Avery, if you think you can run up a sixty day menu in a stan, then I believe you and if you'd send that to my tablet when you're done, I'd appreciate it."

"Sure thing, Captain."

"I'll let you get on with it then, Mr. Wyatt. I look forward to seeing your solution."

I left Mr. Wyatt slipping his tablet into the holster and headed for the lock. I needed to see somebody in "Cargo Dispatch" about a cargo.

DST's fleet admin office was on the oh-five deck and it didn't take me more than five ticks to go from the lock to the door. The counter clerk looked up when I opened the door and stepped in.

"Captain? How can I help you?'

"I'm Ishmael Wang off *Agamemnon* and I'd like to talk to somebody in Cargo Dispatch."

The clerk looked confused. "Cargo Dispatch, Captain? I'm not sure what you mean."

"I was talking to my cargo chief about a cargo for us. He said he gets his cargoes by calling the local office and asking for 'Cargo Dispatch.'"

"Oh, *Agamemnon*! Of course. Mr. Wyatt. A lovely man but he sometimes needs a bit of assistance, Captain."

"What assistance, exactly, do you render?"

"Oh, he calls once in a while and I just pull up the pending freight queue for him and give him the first three on the list that *Agamemnon* can carry."

"It's just luck of the draw? Whatever might be on the free-trade list at the time?"

"Pretty much, Captain."

"Is there any reason why he couldn't do that himself?"

"None in the least. In fact all the other ships chase down their own cargoes and all we ask is that they file a flight plan so we know where they're going."

"All but Mr. Wyatt."

"Yes, lovely man, but as I say, he sometimes needs just a little help."

"Thank you, that clears up a bit of confusion I had. DST wouldn't have any problem if we started tracking down our own cans?"

"Just file the flight plans and don't lose money." The clerk smiled brightly. "Is there anything else, Captain?"

"You've been very helpful. Thank you."

Five ticks later, I was back aboard. When I passed through the lock, Mr. Schubert said, "Welcome back, sar."

"Thank you, Mr. Schubert. Any problems?"

"None, Captain. All shipshape and Bristol fashion."

"Carry on, Mr. Schubert."

"Aye, sar."

I tried not to smile, but then I remembered the freezers and I didn't feel like smiling. The main galley freezers and stores were just aft of the galley. I found the passage easily enough and walked back to do a fast inventory myself.

The canned goods in the pantry were a bit distressing. Not a lot of variety there, then I started thinking about how they might be augmented. Some of the soups would make a good base for something more interesting. A lot of the staples that I'd normally expect to see dried and loose were just cooked and in cans–not my preferred mode, but they could be made to serve. The chillers were almost completely devoid of root crop vegetables and tree fruits. They were almost completely devoid of everything, truth be told. I didn't remember ever seeing ready chillers so empty.

The freezers were my real concern. That was a lot of food and the dates on it were very near. Most of it would be beyond expiration within the next ninety days and all of it would be gone in four months.

When I got to the freezers, though, I almost laughed in relief. Standard freezers operate at about -20C. Food kept frozen there will stay safe from bacteria and decay almost indefinitely. The degradation in food quality really happens when foods become freezer burned–desiccated by extended freezing–or if the temperature isn't maintained at a constant level.

The shipboard freezers were not the standard freezer. If the gauges over the doors were correct, they maintained -50C. At that temperature, the foodstuffs would probably be safe for decades, or until the power was cut.

I opened one and peeked in. It was full. I recognized some of the cartons and they were all pristine. No sign of condensation, freezer rime, or other symptoms that would indicate that there might be a problem. I slammed the heavy door shut before much of the cold air had a chance to escape and vowed to spot check the inventories. Between the canned goods and the freezers, we had plenty of food. We may get bored, but we wouldn't starve, and that gave us time to rotate some of this frozen stock.

The knot in my gut began to unwind before I remembered that it was just the first day and it wasn't over.

CHAPTER EIGHTEEN
DIURNIA ORBITAL: 2372-JANUARY-09

Philip Delman met me at the front door of Jimmy's promptly at 1900. He wore civvies but I hadn't had time to change out of my undress khakis. I was pretty sure we wouldn't evoke the slightest comment. We went in and the *maitre d'* seated us immediately. We were unfashionably early for fine dining on the Orbital, which was just the way I liked it.

I almost felt bad for the crew aboard. Wyatt had taken a chance and stretched his culinary wings for the evening meal. He'd skipped the can of soup and opened a can of beans instead. I very purposefully did not critique his efforts, preferring to acquire adequate information before taking remedial action.

We ordered and while the drinks were being drawn, Philip opened the conversational gambit with a classic. "So, how was your first day at the office?"

"I don't remember the last time twelve stans went by so fast. How about you? The *Tinker* adapting to you?"

"That crew is amazing, Ishmael. You were right, Behr is formidable and Kazyanenko is brilliant." He shook his head in wonder and turned eagerly to allow the waiter to place a pre-prandial cocktail in front of him.

"Any lines on a new second mate?"

"Yes, I'm meeting with one in the morning. The company posted yesterday and his name came up today. So, we're hoping that we'll be sympatico and we'll be getting underway the day after. How about you?" I could have sworn he smirked into his highball. "How's the crew treating you?"

"Not too bad actually. I do have some questions for you."

"I dare say." He smiled at me, as if enjoying some private joke.

"What's with Wyatt and the food?"

"Oh, his opening cans?"

"Well, that and the freezers full of chow that have never been used?"

"Freezers full?"

"Yeah. The three freezers in the galley stores section are full of food that has been there for months. If the inventories are right, there's only a dozen kilograms missing from the original shipments."

"Oh, I'm sure the inventories are right. That man can count with the best. What he can't do is think."

I sipped my own drink as the waiter delivered the first course. I had a nice salad of greens dressed with oil and balsamic vinegar. Philip had the soup.

When the waiter had gone I followed up. "Interesting observation. Do you know why he won't carry a tablet?"

"Oh, yes. He drops them. Repeatedly. Maddening thing."

"Any idea why? I mean we all drop them occasionally." I had, in fact, dropped mine exactly three times since I got my current upgrade almost five stanyers before.

Delman shook his head. "Not really. They're pretty heavily armored so how he manages to break it is beyond me."

I moved on. "What do you think of his cargo picking?"

Delman finished the sup of soup he was taking before replying. "That was probably the single most aggravating thing he did. It seemed like we were always in port six or seven days–occasionally eight or nine while he looked for a cargo. When he found one, it was almost always a low yield box of nothing."

"Almost like he just took the first thing on the open cargo list that the ship could haul?"

Philip brightened. "Exactly! And I never could understand why. I talked to him repeatedly about his initiative and entrepreneurial spirit but nothing I said to him seemed to stick."

"Did you, by any chance, ever tell him that he should be picking his own cargos?"

At this Delman looked confused. "Tell him what?"

"Anything like 'these last few shipments have been really low value and our shares are hurting because of it?'"

"Why in the world would I have done that, Ishmael my lad? The man was a cargo chief. He had to know that."

"Did you ever pick a cargo or two yourself, just to help out, show what you were looking for?"

His eyes went wide in alarm. "Certainly not! I'm a Deck officer, I don't know anything about cargo picking. That's what the cargo officers are for."

"You'll appreciate Mr. Hinds, I think."

"Marcus? That man is genius. You know he had a cargo can lined up on that first day I talked to him?"

"I suspect he did." I didn't get into it, but Marcus usually had our next cargo commitment a least a week before we tied up from the last. He missed a few good ones that he might have gotten if he'd waited, but he also locked down some excellent cargoes that would have gotten away from us otherwise. The *Tinker's* crew enjoyed very reliable shares under his picking.

"What's with Gerheart? Anything odd with her? Other than she looks fifteen and sounds twelve?"

Delman's spoon scraped the last of the soup out of the bowl. "I'm not sure."

"Not sure?"

He shrugged. "She appears to be some kind of idiot savant. Looks at equipment and knows how to make it work. Breakdowns don't happen. If she ever tells you something needs replacing? Replace it. Immediately, if not sooner."

I thought his tone carried a certain bitter voice of experience. "So she's competent? I checked her logs and they're impeccable."

"I have no idea how she got on that ship, to tell the truth. She's much too competent. The only thing I've ever had a problem with is that she talks in that whispery, little kid voice all the time."

I thought about that as the waiter delivered the entrees. I had a nicely flaked white fish fillet and Delman had a steak. We gave homage to the culinary gods for a few ticks while the food was hot and my mind digested.

Delman returned us to the business of captaining. "What can you tell me about Chief Menas, speaking of engineers?"

"Brilliant engineer. Great manager. She keeps that after nacelle neat as a pin. Decks are clean enough to eat off. Her engineering gang dotes on her."

"She seems rather cool toward me."

I gave a little shrug. Mel was also a very astute judge of character, but I didn't mention that. "Give her time to get to see you in action." I also didn't say what the likely outcome of that might be.

"I suspect you're right." He chewed meditatively for half a tick. "Are there any weak spots in the chain of command there?"

"I think you'll find that the people under you on the chain are rock steady, know their jobs, and like to do them. I can't speak for this new guy, but the rest you should find to your liking."

He actually beamed. "Excellent."

"Talk to me about Ms. Thomas? What's her story?"

"Oh, Gwen is invaluable. She'll keep those ratings on their toes, let me tell you."

"Really? I haven't met them all to form an opinion yet, but Mr. Schubert seems to be fairly sharp. Undisciplined, maybe, but sharp."

"Sharp as a knife in the back."

"In what way?"

"Count on him to do something to embarrass the ship every chance he gets!"

"You mean like failing to acknowledge the call button for the owner and then pretending to be asleep on watch until somebody else gets it open?"

Delman blanched. "He didn't."

I nodded.

Delman sighed. "Well, I hope Gwen ripped him a strip of fresh hide for that one. Are you sure he was only pretending to be asleep?"

"I'm pretty sure. Have you ever heard that call buzzer from inside the ship?"

"Oh, yeah. You can hear that thing all the way up into officer country."

"Rather unlikely that he'd have slept through it ringing multiple times, don't you think?"

He seemed startled by that notion. "Does seem unlikely doesn't it?"

"What else can you tell me about the boys?"

"Hill is the ringleader. He's got the gift of gab and an evil mind. Ricks is the space lawyer. He'll cite you chapter and verse every chance he gets."

"And Schubert?"

"Schubert's the class clown. He'll do anything for a laugh. He refilled my teabags with oregano once, and coated the announcer mic on the bridge with something like shoe black. Ms. Thomas looked like she'd been kissing a coal scuttle for two days."

"Yes, on Ms. Thomas. What's with the cabin door?"

He laughed. "Already got you there, eh? I have no idea. She has some very strange ideas on propriety and you will not get her to budge on that."

"Really?"

"Oh, yeah. I don't know if she was abused as a cadet or if she just hopes she will be."

Right up to that point I thought Captain Philip Delman might have been merely a bit dense. That comment told me why he'd been put on the *Agamemnon*. It gave me pause to wonder if perhaps there was a reason that I had been given the assignment.

I concentrated on my food and let the conversation lapse for a few ticks.

"I thought you were going to ask about her voice."

"Her voice? What about her voice?"

"It's loud."

"Oh, really?"

"You hadn't noticed? The blackguards in the crew quarters call her 'Foghorn' behind her back."

I made a show of considering before offering a shrug. "Don't know that I really noticed."

He snorted. "I don't know how you could miss it."

I let the remark pass. "Any comments on Pall. I just met him briefly this evening at watch change. He seems nice enough. A bit young for second."

"Ah, Billy is a dear boy. First in his class at the academy. Got second on his first try. I don't know if he'll ever make first."

"Why not? He looks ok."

"Billy the Buccaneer."

"Excuse me?"

"They call him Billy the Buccaneer. The kid's got pirates under his bunk. Everything that happens, it's pirates. Milk goes bad? Pirates. Jump missed by a few klicks? Pirates. Give him a chance and he'll regale you with tales of the famous pirates of High Tortuga."

"High Tortuga?"

"Yes, he claims there's this mythical place out there in the Deep Dark where the pirates congregate called High Tortuga. He'll tell you all about it if you give him half a chance."

I considered that while I finished off my fish. "That doesn't sound like it would get in the way of his making first mate."

"Normally, I'd agree. There aren't that many questions about pirates on the first's exam as I remember it."

"Then why?"

"Because young Mr. Pall is convinced that the pirates know he knows about them and they'll try to kill him if he goes any higher in the chain of command."

"Paranoia?"

"Let's just say a little light on the stabilizing thrusters."

"When's he eligible to sit for first?"

"Next year sometime."

I made a mental note of that.

We filled the remainder of the meal with background and war stories. At the end of the meal, over a final coffee for me and a sherry for him, he returned to discussing my crew.

"Yes, you've got your work cut out for you, Ishmael my lad. Gwennie will keep the boys in line for you, and Gerheart will get you there. Billy the Buccaneer might keep you entertained if you like pirate stories, but the weak link there is Wyatt. He's barely competent to open a can and he seems to have all the logic and reasoning of a stuffed green pepper."

"Well, I'm looking forward to the challenge. I think we might be able to do something here."

"You watch your back, Ishmael. That crew will break your heart and the boys will stomp you into the deck."

I thought about that as I settled up with the establishment–expensive but worth every credit for what I'd learned. The food was a nice side benefit.

We walked together to the lift and he got out at the dock.

"Good night, Ishmael my lad. Congratulations and best wishes on the *Agamemnon*."

We shook hands. "Congratulations on the *Tinker* as well." I hesitated for a heartbeat before adding. "You've got a great crew there. They'll be a tremendous help to you."

"Oh, I'm certain, Ishmael. After the incompetence of the *Agamemnon*, this crew is a breath of fresh air."

The lift doors closed and I pulled out my tablet to admire the menu that Wyatt had sent me just before I left the ship. Not only did he have a menu, when I went back to him and asked him to plan it using only the food stocks available in ship's inventory, he had it revised in less than half a stan. "Not bad work for a stuffed green pepper," I said just as the doors opened on oh-seven.

The stationer waiting there blinked once. "Excuse me, Captain?"

I smiled and shook my head. "Oh, nothing. Bad habit I have of talking to myself."

She smiled in reply and stepped into the car as I stepped off.

I hurried to our apartment to change into civvies before heading over to The Miller Moth. I wanted to visit with Jen for awhile and she'd be working until 0200. I knew from experience that if I sat on the end of the bar, we'd be able to chat and visit between customers. It was a pleasant way to spend an evening.

In two shakes I'd stripped out of my uniform and started rummaging in the closet. I grabbed my favorite pair of jeans, and went thru the hangers looking for a shirt. I grabbed a handy one and slipped it off the hanger and onto my shoulders in one smooth movement. I looked at it in the mirror while I buttoned and had one of those odd moments of blankness.

I'm good with clothes, but I could not for the life of me remember where I'd gotten it. It fit a bit snugly about the shoulders and loose around my waist, though and I hated clothes that didn't fit right. I must have gotten it so long ago I'd misplaced the mental receipt, and when it didn't fit it got pushed to the back of the closet.

I shrugged off the lapse. It was good enough to suit the purpose. I tugged on my boots and headed down to the pub to chat up the gorgeous woman who I was pretty sure I'd be sleeping with later. That thought gave me a warm smile.

CHAPTER NINETEEN
DIURNIA ORBITAL: 2372-JANUARY-10

My tablet started beeping me awake almost before I got to sleep. I supected I'd made a tactical blunder by sitting with Jen at the bar until she and George closed it up at 0200. We'd come home for what might most charitably have been characterized as falling on each other like animals.

Repeatedly.

The beeping was my conscience and my penance would be a day of duty without sleep. I slapped the shut off and realized that I had enough to do to keep me awake. I probably wouldn't notice.

I grabbed a fast three tick shower, put my uniform mostly on, patted myself on the back for not being hungover as well as exhausted and made my way to the ship. Ricks was on the brow and greeted me pleasantly enough when I stepped aboard at 0500.

"What's for breakfast this morning, Mr. Ricks?"

He seemed surprised that I'd addressed him. "I'm sure I don't know. Captain."

"If you had to guess, what would it be?"

"Packaged cereal, dry toast, and tea, sar."

"Sounds grim."

He shrugged non-committally.

"What would you like for breakfast, Mr. Ricks?"

He answered me instantly. "Pancakes, sausage, and maybe a bit of applesauce on the side."

"Sausage? Not bacon?"

"Bacon would do, sar."

"But you like sausage, Mr. Ricks?"

"With pancakes, yes, Captain. I do. And you did ask."

"Indeed I did and I think your breakfast sounds better than

117

what I'm likely to find in there. Thank you for your feedback, Mr. Ricks. Carry on."

I headed into the ship and up to the cabin. The glow from the station's skin outside was more than enough light for me to change out of my khakis and into a shipsuit. Day two, and high time we began to turn the ship around.

First things first, and food was a key. My old boss on the *Lois McKendrick* used to say something like, "It's the only restaurant they have in the Deep Dark, but they should still want to eat here." Padding into the darkened galley reminded me of him.

The ready cooler had nothing resembling sausage, or even bacon, in it. I took a few ticks to look up the inventory and found both bacon and sausage in the deep freeze. I remembered to put on a pair of work gloves before moving the colder-than-ice packages. In all honesty, they were a pair of oven mitts because I didn't find any gloves handy. I started a list of things I wanted Mr. Wyatt to buy.

I left the case of bacon in the chiller to thaw and took the case of sausage to the galley. I was a little uneasy about what I might find in the case, but whoever had purchased this had done the right thing and gotten portion-controlled, individually wrapped servings. I pulled out enough sausage for ten people and took the case back to the ready cooler to join the bacon.

When I got to the galley I went to draw a cup of coffee, and discovered an empty pot. It was clean enough, just empty. A few ticks of rummaging in the lockers turned up a can of ground coffee, and my buckets of Sarabanda Dark. What it didn't turn up was a coffee grinder. I added that to the list for Wyatt. The can of coffee smelled relatively fresh, and in an emergency one sometimes has to sacrifice. The pot dribbled nicely in a matter of a tick or two and I turned to the sausage. I tossed the packages into the microwave set to defrost. I didn't think it would work completely, but it would move enough molecules that I could probably get the packaging material off it. A hot griddle would fix the rest.

Pancakes turned out to be a bit of a challenge. I found no flour, no baking power, no baking soda. I turned up plenty of salt but couldn't find any fresh eggs.

I checked the dry goods inventory and found a box of pancake mix. It wasn't perfect but it would do for the moment. I added flour and the other missing ingredients to the list.

I had to give Wyatt credit for a painstakingly accurate inventory. Whatever flaws he may have had–and I was convinced they weren't anything at all like people imagined–his record keeping was impeccable. That thought reminded me to update the stock levels for the amount I'd drawn down.

The range was a commercial model that had six burners and even a steel griddle plate. Not large, but big enough for my purposes. While it heated up, I slopped the pancake batter together roughly and smiled as I heard Cookie's voice in my head. *"It's called batter, young Ishmael, so beat it. Just not into submission!"* A few turns with a wisk sufficed to give the correct lumpy consistency to the mix. I was going to add a dash of cinnamon with a bit of sugar, but there was no cinnamon. I put the sugar in anyway, and started a list of spices and herbs.

By then the microwave had beeped and the sausages sizzled nicely when they hit the griddle. The red light on the coffee urn was also on so I grabbed a cup before I started ladling out the batter.

At 0530, Mr. Pall trudged into the galley. "Captain? What are you doing?"

"Good morning, Mr. Pall. I'm cooking breakfast. Anything to report?"

He blinked blearily. "No, long quiet night." He crossed to the pot and drew a mug of his own. "Breakfast, Captain?"

"Yes, meal usually consumed early in the diurnal cycle. Etomologically speaking comes from the phrase 'breaking the fast'–since one doesn't, as a rule, eat while asleep."

"Yes, Captain, but why are you fixing it? Did pirates kidnap Mr. Wyatt?"

"I don't know, Mr. Pall. I just got here a short time ago and I haven't checked his stateroom. When I came aboard I saw that we needed to have breakfast going in short order and Mr. Ricks said he would like to have pancakes and sausage. I thought it sounded pretty good so..." I waved my spatula at the now covered grill and shrugged.

"You sure it's not pirates?" He sounded disappointed.

"Not entirely, no, Mr. Pall. An absence of evidence does not represent evidence of absence but in the face of inadequate evidence, I would suspect that the simplest solution may be the most likely."

"Yes, Captain, I think I agree."

"Think you agree, Mr. Pall?"

"Well, just because nobody's seen pirates, doesn't mean they're not out there."

"Logically sound, Mr. Pall, and a perfect example."

I glanced up at the chrono just as it ticked over to 0545. "Mr. Pall, are you ready to relieve the watch?"

"Yea, I think so, Captain. Are you going to take Third Section or should I wake Greta?"

"I relieve you, Mr. Pall. Please log it at 0545 for me? I have my hands full here."

"Of course, Captain. Anything I can do to help?"

"Syrup and orange juice. I haven't found either yet, but I'm pretty sure there's a can of syrup in the dry goods locker and a crate of frozen concentrate in the number three freezer. If you'd rummage those up, we'll be able to serve breakfast at 0600, I think."

"Sure thing, Skipper." He headed into the stores area and I threw him the oven mitts.

"Don't touch the frozen goods without those on. You'll burn yourself."

He caught them both before they hit the deck and blinked at them before nodding and slipping them on. "Thanks. I wouldn't have thought of it."

"I burned myself before. Not fun but a hard lesson I've never forgotten."

He nodded and disappeared into stores. I thought he was humming a sea chantey, but I couldn't hear well enough to be sure. He was singing *something* to himself.

Before he came back, Avery burst onto the mess deck. "Captain! What are you doing?"

"Just cooking up a batch of pirate repellant. Have you seen any?"

"Seen any what?"

"Pirates, Mr. Wyatt. Have you seen any?"

"No, Captain."

"Must be working then. How many pancakes can you eat?"

"Three, Captain."

"Coffee's ready and Mr. Pall is looking for the orange juice."

"Number three freezer."

"That's where he's looking."

"You sure you don't want me to fix breakfast, Captain?"

"It's okay, Avery. I've got stuff for you to do today and I've got this under control. You haven't called cargo dispatch yet, have you?"

"No, Captain, I was going to call this morning."

"Good. Don't. I'll handle that, while you're out shopping."

"Shopping, Captain?"

"Yes, I've found some things I need you to get for ship's stores. We have supply budget left I assume?"

"Yes, Captain."

"Good. I've got a list started. I think you can get it all at the chandlery down on oh-one."

Pall returned with a case of concentrate balanced carefully across the oven mitts.

I nodded to the counter. "Drop it there while you find the syrup."

Wyatt took a sip of coffee and put the cup on the table. "I know where it is. I can show you, William."

They went back and I could hear them rummaging around. I grinned into my griddle and pulled a few more pancakes off onto a warming pan.

An able spacer I didn't recognize stumbled onto the mess deck. I turned to face him. "You must be Mr. Hill."

"I am. And who would you be when you're at home?"

"Don't get out much, do you, Mr. Hill?"

"Wha–?"

"I'll be your OD this morning, Mr. Hill." I nodded at the chronometer. "And if you haven't relieved Mr. Ricks already, you're late relieving the brow. Oh, and you can call me Captain. It's not my name but use it until you've mastered the knack."

The expression on his face moved from puzzlement to perplexitude but he was obviously not tracking.

I sighed. "Coffee, Mr. Hill. Get some. Now. In that pot. The one with the little red light. Relieve Mr. Ricks at the brow. Do it now, Mr. Hill. We'll sort your chain of command once ship's business is in hand."

To his credit, he did it with only a muttered, "Aye, sar."

Wyatt and Pall returned from stores, Pall holding a plastic retort of syrup triumphantly.

"Excellent. Avery, if you'd get a jug of concentrate mixed up and William if you'd put that case back into the ready freezer? It'll stay frozen and handy there."

Between the two of them, they managed to get the box open without burning or cutting themselves.

At 0600 I slid a big platter of sausages and another of pancakes onto the sideboard. "Ladies and Gentlemen, breakfast is served."

Ms. Thomas burst into the galley. "What's going on in here? What's that smell?" Her voice echoed off the overhead.

I lifted my nose and sniffed delicately. "I believe that's sausage you're referring to, Ms. Thomas. Not quite as redolent or identifiable as bacon but a pork product of some provenance none the less."

It was Mr. Pall who asked, "Captain, do you always talk like that?"

"I'm asked that question a lot. Apparently I do."

Mr. Ricks came into the galley and just shook his head. "I don't believe it, sar. Pancakes and sausage?"

"Well, it sounded good to me, Mr. Ricks. Sorry about the

applesauce. Grab a plate and dig in. Do you happen to know if Mr. Schubert is aboard?"

"He hasn't come back yet, Captain."

"Should we be alarmed?" I looked around the room.

Ms. Thomas said, "The authorities usually contact us, if there's a problem."

"Then we'll assume that he's a big boy and able to take care of himself until we have evidence to the contrary." I stuck my head around the corner. "Breakfast, Mr. Hill. Come and get it."

Greta Gerheart joined us eventually, and I realized that we had the whole crew, less one. The two ratings sat at one table, while Avery, Wyatt, Thomas, and I sat at another. Because she was late, Greta sat with the ratings, giving them each a small smile. They appeared to welcome her with grins.

While we ate, I added to my shopping list including root crops, dry goods, and a case of fresh eggs.

I also added some notes about changes I needed in the ship.

Chapter Twenty
Diurnia Orbital: 2372-January-10

Breakfast cleanup was minimal. The midwatch headed for their
bunks while the off-watch wandered off, and the chief went down
to Engineering. I settled with Mr. Wyatt at one of the tables to go
over my requirements. He accepted the list without question and
headed for the chandlery.

That left me to deal with Mr. Hill.

I ambled out to the brow and Mr. Hill looked up from his reading. The screen in front of him didn't have anything in particular.
It looked like a novel.

"A little light reading, Mr. Hill."

"I'm allowed. Sar."

"Yes, you certainly are, Mr. Hill. Anything to report?"

"No. Sar." His voice carried the sneer that his face showed
clearly.

"Do we have a problem, Mr. Hill?"

"No. Sar. *We* do not have a problem." He put special emphasis
on the 'we.'

"Very well, then, Mr. Hill, do you have a problem?"

"No. Sar. I do not have a problem."

"Are you certain, Mr. Hill?"

"Quite. Sar."

"Excellent, Mr. Hill. I think we'll get along famously."

I turned to go and behind me he spoke again.

"It won't work you know, sar."

I didn't turn back to him, just spoke over my shoulder. "What's
that, Mr. Hill?"

"You comin' in here all buddy-buddy, makin' nice. It won't
work." The pause was deliberate. "Sar."

I did turn to him then. "Mr. Hill, I'm not sure what you're implying but let me assure you that the only agenda I have on this ship is to make it into an effective and efficient money-making machine. I'll need everybody's help to make that happen. So as for making it work, as you so charmingly put it, let me assure you, it will work."

"You think a little pancake breakfast is gonna turn it around?"

"Mr. Hill, that should be 'you think a little pancake breakfast is gonna turn it around, sar?'"

"What?"

"Try again, Mr. Hill. Use 'sar' or 'Captain'."

"Sar?"

"Much better, Mr. Hill. Now as to your question, no, I don't think a little pancake breakfast is going to turn it around. I think we have a lot of work ahead and I believe your role in that effort will be key."

He sniggered.

"What, Mr. Hill? You don't feel like you're a member of this crew?"

"Oh, yeah. I'm a member, sar. Lowest of the low, but a member."

"Actually, I believe that Ordinary Spacer Ricks holds that distinction on this ship, Mr. Hill, but what's your point?"

"Well, sar, you don't see any of us calling the shots do you? And as for being a money-making machine, Wyatt couldn't pick his nose let alone a decent cargo."

"That's Mr. Wyatt, Mr. Hill, and do you think you could pick cargo any better?"

"Sar, a blind lemur could pick cargoes better than Mr. Wyatt."

"Would you care to make a little wager, Mr. Hill?"

"What?"

"Almost ... try again, Mr. Hill."

"Sar?"

"I knew you could do it. I asked if you wanted to bet that you could out pick Mr. Wyatt on cargoes."

"What's the bet?" He remembered after a short pause. "Sar."

"Hm. Good question. What kind of stakes do you think, Mr. Hill?"

"You're serious?" I waited and he added, "Sar."

"Very, Mr. Hill."

He looked at me for a long time. I'm not sure what calculus he was trying to solve in his mind. "Okay, sar, if I win, I get to sit at the captain's table at mess."

I didn't see that one coming. "The captain's table, Mr. Hill?"

"There are two tables in the galley, Captain. Don't tell me you don't realize..."

He sat me back on my heels with that. "To tell you the truth, Mr. Hill, breakfast was only my second meal aboard. I didn't realize, but that's not a good bet for you. Pick something better."

"That's what I want, Captain."

"I'll grant you that anyway. Once we get underway, you can sit at the captain's table, as you call it, at every meal, Mr. Hill. Pick something else."

"You're joking." I waited. "Sar."

"No, Mr. Hill, I'm not joking. You can sit at the same table that I do as soon as we get underway."

He got a sly, calculating look that I didn't like, but he thought a little longer. "A hot tub, Captain."

"A hot tub, Mr. Hill? I rather like the sound of that myself. Where would we put it?"

"In the workout room, sar. I bet if we rearrange it, we could put one in there."

"One moment, Mr. Hill. I'd like to see if it looks feasible to me."

I sauntered down the length of the ship and into the workout room behind the crew's quarters. Just looking at it, I thought there might be sufficient space there. I returned to where Mr. Hill watched me amble down the length of the ship and back. "I will accept that wager, pending Chief Gerheart's assessment on the plumbing and heating."

"Trying to weasel already, Captain?"

"Not at all, Mr. Hill. I intend to wager in good faith and I want to make sure that I can actually pay off, should I lose. If there's a problem with putting the hot tub in that space from an engineering perspective, I'll need to ask you for something else but I'll ask Chief Gerheart's opinion on feasibility before we actually bind the wager. Is that satisfactory, Mr. Hill?"

"I don't know, Captain. Sounds like you're hedgin' before we even start."

"Come, come, Mr. Hill, I'm just trying to be reasonable. I can't make you king of the universe or give you a million credits either. I just want to make sure that what I agree to I can actually deliver."

"And what do you want if I lose?" I waited until he added it. "Sar."

"If you lose, you sit for a specialty rating, Mr. Hill."

"Any particular one, Captain?"

"No. Any division, any specialty. Within six months of the end of the contest you will sit for the test in that rating."

"I don't have to pass it, sar?"

I shook my head. "No, Mr. Hill. You just have to sit for the exam."

He thought about it. I'll give him credit. He looked at me for a long tick before saying, "That's not good enough, Captain. Pick something better."

"That's what I want, Mr. Hill."

He reached over to the console and flipped the screen to a half completed lesson on cargo handling. "I'll grant you the test, Captain. Just let me take it on the next cycle." He grinned at me. "Pick something else."

"Very well, Mr. Hill. If I win, then you become Mr. Wyatt's apprentice for as long as you're both aboard."

"What does that mean, Captain?"

"It means Mr. Wyatt will teach you how to pick cargoes better, and you'll help him with stores."

He thought about it, staring at the half finished lesson on his screen. "Very well, Captain. I think I can agree to those terms. You don't want to add a condition that I have to remain aboard for some period of time?"

"No, Mr. Hill."

"If I pass this exam, I can get another berth, Captain."

"You could, but then I wouldn't have to put in the hot tub if you forfeit, Mr. Hill, and I have a feeling that you're an honorable man. I could be wrong, but you don't strike me as the type to welch on a bet."

"What are the conditions of this bet, Captain?"

"Good question. We can't have this be some kind of hypothetical contest, Mr. Hill, but a real test of your picking ability." I thought about it for maybe a tick. "Here's what I propose. I will give you each a can to fill. On each trip, you will fill that can. We'll keep track of the profit and loss on each can. At the end of—say—ten trips, the winner will be the one with the highest gross profit."

"Ten trips! Captain, that's almost twenty months. I'm not willing to wait that long for my hot tub! Three trips!"

"You raise a valid issue, Mr. Hill, but luck is too much a factor in only three trips. Five trips, and you have to have your cargo picked no later than the end of our first day in port."

"What about the third can, Captain? We're rated to carry three cans."

"That one's mine."

He looked at me skeptically. "Yours, Captain?"

"Mine, Mr. Hill. I'm not part of the contest, but it's not fair to count gross profit and then let Mr. Wyatt have two containers. For the next five trips, I'll pick one can of cargo, you pick one, and Mr. Wyatt will pick the third. I'll pick first and I'll pick mine at least forty-eight hours before docking. You two will have to pick cans going to the same place as mine."

"And we'll start this when, sar?"

"Immediately. I want to get underway tomorrow afternoon and I intend we should have a cargo. I'll pick one as soon as Mr. Wyatt returns and then you two will have to pick by the end of the watch. Not ideal but we're all under the same time constraints so it's equally burdensome. Agreed?"

"That sounds fair, Captain."

"Very well, Mr. Hill. Carry on. I'll check with Chief Gerheart on the plumbing situation to see if we have a valid bet."

I headed back into the ship and took a left turn at the ladder, dropping down one deck to Engineering. When I explained what I wanted to Ms. Gerheart she laughed and clapped her hands in excitement.

"Will it go there, Ms. Gerheart? I'm concerned for plumbing and electrical runs."

"Oh, no, Captain. It'll go just fine."

"You sound very certain of that."

"I am. That space is right behind the crew's head. There's no reason I can think of not to put one in there."

"Thank you, Ms. Gerheart. One other thing. Can we put a repeater console in the mess deck?"

"Like a bridge console, Captain?'

"Exactly, Ms. Gerheart."

Her eyes twinkled in delight. "I have just the thing in spares, sar. It should be no trouble."

"Please replace anything you use up, Chief. I don't want to get underway without a spare."

That chore completed, I needed to contact the chandlery myself, and see about having a little remodeling done, but before I got them on the line I went back to the brow.

"Well, Mr. Hill, Chief Gerheart assures me we have sufficient infrastructure for the hot tub. And I think we have a bet."

I spit in my hand and held it out. He did the same and we shook on it.

At 0930, Mr. Wyatt returned from his stores procurement. "They'll be delivering the whole order this afternoon, Captain."

"Excellent, Mr. Wyatt! I need to contact the ship fitters for a small renovation project, but I need to tell you about a little wager I have made with Mr. Hill. You're going to pick one can of cargo. He's going to pick one can of cargo. If, after five trips, his cans earn more than your cans, I'll install a hot tub."

"What if my cans earn more, Captain?"

"Then he becomes your apprentice. You teach him all you know and he helps you with the stores."

"You wagered this? What do you get out of it, Captain?"

"A more profitable ship."

"Wait! What do you mean I pick a can of cargo?"

"Sit, Avery. We need to talk." I explained cargo dispatch and how all they were doing was picking the first cargo on the list. "You can do a lot better than that, Avery."

He just sat there, his face blank and jaw slack. "That's impossible."

I shook my head. "No, I'm afraid it's not. I talked to the clerk there yesterday afternoon. This is the first chance I've had to talk to you."

Avery screwed up his face and leaned across the table so he could talk softly. "But, Captain, I don't know the first thing about picking cargos." Anxiety had his whole body knotted. "You just bet that I could out pick Mr. Hill."

I nodded with a happy smile. "Avery, he thinks he can out pick you because of the cargoes we've been carrying since you came aboard."

"But I haven't picked any of those cargoes!"

I smiled at him. "That, Mr. Wyatt, is exactly my point. Nobody knows if you can pick cargo or not because you've never done it."

"But you bet a hot tub, Captain!"

"And I'll gladly buy a hot tub if you two can pick some decent cans. The incremental value to the ship and the crew shares will be very much worth it. I also bet on getting you an apprentice and some help with stores. I wouldn't have done that if I didn't think you could do it."

His level of anxiety didn't appear to ease. "But, Captain, I have no idea if I can do it or not."

"I do."

"How can you be so sure, Captain?"

I pulled out my tablet and showed him the menus. "This proves it. You took a huge amount of data, distilled it down to a few likely choices, applied some judgment, and built a menu for sixty days using just the stores we have aboard. I'm going to want a bit of change to it based on the incremental stores you bought this morning, but if you can do this, you can pick cargo."

He started to calm down. "Well, that wasn't very hard. I knew all the variables."

"True. Cargo picking is a little more complicated. You don't know all the variables, but you don't need to. The more data you can use, the better you'll be, but even having a little control will let you do better than cargo dispatch. That was purely random assignment."

He uncoiled a little more. "What do I do?"

"You already know most of it. Cargo dispatch gave you a manifest number. You logged in and booked that manifest by the number. It was almost always a three can unit, because that's what they searched for. You'll be searching for a one can unit. Once you have the number, you'll log it just like before. Everything else works exactly the way you know how to do. The only difference is that instead of waiting for Cargo Dispatch to give you the numbers, you'll get them from your own research."

"And Mr. Hill."

"Yes, Mr. Hill will give you his number, and you'll book it, just as if it were cargo dispatch giving it to you."

"Who will pick the third can, Captain?"

"I will. In fact, I'll pick first. You two will have to pick cans going to the same place. Furthermore, you have to pick your cans within twenty-four stans of docking. I'll lock mine at least two days before docking so you'll have three days to pick your cans."

His eyes lost focus for a few heartbeats while he mulled it over. "I really can't lose, can I, Captain?" he said at last.

"No, Mr. Wyatt, you can't lose because you have no dog in this fight. I'm the one who's betting with Mr. Hill. You're just the innocent bystander. And I can't lose either, because no matter who makes more money, the ship wins. I do have one immediate problem. I need to pick a can going somewhere because you need to pick your can before the end of this watch."

"What? How am I supposed to do that?"

I pulled up my tablet and had it display the current cargoes on the station net. I filtered for one-can loads for immediate shipment. I scanned down the list looking for a value higher than the average. There were several and one carried a small priority. I grabbed that one and forwarded the manifest number to Mr. Wyatt's tablet, which I was pleased to hear bip from across the table.

"If you'd book that number to the ship, Mr. Wyatt, we've got the first can and it's going to Welliver."

I looked up to see Mr. Wyatt staring at me. "Is that all we have to do?"

"If you'd book that can, Mr. Wyatt? It won't be available long and I don't want to lose it. I'll explain after we have the contract."

"Of course, Captain." He stood and hurried off.

I followed him out of the galley but headed for the brow. "The game is on, Mr. Hill. Welliver. And that priority can of machine parts is mine."

He snapped to his screen and pulled up the open cargo list. I was close enough to see that it was almost the same display that I'd just had on my tablet, with a few more columns of information. He adjusted his display with a couple of keystrokes. "This one, Captain?"

I looked over his shoulder. "Yes, that's the one." While we watched, the status changed to show it under contract to us.

"Nice snag, sar."

"Thank you, Mr. Hill. We need two more cans as good or better than that by end of the watch. I'll get Mr. Pall on the flight plan for departure on or about noon on the eleventh."

Mr. Hill's screen updated and new cargoes showed up. "How do I tell Mr. Wyatt, sar?"

"Just send it to his tablet, and dupe to me. We'll need to figure out a more elegant solution, but I have some ideas."

A new priority shipment appeared on the list, and it looked like a good one to me. Mr. Hill barked a short laugh and pounced on his keyboard, but before he could capture it, the status changed to show it already under contract to the *Agamemnon*.

"Well, Mr. Hill. Looks like we already have that one." I mentally applauded Mr. Wyatt.

"Hmm. This could be trickier than I thought, Captain. The delay in notification and booking could jimmy the deals."

"My thoughts exactly, Mr. Hill. Perhaps we three can put our heads together on how best to deal with this. Things should go more smoothly now we've got the cycle underway, but still it seems cumbersome, even to me." I left Mr. Hill watching his screen. I wasn't sure that the delay would be all that significant once the process got started, but I made a note to look into how to make it fairer to Mr. Hill, short of giving him the booking codes.

I met Mr. Wyatt coming down the ladder with a smile on his face. "I booked a can, Captain!"

"Excellent catch, too, Mr. Wyatt. When Mr. Hill sends you a manifest number, please be sure to book it as soon as possible. Time, as you may have guessed, will be critical on the better cans."

"Aye, aye, Captain. I understand."

I wasn't too worried about hanky-panky because the final value of the can wouldn't be determined until we actually delivered it, the numbers on this end were speculative and subject to variation in market conditions on the other end. Still, the two cans we had booked showed promise for an excellent return.

"Next for you, Mr. Wyatt, lunch." I pulled out my tablet opened the menu list. "Says here lunch will be braised chicken, rice, and sautéed beans, with a minestrone soup first course and apple pie for dessert."

Mr. Wyatt blanched. "You said I didn't need to know how to cook the meal, Captain. Only that we have the stores on hand to make it."

"Indeed I did, Mr. Wyatt. I don't want you to cook it. I want you to round up the stores we need to make it. Where is this stuff?"

We spent a fast five ticks having Mr. Wyatt pull the necessary supplies out of stores. While we were there, I had him identify and retrieve what we'd need to make dinner. He understood the idea of pulling full cases to the ready lockers well enough so I left him staging the next few days' worth of meals.

As I headed up to the cabin, he called after me. "Can I adjust my menu a bit, Captain? I'd like to load it so that these materials get used up more rapidly than things still in deep freeze."

"You may, indeed, Mr. Wyatt. While you're at it, factor in the stores you bought this morning. The root crops in particular will have a large effect on the menus."

In the cabin I settled down for a little chat with the fine people in the ship fitting department of the chandlery and they promised to send up the requisite materials and manpower first thing in the morning.

I grinned as I disconnected and looked around the empty cabin. It was 1000 so I took half a stan to hang up a couple of ship suits and put my personal items in the head. I'd never been one to put up a lot of stuff on the bulkheads but my eyes went to a spot over the desk and I made a note to get my Master's License framed.

I pondered the irony of a land rat teaching spacers how to sail, but shook it off. Sometimes you needed to be an outsider to really appreciate how things worked. Otherwise you took it for granted. My mother used to say something about having fish describe water. That seemed to make more sense to me as I headed to the galley to begin cooking lunch.

Chapter Twenty-two
Diurnia Orbital: 2372-January-10

Lunch was attended by the officers, but neither of the off duty ratings joined us. The meal reinforced the awkwardness of two tables
and I was even more pleased with the plans I'd made. We discussed
the placement of the repeater while we dined and agreed on a location. Chief Gerheart surprised me by suggesting an oversized screen
and remote combination that would allow a much greater flexibility
in use.

"And do you have these just laying around in spares, Chief?"

She giggled delightfully, and talked quietly at her plate. "Oh,
you know, boys aren't the only ones who like toys. I picked these
up a while back, Captain. I thought they might be useful one day."

"Captain Delman didn't want to use it?"

She shook her head. "He didn't spend much time on the mess
deck, so didn't see the need I guess, Captain."

After lunch, Mr. Wyatt helped me clear and clean while Mr.
Pall went ashore and Ms. Thomas retired to her stateroom for a
nap. She'd be taking the overnight at 1800 and needed the rest.
Chief Gerheart entertained us by bringing in a huge monitor on
a dolly and proceeded to quickly and efficiently mount it on the
bulkhead where it could be seen from anywhere in the galley.

Mr. Wyatt chuckled. "My goodness, Greta, is it big enough? I
think I've seen smaller screens at the movie theater."

She giggled again. "It's not that large, Avery. It just looks big
in this space." She stepped back and admired her work. "It is about
three times larger than a standard console, but that's good if you're
trying to read it while you're cooking."

She bundled up all the packing materials and disposed of them
before coming back with a detached console keyboard. It was pow-

ered by rechargeable batteries and communicated with the screen wirelessly. Not exactly cutting edge technology but not the usual configuration of shipboard consoles, more like a home entertainment unit. It took a little jiggering but we found a place to lock the docking station so that the keyboard could be docked for charging when not in use.

This unit wouldn't be all that useful while docked, but remembering my voyage on the *Bad Penny*, I could certainly see where having this kind of data available on the mess deck would make being underway less problematic while short-handed.

Chief Gerheart seemed very pleased with her work, and I had to admit she'd done a terrific job of it.

"We do still have a spare console in stores, don't we, Chief?"

"Yes, we do, Captain. If something happens, I've got one whole bridge console as spare, and a few extra monitors and keyboards as well. We're well stocked."

"Good to know. Thank you, Chief."

She had almost finished when the extra stores arrived. I left Mr. Wyatt to deal with the shipment and went up to the bridge to file the flight plans. I intended to get underway for Welliver the next day at 1500. All we needed was our third can, and the final touches that the ship fitters would be doing in the morning.

I remember thinking that things were coming together nicely about the time I got the call from Orbital Security.

"You the new skipper on the *Agamemnon*?" The officer was pleasant enough.

"Yes, Ishmael Wang, at your service, officer. Is there a problem?"

"Mr. Ricks and Mr. Schubert have been remanded here for drunk and disorderly on the oh-two deck, Captain." He had a particularly bored air.

"Not unusual, I take it?"

"Not terribly, Captain. You can bail 'em any time. There's fines, of course, and they're pretty hefty, or you can take it to court and see if you can reduce 'em."

"But we'd need to be here for that."

"Yes, Captain. 'Fraid so."

"Any purpose in fighting it, Officer?"

"Not really, Captain. The evidence is pretty convincing. Nobody's pressing charges on assault and battery, or indecent exposure. Just the d-and-d."

"This sounds like it's pretty routine."

"All too routine, Captain."

"Thank you, officer. I'll have my cargo chief come relieve you of the carcasses within the hour. I'll pay the fine."

"Okay, Captain, shall we bill the ship?"

"No, this is personal. I'll pay it."

"Are you sure, Captain." The officer sounded surprised. "Captain Delman always had me bill the ship."

"I'm sure."

He sent me the ticket and I returned the payment authorization. The total made me wince a little.

"Thank you, Captain. And good luck with them."

"Thanks. I have a feeling I'm going to need it."

When he signed off, I did something I should have done the first day and had forgotten. I looked up the balance on the ship's pooka. When I first signed on to the *Lois McKendrick* back in '51, I'd been surprised to learn that there was a crewman on the roster named Lois McKendrick. They told me that the ship had an account set up for random acts of kindness and aid. When somebody in the crew needed something that fell outside the pale of normal operations, that something was sometimes handled by the pooka. There was a fund set up, and some extra mass allotment so most things could be accommodated anonymously in a way that permitted largesse that couldn't be traced. There was a William Tinker crewman on the *Tinker*. He'd been a bit neglected and overlooked when I first joined the ship, but I left him healthy and well tuned. I wasn't surprised to find Agamemnon had almost no money and an allocated mass allotment equal to about five full shares. I made a note to follow up with Wyatt on that. I took solace in it being there at all and chalked it up to *status quo*.

In the meantime, I needed to get Mr. Wyatt up to security to retrieve our wayward boys.

I headed down to the mess deck but met him coming up the ladder. "I've got the new stores stowed, Captain. And Mr. Hill has a can. It looks good."

"Excellent. Go book it fast and then go up to security and retrieve our missing crewmen, if you would, Mr. Wyatt?"

"Oh, no." He stopped on the ladder.

"Yes. Well. Grab that can before somebody else does. Then go up and get the lads. I'll have a little talk with them when you get them back here."

"Aye, aye, Skipper." He raced up the ladder and I went down to the mess deck. I'd ordered a new coffee grinder and I wanted to try it out on some of the Sarabanda Dark.

I had a pot brewed and was just savoring my first mug full when Wyatt returned with a pair of rather bedraggled looking, civvy-clad crewmen. I had him line them up on the mess deck. Ricks had what looked like a bruise on his cheek and Schubert looked like he'd vomited down his shirt. They both smelled rather bad.

"You gentleman seem a bit worse for wear."

Ricks smirked. "We try not to do things halfway, sar."

"Well, gentlemen, I'm glad to see you've retained a sense of humor. You may find that handy. You're confined to ship, of course, until departure. You're too expensive for me to have wandering around loose. And I'm claiming your shares to pay back the fines I just paid on your behalf."

Schubert sniggered and cast a sideways glance at Ricks.

"You have a comment, Mr. Schubert?"

"Good luck with that, sar. The way our shares have been, you'll be a long time recovering."

"I appreciate the sentiment, Mr. Schubert, but I calculate that your share value on this next trip might be as much as, if not more than, the princely wage we pay you. Two trips and I expect to recoup the losses to my purse."

They looked startled.

"Mr. Wyatt and Mr. Hill are having a bit of a competition to see who can pick the better cargo. I've upped the ante by agreeing to put in a hot tub if Mr. Hill prevails, and Mr. Hill will become apprentice to Mr. Wyatt should that work out the other way. I'm picking the third can, and if I'm any judge of cargo, the share value on this trip should be something on the order of five times bigger than the last."

They looked doubtful. I didn't blame them.

"Gentlemen, let's be clear. I'm the captain now. Things will change. Because *I* am the captain things will change the way I want them to. What I want is to make money. I want to make lots and lots of money. We do that by carrying cargo from here to there and back again very cheaply. We don't do it cheaply if the ship has to pay the fines for idiots who can't hold their liquor or control their tempers. Am I clear so far? Just nod."

They nodded.

"Good. Toward that end, you'll find that the ship did not pay your fines this time. I did. Personally. You owe me, not the ship. I intend to make sure you pay me back. Please consider this a business relationship and nothing personal. You two, and looking at the records I should probably include Mr. Hill in this, have been playing this game too long. It ends. Here. You will not get in the way of my profit margins. Are we clear on this? Just nod."

They nodded. They didn't really look like they believed me, although I saw Mr. Schubert eying the new repeater on the bulk-head.

"Excellent. We're getting underway tomorrow afternoon at 1500. We'll have more time to get acquainted on our trip out to Welliver. And just so you're aware. The only way you two are getting off this ship is if your contracts expire or you take berths on another vessel."

That hit them out of left field somewhere. Mr. Ricks had enough on the ball to question. "Sar?"

"Look, I'll take the gloves off here, lads. You've been trying to get put ashore so you can sue the company for what? A couple of stanyers? While I admit that I admire your stamina, I question your strategic ability. The lawyers won't let the company put you ashore because of a union rule. You know it. Captain Delman knew it. I know it. Unlike the company lawyers, I happen to know that you three may be the best three spacers in the whole fleet, and I have no intention of letting you get away."

Mr. Wyatt looked shocked at that, but he had sense enough not to speak.

"I also have no intention of letting you squander your not inconsiderable talents on bar brawls and d-and-d charges. You two are going to help us make this ship the best in the fleet and we're gonna thumb our noses at the rest."

Ricks recovered faster than Schubert. "Okay, Captain, and how do you propose we're gonna do this miraculous feat of financial engineering?"

"I'm glad you asked that question, Mr. Ricks. This ship has no morale officer, as I understand it. Is that true, Mr. Wyatt?"

"Yes, Captain."

"Well, that's changed. Mr. Ricks, you are now the ship's morale officer."

Mr. Wyatt's eyes widened in shock, but he didn't speak. He didn't need to, because my space lawyer chimed in right on cue.

"Sar? I'm the lowest ranked member of the crew. You can't make me morale officer."

"Really, Mr. Ricks. Can you find me a rules citation for that? Something in Title J under other duties as required maybe?"

Bless his little heart, I could almost see his brain cranking over as he mentally reviewed the appropriate sections.

"We can pull up the manual on that screen if it would help, Mr. Ricks."

He knew I had him. "No, Captain. There's no citation."

"Thank you, Mr. Ricks, then I would think being the lowest of the low, you'd have the best perspective on what would make life better for the crew as a whole. With that logic I believe you to be the appropriate person to hold the post."

He didn't look convinced.

"You don't need to do anything right now. We'll iron out the details once we're underway. You'll have a budget and some discretionary authority over how it might be spent."

He perked up at the mention of budget. He'd probably be disappointed when he saw how much it would really amount to, but small steps can complete long journeys.

"Mr. Schubert, are you tracking?"

"Yes, Captain."

"Good, because I've got a collateral duty for you as well."

"Me, sar?"

"You, Mr. Schubert. You're going to be in charge of the ship's co-op."

"Co-op, Captain?"

"Yes, Mr. Schubert, the co-op. We'll talk more about it when we get underway. We're out of time here but I expect good things from you."

They both looked very confused.

"Dismissed, gentlemen. Get cleaned up. There's fresh coffee and dinner mess will be promptly at 1800. I've got a date with an angel, so I'll be missing that, but we'll have plenty of time to get better acquainted when we get underway."

They trooped out of the mess deck and crossed the passage to crew berthing.

Mr. Wyatt looked at me with a question in his eyes that he didn't ask.

"Ask it, Mr. Wyatt."

"Captain? Are you sure?"

"Very, Mr. Wyatt."

"The best three spacers in the fleet, Captain?"

I smiled and shrugged. "Okay, that might have been a bit of hyperbole on my part but do you know any other three spacers in the fleet who could have been in so much trouble for so long without being put ashore, or busted to Spacer Apprentice?"

"Oh, they have been busted, Captain. They just keep coming back."

I smiled at him. "You begin to see my point, Mr. Wyatt?"

I could see the light dawn and he looked at me oddly. "Yes, Captain. I think I do."

"Good. Then let's get the dinner mess going. I'll need to leave it to you this evening, because I'm spending my last night in port with the Missus."

"Are you sure I can do this, Captain?"

"What? Dinner?"

He nodded.

"Yup. Positive."

We started pulling up the menu and getting things organized. It was a simple meal and one that was mostly opening cans and adding the fresh herbs and spices that had been delivered earlier in the day. The one serious bit of cooking was roasting a pork loin and I walked him through that process easily.

As the clock ticked down, we started planning breakfast, so that the 0600 watch change would have a full meal. I planned to be back aboard by 0800 myself. He seemed to adjust pretty well. He'd been doing all the cooking before, so this was not something new for him, even if what he was cooking was a bit more complicated. I hoped he would find it more satisfying.

Ms. Thomas came down to the mess deck at 1745 and we relieved the watch amid the delicious smells of roast pork and baking biscuits. I was almost sorry to be leaving.

She eyed the new terminal on the bulkhead, but made no comment. We exchanged reports and I noted that Schubert and Ricks were confined to ship.

"You're not going to confine Hill?"

"No, Ms. Thomas. He didn't do anything to warrant it. And he's snagged us a nice cargo."

She looked startled at that.

"Ask Mr. Wyatt to explain it over dinner. I've got a date."

I smiled all around. I ran into Mr. Hill on the way off the mess deck. "You won't be causing me any grief overnight, will you, Mr. Hill?"

He looked at me and I'm not sure what he saw, but the look went from challenging to contemplative while I watched. "No, Captain."

I smiled. "Thanks, Brandon. I'm counting on you."

I turned and scampered up the ladder but not before I caught the look of surprise on his face. As I skinned out of my shipsuit and into civvies, I was caught between the feeling of pleasure that things might actually turn around on this boat and anger that the crew should have been so abused.

When I signed out for the night, an odd thought crossed my mind.

"Mr. Schubert? Do you think we should get a cat?"

Chapter Twenty-three
Diurnia Orbital: 2372-January-11

I dreaded getting underway. Not the getting underway part. I actually looked forward to that. There's something oddly exciting about getting out there. Mostly it's nothing to write home about. Lots of watches. Lots of hours trapped in a can. A few ticks of magic when you're going someplace really different and then more hours, more watches. A few days in a new port and then back out again. I'd been doing it so long, being docked seemed odd to me.

No, I dreaded the leaving Jen part. It didn't matter what time I got underway, she'd get up while I showered, and would accost me in the kitchen with The Look—part accusatory, part puppy dog. We'd have The Scene. And I'd leave feeling like a selfish jerk and she'd sit there cursing me as the door closed. And worse, I couldn't be sure she wasn't right.

For stanyers, every time I got underway, we had The Scene. Except that morning, she didn't. She didn't even get up. She lay there in bed looking so delightfully rumpled I nearly crawled in with her again. It had been a truly memorable night and early morning. I had several gouges in my hide and a silly grin on my face to prove it.

I sat on the edge of the bed. "We're getting underway this afternoon. Heading to Welliver."

She smiled up at me sleepily and wrapped those strong arms around my neck and pulled me down for a kiss. "Mmm, yeah. I 'member. You be safe out there, 'k?"

"I'll do my best." I was melting inside.

"You have any idea when you'll be home?"

I thought about it. With our mass and sail, we should carve weeks off the round trip. "Something around mid-April, I should think."

She seemed to wake up a bit for that. "Oh, that's quick! I was thinking May."

"Smaller boat, shorter run."

She nodded. "Okay." She pulled me down for one last smooch. "Go. Your ship's waitin', Captain."

"See you in a few weeks, my love."

"Turn the light off on your way out. I don't have to get up for a coupla stans yet." She giggled and burrowed back under the covers.

I chuckled, grabbed my kit, shut off the lights, and headed for the door. It felt good to be leaving for once when I wasn't under a cloud. I arrived at the ship at 0730 and the real fun for the day began.

When I popped the lock and stepped aboard, I had a bad feeling. You can tell a lot about a ship by the smell. I'd been pleased when first coming aboard that the smell had been clean and only slightly mechanical. This morning, the ship smelled more like . . .

"Burned bacon, Skipper." Mr. Ricks supplied the missing identifier.

"Thank you, Mr. Ricks. And I take it breakfast mess didn't go as smoothly as I'd anticipated?"

"Um, no, sar. But it was entertaining for a time."

"As morale officer, you should note these instances in order to capitalize on them in the future." I stood on the scale while he did the mass adjustments.

"Not that entertaining, sar, if you catch my drift."

From the direction of the mess deck I could hear Ms. Thomas proclaiming loudly although the echoes in the ship made her actual words indistinct.

"Yes, Mr. Ricks, I believe I do." I sighed. "Carry on, Mr. Ricks."

"Sar? About this morale officer business?"

"Yes, Mr. Ricks?"

"Are you serious?"

I waited.

"Sar?"

"Quite, Mr. Ricks. You are the lowest rating on the ship. Traditionally morale officer falls to the lowest ranking officer, but we're a small crew and we all need to contribute." I paused while the loud clatter of some metallic object rattled off the deck from the direction of the galley, followed by some more imprecations in the key of Thomas. "And I have it on good authority that you're something of a space lawyer. I intend to use that, Mr. Ricks."

"Use it, Captain? Space lawyer isn't a phrase most folks take as a compliment."

Several smaller clatters that sounded suspiciously like flatware echoed down the passage.

"No, but usually the people who use space lawyer as pejorative do so because they're caught out on the wrong end of a rule. While there are those who abuse the issue by splitting semantic hairs and parsing every sub-clause, you didn't do that when I put you on the spot yesterday."

"But you'd already made me morale officer by then, Captain."

"Yes." I smiled at him. "Yes, Mr. Ricks, I had. Contemplate that timing of events while I see if any medical attention is required–" I had to pause for another loud clang "–in the galley."

"Of course, sar. Thanks for your time."

"My pleasure, Mr. Ricks. Carry on."

"Aye, aye, sar."

I wasn't really certain I wanted to see what all the noise was about but, knowing the mess that bacon fat can make on deck plates, I considered it my duty to try to get things shipshape before the fitters arrived. I stopped at the entry to the galley and leaned against the jamb. I was still in my civvies and my presence seemed to make no impression on the mêlée in progress.

Mr. Wyatt stood with his back to the door. Even from behind, he looked a bit smoked out and greasy. That, coupled with the burned bacon smell, made me think that I'd over estimated his culinary ability. I kicked myself mentally. Mr. Pall should have been OD but he managed a swab and a bucket of water near the range trying to clean up a blackened runnel of what could only be bacon fat, smeared across the deck and congealed. The center of attention was on Ms. Thomas and Mr. Schubert.

Ms. Thomas was in fine fettle, leaning down over Mr. Schubert— giving him both barrels—as he tried to pick up loose pieces of burned bacon, flatware, and what looked like a half-meter stainless steel roasting pan. Every time Mr. Schubert would start to make some progress, Ms. Thomas would kick loose pieces around and increase the not inconsiderable volume of her diatribe.

Neither Mr. Hill nor Ms. Gerheart were in evidence, a fact which I chalked up to either good fortune or good sense.

After several ticks of observation, I dropped my kit loudly to the deck during one of the infrequent lulls in the action. It made a satisfying thwack when the bottom hit the deckplates.

Mr. Pall had the presence of mind to notice the sound and snap, "Captain on deck."

I don't take much to the more military aspects of rank and most ships ran rather looser than the academy made cadets believe. In extremes, however, the training kicked in and I was grateful that Mr. Pall's instincts were on the mark. If the assembled company didn't exactly jump to attention, they stopped what they were doing and silence descended.

I let it lay there undisturbed for more than a few heartbeats.

Ms. Thomas had a look of "you're gonna get it now" on her face. Mr. Schubert looked grateful for the interruption but froze where he sprawled on the deck. Mr. Wyatt stood at attention, still with his back to me, frozen ramrod stiff by Mr. Pall's call. Mr. Pall stood almost at attention and seemed to be having trouble figuring out what to do with the mop. I interceded before he tried "port-arms" with it.

"Good morning, lady and gentlemen. Is there coffee?"

Ms. Thomas was the first to speak. "Coffee, Captain?"

I ambled across the mess deck, walking around Mr. Wyatt, and snagged a mug out of the rack. "Yes, Ms. Thomas, coffee. Dark beverage made by dripping nearly boiling water through the ground seeds from the fruit of the coffee plant. You've heard of it?"

She had the grace to flush as I drew a cup from the ready urn. "Yes, Captain. I've heard of it."

"Good, Ms. Thomas." I tasted it and it was, frankly, in need of assistance. "May I ask who made this pot?"

Mr. Wyatt spoke up. "I did, Captain."

"Not bad, Mr. Wyatt. Get with me later and I'll give you some pointers." When I looked at him closely from the front, I winced. "Do you need medical attention, Mr. Wyatt?"

His hands went to his face. "No, I don't think so, Captain. It flashed up and caught me by surprise. I think it only got my eyebrows."

"Please do me a favor, Mr. Wyatt. Report to the first aid station on oh-one right now. It's probably nothing serious but I want to get underway this afternoon, and I'd like to take a healthy crew with me."

"Oh, dear, is it that bad, Captain?" Mr. Wyatt looked alarmed.

"It looks minor to me, Mr. Wyatt, but grease burns aren't anything to take a chance with. We have the time and the facility. Please make sure that it's as minor as it looks by checking with the appropriate medical authorities?"

"Yes, sar." He said it but he stood there.

"Now, Mr. Wyatt."

"Don't you want my report, Captain?"

"In good time, Mr. Wyatt. Health and safety before blame and finger pointing. Scoot."

He scooted.

I rested my haunches against the counter and sipped as I very obviously took in the scene. To their credit, nobody interrupted my inspection.

"Mr. Schubert, that looks uncomfortable. You could stand."

"Thank you, Captain." He did so and braced to attention when he regained his feet.

"Mr. Pall? You're OD. Please report."

"Pirates, Captain!"

Ms. Thomas turned red and barked. "Pall, will you–"

"Ms. Thomas!" I interrupted her before she could get up to speed. "I asked for Mr. Pall's report. Please grant him the courtesy of letting him make it." I turned to Mr. Pall. "You were saying, Mr. Pall."

"Pirates, Captain. They sabotaged the range where Mr. Wyatt was trying to cook the tray of bacon. When he went to pull it out, it flashed up, and he got singed. Quick thinking on Mr. Schubert's part here. He dropped a second pan on it, snuffing the fire."

I turned to him. "That *was* quick thinking, Mr. Schubert. Thank you."

Schubert shrugged. "I got lucky, Captain."

I smiled at that and nodded for Mr. Pall to continue.

"Things started going wrong after that, Captain. Mr. Schubert tried to pick up the pan and dropped it."

I looked at Mr. Schubert. "Show me your hands, Mr. Schubert."

I hadn't been able to see them before but he had angry looking burns across the palm of each hand. "Usually one uses pot holders, Mr. Schubert. Please follow Mr. Wyatt's footsteps immediately. Go."

"Aye, aye, Captain."

"And then there were two." I looked them over.

"Mr. Pall, that mop won't do much against the congealed grease. Use a spatula and scrape up what you can. Then report to Ms. Gerheart with my compliments and ask for a little of her Blu-Goo. She'll know what that is. Use that to clean the residue off the deck."

"Aye, aye, Captain." He stashed the mop and began corralling the loose bits of hardware and burned food off the deck.

"Ms. Thomas? The cabin, if you please."

"Aye, aye, Captain."

She followed me out of the galley and I snagged my kit on the way. She started to speak a couple of times as we climbed the ladder, but I held up a hand. She was wise enough to heed the warning. I opened the door and walked through into the sleeping space to toss my kit onto the bunk before returning to the main cabin.

Ms. Thomas stood just inside the door.

"If you'd close the door, Ms. Thomas?"

"I don't think that's wise, Captain."

"Right at this moment, Ms. Thomas, I don't really care if you think it's wise. Close the door. Do it now. Stand at attention right there." I pointed to a spot on the deck in front of the desk. "I'm going to go into the next room to put on a shipsuit. You're going to wait for me. While I'm gone, I'd like you to think of why I shouldn't put you off this ship for dereliction of duty, endangering the health and safety of the crew, and conduct unbecoming an officer."

She started to speak, but I cut her off. "Shut up, Ms. Thomas. Close the door. Stand there. Do it now, please."

I went into the sleeping space and pulled the screen closed without waiting to see if she did it, or giving her a chance to question.

It took me no time to skin out of civvies and into the shipsuit. I'd left one hanging in the head before leaving the ship. I gave Ms. Thomas a few extra ticks to think about what I'd said by washing my face and hands. It gave me a few ticks to think as well. Ms. Thomas was an enigma. There had to be more going on with her. Call me naïve, but I really wanted to believe that there was more to her than met the eye–or ear.

I returned to find her properly braced and standing where I had left her. I didn't sit behind the desk but stood in front of her to take her face on. She was short. I was shocked to see how short. Of course, I knew she was a heavy-worlder, she probably out massed me by half again, but she barely came up to my shoulder. I'd known that, but lost sight of it.

"Do you have any idea why you are here, Ms. Thomas?"

She seemed confused by the question. "Here, Captain?"

"Yes, Ms. Thomas. Do you have any idea what you may have done to invoke my ire?"

"I would suspect it has something to do with the injuries to the crew and my failure to address them, Captain."

"Points for you, Ms. Thomas. Can you explain your actions in failing to deal with the immediate and urgent issues of injured crewmen?"

"No, Captain."

She seemed contrite and actually at a loss. That set me back. I paced around behind her to give her a little thinking space. "What happened to start this all off?"

She cocked her head slightly, "Captain?"

My pacing brought me back in front of her and I faced her once again. "What happened to start this all off, Ms. Thomas?"

"Oh, that buffoon–"

I interrupted. "Which buffoon, Ms. Thomas?"

"Mr. Wyatt, Captain." She looked a bit exasperated that I should have to ask for clarification.

"The crew have names. Please use them. Name calling is beneath you, Ms. Thomas."

"It's beneath them, too, Captain, but they don't seem to have any trouble doing it."

"No doubt, Ms. Thomas. Is there a name you're particularly sensitive to?"

"Come, Captain. I'm no idiot. I know they call me 'Foghorn' and 'Ole Fireplug' and gods alone know what else."

"Ouch. That's cold. And you've heard them?"

"Well, not this crew, no, but I've heard it enough that I know it's what they're saying, sar."

"How do you know, Ms. Thomas?"

"The lack of respect, sar. It's insulting. They may make fun of me for my height or my voice, but by the gods they should at least respect the office of first mate and these chucklewits show all the respect of–"

I interrupted her again. "The crew, Ms. Thomas. Not 'these chucklewits' or any other derogatory epithets you might be contemplating. The crew."

"Captain, I have a hard time being respectful of individuals who show so little respect themselves."

"Did it occur to you, Ms. Thomas, that they may be having the same problem?"

She took a breath and thought before speaking. "Sar?"

"Ms. Thomas, it's been my experience that nobody respects an office if they cannot find it in themselves to respect the officer who fills it. Furthermore, that officer cannot simply demand the respect due the office without demonstrating that he or she deserves it."

"Well, of course, Captain."

"And do you consider referring to your fellow officers and crew as 'buffoon' and 'chucklewits' as demonstration of deserving their respect, Ms. Thomas?"

"It's all they deserve, Captain. It's what I get, why shouldn't I give it back? It's not like I call them that to their faces."

"No, Ms. Thomas, but it's how you think of them and that shows up in your treatment of them. And you're the first mate. You're supposed to be in command, but before you can command them, you have to command yourself. You got mad when Mr. Wyatt burned the bacon and became incensed when Schubert dropped it on the deck and made a mess, didn't you, Ms. Thomas?"

"Well, of course, Captain. Cooking bacon is not exactly complicated. He's an officer! He can't manage a simple task like cooking breakfast? And that oaf–errr–when Schubert dropped it on the deck, I just saw it as my duty to teach him a lesson. The man is so clumsy!"

"So your first instinct wasn't to see if, perhaps the ship were in danger, or the crew might be injured, but rather that you needed to assert your authority by punishing Mr. Schubert for his clumsiness?"

"Exactly, Captain."

"For over a full stan?"

"Sar?"

"Ms. Thomas, I came aboard at 0730. Breakfast mess traditionally begins at 0600. Allowing for a bit of delay because of the new experience of actually cooking a meal instead of decanting it, I'd guess this all started between 0600 and 0630."

"Yes, Captain."

My tablet bipped. I glanced at it and it was a note from the brow. The ship fitters had arrived. I punched an acknowledgment and returned to the problem at hand.

"Think about the fact that you kept injured crew from medical treatment for a stan while you exercised your authority and showed them just how much respect you have for them. I need to deal with an issue below for a few ticks. I'll be right back."

I left her at attention and headed for the lock. The head of the shipfitter crew waited with a couple of hands and some packages. "Good morning, Captain. I'm Charlie, this here's Sam and that's Terry. Understand you got a bit of remodeling you'd like done?"

I shook each hand in turn. "Yes, thank you, Charlie." I turned to Mr. Ricks. "My compliments to Chief Gerheart and would she join me on the mess deck at her earliest convenience, Mr. Ricks?"

"Aye, aye, Captain."

I led the work gang onto the mess deck and explained what I wanted done. Before I got halfway through the explanation, Chief Gerheart skidded through the door with a bright look and a big smile for Charlie. I backed up slightly for her benefit and within two ticks I knew I was in trouble.

Charlie looked at the chief and she shrugged.

He turned back to me. "Captain. I can do what you're asking or I can do what I think you want."

"Please explain the difference, if you would, Charlie?"

"Of course, Skipper." He proceeded to give me chapter and verse in appropriate detail with encouraging nods from the chief. He finished with a flourish. "To do what you want, I'd have to burn out those two deck flanges. We can do it but it would be ugly. If we substitute a couple parts, we can use those flanges and give you a really nice solution without cutting up your ship."

It sounded pretty good to me. "Differential in cost and time?"

"Costs less. The parts are less expensive and we'll use more of what you got. Time is the problem. We didn't bring the parts we need, Captain."

"You brought what I asked for?"

"'Fraid so, sar."

"I want to get underway by 1500. What can you do?"

"We're talking a stan, tops. I can be back with the parts and all by 1300. You should have an hour to spare if you wanna cut it that fine, Captain."

I looked at Chief Gerheart.

She nodded back.

"Make is so, Charlie, and I'm sorry for not asking the experts before making up my mind."

"No problem, Skipper. Happy to do it."

They took their tools and boxes and left. Ms. Gerheart remained on the mess deck measuring it with her eyes.

"Measuring for drapes, Chief?"

She grinned and shook her head before scampering back down to engineering.

Mr. Pall was still working on the clean up but he'd heard it all. "Your thoughts, Mr. Pall?"

"Yo ho ho, Captain. Should we stock a few bottles of rum?"

"Not a bad idea, Mr. Pall. Let me get back to you on that."

In the meantime I needed to get back to the cabin and I scampered up the ladder at a dash.

I walked into the cabin to find Ms. Thomas still braced. "I'm sorry for the delay, Ms. Thomas."

She jumped as if startled as I walked past her and took a seat at my desk.

When I looked at her face, I knew she'd had time to think. "Comments, Ms. Thomas?"

"I didn't know they were injured, Captain."

"I'm glad, Ms. Thomas, because if I thought you had known and had kept them from treatment even knowing, I would have been very sorry to have to cancel our departure while I found a new first."

"I should have known, Captain."

"Yes, Ms. Thomas, you should have."

"I have no excuse, Captain."

"I know that, Ms. Thomas. And I'm glad you do, too." I let that settle in for a couple of heartbeats. "Here's what we're going to do. You are going to go to your stateroom, take a hot shower, and rack out until I call you to the bridge for navigation detail. You're just off the mid and we're getting underway at 1500. I need you fresh and ready to help me get this ship underway. You know better than anybody else aboard how she handles and I'll need your assistance."

"Actually, Mr. Schubert knows better, Captain."

"Excuse me, Ms. Thomas?"

"Mr. Schubert, Captain. The man has the touch."

"I thought you said he's clumsy, Ms. Thomas."

"Oh, he is, Captain, with everything but the helm. Put him on helm and he knows just how to move her to put her right where we need her. He's got the touch, sar."

I almost had to bite my tongue and it took several long breaths to get myself under control. In the end I managed not to laugh, but I thought I had a pretty good handle on one of the issues facing Ms. Thomas.

"Thank you, Ms. Thomas. I'll take that under advisement. Now, please, get some sleep."

"Captain?"

"Yes, Ms. Thomas?"

She looked embarrassed but she plowed ahead. "Food, Captain. I–um–missed breakfast and with my metabolism, I need something to eat. Rather badly."

"Oh, crap." I jumped to my feet and probably startled her. "I'm so sorry. I know about heavy worlders but I completely lost sight of that. Please accept my apologies, Ms. Thomas!"

"Of course, Captain. I'll consider it my penance. And I am sorry. You're right. I was over the line and I don't really know why."

She did seem contrite.

I felt like a heel for keeping her standing there while her stomach ate its way to her backbone.

"Do you know Over Easy?"

"Down on oh-two, Captain? Of course! Everybody knows Over Easy."

"Before you rack out? Go eat. Top yourself up. Bring me the bill."

"You don't need to do that, Captain."

"Consider it my penance for not taking the physical well-being of my crew–no matter how ill behaved–into consideration. It wasn't an obvious ill, but I overlooked it. I'll take it as a lesson and be grateful that it didn't come at any higher cost than one of Frank's breakfast specials."

"Or two?" She looked a little sheepish.

"As many as you want, Ms. Thomas. I know heavy worlders. You're just built that way. It's nothing to apologize for. Dismissed."

She left and I slumped at my desk. I didn't really want to think about what else might go wrong. So far I was getting tossed a lot of soft pitches. I was pretty sure I'd be able to hit a few of them.

But I worried about the ones I'd miss, and what I'd do when they started throwing fastballs.

Chapter Twenty-four
Diurnia Orbital: 2372-January-11

Around 0900, after a bit of quiet soul searching of my own and a brief kick in my own behind for being an idiot, I went down to the mess deck to find the chief and Mr. Pall finishing up the degreasing of the galley.

"Did anyone get breakfast, Mr. Pall?"

He looked startled by the question. "Not that I'm aware of, Captain. The excitement started and then just kept going until you showed up."

I sighed and scrubbed my face in my hands. "Okay, priorities, Mr. Pall, feed the crew. Do we have anything left from breakfast?"

He looked around a bit bewildered. "All I saw was the bacon. What was supposed to be here, Skipper?"

"The menu called for bacon, scrambled eggs, juice, toast, and some of that honey melon that came up yesterday from the chandlery."

He pulled the handle on the ready cooler and all the rest of the ingredients for breakfast were in there. He held the door wide so I could see.

"Can you scramble an egg, William?"

"Captain?"

"Some people can't. I'm just checking. Can you scramble an egg? No. Can you scramble, say, a dozen? There's a skillet under the counter there and bowls above the work counter. Wisks in the drawer with the spatulas which you've already found. Can you handle it?"

"Of course, Skipper."

Chief Gerheart surprised me. "Can I help him, Skipper?"

"That's up to him, Chief, but sure. Many hands make light

work."

I heard footsteps in the passage and turned to see Ms. Thomas coming back from breakfast. She nodded to me, somewhat sleepily I thought, and continued up to officer country. Not long after that Wyatt and Schubert returned from the medical station. Wyatt had a light salve on one cheek bone but Schubert's hands were wound with bandages and I got a sinking feeling.

I pointed to the chairs. "Sit, gentlemen. You've had a busy morning."

They sat.

I nodded to Mr. Schubert first. "This doesn't look good, spacer. What's the status?"

He held up his wrapped hands and twisted them with a bemused expression on his face. "I don't think it's as bad as it looks, Skipper. They got a little carried away with the dressing."

"I was counting on you for helm this afternoon, Mr. Schubert."

He shrugged and rested his wrists on the edge of the table. "Shouldn't be a problem, sar. I only need my fingers really so I can feel the helm. I think, with a little help, I can probably free enough of them to do what I need."

"What did the medico say, Mr. Schubert?"

"Light duty, three days."

"You get us out, we'll keep you covered, Mr. Schubert."

"Can do, Skipper." He was way too chipper for a man with burns on his hands.

"Mr. Schubert please pardon my talking around you, but Mr. Wyatt, did they drug him?"

"No, Captain. Not that I am aware of and they briefed me on his condition. Three days, light duty. He's got a tube of goop in his pocket and they gave us some spare dressings." Wyatt held up a bag.

"Thank you, Mr. Wyatt." I looked back at Mr. Schubert. "You seem pretty chipper for a man with burned palms, Mr. Schubert."

"It's really not that bad, Skipper. I tried to tell them at the aid station. It was red but not deep. I've been burned before and this didn't even blister. They were acting like I had smoked hams on my wrists."

Mr. Wyatt nodded in confirmation. "It's true, Captain. I saw his hands before they started working on him. I think they had a training day down there today or something, because the candy striper working on him seemed to think he was all but dead."

"How'd you get away with just a little salve, Mr. Wyatt?"

Mr. Wyatt shrugged. "The corpsman working on me didn't think I was cute enough for him, perhaps, Captain."

Enlightenment comes slowly sometimes, but is usually worth the effort. "I begin to see, Mr. Wyatt. Thank you for that extra bit of information."

He grinned. "You're welcome, Captain."

"Mr. Schubert? They should have some scrambled eggs and toast ready in a moment or two. You ready for breakfast?"

"Yes, Captain, I am."

"Okay. Hang in there. Should be but a couple of shakes."

"Chief Gerheart? Mr. Pall? Can I count on you to take care of Mr. Schubert here. Feed him up and send him to bed?"

Mr. Pall looked up from the pan of eggs. "Of course, Captain."

Chief Gerheart nodded her silent confirmation.

"Mr. Wyatt? If you're up to it, could you join me in the cabin?"

"Of course, Captain."

We climbed the ladder to officer country and I pointed to the conference table. "Have a seat, Mr. Wyatt. I'm ready for your report."

I sat at the head and he took what I assumed must be his normal seat at the port side foot.

"We were running a bit late on breakfast but I wanted to make sure the bacon was cooked thoroughly, Captain." He stopped and looked at me for reassurance. "I looked up how to cook it and I was pretty sure that I had it right. I put it on a raised rack in the oven with a pan under it to catch the drippings. The smell was amazing and everybody but Mr. Hill and Mr. Ricks was in the galley waiting for breakfast. I don't know what went wrong because all of a sudden things started smelling burnt. I opened the door, pulled out the pan and poof! The flame just came right up in my face."

I nodded encouragingly.

"Well, sar, Mr. Schubert was there almost before I got straighted up and he'd grabbed another roaster from the rack and dropped it upside down on the flames. It snuffed the fire but it was still smoldering pretty good. He went to grab it and, of course, the pan was blazing hot, and he got it just far enough for it to clear the range before he dropped it. By then, all we really had was a lot of smoke and Chief Gerheart went down to crank up the scrubbers a couple of notches while the rest of us watched Ms. Thomas." His report petered out a bit at that point.

"Thank you, Mr. Wyatt."

"I'm so sorry, Captain. This was all my fault." He looked positively miserable.

"Mr. Wyatt? If this is the worst thing that happens on this ship, we're going to be in very good shape, indeed. Take the lesson, and be thankful the cost wasn't higher. If that burning fat had spilled onto your clothes, we'd have been canceling this trip while we waited for a replacement cargo officer."

He blanched.

"I've learned a lesson or two myself this morning, Mr. Wyatt, so don't beat yourself up over it. When the captain changes, especially on a crew this size, the whole ship changes. And I'm not slipping in quietly. There's a lesson in there for me, but it'll probably be awhile before I figure out what it is."

He seemed a bit mollified. "If you say so, Captain."

"I do, Mr. Wyatt. What I need you to do now is go get something to eat. We've got a date in Welliver."

He smiled at that and nodded his thanks.

"Dismissed, Mr. Wyatt. Save me some toast."

He left and I crossed to my desk. The console there was the same as any on the bridge. At least I didn't have to remove the block that prevented me from looking at any of the ship's status displays that I wanted. There was one more display here that I'd never seen on any console, and a little digging showed it to be local to the device in the cabin. It was the captain's log. I thumbed through the last few entries and saw nothing that caught my eye. Delman's log style was sparse to the point of terse, with bare minimum notations on ship's status, crew, ports, and so on.

Record keeping. I'd forgotten about that part of being the captain. I checked the captain's inbox and found all the reports and documents that would need my review and approval before they could be put away. I groaned and closed my eyes against the tide of unread reports. Well, we'd be underway in a few stans. There'd be plenty of time to deal with the backlog then.

The little voice in the back of my head told me there'd be a whole new batch to deal with by then. I told it to pipe down and checked to make sure the flight plan had been approved and that the tug was on schedule for a 1500 pull out. It all looked good, and I went in search of a piece of toast and a cup of coffee.

What I found at the bottom of the ladder was a rather worse for wear looking Mr. Hill being held up by a pair of Orbital Security guards. Mr. Pall was with them and he nodded apologetically. "These nice officers brought us a present, Captain."

"Mr. Hill? I thought I wasn't going to have any problems with you."

"Not my fault, Captain." I believed him. I don't for the life of me know why.

I looked to the Security men. "Gentlemen?"

"We found him in an alcove down on oh-five, Skipper. He'd

been pretty well rolled. We got the images on the security cams but..." he gave a one shouldered shrug. "Hoods and masks. Not random and, as much fun as we've had with this rascal in the past, I'd have to agree. Not his fault."

"Medical?"

"Been. He's got a few bruises. Nothing seriously broken. There's a bandage under his arm there where one of 'em kicked him, but it's a scrape."

"Can you walk, Brandon?"

"Yes, Captain. It's not as bad as it looks."

"I'm getting kind of tired of hearing that this morning, Mr. Hill. Go lay down. We'll call you for nav detail."

He turned and shambled into crew quarters.

I looked up at the two guards. "Your opinion, gentlemen?"

They looked at each other and shrugged. "Nothing official, Skipper."

"Of course not. What's your guess?"

The taller one shrugged and looked down at his feet. "Karma, Skipper."

"Past sins coming home to roost?"

They both nodded. The short one tugged an earlobe. "You can't play games on the dock for as long as these boys have and not pick up a few scores that aren't quite final, if you know what I mean, Captain."

"Thank you, gentlemen. I do, indeed."

Mr. Pall showed them off the ship and I turned to go into the galley. It was small consolation, but I now had plenty to write about in the captain's log. In a way I envied Delman's lack of narrative, but had to wonder if it were the case that he found nothing to write about.

Or if he had just not bothered.

Chapter Twenty-five
Diurnia Orbital: 2372-January-11

I found Wyatt, Pall, and Gerheart on the mess deck. Wyatt was happily scrubbing pots in the deep sink, Pall and Gerheart were finishing what looked like a nice mess of scrambled egg and toast. My stomach rumbled a bit to remind me that I hadn't stopped at Over Easy in my haste to get aboard.

"Any of those eggs left, Mr. Pall?"

"We left a plate on the sideboard for you, Captain." He nodded in the general direction.

"Bless you, Mr. Pall."

"You're welcome, Skipper."

I swung by the toaster and dropped two before checking in with Wyatt at the sink. "You doing okay, Avery?"

"Yes, sar. Feeling a little stupid and helpless. That really got out of hand there and I really should have done something." The soapy water did little to hide his frustration.

I patted him on the back of one shoulder. "Hang in. We're all getting used the new way of things. I'm afraid you'll get a chance to try to do better." I chuckled a little. It wasn't really funny but more like one of those laugh-or-you'll-cry things.

He bit back a laugh of his own and I collected my eggs. By the time I'd drawn a fresh cup of coffee, the toast had popped and I joined Mr. Pall and the chief at the table.

"Think we'll have any trouble with pirates this trip, Mr. Pall?"

"No, Captain. They're not operating in this sector just now. Mostly over on the border lands between Halpern and Ciroda."

"Didn't stop them from mucking up breakfast, Mr. Pall."

Chief Gerhart giggled.

Mr. Pall wasn't fazed. "Well, there's the odd pirate here and

161

there, Skipper, as you well know."

"Of course, Mr. Pall."

"Any reservations about getting underway, Chief?"

Gerheart glanced up from her plate to make sure I was talking to her before answering. "The ship is ready to go, Captain. I'm betting my life on it and I expect to win." She never lost the singsongy, little girl voice but I knew she had to be nearly my age, even if she looked ten stanyers younger.

"That's an interesting way to put it, Chief."

She smiled a real smile and, until she did, I hadn't realized that it might have been the first one I'd seen on her face. "My father used to say that. Probably still does. A man of certain habit is me dah."

"Your father's an engineer, then, Chief?"

"Yes, Captain. Chief Engineering Officer on the *Halldor Laxness*, operates out of New Mannheim in Venitz."

"You're a long way from home, Chief."

She smiled again, another real one. "Home is where your tool chest is, Captain. I'm less than twenty meters."

Mr. Pall looked surprised at that. "Don't you mean your heart, Chief?"

She giggled. I confess, having an engineering chief who giggled was a little unnerving. Still, it was a delightful giggle. "I think I said that, William."

"You said 'tool chest.'"

She looked at him with a silly grin pasted on her face. "Yes!"

Mr. Pall looked like he was going to speak again, so I forestalled him. "Course laid in, Mr. Pall?"

He gave up on the elusive Chief Gerheart and focused on me. "Not yet, Skipper." He shrugged apologetically. "I was going to go do that right after breakfast."

I looked at his empty plate.

He looked at his empty plate.

"That would be about now, I think. If you'll excuse me, Skipper?"

I nodded and raised a cup in salute. "Thread me a needle, Mr. Pall. Carry on."

He looked a little startled but gathered his dirties and racked them for the washer before heading up to the bridge and his astrogation station.

I pushed my own empty plate away and leaned forward over the last of my coffee. At the small tables it brought my head close to Chief Gerheart's. She was aware of it, but didn't withdraw. I didn't turn toward her and I spoke softly. "I asked if you had any reservations about getting underway, Chief. You said the ship was ready. Do you have any reservations about the crew?"

She raised her face and looked at me. Firm muscle and rigid bone subsumed the soft little girl face. The pale, watery blue eyes turned to piercing, hard sapphire. For the first time since coming aboard, she looked me square in the face. "Not any more, Captain." The voice was as clear and strong as a mountain river, and as quiet as wind over grass.

And like the shadow of a wind-driven cloud, gone.

The little girl came back and the chief giggled.

I smiled into my mug and tried to breathe. "Thank you, Chief."

"Sure thing, Captain. I better get on with my prep." She gathered my plate up with hers and took the whole lot to the washer.

A sip of coffee helped me focus again and I started with basics. "First, feed the crew."

"Excuse me, Captain?" Wyatt was just finishing up in the deep sink.

"Basics, Mr. Wyatt. Our mess schedule is a wreck. Here it is almost 1000, we're supposed to serve lunch at 1200 but most people have just finished breakfast or will be sleeping. We're going to go to nav detail at 1400 for a 1500 pull out. We'll be at stations until–what? 1800?"

He shook his head. "More like 1900. The tug has to give us a good push to get us started since we don't have the kickers. Takes us a little longer to get going."

The morning was full of surprises. "Good to know, Mr. Wyatt. Thank you."

"Were you planning to have a pre-flight, Skipper?"

Pre-flight was a meeting of all the command staff to review ship's status prior to going to navigation stations. "I should, but we're scrimping on time. Ms. Thomas needs the rest and so do Hill and Schubert. We'll go with the seat of the pants this time and see how it goes."

He dried his hands on a side towel and grinned, leaning back against the sink. "You like playing close to the edge, Skipper?"

"No, Mr. Wyatt. I surely do not. But sometimes close to the edge is all you got and it's better than over it."

"Good point. What do we do about meals?'

"Mind playing messmate for this evolution, Avery?'

"Not in the least, Captain. What would you like me to do?"

"Do we have any boxes aboard?"

"Boxes, Captain?"

I pulled up my tablet and accessed the chandlery's catalog. "Bento boxes, like these." I showed him the screen.

I saw him study the picture but I had the uncanny feeling that he was actually reviewing the ship's inventory in his head as he looked at it.

"No, Captain, we don't."

I looked at the unit codes, ordered a case, charged the ship, routed the bill to Mr. Wyatt's inbox, and marked the order for pickup. "Okay, Avery. I know it's your job to order stuff, but I had it up and we need 'em fast."

He laughed. "You're the captain, Captain. Last time I checked I stand on ceremony for you, not the other way 'round."

"Yeah, well, true to a point, but you're the guy who has to keep this pile all sorted out and having unfamiliar fingers in the files doesn't help you."

"I appreciate the concern but aren't we in a hurry, Skipper?"

"Yes, we are. Here's what I want."

It was a simple logistical problem that Mr. Wyatt grasped immediately. Truth be told, I think he knew the solution as soon as he saw the boxes. Lunch mess would be a "one-can classic" since not many people would be partaking. It was mostly *pro forma* for the watch section and easy to clear away. Dinner would be the boxed lunches served on station. We'd done it a lot back on the *Lois*. Being driven by a larger schedule, she got underway when the company said move. DST worked on a different clock and ships had a little more flexibility in their movement.

I left Mr. Wyatt laying out the assembly line while I made the run to the chandlery.

"Shouldn't we send somebody else, Captain? Have them delivered?"

I paused halfway out of the mess deck. "I'm in a hurry, Mr. Wyatt, and who would we send?"

He thought about it for about three heartbeats and shrugged. "Good point, Captain."

It really was only a matter of a few ticks to make it down to the chandlery and back. By going myself I had the chance to rummage in the produce section a bit. I snagged a few nice looking pieces of fruit, a box of candy bars, and a bag of hard candies, before I picked up the heavy flat of boxes. I garnered a few odd looks riding the lift back up to the dock, but if the stars on my collar provoked the looks to begin with, they also prevented comment. It's not every day you see a clipper captain acting as delivery boy, but it's not something anybody in their right mind would question.

Mr. Ricks was expeditious in booking the mass to stores as I came through the lock and, if he was curious, he didn't ask any questions. I reached into the bag of hard candies and flipped him one as I went by. He caught it neatly on the fly with a "Thanks, Skipper," and I hurried back to the mess deck.

Mr. Pall had returned from the bridge by then, and helped Mr. Wyatt assemble sandwiches. I unloaded my bundle on the other work counter and broke open the pack of flattened boxes. I held one in my hands and the smell of the pasteboard, even the texture of it against my fingertips, took me back twenty stanyers. I could almost hear Cookie's voice in my head. My hands flexed in an old but unforgotten pattern and the completed box stood in my palms.

I didn't pause to admire it, but rather did it nine more times, stacking the empties on the counter until I had enough. They were easy enough to gather up and lay out for the assembly line to fill. While they finished the sandwiches, I added fruit, candy bar, and a few hard candies to each box. I pulled a twelve pack of water from the bottom of the ready cooler and put one of those in each box as well, cracking the lid off the eleventh and downing it myself in almost one go.

By then the sandwiches were ready and we started the final packing.

Mr. Pall looked at the line up curiously. "Why ten, Captain? There's only eight of us."

"Spoilage, Mr. Pall."

"Spoilage, Captain?"

"Pirates, Mr. Pall."

"Ahhh. I see, Captain. Yes, of course."

I stood looking at the boxes and I knew I was forgetting something. It came to me very suddenly. "Ms. Thomas." I said it aloud.

Mr. Wyatt looked to see if she were coming, but Mr. Pall looked at me. "Sar?"

"Ms. Thomas, William. She's a heavy worlder. We can't feed her this. It's not enough."

They looked startled.

Mr. Wyatt twigged first but Mr. Pall didn't need further explanation.

Mr. Wyatt asked, "Do we give her two, Skipper?"

"How would that make you feel, Avery?"

"You're making a lot of good points this morning, Captain."

"Thanks. I'm trying to make up for missing a few easy ones this morning. Make about three extra sandwiches. Put them in one of the boxes and mark the box. Put in an extra bar of chocolate, too."

"Extra water, Captain?"

I thought about it and shook my head. "Won't be room and we'll all need extra water so maybe I can ask you to ferry a cold twelver up to the bridge when we need it." I looked at Mr. Wyatt.

"Of course, Captain. Mr. Ricks will be here with me. He has the forward lock duty. I'm sure he'll help."

I nodded. "Good thinking, Mr. Wyatt."

We set to with the final details, Avery packing the bagged sandwiches, William closing up the finished boxes, and stacking them in the ready cooler. I showed him Cookie's old trick of using sheet cake pans as trays. He made up two trays of five and we made sure to put the marked box on the front so they'd take the right tray to the bridge.

The sudden lull took me by surprise.

If my limited experience aboard had taught me anything, though, it was that it was probably just the calm before the real storm.

The chrono clicked over to 1130 and I tried to focus.

"Avery? Soup time. William, I've got fitters coming at 1300. The mess deck needs to be clear by then. They promised me they'll be secured by 1400."

"Yo ho ho, Skipper. I remember."

I grinned. "Arrgh. Good lad."

Mr. Wyatt looked a bit startled. He didn't say anything but turned to warming a pot of soup. I was delighted to see that he'd snagged a pack of ready-bake rolls from the freezer and he snapped them into the baking oven and set the timer.

I grabbed my empty mug and headed for the coffee pot for a refill. "Carry on, gentlemen. I must off to battle the bane of every captain's existence. Reports."

Mr. Wyatt made a warding sign with his free hand and Mr. Pall had the decency to laugh.

I sipped the coffee and remembered one more detail. "Oh, Mr. Wyatt?"

He looked up from the soup. "Yes, Skipper?"

"Next pot of coffee? Make the grind about 20 percent finer, add about half again the amount of coffee to the basket, and use cold water."

"Plus 20, plus 50, and cold as I got, Skipper. Aye, aye."

As I climbed the ladder to officer country, I heard Mr. Pall volunteer to make a pot using the new formula.

Billy the Buccaneer or not, I was impressed.

Chapter Twenty-six
Diurnia Orbital: 2372-January-11

Charlie was as good as his word and showed up at the lock with his crew promptly at 1300. Mr. Wyatt had the galley spaces cleared and secured for them and Mr. Pall pinged me at 1350 to let me know the work had been completed.

I came down from the cabin to find the new table in place and gleaming. Charlie's work gang was policing the area for loose bits and tools. Charlie himself beamed with pride.

"Told ya, Captain. We beat your time." He turned to look at the table. "Is this what you wanted?"

"It is what I wanted and more, Charlie. My compliments to you and your crew. Thank you."

"My pleasure, Captain. We'll just clear this away and get outa here. I think you might have things to do and places to go today?"

"We do, Charlie. We do, indeed."

I thumbed the offered work order and he shepherded his gang off the ship, taking the leftovers, spare parts, and trash with him.

The new table was the perfect fit for the two deck mounting flanges. Each flange held one of the two sturdy legs of the single, long table. A bench ran down the length of each side. The whole assembly bore a striking resemblance to the picnic tables I'd grown up around on Neris. It also matched my fond memory of the table aboard the *Bad Penny*. It was exactly what I wanted.

Mr. Pall stood to the side looking the table up and down. Mr. Wyatt leaned against the sink with his arms folded across his chest and an amused expression on his face as he looked from me to the table and back.

"What do you think, Mr. Pall?" I asked.

He glanced up at me. "Fine piece of workmanship, Skipper."

"As nicely phrased a non-answer as I've heard, Mr. Pall."

"Thank you, Captain. I've been practicing."

"Mr. Wyatt?"

"It takes a little getting used to, Captain."

I nodded an agreement to that.

I heard Chief Gerheart come up behind me. "Oh, good. They got it in." She looked up at me with the little girl face. "Did you know this is the original configuration, Captain?"

"Chief?"

She turned back to the table and waved her arm. "This is how she's s'posed to be, Captain. The original plans show one table on the two flanges."

"I didn't know that, Chief. Good piece of information."

"Kinda makes ya wonder why they changed it, don't it, Captain?" It was the little girl voice, but the question struck a lot deeper.

"Yes, Chief, it does."

We admired for a couple heartbeats before I roused myself to focus.

"As nice as it looks, people, we got cargo to haul. Mr. Wyatt? Where are my cans?"

"Latched and locked, Captain. They came up last night about 2000."

"Excellent, Mr. Wyatt. Mr. Pall? Where is my crew?"

"Crew present or accounted for, Captain."

"Chief, ship ready for space?"

"She is, Captain."

I stuck my head out into the passage. "Mr. Ricks? Secure the lock for departure, if you would, please?"

"Aye, aye, Skipper. Lock secured for departure." His voice echoed down the passage from the bow.

"Thank you, Mr. Ricks."

I turned back into the galley and crossed to the urns. I pulled a fresh cup from the new urn and tried it. "You made this pot, Mr. Pall?"

"Yes, Captain. Followed your suggestions."

"Did you taste it, Mr. Pall?"

"Yes, Captain."

"And what did you think of it, Mr. Pall?"

"Arrgh, Captain. Now that's a cuppa coffee." He was grinning.

"I think so, too, Mr. Pall. Nicely done. And thank you, Mr. Wyatt, for your able assistance here."

Mr. Wyatt smiled. "Most welcome, Captain."

Chief Gerheart checked the installation job one last time.

"Does it pass inspection, Chief?"

The little girl smiled up at me and nodded shyly.

"Excellent, well, we have a stan or so before we call navigation stations. OD, if you'd rouse the crew and give them a chance to refresh themselves? I'll knock on Ms. Thomas's door on my way up to the bridge."

"Aye, aye, Captain."

I headed out of the galley and took a side trip to the ready cooler. I snagged one of the extra bento boxes from the offside tray and tucked it under my arm.

"Expecting pirates, Captain?" Mr. Pall smiled at me.

"Better safe than sorry, Mr. Pall."

"Good planning, Skipper."

"Thank you, Mr. Pall."

I scampered up to officer country and stopped to knock on the first mate's door. "Room service."

Three heartbeats later, a slightly disheveled Ms. Thomas opened the door, and I offered the boxed lunch. "A little something to tide you over till dinner, Ms. Thomas. You missed lunch."

She took it with an oddly shy smile and a nod of thanks. "Much obliged, Captain."

"You're quite welcome, Ms. Thomas. If you'd join me on the bridge, we'll set nav detail at 1445."

I headed up one more ladder to the bridge and took a few ticks to savor the moment. Strictly speaking, I should have been the last one entering the bridge and the first one off. A captain with more experience would trust his crew to prep the ship while he continued on with his august duties safely ensconced in the sanctity of the cabin. I wasn't that experienced yet, and while I certainly didn't want to make the crew feel like I didn't trust them, there's such a thing as being too certain of an unknown command.

Besides, this was just too darn much fun.

I took a tick to look aft to check out where the cans attached. Each cylindrical can was rated at fifteen metric kilotons. The tractor could carry up to three of them strung together like beads. Each can had a central locking shaft that was hoop on one end and hook on the other. The hook on one can latched onto the hoop on the next. A special terminal fitting went into the final hook out there at the far stern, and gave us an anchor on the end so the cans couldn't slide off. The *Agamemnon's* cargo latch fitted into the hoop on the closest can. Each can had pads and buffer latches at three corresponding locations so that, with the cargo latch engaged, the cans locked snuggly against each other and the ship. Not a terribly pleasing design to look at, but the functionality was undeniable.

Ms. Thomas was first up the ladder at 1435 and we were joined shortly by Mr. Pall who took the systems and astrogation console, Chief Gerheart sat at engineering, and Mr. Schubert assumed the helm. I sensed the party was about to start so I took my seat in the captain's chair for the very first time. There was a handy cup holder on the right side and I slotted my half empty mug into it. An air of expectancy permeated the bridge. I'd felt it on every pull out since that very first time on the *Lois McKendrick*. I tried to channel Alys Giggone as I gave a little nod to Ms. Thomas. She used the toggle on the duty watchstation to activate the squawk box and made the announcement.

Down in the ship, I knew Mr. Ricks should be taking his position on the forward latches in case of emergency. Mr. Hill was standing by the console down in Engineering. He was just the local set of olfactory sensors with orders to report anything that didn't look or, especially, smell right. Quite often the odor was the early warning clue, not the look. Hot metal doesn't look very different until it's very hot, but it smells different almost right away. Chief Gerheart would be going below as soon as we were on ballistic and would be present to fire up the grav keel and sails herself. Mr. Wyatt's role was supercargo, and he stood by in the galley, just in case.

Around 1450 the tug scooted into view around the curve of the orbital and eased in close to lock onto us. They were so close I could see into their bridge and watched the flickering lights of their maneuvering thrusters over my shoulder. The tug would be our temporary engine and pilot to get us out of the orbital's local space and kick us out into the Deep Dark.

I could see the astrogation station updating the ship's systems as the two hulls, in effect, became one vessel. The data streams merged and stabilized.

Mr. Pall turned to me. "Tug's locked in, Captain, and is ready to assist us."

"Thank you, Mr. Pall. Make ready for pull out, Ms. Thomas."

"Making ready for pull out, aye, Captain." She pressed a few keys on her console, and I saw the telltales shift from red to amber to green. "Locks are secured, docking clamp interlocks are offline, Captain. Ship's board is green once." Her voice was as loud as ever but it sounded like magic to me.

"Thank you, Ms. Thomas. Is astrogation ready, Mr. Pall?"

He reviewed his screen, formally running his finger down a long list of green indicators. At the end he nodded as if to himself. "Astrogation online and running stable, Captain. Board is green twice."

"Systems status when you're able, Mr. Pall. Cross check and

verify, Ms. Thomas."

She stepped over behind Mr. Pall and watched as he pulled over the systems and communications screens. "Systems are online and running Captain. Ship's board is green thrice."

Ms. Thomas returned to her position and pulled up both astrogation and systems displays. "Cross checked and verified, Captain."

"Ms. Thomas, are we ready?"

"All ship's boards are green. We show ready for departure on your command, Captain."

"Pull out in ten on my mark, Ms. Thomas." I didn't pause very long in real time, I don't think, but the realization hit me in that very moment that I would be in command of a ship free in space–my ship in any way that mattered until I returned to dock–for the first time in my life ten seconds after I uttered the very next word. I don't know what I felt, exactly. It was some combination of jubilation, dread, confidence, and terror. It exploded across my whole body.

"Mark."

There was a certain inevitability to it. The decisions had been made, the die cast. We needed to wait out the roll to see how well we'd done.

I felt the familiar clunk as the docking clamps released and the moving lift feeling for just a few heartbeats before the inertial dampeners kicked in.

"Log departure 2872-January-11, 1459, Mr. Pall."

"Aye, aye, Captain."

The tug pulled us free and within half a stan we sailed well away from the confusion of shuttles, cargo, and ship traffic. The tug spun us about, turning toward the Deep Dark, and ratcheted up the pusher to give us a good toss outward. We slowly gained velocity relative to the gravity well and soon left the most heavily trafficked areas behind.

At 1745 the tug signaled that he was ready to drop off. "My compliments to the skipper for the smooth ride and fine service, Mr. Pall."

"Aye, aye, Captain." There was a short pause. "Tug sends, 'Safe voyage. Next beer's on you,' Captain."

Everybody on the bridge chuckled. "Acknowledge, Mr. Pall."

"Acknowledged, Skipper."

We still had a way to go before we could open our sails safely, but the tug cut us loose and left us coasting along like a rock from a slingshot.

At 1800, Mr. Wyatt brought up the tray of boxes and Mr. Ricks carried a spare rack of water. There wasn't a lot of activity on the bridge as we monitored systems and made sure we were on track, so he had no trouble slipping on to the bridge and leaving a box on each console. He handed me one with a smile and slipped back off the bridge without a ripple.

As the bridge crew opened and examined the boxes, I caught Ms. Thomas out of the corner of my eye. I turned to look at her. She nodded once and mouthed the words, "Thank you, Captain," before pulling another sandwich out of the box beside her.

I just smiled, winked, and dug into my own. The sandwiches had gotten a little dry, but the fruit was good. I set the candy aside for later. I wasn't much of a chocolate eater myself, but perhaps it would come in handy before we secured.

Around 1830 we finished up with dinner and Mr. Pall nodded to Chief Gerheart. "Captain, we'll reach the safety perimeter at 1845. We'll be able to set sail at that time."

"Thank you, Mr. Pall. Chief? I think you're up."

She smiled gently and bobbed her head in acknowledgment with a quiet, "Aye, aye, Captain." She slipped from the bridge, thoughtfully taking the used boxes with her.

For the first time I noticed that Mr. Schubert's hands were not swaddled in bandages. I felt a pang of remorse for not noticing sooner but as he moved about the helm, it became clear that the single pad across the palm was doing quite well and my earlier fears might indeed be chalked up to an enthusiastic candy striper.

There was a point in this maneuver that is guaranteed to give nightmares to every person who has ever captained a tractor. We were out bound, certainly, but with no keel, no sail, and only maneuvering thrusters for motive power. If the sail generators failed to come online at the proper time, we would be in a bit of a pickle. On the other hand, we had multiple redundancies. For us to be in a real jam, they'd all have to fail. We still kept our fingers crossed as we approached the point where we'd find out if we were flying or if we'd just keep falling.

"We've passed the safety perimeter, Captain."

"Thank you, Mr. Pall. Signal Chief Gerheart that she may deploy keel and sails when ready."

"Aye, aye, Captain. Signal passed."

"Thank you, Mr. Pall."

A few ticks later, I could see the results on the display as the first sail generator spooled up and the field deployed.

At 1905, Ms. Thomas turned from her screen. "Chief Gerheart reports all sail and keel generators are operating nominally, Captain. Sails and keel are deployed."

"My compliments to the chief, Ms. Thomas. Helm report?"

"Ship has steerage and answering smartly, Captain."

"Thank you, Mr. Schubert."

"Ms. Thomas secure from navigation stations. Set normal watch. First section has the duty, I believe?"

"Aye, aye, Captain. Secure from stations and set normal watch. First section has the duty." She made the appropriate announcement to the rest of the ship.

I stood up, and smiled around the bridge. "Thank you, people. We should do this more often."

I was a little nervous that I'd stumble on the way back down the ladder, but I didn't, in spite of the weakness in my knees and a rather pronounced lightheadedness as the reality of what had just happened sank in. As I approached the cabin, I became a bit more concerned that I might lose my dinner as the enormity of that reality chased along behind.

Then I opened the cabin door and that huge port showed the rich, sparkled darkness of the Deep Dark strewn ahead of us. I stepped into the cabin and closed the door behind me so I'd have something to lean on as I drank it in. For what must have been five or six full ticks I was washed with thoughts and fears, emotions and endorphins. I'm not sure I'll ever be able to describe it, that ineffable feeling that I, myself–not in the ship, or part of the ship, but me–I flew outward, racing into the Deep Dark.

No, I don't think I could ever really describe it, but I was sure I'd never–as long as I lived–forget it.

Chapter Twenty-seven
Diurnia System: 2372-January-12

My tablet bipped me awake at 0500. I grabbed a quick shower and threw on a fresh shipsuit before heading down to the galley. I found Mr. Wyatt already up and about, with that heavenly aroma of fresh brewing coffee filling the mess deck and what looked like ten kilograms of flour spread around the work surface. He looked up at me with a sheepish shrug. "The biscuits are winning this morning, Skipper."

"I see that, Avery. How many were you planning on making?"

"I tripled the recipe so we'd have some for biscuits and gravy tomorrow morning. It didn't work out too well."

I crossed to the urns and snagged a fresh cup before trying to diagnose the problem. "Looks to me like you tripled the dry but only doubled the buttermilk."

He frowned down at the mess. "How can you tell?"

"It's just a guess. But you've got a lot more dry than batter there. I've done it myself often enough. Pile it up, make a little hollow in the middle and pour some more in. Mix it on the board and repeat until you get a good dough."

"Won't that make them tough, if I knead them too much, Skipper?"

"You've been reading again, Avery?"

He shrugged. "Seemed like a good idea, Skipper."

"You got the choice of tossing it and starting over or making them a little tough. Nobody here will complain–or probably notice. At the moment, there's not enough liquid in it to activate the gluten. You're not really kneading it yet. Just getting it to the point where you can."

I watched him considering it and I crossed to the work counter to get a better look.

"You might wanna consider a tad more shortening next time. Recipes seem to keep it to a minimum and I don't know if it's the recipe or the shipboard air conditions, but Cookie always used about a third more shortening and maybe a bit more of the baking soda."

"Skipper? Can I ask you a question?"

"Sure. I reserve the right not to answer, but you can ask anything you like."

"You know a lot about the galley for a Deck officer."

"I started as an attendant in the Steward Division, Avery. *Lois McKendrick* out of New Farnouk. Operated over in Dunsany Roads before I went to the academy."

"You were a rating, Skipper?" He sounded surprised.

"You didn't look me up?"

"Look you up, Captain?"

"I do have a fleet record. You can see it. Not all of it of course, but my pertinent details are listed."

"Oh." He looked a little crestfallen. "I didn't think of it."

"Don't feel bad. I've reviewed all your jackets, but I haven't looked at public records yet, either. We've been rather busy."

He chuckled at that and proceeded to scrape the floury pile up and work it into something approaching biscuit dough. I itched to get my hands in it, too, but I needed to let him find his own way there.

"So you were a steward? How did you wind up in Deck Division, Skipper?"

I sat on the bench and sipped my coffee. "Well, actually, I was a Systems Two when I left the *Lois*."

He goggled at me, freezing with his hands in the dough. "How many ratings do you hold?"

I shrugged. "Technically, none right now, but when I went to Port Newmar I was full share in all four divisions, in one capacity or another."

He resumed his biscuit recovery operation and continued to glance at me occasionally. "That's not that common, Skipper."

"Well, maybe, but I'm not spacer-born, so I had to make up for lost time."

"You're a land rat, Captain?"

"Born on a planet—Diurnia, as it happens—and neither of my parents were spacers. My mother was an ancient lit professor at the University of Neris. She got killed and I took a berth on the *Lois McKendrick*. The rest is twenty stanyers of mistakes and the occasional good meal."

I glanced over to the chronometer on the bulkhead as it clicked over to 0530.

"I've got a few ticks here before I have to get up to the bridge. Can I give you a hand, Avery?"

He nodded at the ready cooler. "If you could mix a pitcher of egg mix for omelets, Skipper? Eggs are in the cooler."

It was a matter of moments to crack two dozen and get them whisked up with a little cold water, salt and pepper. I snapped an airtight lid on it and left it on the side board. "You want me to heat a pan?"

"No, sar, but if you'd like to pull out the filling–"

Ms. Thomas's voice cut across the mess deck. "What happened in here?"

Avery and I both snapped around, taken aback by the volume and alarmed by the content.

Ms. Thomas was just inside the mess deck and staring like there was something truly terrifying and horrible about to engulf her. She seemed to be staring at the table.

"What, Ms. Thomas?"

"Captain, the–the tables!" She seemed almost in despair.

"Yes, I had them pulled and replaced with this just before we got underway. Why?"

"But–?"

"But what, Ms. Thomas?"

"Where will officers sit?"

"I don't understand, Ms. Thomas. At the table, of course." Actually I was afraid I did understand but I wanted to give her the benefit of the doubt.

She paused for a moment, still staring at the table, but processing. She looked at me after a moment. "Oh, well. Then where will the enlisted sit?"

"At the table, Ms. Thomas." I forestalled her next question. "Yes, at the same time. There's plenty of room."

"But that's impossible, Captain. We can't encourage that level of familiarity between officers and crew!"

"Ms. Thomas? Before you get too far down that unfortunate path, let me remind you that you're standing outside of crew quarters where, unless I'm very much mistaken at least one of said crew should be getting ready to join me on the bridge and to whom your commentary is going to be clearly audible."

"The crew is perfectly aware of my feelings on fraternization, Captain."

Mr. Hill stepped around Ms. Thomas on his way to the coffee pot. He nodded respectfully to Ms. Thomas. "Indeed we are, sar."

He seemed completely unfazed by the encounter and continued to the urns. He nodded to me and then Mr. Wyatt. "Morning, Skipper. Howdy, Mr. Wyatt."

I sighed and scrubbed my face with my hands. "Cabin, Ms. Thomas. Mr. Hill, at the appropriate time would you report to the bridge to relieve Mr. Ricks and relay my compliments to Mr. Pall and my apologies for delay in relieving the watch?"

"Aye, aye, Captain."

I turned back to Ms. Thomas. "Cabin, if you please, Ms. Thomas."

She went and I followed. She paused at the top of the ladder to let me lead the way into the cabin and I forestalled our normal dispute over the door by holding it for her as she entered and closing it myself.

"Captain, I must protest."

"Sit, Gwen." I pointed to the chair at the desk and I took mine on the other side.

She looked shocked at the familiarity. "I'd prefer to stand, Captain."

"Sit, Gwen. We need to talk and it's gotta be fast because I've got to relieve Mr. Pall."

She gathered into herself and took the chair.

"Okay, Gwen, what's the problem? Crew cooties? You can't eat at the same table? What?"

"Captain, it's not right that ratings and officers share the same facilities."

"Says who?"

"It's–It's–It's just not done, Captain." She was off balance but still truculent.

"What's got you so spooked?"

"Captain?"

"Look. Gwen, you're my first mate. I really rely on your knowledge of the ship to keep things moving smoothly. Getting underway yesterday proved to me that you have the skills and knowledge I need and that we can work together. We're still getting used to each other at the moment. We're on the first day of what might be a six week blind date from hell. We need to take some of the masks off and get down to the real parts before we make any more blunders. What's going on?"

"I don't understand, Captain."

"What's with the fraternization crap? And what's with the cabin door? I have never given you any cause to fear any kind of impropriety and you're strong enough to break me in half. Are you afraid I'm gonna call rape or something?"

"No, Captain. I'm just–"

I waited for her.

She shifted uncomfortably in the chair. "I don't get along well with men."

I shrugged. "Okay, that's not a problem with me. My mother preferred women, too."

"No, Captain." She flushed bright red. "It's not that I prefer women. Quite the opposite. I just–don't get along with men."

The light was dawning for me. "But you'd like to and it's not really working out well?"

"Yes, Captain."

"So you don't, what? Trust yourself alone with men?"

She looked startled. "Well, not exactly that, but–" She was really looking embarrassed. "Why add temptation I can avoid?" She was looking at her hands where they writhed in her lap.

"Okay, well, I'm not available. Don't be tempted and stop giving me grief about the door. I'll leave it open if it's ship's business but closed if we need to have a private discussion that I'd rather not share with the whole crew, okay?"

She took a deep breath and looked up at me. "Okay, Captain."

"Now what's with the table?"

"Well, that just struck me odd, Captain. I've never been on a ship where officers dined with ratings."

"They had two tables on the Hector?"

She shrugged and nodded. "Yes, Skipper, they did."

"Small ships have different rules, Ms. Thomas. Organizationally, these ships are a mess. We're desperately top heavy. They're just big enough to need a specific officer corps and not big enough to warrant sufficient ratings. That's why Mr. Wyatt is acting like a commissary man and I've been cooking meals."

"I can see that, Captain."

"We, as officers, need to acknowledge the value and contribution of the ratings. None of us gets home alive if we don't all pull together. That larger table is part of it. It represents something significant–as your reaction to it underscores."

She looked down at her hands but nodded. "I can see that, too, Captain."

"And besides. It's just a more efficient use of the space. Having another large surface where we can all work may come in useful for some of the other projects I have in mind, and the way it's situated in the galley, it's a place for crew to come in and hang out, help out with the cooking, kibitz with the cook. It's just friendlier."

She took a deep breath and then let it out slowly and shifted in the chair again. She didn't say anything.

That was when I noticed that her feet did not reach the floor. "Oh, dear."

"Captain?"

"I'm sorry, Gwen. I've been insensitive again. It's not the table, is it?"

"Not really, Captain. No. It's the bench."

"How did you sit at the smaller tables?"

"The seats had a little bar down below where I could hook my heels." She looked embarrassed.

"If I can fix that problem, will you be ok with this new arrangement?"

She looked startled at that. "How can you fix it, Captain? Stretch my legs?"

I grinned. "No, Gwen, I'm gonna raise the deck." The chrono on my desk clicked over to 0555. I nodded to it. "But I really need to relieve the watch now. Can you tough out breakfast and trust me to get it resolved before lunch?"

"Sure, Captain. But I'm really curious how raising the deck will help, and how you're going to accomplish that."

"You'll find out." I reached across the desk and offered my hand. "Call me Ishmael."

She had to stand up to be able to reach across to me, but she did and when she shook, there were no strength games involved. "Thank you. Ishmael."

"Git. I have a watch to relieve."

She really did have a lovely smile.

Chapter Twenty-eight
Diurnia System: 2372-January-12

I scampered up the ladder a tick before the top of the hour. "My apologies, Mr. Pall."

"No problem, Skipper. Ship is on course and on target. No incidents or actions. Standing orders are unchanged since you haven't changed them. You may relieve the watch, Captain."

"I have the watch, Mr. Pall. Logged on 2372 January 12 at 0601 per standing order."

"Thanks, Skipper."

"My pleasure, Mr. Pall."

"Mr. Wyatt will be bringing up a tray shortly, Captain."

"Ah, thank you, Mr. Pall. I trusted there was a procedure in place."

He smiled and dropped down the ladder.

"Good morning, Mr. Hill. Anything on the helm?"

"Full sails and fair sailing, Skipper."

"Excellent. I assume they'll bring us both trays?"

"If history is any predictor of the future, Captain, I believe they will." He grinned over his shoulder at me.

"Not long standing policy and practice then, Mr. Hill?"

He snorted. "At the risk of impertinence, Captain, have you seen the standing orders?"

I looked at him and I'm sure a certain level of embarrassment must have been evident on my face.

He gave a little shrug but said no more.

"Thank you, Mr. Hill. I'll–ah–take that under advisement."

"You're welcome, Captain."

I dug into the overnights and found no immediate red flags. I took the opportunity to initial them and send them to archives, clearing at least that much of my bureaucratic backlog. With a glance at the back of Mr. Hill's head, I pulled up the current standing orders file and began reviewing it.

Mr. Wyatt slipped in about 0620 with a couple of trays. "I took the liberty of throwing a little of this and that into an omelet for you, Skipper. Hope it's ok."

"Food. Warm. Good, Mr. Wyatt." I smiled up at him from the station. "At this point, I'm grateful for all small blessings."

"And for you, Mr. Hill. Same menu as the captain. Can't get any better'n that."

Mr. Hill laughed a little. "Thank you, Mr. Wyatt. I'll eat pretty much anything."

"I'll be back for the trays after we get the galley secured, Skipper."

"First things first, Mr. Wyatt. You're doing great. Don't stop now."

"Thank you, Captain." He headed back to the mess deck and I started to eat while I continued reading the standing orders.

The eggs and biscuits were gone long before I got to the end of my perusal, but I kept plowing. Any error in standing orders could spell catastrophe and Mr. Hill had me dead to rights. I hadn't really paid much attention to them.

After nearly a stan and a half, I finished the last paragraph. They didn't seem too bad. There were a couple of raggedy bits that I would have changed–should change eventually–but nothing I found objectionable.

"You have some critique of the standing orders, Mr. Hill?" I'd been quiet for a long time.

"The section on meals and coverage of the watch seems a bit on the sparse side to me, sar."

I didn't remember that section, but I'd read through a lot of material in rather a short order. I scanned the index again and didn't see a listing. What he was saying was suddenly crystal clear. "A bit on the spare side does appear to be a bit of an understatement, Mr. Hill."

"Well, yes, Captain. Probably so."

"Thank you for pointing it out, Mr. Hill."

"Quite welcome, Captain. I expect you've had a few things to worry about since coming aboard."

"I have, indeed, Mr. Hill. And, speaking of things to worry about, how are you feeling today?"

He smiled. "I'm okay, Skipper. I had it coming. I just didn't think they'd pay off so soon. I'm sore in a few places and my skin is turning technicolor, but there's nothing serious. Sorry, about that."

He actually sounded it.

"Apology accepted, Mr. Hill. We all have debts that need to be paid one way or another." That brought up an unexpected thought of Jen and a pang of regret for what my being in space was doing to her. I brushed it aside. "Are there any other 'sparse' sections of the standing orders that you're aware of, Mr. Hill?"

"I'm hardly an expert, Skipper."

"Entertain me, Mr. Hill."

He did. On several different topics. He ran down after two solid ticks.

I kept a list as he went and then compared it to the existing standing orders. I found one mismatch, but when I dug into it a bit deeper I found that he had been right on practically every point.

"Mr. Hill, have you ever considered the Academy?"

That startled him. "Of course not, Captain. I'm an Able Spacer!"

"So, was I once. Briefly."

He looked very startled at that, but offered no comment.

I went back over the list and looked at how well he'd filled in the critical holes. There weren't any of them that would have put the ship at risk or were particularly serious in terms of ship's services, but they were the kinds of standing orders that assured the smooth running of the ship during normal operations and largely addressed the comfort of the crew.

I sat back in my seat and stared at the list. "Mr. Hill, I have another collateral duty for you."

"Yes, Captain?"

"Sorry. This really does seem like it comes right from the No Good Deed Goes Unpunished Department but I'd like you to head up a group to revise the standing orders."

"Me, Captain?"

"Yes, Mr. Hill. You've already given this a great deal of thought and I'd like to capitalize on that good work. Tap Mr. Ricks, Mr. Wyatt, Chief Gerheart, and Mr. Pall, with my compliments. What I'd like is a review of existing standing orders. Come up with any revisions to those orders that may be required to keep them consistent with the current state of the ship and her systems, as well as any additional orders that might be required to fill in the gaps." I paused for breath. "You've identified some gaps already. I'd like to do what I can to fill any that you may not yet have thought of."

He nodded slowly. "There are officers in that group, Captain."

"I'm aware of that, Mr. Hill. Use them well, but abuse them at your peril."

"What if they don't like it, Captain?" He seemed uneasy.

"They'd like heading up the committee much less, Mr. Hill."

"Captain, were you always this vicious?"

"I've worked hard to develop the talent to its current level, Mr. Hill."

"I don't doubt you for a second, Captain."

"Thank you for the vote of confidence, Mr. Hill."

"Any time, Skipper."

I grinned and he turned back to his helm.

Mentioning Chief Gerheart reminded me. I needed to talk to her about raising the deck. I sent her a quick note asking her to join me on the bridge when she had a moment. I hadn't done much more than send it when she popped up onto the bridge.

"I was on my way anyway, Captain." The little girl smiled out at me this morning.

I pulled out my tablet and began a rough sketch of the table and it's context in the galley. "I need a favor, Chief. If you could do this before lunch, I'd appreciate it."

She frowned seriously at the sketch. I explained the situation briefly and she chewed on the corner of her lip, never taking her eyes off the sketch in my hands as if fearing that it might disappear if she looked away.

"Do you know how high, Captain?"

I shook my head. "The most direct approach would be to ask, but Ms. Thomas is asleep."

She nodded her understanding. "I've several ideas, Captain, but . . ." She started to reach across me to my console before she realized what she was doing. She froze halfway and looked a question at me. I sat back out of the way with a gesture for her to continue. She pulled up Ms. Thomas's jacket where it listed her height. "This will give me a solid place to start, Captain. Thank you."

She flipped the screen back to the exact place it was before she'd touched it and turned to frown at the sketch once more. She was concentrating heavily now and I recognized the symptoms. "I know what but I don't know where, Skipper." I don't think she realized it but the little girl voice had a bit of an edge. Mr. Hill heard it. He didn't turn but he stiffened in his seat.

I used the stylus to put an X on the diagram on one corner of the table. "That position. Fix it so the person sitting here can use it."

She pulled back a bit, straightening and gazing. She looked at me with an almost sapphire gaze. "There?"

I nodded.

"Not beside you?"

I shook my head.

She looked at the sketch again very intently before smiling. "Insight, hunch, or edict?"

"Hunch."

"I like your style, Skipper."

"I like yours, too, Chief."

That brought the little girl back. She giggled a bit with a nervous glance in Mr. Hill's direction.

"Carry on, Chief."

She did.

After the sound of her footsteps made it clear she was gone, Mr. Hill turned to me. "Captain?"

"Yes, Mr. Hill?"

"What's with her voice, sar?"

"Her voice, Mr. Hill?"

"Yes, Captain. Her voice. I've been aboard for what? Five stanyers? I've never heard her speak much above a whisper and always in that little girl voice she has."

"Your point, Mr. Hill?"

"Captain, that was not a little girl voice."

"Really, Mr. Hill? I hadn't noticed."

The hairy eyeball he gave me back was one lash short of insubordination and masterfully done. "Captain, has anyone ever told you—?"

"Yes, Mr. Hill. I am a very bad liar. I try to avoid it where possible. Please, don't give me more practice."

"You know, then, sar."

"Yes, Ms. D'Heng and Ms. Jaxton on the *Tinker* kept me appraised of my progress on a regular basis. I'm a slow learner, Mr. Hill. What can I say?"

He took the hint and turned back to his helm.

I turned back to my own console and ran through a routine scan of ship's position, velocity, and overall status. On the bottom of the screen, ETA to jump caught my eye. 2372 February 15.

"Mr. Hill, do you have an estimated jump date on your display?"

"Yes, Captain, the fifteenth of February."

"What's the date today displaying as, Mr. Hill?"

"January 12, Captain." He straightened up in his seat and looked over at me with little glances. "Something wrong, sar?"

"Do you have any idea why it's going to take us almost five weeks to hit jump, Mr. Hill?"

"No, sar. I'm just the helm. Mr. Pall does the plotting."

I forced myself to take a breath before I spoke again. It wouldn't do to lose it on the bridge. "And does five weeks seem a reasonable run out to you, Mr. Hill?"

He shrugged, still scanning his board. "Seems like it's always about that, Skipper."

"Always on the run out of Diurnia?"

"No, Skipper. Always. We run out about five weeks, jump, run in about five weeks. It's just what we do."

"Thank you, Mr. Hill. Valuable insight."

"Is something wrong, Captain?" He asked again, looking over at me with concern on his face.

"No, Mr. Hill." I kicked myself mentally. "If this is the norm, then there's probably a good reason."

He settled back into his chair and turned to the helm. "You'll need a lot more practice, Captain."

"No doubt, Mr. Hill, but let me check my assumptions before I commit my blunders. I prefer to make my mistakes on purpose rather than by accident."

"An interesting philosophy, Captain."

"Thank you, Mr. Hill." I started slapping keys and he was smart enough to leave me alone while I ran a few numbers of my own. I got to the end and had a date in March. I sighed and started checking it again. I didn't spot the error so I erased the work space and filled it in from scratch. Unfortunately, in my zeal, I had erased all the default values for ship's systems as well and had to reload them all from current status. I got to the bottom and had a date in early February which seemed much more likely. I was still concerned that I didn't have some key piece of the puzzle. I sat back in my chair to think.

"Find it, Skipper?" Mr. Hill hadn't turned his head before speaking.

"I don't know, Mr. Hill. I think so, but I need more information."

He glanced at me out of the corner of his eye. "This is going to be an interesting cruise, Captain."

I grinned. "You just figuring that out, Mr. Hill?"

He snickered a little. "I've had some hints, sar, but I think this is the first time it's really hit home." He shrugged a little apologetically. "Slow learner, sar, what can I say?"

"As long as we learn eventually, Mr. Hill, that's the key."

He nodded in agreement. I looked at the chronometer and my empty mug. "How do we get a fresh cup of coffee up here, Mr. Hill?"

He looked at his mug, too. "I don't know, Captain. I've never really been tempted by a second so I've never bothered to find out."

"In five stanyers, Mr. Hill?"

He shrugged. "Captain, you may have noticed that the coffee aboard wasn't all that good."

"I did notice some improvements in recent days now that you mention it, Mr. Hill."

I pondered for a moment. "How long do you think it would take you to scamper down to the galley, fill two mugs, and come back?"

He looked over at me to see if I was serious. "Three ticks, max, Skipper. Why?"

I held up my mug. "Just a splash of milk, if you please, Mr. Hill. Go."

"The helm, Skipper?"

I stood up and crossed to his post. "Scoot, man. I'm qualified."

He scooted, taking his own mug with him, and trailing an "aye, aye, Captain," in his wake.

I hadn't gotten a chance to settle into the seat before he was back with a grin and two mugs. He handed one to me as I slipped out of his chair and into my own.

"Make a note to deal with that, Mr. Hill."

"Captain?"

"In the standing orders. Bridge watch needs refreshment and we have no messengers to help. That needs to be addressed."

He actually pulled out his tablet and, as I watched, made a note. I grinned and opened my own comms channel at the console and sent low priority messages to establish the work group to review standing orders.

"Captain?"

"Yes, Mr. Hill."

"You're humming."

"Interesting, Mr. Hill. I wasn't aware. Does it bother you?"

"No, Captain. Just–never had a captain who hummed."

"I usually whistle, Mr. Hill."

He glanced at me out of the corner of his eye once and settled into his seat with a wry smile. "Yeah. Interesting trip, indeed."

"Did you say something, Mr. Hill?"

"No, Captain."

"Very well, Mr. Hill. Carry on."

"Aye, aye, Skipper."

CHAPTER TWENTY-NINE
DIURNIA SYSTEM: 2372-JANUARY-12

Mr. Pall popped up the ladder right on time at 1145 with Mr. Ricks in tow. We did the needful and I vacated the bridge in favor of the mess deck. As I walked in, Ms. Thomas stood beside the table, bent over peering under it at a raised, and slightly tilted box. If Chief Gerheart's calculations were correct, she would be able to comfortably rest her feet while seated.

Mr. Wyatt was very busy not noticing as he bustled around the ovens, pulling out a very credible casserole of what smelled like chicken, and a tray of ready-bake rolls.

"What do you think, Ms. Thomas? Will it work?" I asked.

She straightened from her examination and beamed at me. "It does work, Skipper. I tried it already and was just looking to see how she'd managed it."

Chief Gerheart showed up at my elbow then. "Mastic, Gwen. Stick'um works good." Her voice had that bright little girl tone and she sounded as proud of herself as any four year old with a mud pie.

Gwen slipped up onto the bench and placed her feet on the box. She gave a kind of settling shake to her body and placed her hands, palm down on the table. She looked up then and actually whispered. "Thank you, both."

Chief Gerheart grinned and I nodded my acknowledgment, before crossing over to the ready cooler. "How can I help you, Mr. Wyatt?"

He glanced over from arranging the casserole on a hot pad and nodded at the cooler. "You should find a large bowl of salad and a couple of bottles of dressing in there, Captain. It all needs to come out and go on the sideboard."

"Got it, Mr. Wyatt."

We bustled around setting up the buffet while the crew gathered. When it was all ready, Mr. Wyatt nodded to me. "That looks like it, Skipper."

I stepped back and admired the spread. "Nice job, Mr. Wyatt."

"Thank you, Captain."

The clock ticked over to 1200 and I took captain's privilege, grabbing the first plate and starting down the line. Ms. Thomas came right behind me and Chief Gerheart behind her. After that I lost track but the boys seemed to sort it out among themselves and in a matter of just a few minutes I'd taken my place on the left side of the table on one end, thereby establishing, once and for all, the head. It happened to be, through absolutely no coincidence at all, directly across from Ms. Thomas. The chief engineer sat next to the first mate, and as I expected, Mr. Hill sat on the opposite end of the bench from me, while Mr. Schubert sat opposite him, establishing the foot of the table. With the order established, I felt certain it would remain.

Chief Gerheart watched covertly as the seats filled. When Mr. Wyatt took the trays up to the bridge, she hid a wink and a nod in my direction behind her coffee mug.

"I think Mr. Wyatt would take it amiss if we let his excellent efforts get cold." I announced it to the table at large and took the ceremonial first bite. My first lunch mess underway got off to a good start. I had hopes that it would finish well. There was a certain amount of tension for me, and I think for the rest of the crew as they began to get used to the idea that we were, indeed, one crew. Even Mr. Wyatt's return failed to bring doom upon the party as he took up trencher and mug and after a single heartbeat's consideration took the seat beside Chief Gerheart and not the one next to me.

The Chief grinned, licked one fingertip delicately, and made a kind of tally mark in the air with a nod in my direction. I gave her a small toast with my coffee cup and the meal progressed swimmingly.

For dessert, Mr. Wyatt brought out small cups of frozen custard, each garnished with a strawberry and a drizzle of chocolate syrup, and by 1245 we were all pushed back and replete. Even Ms. Thomas.

As the last of us finished and the meal drew to a close, I held my mug in toast to Mr. Wyatt. "My compliments to the chef!" It was followed by a general round of raised mugs and glasses with echoes of "Hear! Hear!"

He looked embarrassed but pleased, and was gracious in his acceptance.

When lunch started to break up, I was pleased and surprised to see Ms. Thomas and Mr. Schubert stand to help Mr. Wyatt with cleanup without being asked. I hoped this would be a pattern that would continue as well. I stood, bussed my dirties and, with a suggestion to Mr. Hill that he make an effort to get some rest before he reported to watch, left the mess deck with what I hoped was a cheerful, "Carry on."

It was the tight turnaround slot in my watch schedule. We'd done six stans on, and were off for six. We'd be back on watch from 1800 until midnight when we'd go off watch until midnight the following day. I thought I really should take a nap myself, but I had a nagging problem that I needed solved before I would be able to rest.

I scampered up to the bridge and took a seat at the engineering station which was handiest to the main watch console.

"How's the watch so far, Mr. Pall?"

"No hostiles as yet, Captain. We've a weather eye peeled."

"Excellent news, Mr. Pall. If you can spare a moment from pirate patrol, I've a bit of a confusion that I'd like you to clear up."

"Certainly, Skipper. Keep a sharp lookout, Mr. Ricks."

"Aye, sar. Keeping a sharp lookout, sar."

Mr. Pall turned to give me his complete attention.

"I was running some astrogation exercises and I came across an odd anomaly that I hope you can explain to me, Mr. Pall."

"I'll try, Skipper. What's up?"

I pointed to a worksheet on the console's local storage. "Open up that plotting calculator, if you would, Mr. Pall."

"Aye, aye, sar." He was already opening it before the words were out of his mouth.

"If you'd check the jump estimate, you'll see a date that's substantially different than ours, Mr. Pall."

He was deep in the calculation and that's where I wanted him. "Aye, Skipper. I see that. What I don't see is why you think this is our ship."

"What do you mean, Mr. Pall?"

"These setups are all wrong."

"Why are they wrong, Mr. Pall?"

He held that sheet open while he slipped the formal astrogation displays open behind it. A few flicks of the keys and he had an identical worksheet open with defaults set that were radically different from the ones I'd pulled from the current ship's systems.

He pointed to the screen. "That's our ship, Captain."

"Where do those numbers come from, Mr. Pall?"

"Template file, Captain. It's our baseline for all astrogation calculation."

I blinked at him. "But the ship is different each trip. How can you use a template for astrogation?"

He shrugged. "It seemed odd to me, too, Skipper, but when I came here, Captain Delman showed me the set up and gave me the standing order. It's what he wanted, so that's what I've been doing. Why?"

"Standing order, Mr. Pall?"

He nodded and pulled up the file with the requisite order and opened it for me to read. I remembered reading it but the implications of it hadn't really sunk in because it looked like a pretty standard 'follow the established procedure' order.

"And the established procedure is to use this template every time."

"Yes, Captain. Those are the settings for the ship's baseline."

"Who told you that?"

"Captain Delman, Skipper."

"Tell me, Mr. Pall. Did it ever seem odd to you that every trip was exactly ten weeks long?"

He thought about it for a few ticks. "Well, no. I guess I never noticed. Are you sure, Captain?"

I shook my head. "No, I'd have to check the logs, but do me a favor, run up an exercise sheet. Plot Diurnia to Jett using your template."

"Aye, sar." He tapped keys for a few ticks and sat back in the chair staring. "Ten weeks, Skipper."

"Try Diurnia to Breakall."

A few more ticks and he looked at me strangely. "Ten weeks, Captain."

I nodded. "Those baseline numbers are not the *Agamemnon*. Or at least not the ideal plot for the *Agamemnon*. I'm not sure why, but somebody wanted every trip to be exactly ten weeks long."

Mr. Pall turned to me, his eyes wide. "Pirates, Captain?"

I shook my head. "I don't know, Mr. Pall. It's certainly possible. Where did this template come from, can you tell?"

He grinned. "I'm not just the astrogator, Captain. I have access."

He turned back to the console, pulled up the system's displays, and started rooting about in archives. After a few ticks he frowned, and started typing faster. I could see his eyes tracking something on the screen as folders and files opened and closed, but I didn't interrupt him to find out what it might be. I knew he was getting close when his eyes tightened and I saw his eyeballs slow in their sockets. "Gotcha." He turned to me. "Skipper, this template has been in place for going on twenty stanyers."

"Well, I like to see well established policy, Mr. Pall, but it would be good if that policy were established for some reason. Any clues as to who put that template up?"

"It's listed to a David Burnside, Captain."

"Burnside, Mr. Pall?"

He nodded and pointed to the screen. "Right there, Skipper. Operator of record for this file was David Burnside, Second Mate." He looked up at me as I came around to look over his shoulder. "That name mean anything to you, Skipper?"

"Pirate, Mr. Pall. I've run into him before. I think if you cross reference that date against the command list you're going to find that the skipper who put the standing order in place was Captain Leon Rossett."

His fingers dodged around the keyboard for a few moments. The list of *Agamemnon's* captains spooled down the screen from most current, me, to Delman and on down the list. Some I recognized. Most I didn't, until the pointer rested on the name Leon Rossett.

"Damn, you're good, Skipper."

"Thank you, Mr. Pall, but that answers my question. My suspicion is that Captain Rossett wanted to have some order in his life, and Mr. Burnside supplied it."

"The template is wrong, Captain?" Mr. Pall sounded alarmed.

"No, Mr. Pall. It does what that captain wanted and it's done it very well. The wonder is that nobody since has thought to change it."

"Nobody wants to challenge a standing order, Captain."

"Yo ho ho, Mr. Pall. I think it's time we kicked a few butts, took a few risks, and called the cat rude names."

"We have a cat, Captain?"

I laughed, because I wasn't really sure he was joking. "I'm considering it, Mr. Pall. Do me a favor, and bring up a blank plotter."

He clicked a few keys, but the plotter he showed was filled with the suspect template. He frowned at it. "That's as empty as I have, Skipper."

"Use the console commands to erase all data, Mr. Pall."

He did so.

"Now, if you'd use your fine understanding of ship's systems, modern astrogation techniques, and any other little tricks, traps, and foibles you've concocted along the way to plot me a run from here to Welliver, best time, current configuration. Assume a climb out to the burleson limit with a five percent safety factor on this end and drop us outside the wall with ten percent margin on the other, Mr. Pall?"

"I love it when you talk dirty, Captain."

"I do, too, Billy. Plot me a course no buccaneer would dare follow."

Mr. Ricks was trying not to stare openly.

"Aye, aye, Skipper." He was already moving. Familiarity with the screens and current practice in the tools made my earlier efforts seem almost childish. He worked for the better part of a quarter stan. Every once in a while he'd grunt and his left cheek would twitch, but other than that only his fingers and his eyeballs moved. He didn't even jiggle a foot. Every erg of energy was focused on the task. The frenetic activity ended suddenly and he pulled his hands back from the keyboard.

"That can't be right." He was talking to himself and not to me. The date on the screen was two days earlier than mine–February 2.

"Why not, Mr. Pall?"

He slapped his sheet against mine and then compared them, line by line. Where there was a difference, and there weren't many, the error was mine.

"Cross checked and verified, Mr. Pall." I said it softly but I saw Mr. Ricks twitch.

"I'm–speechless, Captain."

"Okay, so we have two experienced astrogators who believe that this date is correct. All we need now is to find the course that takes us there."

"Mr. Ricks? Come right five degrees and yaw plus fifty-two. Hold her because I'm going to ask for some more sail." His fingers moved as he spoke and the engineering display showed the action matching the word. When the fields had stabilized and the new track established, he looked up at me. "Any suggestions, Captain?"

"Two, Mr. Pall." I smiled down at him. "File that corrected course with Diurnia traffic control and keep a weather eye peeled."

He grinned. "Aye, aye, Skipper."

There were a few more details I needed to deal with before I could find my rack, and first was a stop in Engineering. I found Chief Gerheart grinning at the sail generators and in a way that had nothing to do with little girls. She saw me enter the generator room out of the corner of her eye and turned those sapphire daggers on me. "About damn time, Captain."

"How are they doing, Chief?"

"The generators? These baby's have been dying to cut loose for a long, long time, Skipper." Her eyes went back to the machinery and I could see her tracking back and forth in ways that I didn't understand, watching the cues that meant something to her, but not to me. There was an almost predatory glee in her face as she watched the machines working.

"This isn't normal then, Chief?"

She shook her head, never taking her eyes off the displays. "I don't think we've ever had them out past forty percent, Skipper. Not in the two stanyers I've been aboard."

"Any idea why?"

"Delman always said it was standing orders. I tried to tell him it was causing them more damage to run damped down like that, but he just told me to deal with it."

"How much leg does the ole girl have?"

"Lot more than we're using, but Billy's a good sailor and Ricks knows his helm. They'll call for what they need. And we're still close in. We get further out and we'll need more sail to maintain delta-v."

We stood there in the belly of the beast, feeling the new tension in the hull, a new tempo in the beat of the ship's heart. Chief Gerhart laughed–high and musical and filled with delight. "Yes, Cap'n. The girls are doing just fine and thankee, sar, fer askin'."

I really wanted to know but I was afraid to break the spell, and I wasn't sure it mattered.

She answered the unspoken. "It's camouflage, Captain."

"Does it work, Chief?"

She arched one raggedly perfect eyebrow with a sardonic grin. "Do you need it?"

She stopped for a heartbeat and started to answer, but stopped again. "Good question, Captain. Can I get back to you on it?"

"Of course, Chief. Take your time." I stopped to take a quick look around the space. "Any issues in the other systems? The bacon fire cause any problems with the scrubbers?"

She shook her head and gave a little sideways shrug. "Mighta knocked a day off the life cycle, but nothin' serious, Cap. I may have to swap out a cartridge a day early but these things are massively over engineered for the size of crew we have."

"That's what I thought when I saw the specs. Any idea why, Chief?"

"Old design. They built to different standards then and I think they engineered environmental on the volume of the nacelle and not the anticipated crew load."

"Good point, Chief."

"S'my job, Cap'n."

"You do it well, Chief, and I'm truly grateful."

"My pleasure."

I left her running status checks on the fusactors and headed up to the galley. I needed to make sure Mr. Wyatt was okay with dinner before I took my nap. It was already pushing 1400 and I needed to lie down soon or it wouldn't be worth it.

I found the mess deck already shipshape and bristol fashion. Ms. Thomas and Mr. Schubert weren't there but I found Mr. Wyatt putting the finishing rub down to the work counters. He smiled when he saw me coming. "Did I feel the generators spooling up, Captain?"

"You did, indeed, Mr. Wyatt. We put on a bit more sail and took a new tack."

"Pirates, Captain?"

"In a way. We'll be getting into Welliver a bit earlier than expected."

He looked curious but didn't press it, for which I was grateful.

"You okay for dinner mess, Avery? I'd like to take a nap before it gets too late, but I'm asking you to do a lot that's not in your pay grade, and I don't wanna leave you hanging in the wind. Again."

"I'm fine, Skipper. Dinner's a roast with some tubers and veg. Using one of the cans of soup, with a little help from the pantry like you showed me. Dessert's a frozen pie tonight, but ..." He shrugged apologetically. "Gotta use 'em up."

I nodded my agreement. "Well, if there's nothing you need from me, I'm gonna try to get a couple stans rest before watch."

"Sleep while you can, Skipper."

"First lessons, eh, Mr. Wyatt?"

He chuckled and I headed out of the galley but remembered one other point. "Mr. Wyatt, you know about the ship's pooka?"

"The Agamemnon account, Captain? Of course. What about it?"

"Has it ever been used?"

"Not that I know of, Captain, but I might not be in the loop on that one."

"Thanks, Mr. Wyatt. I'll look into it and let you know what I find."

"Get some rest, Skipper."

I went up to the cabin and was almost tempted by the paperwork, but I had a long evening watch ahead that I could use for some of it and I needed to be careful to sleep enough. I went into the sleeping cabin, slid the privacy screen closed, skinned down to my boxers, and slipped into the rack. I was concerned that I might not be able to fall asleep, but good training tells. Before I could even wonder too seriously if I'd be able to sleep, my tablet bipped me awake at 1700.

Mr. Wyatt was puttering in the galley when I got down there at

1730. "Any problems, Mr. Wyatt? The roast smells marvelous!"

He shook his head with a smile. "All ops normal, Captain. Dinner's on course and on schedule."

"Good to know, Mr. Wyatt. Thanks for this." I waved my hand at the galley and mess deck.

He paused for a moment before speaking. "You're welcome, Captain. It's funny, but when all I was doing was opening cans? I hated this part." He nodded to indicate the galley. "It just seemed like so much work." He laughed. "Now I'm working ten times more, and enjoying it. All of it." He shrugged. "It fills the time and–this probably sounds corny–it feels like I'm helping."

"You are, Avery. More than you may realize. If you need anything, make sure I know about it, okay?"

"I will, Captain."

I crossed to the urns and decanted a mug before climbing the two ladders up to the bridge. I really felt like it was coming together and I regretted that feeling with every step. If experience taught me anything, it was that feeling like I had things under control was usually the first symptom of a complete and utter lack of understanding. It was a lesson I thought I had learned well, but which continued to show me new variations with every iteration.

Chapter Thirty
Diurnia System: 2372-February-02

After the initial excitement, the run out to the burleson limit settled into a comfortable rhythm. The predictable procession of watches soothed any jangled nerves and we slipped collectively into a Zen-like state. We lived in the moment. We looked to the next task, the next watch, the next meal, the next shower, the next sleep. I started using the treadmills in the workout room, surprising Mr. Hill on the rowing machine one morning by joining him. He rowed. I ran. The universe unfolded.

Three minor excursions marked the outward leg. The Confederated Planets Joint Committee on Trade required us to exercise the crew in emergency procedures once each quarter. Spacers soon took these little alarums as just part of the routine, even though they were generally offered at some odd time on a semi random basis. The *Agamemnon's* crew sailed through with nary a hitch, other than a few ticks of lost sleep for the off watch. They executed lifeboat, suit, and fire drills flawlessly and with some degree of good grace.

Jump, on the other hand, was one of those evolutions that could break the routine on any voyage and rouse the crew from the pattern. It marked the only tangible milestone in the journey from here to there. It represented the point where we were no longer leaving here and started approaching there.

Mr. Pall had, indeed, threaded me a needle, when he finally realized that he could hold the thread. We actually crossed the burleson limit in the middle of the morning watch on February 2, 2372. I purposefully held off calling the navigation detail until 1130. It was one of those little things that often got in the way on larger ships that ran on somebody else's deadline. I had the luxury of delaying the jump for a convenient point in the watch cycle–where waking everybody in the ship, dragging them to duty for half a stan, before going back to the mind-numbing cycle would have the least effect.

It promised to be a special day for all. Mr. Wyatt had been planning a celebration dinner for days and refused to tell me what was on the menu, but assured me that going to navigation stations wouldn't effect it in the least. After we secured, there'd be a feast awaiting us on the mess deck, assuming that the jump went as predicted, of course. If it didn't go as predicted, that would be another issue. In the twenty-odd stanyers I'd been making jumps, I think I could count on the fingers of my hands the number of times they'd gone wonky. Typically, it was a minor over or undershot. One memorable jump on the *Tinker* dropped us almost on top of an outgoing tanker.

To be clear, in the universal scales of the Deep Dark, "almost on top of" consisted of within ten kilometers. We could see his running lights. It was that close. Not "we could see into the bridge windows" close. He'd been out of his lane and was more embarrassed than we were.

There wasn't really any way to know if there was something already in the spot we were jumping to. The probability of there being anything there was very small, but not zero. So we woke everybody and got them where we'd need them in case of emergency.

Promptly at 1100, Ms. Thomas, Mr. Pall, and Mr. Schubert joined Mr. Hill and me on the bridge.

As they trooped up the ladder, I stood from the watch stander's station, logging Ms. Thomas on as I did so, then crossed to the captain's chair. "Let's go somewhere else, Ms. Thomas? Shall we?"

She smiled in real amusement. She'd settled down in the weeks we'd been chasing each other around the watch stander merry-go-round, and my instincts seemed to be holding up. She gave every impression of being a first-rate first mate, and I thought she might make a good captain–if she weren't so loud. I knew she struggled to control it, but with limited success.

"Did you have any place in mind, Skipper?" she asked.

"I'm thinking Welliver, Ms. Thomas?"

She turned to Mr. Pall who was already setting up the astrogation board. "What d'ya say, Mr. Pall? Welliver work for you this morning?"

"Yes, Ms. Thomas. I think that would be an excellent choice."

"Mr. Pall agrees, Captain. Shall we?"

"Oh, let's. We're already this far along. Log it up, Ms. Thomas."

She called the hands to navigation stations as a formality. Most of them were already in position, and Mr. Hill was probably halfway to Engineering by the time the call went out.

We settled down and ran the checks, locked down the ship, and generally braced up as well as we could. I'd done this so many times I'd lost count, but I always got a frisson of thrill from the possibilities of what lay just a few ticks ahead.

"Ship is green, thrice, Captain."

That was my cue to give the command to jump. There wasn't a prescribed command in the manual. It was one of the curiosities of the ages. In virtually every circumstance where command and control relied on living people talking to one another, tradition and experience created a prescribed set of commands and responses. Those commands get drilled, and the responses rehearsed endlessly. Lives depended on the commands being heard, interpreted, and understood correctly as fast as human synapses allowed. Yet in this one circumstance there was only a suggested command word. Each Captain I'd served under had their own way of doing it. Some, like Captain Giggone just said, "Go." Leon Rossett had always said, "Jump." Fredi deGrut used to say, "Punch it!"

I confess. I had thought more than once about what I would do when the time came. I'd spent more than a few idle moments on watch wondering what command I'd use. I couldn't make up my mind whether to be staid and by the book or say something flamboyant and memorable. I felt like a total ninny for even considering it. Right up until the point where Ms. Thomas gave me my cue and Mr. Pall looked up from astrogation.

The whole ship paused, waiting for me to say something.

"Ready about, Mr. Pall. Hard a-lee."

He punched it and we were somewhere else.

Ms. Thomas queried the scanners and Mr. Schubert kept us steady ahead until we could find a course. I had nothing to do, but Mr. Pall's hands almost blurred as he cranked through the process of finding where we were, exactly.

Ms. Thomas reported first. "No proximity warnings, Captain."

"Good to know, Ms. Thomas. Thank you."

She straightened from the terminal and looked out the armor glass to space around us.

Ahead was a pin head's dot of light in the field of dark. It seemed slightly larger than the other points of light and carried a faint yellowish hue, even to the naked eye. It looked like Welliver to me, but Mr. Pall had not reported. I wasn't worried.

Yet.

He spared a glance in my direction. "Sorry, Skipper. I'm used to landing about two weeks further out."

"Take your time, Mr. Pall, but remember Mr. Wyatt is holding lunch."

He snorted a laugh and punched the enter key. "Sorry, Skipper. I over shot by two percent. We're in Welliver. Location updates completed. Course plot solution working, estimated new course in less than a tick."

"Thank you, Mr. Pall. Try to do better next time." I was smiling. A two percent jump error was as close to nothing as didn't matter.

"Course plots completed, Ms. Thomas."

"Thank you, Mr. Pall. Helm, come to new target heading, port forty-two and yaw us down three points if you please Mr. Schubert."

"Aye, sar, port forty-two and down three." The helm display showed the corrected course as the astrogation system updated both helm and autopilot.

"Make all appropriate sail, Ms. Thomas. I hear they have good beer here. I'd like to find out as soon as possible."

She punched up the sails, but frowned at me sideways as she did it. "You've never been to Welliver, Skipper?"

"Not this month, Ms. Thomas."

Ms. Thomas giggled. She actually giggled.

That alone was almost worth the trip.

It took next to no time at all for the final course and position updates to cascade through the systems. When we secured from navigation stations, we relieved the watch as well.

We were at the familiar place in the watch cycle where I ate breakfast on the bridge, got to eat lunch with the crew, but I'd be back on the bridge for dinner. I stopped in the cabin on the way through officer country. I wanted to let the crew get ahead of me so I felt less like I was leading a parade and I usually stopped after watch for biological reasons.

When I walked onto the mess deck, the off-watch crew were all standing around and the aromas of cooked food drew a wash of anticipation to my mouth. The ship did a good job of isolating the smells from the galley. I chalked it up to the over-engineered scrubbers. Mr. Wyatt had done himself proud with a roast of beefalo, white and sweet potatoes, a collection of green vegetables as well as a rich-looking tomato soup first course, and three pies for dessert.

I made a show of counting noses before calling loudly. "Mr. Wyatt, where are the other twelve people you intend to serve with this feast?"

"Sorry, Captain. We're all the help you'll get, but I'm sure we'll all do our best on this particular evolution."

There were general cheers all around, I took the ceremonial first plate, and lunch mess began. Over the days we'd been underway, I'd been gratified to see that my assumption of seating had been correct. Over the stanyers I'd noticed that people picked the places they felt they should be in and they stayed there. The arrangement of officers was only slightly skewed from what it might have been at a wardroom table, but with no Captain's chair at the head, it made sense for senior department heads to sit where we could talk face to face. Mr. Pall took the seat to my right when we dined together, and the ratings each seemed to have picked places and kept them, even to the point of leaving open space when a member was on watch.

Over dessert we slowed our mass ingestion and began to be more social. With most of the crew present, and with some awareness that we'd soon dock in Welliver, it seemed a propitious time to raise an issue that we'd not yet discussed. "Mr. Schubert? We need to talk about the ship's co-op."

None of the officers, except Mr. Wyatt, had been there when I'd made the arrangement with Mr. Schubert so they looked on with interest to see what rabbit I was about to pull out of my cap.

"When would you like to do that, Captain?" Schubert asked.

I looked at the assembled company. "Given that it involves at least some of the crew, Mr. Schubert, I'd suggest now to be a good time. Are you familiar with the long held and respected tradition of private trading, Mr. Schubert?"

I was surprised to see him shoot a glance at Mr. Hill across the table before he answered. "Yes, Captain. I am."

The officers looked on with obvious interest but made no comment. Mr. Hill kept his fork moving, but I wasn't sure he was actually moving food with it.

"And do you engage in this practice, Mr. Schubert?"

"I've been known to dabble a bit, Captain, yes."

"Mr. Hill?"

He jumped as if I'd stuck a fork in him. "Captain?"

"Private trade, Mr. Hill? Ever done any?"

He smiled and nodded. "Skipper, I think every rating in the fleet has at one point or another."

"Good, then we have some current perspectives. Would it surprise any one to learn that I used to dabble a bit, as Mr. Schubert calls it?"

Ms. Thomas looked fascinated and Chief Gerheart was in danger of losing her mask as she gazed at me with an intensity I wasn't used to seeing. Mr. Wyatt enjoyed his second piece of pie and the floor show.

Schubert and Hill exchanged those odd glances again. It was Mr. Hill who spoke. "When you were on the *Lois McKendrick*, Captain?"

"Yes, Mr. Hill. I did pretty well at it, but that was a long time ago and a long way away."

This time the look they passed was more smug than concerned.

"Really, Captain?" Mr. Schubert seemed almost amused.

"Quite well, Mr. Schubert. The profits paid for my first two stanyers at the Academy."

The mess deck went still.

It was Mr. Wyatt who asked. "Captain? You made enough from private trade to pay for ... what?"

I smiled into my mug. "My first two stanyers at Port Newmar. Books, board, tuition, fees, and uniforms."

I was sure the officers knew approximately how much money I was talking about but Hill and Schubert were probably only aware that it was a great deal of money. On a grand scale, it wasn't really, but enough to give them pause.

Ms. Thomas looked like she wasn't sure if I was telling a tale or not. Chief Gerheart was holding back a laugh that I suspected she could only safely let out in Engineering, and Mr. Wyatt was practically slack-jawed. Oddly, the two on the end of the table were staring into each other's eyes so intently I thought they may be working on some telepathic experiment.

"I didn't do it alone, Mr. Schubert." At the mention of his name, the eye lock broke and they both turned to look up the table at me. "The *Lois* had a co-op, a co-operative selling arrangement, where all the ratings on the ship could put their private trade goods on consignment and the co-op brokered the goods and distributed the profits."

Mr. Hill was following this very intently. "Where did they do this brokerage, Captain? And how?"

"They rented a table at the orbital's flea market, Mr. Hill. All the crew's trade goods would be available to the public who usually paid top credit for some of the more exotic goods. The co-op arranged for somebody to tend the table for as long as the market was open, and in exchange took a small share of the sales to fund their operation."

Ms. Thomas finally found a question that she needed answered. "Why did you form a co-op?"

"More profitable. Many of the crew engaged in trading but the difficulties in finding buyers on short notice often meant that the goods went for only a fraction of their real worth, because buyers knew the crew had time limits. Being beaten up and robbed was also far from a theoretical happenstance." I felt Mr. Hill stiffen, but didn't look at him.

Ms. Thomas pressed for more details. "So you–and I'd bet my next sandwich that it was you, Skipper–organized the crew to form this co-op and convinced the ship to go along?"

"No bet, Ms. Thomas, but I had help. My friend was mugged and lost his trade. I just found a different way to do it where crew didn't run the risk of being mugged and together we convinced enough people to go along with us that it just took off. Once people saw how well we did, we had plenty of participants."

Mr. Wyatt recovered by then. "Skipper, you did not make enough money doing private trades to pay for two stanyers at the Academy. You must have had something else."

I grinned and shrugged. "Okay, yes. That's true." There was a general air of relief around the table, as if they really didn't believe I'd done it, and were just waiting for the truth to come out. "The private trading gave my buddy and I enough capital to begin buying and selling cargoes. That was really where most of the money came from."

Mr. Wyatt got the point immediately. It was his field after all. "Buying and selling cargoes, Captain? As in... containers of goods?"

I smiled a little. It was rather insane when viewed in hindsight, but it seemed logical at the time. "Yes, exactly, Mr. Wyatt. The *Lois* was a Manchester-built freighter that carried the twelve meter canisters."

Mr. Schubert had lost the thread by then and struggled to regain it. "How much cargo can you put in only twelve meters, Captain?"

Mr. Wyatt turned to him with the answer. "Six hundred metric tons, Mr. Schubert."

Mr. Schubert frowned. "That's a lot of cargo, sar."

"We had to buy low value cargoes at first. It takes a lot of money to fill a twelve-meter container."

The group took a collective breath and then resumed eating. Chief Gerheart kept giving me furtive little glances from under her eyebrows and Ms. Thomas muttered, "No wonder they sent you to the Academy."

Mr. Hill laughed and almost choked on his pie trying to hold it back.

"So, Mr. Schubert, I'd like you to take charge of starting the ship's co-op. Organize it, see how it might work. We don't have the crew that the *Lois* had, but there must be a way we can do it."

Schubert and Hill exchanged glances once more before Mr. Schubert turned back to me. "Aye, aye, sar."

"Do you have any trade goods aboard with which you might prime the pump to get started in Welliver, Mr. Schubert?"

He gave a little sideways shrug. "I may have a few odds and ends, Skipper."

"Mr. Hill? Are you in?"

I looked up the table at him. I couldn't tell if he was enthusiastic or just acting that way. "Sounds intriguing, Captain. Count me in."

"Okay, then, I'll leave it in your hands, gentlemen. Please ask if you have any questions."

The two ratings answered as one. "Aye, aye, Captain."

Lunch ended pretty quickly after that. Just as well, really. It was getting on to 1300 and after that feast, I needed a nap. We all chipped in to help clear away the additional mess caused by the extra food. With all of us helping, the galley was shipshape again in no time. As I drifted off to sleep, I kept remembering those glances and wondering what the boys were up to.

CHAPTER THIRTY-ONE
WELLIVER SYSTEM: 2372-FEBRUARY-16

We were still almost a couple of weeks out of Welliver when I found out why my two young gentlemen were so skittish around the subject of private trading. I'd finally caught up on the paperwork at the trailing end of an otherwise unremarkable midwatch. Welliver grew ahead of us and I knew I'd need to start picking cans soon.

On a whim, I pulled up the available cargo list for Welliver. It was blank. "Mr. Hill? Have you any idea why the cargo availability list for Welliver is blank?"

Bless his heart, he'd grown used to long stans of silence punctuated by odd questions from me. He looked over from the helm and shrugged. "It's always blank until Mr. Wyatt gets the updates from the inner beacons, Skipper."

"That'll be only a day or so before we dock." Yes, I was stating the obvious.

He shrugged again. "Not much we can do until then anyway, is there, Captain?"

My disbelief must have shown on my face.

"Captain?"

"Mr. Hill, you do realize that we don't need to actually be docked to buy and sell, correct?"

"Of course, Captain, but I don't get it. We don't get up-to-date market data until we're a lot closer in."

I sat there for a moment as the implication of what he had said washed through my incredulous mind. I couldn't even respond for a full tick. "Mr. Hill, after we get the breakfast mess secured, you and I and Mr. Wyatt need to have a serious talk about making money."

"We're missing something, aren't we, sar."

"I'd guess about ten to twenty percent on profit."

He goggled.

I debated running the update myself, but the chronometer clicked past 0515 and a stan or two wouldn't matter. Running Mr. Wyatt through the whole process from the beginning would expedite understanding.

"After breakfast, Mr. Hill. We'll talk."

"Aye, aye, Skipper." He smiled and settled back to his watch.

Thinking of cargo reminded me of Schubert and the co-op. The gang of three hadn't come up with a name. They were still debating on what the appropriate percentages should be. Mr. Schubert's wit and good humor stood him in good stead as he chivvied the other two into position. I'd overheard them discussing it on more than one occasion and realized that the lack of personnel would make things more difficult than I first expected. Still, if they could cover even half a day on the tables, I was certain they'd do better than whatever they'd been able to scrape together on their own.

My train of thought pulled into pooka station and I pulled up Agamemnon's record on my screen. I'd almost forgotten about the extra mass but with the possibilities looming in the near future, I wanted to find out if the stuff was still aboard or if it were just accounting error.

The main record was as I remembered, but when I clicked on the transaction details, I began to get an idea of why my two young colleagues were so uneasy about the idea of the captain becoming interested in their private trades. The most recent date corresponded to our next to last day in Diurnia. Mr. Schubert had logged a dozen kilos out of Agamemnon's account. Scrolling back through the transaction details I saw postings in and out of the account by all three of my brow watch standers.

"Did they get it all, Mr. Hill?"

"Captain?"

"The trade goods. Did they get it all when they rolled you in Diurnia?"

He stiffened slightly, caught himself doing it, and tried to relax. "I'm not sure I understand what you mean, Captain."

I snorted. "Good man. Don't admit to anything until you know what you're accused of." I had to smile and give him credit for that. "I'm looking at Agamemnon's mass allotment transactions, Mr. Hill."

"Yes, Captain?"

"It shows that Mr. Schubert signed a dozen kilos of mass out at a time which might reasonably coincide with your leaving the ship. There is no corresponding record showing that mass–or any other–returning before we got underway. What I do recall is a rather worse-for-wear crewman being returned to me sometime the next morning, Mr. Hill."

He sighed but kept his attention on his helm. "Yes, Captain. They got it all."

"Is all this stuff yours, Mr. Hill?"

He shook his head without looking at me. "No, Skipper. All three of us have some of it. I may have the most, but we don't really keep track."

"Where do you store it, Mr. Hill?"

"Here and there, Captain. Bottoms of lockers. Under the mattresses."

"Anything dangerous to the ship?"

"Empty data cubes, some electronics parts, the odd bit of this and that. Nothing really too far out there."

"Entertainment cubes? Consumables?"

"Entertainment, yes, Captain. Drugs or stuff like that? No. Chooch–Mr. Schubert–brought a few bottles of wine once and they broke in the bottom of his locker. We've tried to keep with durables since then."

"Alcoholic beverages are tricky to do well. You have to know what you're doing, Mr. Hill."

He glanced at me out of the corner of his eye, but I was staring at the transaction record on the screen. The lads had been very industrious, if the number of transactions were any indication. After a few ticks I sat back and looked at the side of his head. "How's this worked out for you, Mr. Hill?"

"Not great, Skipper." Defeat hung heavy in his voice. "You nailed it during mess the other day. High risk, low yield."

I made a tsking sound in my teeth. "Been there, Mr. Hill." I had a half baked idea that wasn't quite ready to come out of the oven. "Let me ponder this a bit, Mr. Hill. Thank you for being forthcoming. Would you pass to your trading partners that the jig is up and that there'll be a ruling soon?"

He slumped. "Of course, Skipper."

"Thank you, Mr. Hill."

The chronometer ticked toward the end of the watch and I turned to making sure my logs were up-to-date while I pondered. I couldn't just let them add to the ship's mass without some kind of oversight. On the other hand, the amount of mass they had accrued was lost in measurement error on the scale of things we worked in. I was also a little leery about letting them deal in just anything. Having the co-op deal at the table would obviate some of that. Limiting trade goods to those things which would be sold by the light of day and not in some out-of-the-way corner of the orbital would relieve most of my worries. Still, there was a better solution lurking in my hind brain. I just needed to pretend I wasn't looking for it so it would come out.

Luckily, Ms. Thomas and Mr. Schubert came onto the bridge then and I was completely distracted from the issue by the watch change. While Ms. Thomas relieved me, Hill and Schubert had their heads together at the helm. I saw Schubert flinch once and stop himself from looking at me. He leaned in to say something and Mr. Hill shrugged.

Formality served, I headed to the cabin for a quick splash of the face and then on to breakfast. Mr. Wyatt was turning into an extraordinarily good omelet maker and I felt the need for one of his sausage and mushroom masterpieces.

As we cleaned up from breakfast mess I broached the subject with Mr. Wyatt. "I tried to access the available cargo listing this morning, Mr. Wyatt. It's blank and Mr. Hill informed me that you don't pick up the outer marker data. Is there a reason for that?"

"It's out of date, Captain. It just never seemed like it was worthwhile before."

"Why is that, Mr. Wyatt?"

"In part because of the time involved, Captain. We rely on cargo dispatch for our cargo and it's five weeks." He stopped wiping down the work table and his head snapped around as comprehension dawned.

"Used to rely on cargo dispatch and it used to be five weeks, Mr. Wyatt."

"Still, we're almost two weeks out now, Captain. There's something I'm missing, isn't there."

"Yes, Mr. Wyatt, there is." I grinned and he caught my excitement. "If you'd ask Mr. Pall to run the updates with the best data he can find, I'll show you what it is."

He pulled out his tablet and ran a few commands. "Three ticks, Captain. He's running up to systems now."

I drew a mug from the urn and snagged the keyboard from its dock before settling on a bench where I could see the repeater screen and have room to work. I brought up the cargo lists and waited. As good as his word, in just a few ticks the list refreshed and a long list of cargo availabilities scrolled down the screen.

Mr. Wyatt walked over to the screen so he could point to it to demonstrate his issues. "The dates on these postings are quite old, Captain. Many of them days old."

"Yes, Mr. Wyatt, but how long do cargoes stay on the list when we're in port?"

He looked startled. "Oh. Well, yes. Several days if they're not bid out."

I highlighted a field on the top of the screen. "That's the number you want to watch, Mr. Wyatt."

Mr. Hill brought his coffee and settled on the bench beside me so he could watch as well.

"Time of last update, Skipper?"

"That's the date and time that this list was captured and spun out to the beacons."

He looked at it, but objected. "It's still a day out of date."

I flicked a few keys and the date display changed. Mr. Wyatt's eyes almost bugged out of his head and he glanced at the chrono on the bulkhead. "What happened, Captain?"

"I accounted for the difference between Welliver standard and ship local time."

"It's only three stans delayed?"

"It varies, but it's seldom more than five."

Mr. Hill was taking it all in and looked at me for permission to speak.

"Please jump in, Mr. Hill. You're part of our little troika."

"How does this help us, Skipper? Sometimes you lose a cargo because you're a tick late. These numbers are three stans."

"True but they give you a feel for how the market flows. Some ports, you can't keep up with the flow. Some ports, priority cargoes wait for contracts for days. Getting a feel for how it flows is part of it. But even out here, if you see a good cargo, grab for it. Maybe you'll miss, but maybe you'll hit. By starting early, it takes the time you have available to search from a day or two to a week or two. You only need to be successful once on a really fat cargo and there's no penalty for missing one because of the time delay."

We stared at the list. I hit a few keys to winnow out all but the fifteen metric kiloton cans. The remaining list was shorter, but still impressive. I sorted by priority and a three can string went to the head of the list.

Mr. Hill spotted the value on it first. "Mr. Wyatt, does that number mean what I think it does?"

"If you're looking at the delivery bonus, yes, Mr. Hill. It does."

I had to admit. It was impressive. The bonus alone on that set of cans was more than we'd likely clear on the three we had. Several other cargoes were on the list, but none had that value on them.

"Why is it so high, sars?"

"Look at the destination and cut off date, Mr. Hill."

The string was going to Jett and they were asking for delivery in seven weeks. I sighed. "We'd have to be almost docked and ready to pull out immediately to bid on that one, Mr. Hill."

He nodded slowly, lost in thought. "I see that, Captain."

Mr. Wyatt pointed out the other limitation. "We'd also have to jump twice, Skipper."

"Yes, we would, Mr. Wyatt."

The chrono ticked over to 1000 and I realized that I had better hit the rack for a snooze. Mr. Hill and I had been up all night on the midwatch and we'd be back on the bridge at noon.

"Watch in two stans, Mr. Hill."

He roused himself from his reverie. "Yes, Captain. Thanks for the reminder."

We bussed the empties and headed out of the mess deck, he for crew berthing and I to the cabin. As I stretched out on my bunk, that string of cans weighed on me. We weren't close enough in to bid on it, but what if we were? Would I need to end the bet so the ship could profit? Was that wise? In the short term, perhaps, but things were beginning to shape up nicely and how would my lack of faith in them be perceived? Or would it even matter? And what about Jen. I told her I'd be home in mid-April. This would push my arrival home until May or June. The thoughts were not easy ones and they chased themselves around in my head–even while I slept, apparently. When I awoke, I felt more tired than when I'd laid down. Fortunately, the set of cans in question was beyond our capacity to deliver. We wouldn't make it to Welliver in time to take them to Jett.

Chapter Thirty-two
Welliver System: 2372-February-17

The watch cycle included two extended periods of downtime–one twelve stans long and the other twenty-four. The twelve fell across the 1800 to 0600 time slot, giving the watch stander one good ship's night every third day. It worked out pretty well. Get off watch, have a relaxing dinner on the mess deck, and even have a little time for relaxation before hitting the rack for a solid eight or nine stans of sleep. Of course, then the cycle began again, but that's life no matter where you are.

My body woke me at 0515 for rather pressing bladder capacity issues and once vertical just continued on to the shower, a clean shipsuit, and down to the galley for a fresh cuppa. I found Mr. Wyatt doing a very creditable imitation of a steward, complete with fresh quiches in the oven and a second urn of coffee just coming off the brew cycle.

I had to give the man a lot of credit. Once he had the scope of a problem and clear understanding of his operational authority, he was an amazingly resourceful individual. He was particularly adept at logistical issues like meals. Somewhere around the end of the first week underway, he'd come to me with some revisions for the menu. My stipulation of frequency was actually a bit problematic, particularly around breakfasts. When I thought of my own preferences, I had to agree. Having omelets every morning was certainly not advisable, but being able to offer them more than once every two weeks certainly was. I accepted his changes and had been very pleased with the results. Even Ms. Thomas seemed less pinched about the eyes. Not only was she getting larger portions at meals, but the ready cooler held a bottomless supply of individually wrapped meat and cheese sandwiches. He'd even added some redi-heat canisters of soup she could grab on the way to the bridge.

I drew off my first mug of the morning and leaned back against the counter for a few heartbeats while Mr. Wyatt checked the status of his quiche. I looked up at the cargo list on the big screen and those three canisters still occupied the top slot. The list had refreshed recently, judging from the status display. I kept thinking about the bet and what those three cans would do for us if we could take them. I couldn't very well suspend our arrangement without jeopardizing what I was working so hard to accomplish. On the other hand, the profit was sorely tempting.

Of course, I also felt guilty about not getting home to Jen for another six weeks, if we took them. Standing there on the mess deck in the cold Deep Dark I felt more than a bit guilty about the reality of the life we weren't really sharing.

"Frustrating, isn't it, Skipper?" Mr. Wyatt was resting his forearms on the top of the work island and looking up at the screen with me.

"See anything else come by that was worth grabbing, Avery?"

"No, Captain. There have been a lot of mid to low value cargoes but they all look pretty puny next to that one. I wonder why nobody has snagged it yet."

I shrugged. "Hard to say. Maybe no tractors in port, or maybe nobody wants to take the double to get it there in time."

A timer dinged and he bustled about pulling hot egg pies from the oven to cool a bit before serving. Mr. Hill joined me at the coffee urn with a smile and a nod. He glanced up at the screen but offered no comment. We climbed the ladders to the bridge and settled into our watch.

I kept thinking about those cans off and on through the morning watch. Mr. Wyatt's quiche was delivered up and consumed, each of us lost in our own thoughts. I scanned the overnight logs and checked the ship's status. Being captain and OD gave me a bit of advantage in terms of having many of the same responsibilities. In a lot of ways, OD was a kind of surrogate captain so I found that the extra workload wasn't all that egregious, other than not being able to walk about the ship as often as I'd seen other captains do. No matter what else I did, my mind kept coming back to that string of three cans and the amount of profit it could bring the ship, and what the costs might be if I did what I'd need to do in order to take them.

"Have you reached any decision, Captain?"

It was unlike Mr. Hill to initiate a conversation on the bridge. He was an excellent helmsman and we'd developed into a good team over our brief time together. He'd been Captain Delman's helmsman so perhaps that colored our relationship and may have made him more reticent to break into my silences. He did startle me with the question, however. "Decision about what, Mr. Hill?"

"The irregularities in Agamemnon's mass allotment, sar."

"Ah, of course. Sorry, Mr. Hill. I've been a bit distracted by other issues." Even as I spoke, I realized that the solution to one problem had come to me while I was focused on the other.

"I understand, Captain." He sounded disappointed.

"Ten percent, Mr. Hill."

"Captain?" He turned to look at me.

"I want ten percent of the profits rolled back into Agamemnon's credit balance. There'll be some other restrictions as well, I think, but we can start there."

His face took on a frown of concentration. "You want us to do what, Captain?"

"Sorry, Mr. Hill. You came in on the middle of a conversation I was having with myself."

He seemed a bit confused and I didn't really blame him. It's hard to follow conversations that veer so unpredictably from course.

"Here's what I want, Mr. Hill. You gentleman can continue using Agamemnon's quota up to but not to exceed the amount you currently have tied up. I estimate that to be about five full shares worth—something on the order of two hundred kilograms."

He nodded. "About that, Captain."

"In return, all profits from the use of that mass will be accounted for and ten percent of the profits will be donated to Agamemnon's credit balance."

"Ten percent, Captain?"

"It's the traditional captain's share, Mr. Hill. It seems appropriate. You're using ship's resources and the ship should profit from it."

"Is that before or after co-op charges, Captain?"

I considered that one. One of the bits of advice I'd given the group organizing the co-op was that they should invest in themselves first by rolling some amount of the profits back into the organization so that they'd have funding to take care of all the odds and ends of expenses they'd incur through the course of doing business. "After, Mr. Hill."

"That's very generous, Captain."

I shook my head. "I think it's fair. All Agamemnon is providing is some storage and the transport. Incrementally, it's nothing she's not going to do already, so there's no additional expense involved, and in return we serve a greater good by creating a revenue stream for the good of the ship that doesn't depend on voluntary contributions of a very small crew."

He thought about that for a time.

"One other thing, Mr. Hill."

He braced for the bad news.

"I need to be able to inspect the goods on demand."

"You want us to approve them with you, Captain?" I heard the concern in his voice.

"No, Mr. Hill. I have too much to do to approve or disapprove of these transactions individually and you gentlemen need some operating room to be able to take advantage of market conditions."

"Then what, Captain?"

"When it strikes my fancy, I want to be able to see all the goods you've booked in the ship's name. If push comes to shove and I get called to answer the question, 'Did you know this was aboard, Captain?' I do not want to have to say, 'No.' That would look very bad."

He looked a bit troubled by this. "I understand the need, Skipper, but right now, I think it would take a stan for us to find it all to show you. How do we do this?"

We frowned at each other in concentration. "I don't know, Mr. Hill, but I know who to ask. Let's table that point until we can put together a workable solution, shall we?"

He nodded an agreement. "That sounds reasonable to me, Captain." He continued to look at me, as if waiting for the conversation to continue.

"Mr. Hill?"

"Is there more, Captain?"

"More what, Mr. Hill?"

"More conditions, Captain? So far you want ten percent and the ability to inspect the goods."

I thought about it. "Yes, Mr. Hill. If I find goods that seem to be a danger to the ship in any way, I reserve the right to dispose of them immediately, without dispute or recourse. That includes dropping them out the lock."

"Well, of course, Captain. I sort of took that as a given."

I considered the topic a while longer. "I'm sure the details of the arrangement will evolve, Mr. Hill, but if you see anything I've missed?"

He took a deep breath before continuing. "I was thinking that perhaps the captain might want to exact some punishment, sar."

I made a big show of considering it. "I appreciate the offer, Mr. Hill, but I can't think of anything the captain might want to do in that regard."

He looked at me with an expression I couldn't really read. It looked a little like disbelief.

I relented and offered the explanation. "You found a hole and you used it, Mr. Hill. Shame on me–on the procedures really–for having the hole. I'm not going to lower the boom on you for exploiting it. There may or may not be some ethical issues involved, but they occurred on somebody else's watch and I won't try to second guess with the advantage of hindsight."

He looked relieved. "Thank you, Captain."

"No thanks needed, Mr. Hill, but you're welcome. Just don't violate my trust. It's all I ask. We're one ship, one crew. We need each other and trust is the glue that'll bind us–or break us."

He considered that. It stabbed me that he looked like he wanted to believe it, but wasn't sure he could.

The rest of the routine watch passed without additional incident or commentary. Mr. Pall relieved the watch on time and we went down to lunch on the mess deck.

Mr. Wyatt had prepared a very nice grilled chop for lunch with rice and two vegetables. He had every right to feel very pleased by the enthusiastic reception. We were still working through the frozen pie inventory but he offered a side of ice cream which was generally greeted with approval around the table. All through the meal, I had to fight to keep from looking over my shoulder at the cargo display, but I could tell from Mr. Wyatt's occasional glance that it was still there.

We cleared away the rubble and I took Mr. Wyatt aside and explained my requirement. He thought about it for only a moment.

"I think I know just the thing, Skipper." He led us out to the main lock. Fitted into one side of the lock was the embargo locker. That was where the ship sealed anything that might be aboard, but considered contraband in any given port. Fitted into the other side was another large, empty, double locker. He slipped the catch and swung it wide. "Guest locker, Captain. For visitors to the ship who need a place to park while they're aboard."

I considered the space. "Do we get many guests aboard, Mr. Wyatt?"

"Not that I've noticed, Captain."

I turned to Mr. Hill. "What do you think? If I add the condition that everything you book to Agamemnon has to fit in this locker? Is that acceptable, Mr. Hill?"

He was measuring the space with his eyes and he nodded slowly as he took it all in. "Absolutely, Skipper. And thank you."

I held out my hand. "Then we have a deal, Mr. Hill. If you'd notify your compatriots and have the goods transferred here over the next couple of days...?"

He looked at me and the hand as if confused for a moment, but he shook the offered extremity and nodded. "Yes, Captain. We have a deal. We'll get the stuff moved ASAP." He looked a little sheepish. "Frankly, I'll be glad to sleep on a flat bunk again."

Chapter Thirty-three
Welliver System: 2372-February-22

Mr. Pall picked data off the inner markers while we were still six days out of Welliver. The rest of the crew was, by then, in on the bet and with the new updates came renewed interest. I felt the pressure to pick a can so we'd know where we were going next. The obvious choices involved grabbing three and heading back home, but the manifests heading in that direction were nothing to write home about, let alone carry along with us. Everybody got into the act. I was as likely to find Ms. Thomas sitting at the table staring at the list as Mr. Hill.

It didn't help that those three high priority cans still sat on the dock. The delivery date had shifted as we worked our way slowly down the gravity well. It was still too close for us to make, but it was tantalizing to watch.

It was almost 2200 when Mr. Pall caught me on the deserted mess deck, leaning against the counter with a fresh cup of coffee and staring at the screen. "You're up late, Skipper." He nodded at the coffee mug. "You planning on pulling an all-nighter?"

I smiled. "No, Mr. Pall. I've never had any trouble sleeping, coffee or no. I just felt the need for something warm. I'll probably hit the rack soon."

He crossed the mess deck and nodded at the screen. "They keep changing the delivery date, Skipper." He joined me, drawing a cup and leaning on the counter beside me. The current date was April 3, 2372.

"I noticed that, Mr. Pall. How far do you think they'll go?"

I felt him shrug beside me. "Till they get a carrier or until the point is passed on the other end, I guess, Skipper."

I glanced at him out of the corner of my eye. "What's your best guess of run time from here to Jett, Mr. Pall?"

"Best guess, Skipper? Forty days, seven stans and the odd tick for maneuvering–pull out to clamp down." He paused to blow on his coffee. "Approximately. Captain."

"Pretty accurate guess, Mr. Pall."

He shrugged. "You know how long watches can get sometimes, Captain."

"I do, indeed, Mr. Pall." I looked at the screen some more. "Any variability in that estimate due to astronomical changes?"

He blew across the top of his mug again as he thought. "Not enough to matter. Call it 40 days in round numbers and we might slide a day off it, but not much more."

"And when would we have to leave to be able to take it?"

"We could meet the deadline if we left tomorrow, Skipper. Not being docked yet is probably going to be an obstacle."

"You have a penchant for understatement I had not expected, Mr. Pall."

"Thank you, Captain. I try."

"You're doing well, Mr. Pall."

"Thank you, Captain."

We stood there for a few more ticks.

"Would you do it, Skipper?"

"Void the bet, Mr. Pall?"

"Take the cargo, Skipper."

"At the moment, it's all hypothetical, Mr. Pall."

"We're the only tractor due in the next week, Skipper."

I turned my head to look at him.

He glanced up at me with a shrug. "Picked up the shipping status updates off the inner beacons, Skipper. Just happened to notice."

"Is that normal? DST has a lot of tractors and we're hardly the only ones operating here, Mr. Pall."

"Honestly, Skipper? I don't know. We've always been in a kind of cocoon here. Captain Delman never seemed to be too interested in what's going on around us." He shrugged. "I don't have any baseline. Shipping status shows five tractors outbound–four for Diurnia, one for Breakall."

"Wonder why one of them didn't take it." I said it aloud but I didn't really expect an answer.

"Three were already underway when it posted last week. And the other two had booked cargoes. We're just in the right place at the right time."

"But I'd have to void the bet and we'd have to take a double jump over to Jett."

Mr. Pall nodded.

We stood there for a few more heartbeats. I have no idea what Mr. Pall was thinking but my brain did in a great deal of wheel spinning with precious little traction. Getting home late to Jen was high on my list of Bad Ideas because it set a precedent that I didn't really want to set. Booking the cans over the top of my agreement with Mr. Hill was likewise a bad idea. I'd be with this crew, with any luck, a lot longer than the benefits of this one trade might yield. Balanced against that was my obligation to the company to maximize profits where possible. That's what they paid me for and why they gave skippers as much leeway as they did. The run out to Welliver was going to be the most profitable this ship had seen in a decade. Expenses were going to be reduced by at least ten percent, if not a lot more, because of the reduced run time. Revenues should be a lot better because we'd picked three really good cans off the dock on Diurnia. The balance sheet on this one was going to total out at a very nice number for the crew share value.

Any direction I went had a serious downside and short of flipping a coin, I couldn't see any rational way of choosing.

To make the whole matter worse, it was all hypothetical. At the moment, we couldn't commit to the cargo. We were still too far out and the deadline would pass before we could be expected to deliver the goods. The information that Mr. Pall had given me didn't really contribute to my peace of mind, nor did the lack of good alternatives for single cans. This cargo was the plum. I wondered if it would stay on the tree long enough for me to have to decide whether or not to pick it for real.

I sighed and headed for the cabin. I wasn't sure I could sleep, but I had to try. I shouldn't have worried. My tablet bipped me awake with barely enough time to grab a quick shower and fresh shipsuit before relieving Mr. Pall on the bridge.

Mr. Hill was there ahead of me and he handed me the cup of coffee that I would have gotten if there'd been time. "Thank you, Mr. Hill. I owe ya one."

He grinned, but offered no comment and we proceeded to relieve the watch.

It was around 0610 when Mr. Wyatt came up to the bridge with our breakfasts. Mr. Hill gave him a Look and Mr. Wyatt nodded once as he slid the tray onto the console.

Mr. Hill looked very nonchalant as he took fork to food and began to eat. "Has the date changed, Mr. Wyatt?"

"Yes, it has, Mr. Hill."

I chuckled. "Okay, gentlemen, just a moment." I crossed to the system console and brought up the current lists on that display so I could leave it running while maintaining my own screen. The date had changed. They'd added a week to the deadline and raised the priority. The new date was April 10th.

Behind me at the helm, I heard Mr. Hill laugh. "They're getting desperate."

I was running numbers in my head and the sums didn't add up. "It's close, but we still can't take it." I turned to look at them. "I talked to Mr. Pall last night. He says if we left today, we could do it, but we can't leave today. We're still five days out and we'll need at least three days to turn the ship around." To make this deadline we'd need to leave on the second day in port and that's not enough time to top off tanks."

The two of them looked deflated and I began to smell a rat.

"Why? You two gentlemen shouldn't be all that interested in this string of cans. We need three individual cans for the bet."

They looked at each other and Mr. Hill shrugged in my direction while looking at Mr. Wyatt as if to say, "You're the officer. You tell him."

Mr. Wyatt took a short breath and turned to me. "We've been chatting, Skipper. There is a way we can do this and keep the competition going, if you're willing to take the double jump."

I crossed to my seat at the watch station and sat down. Even I was smart enough to recognize a double-team when I saw it. "Go on, Mr. Wyatt. You've got my attention."

He smiled. "It's easy, Captain. According to the rules of the bet, we each have to pick one can."

"Go on, Mr. Wyatt."

"So? We each pick one can."

"Yes, but which cans, Mr. Wyatt? We've been watching for good cargoes all the way in. I'm going to have to lock a can in the next couple of days, but I don't see anything really good except that string."

They were both grinning at me then. Mr. Wyatt pointed to the screen. "No, Captain. You don't understand. We each pick one of those cans."

"But there's no competitive advantage to that, Mr. Wyatt! Why would you want to do that? Neither of you will get ahead that way."

Mr. Hill delivered my wake up call. "No, Skipper, but the ship will."

The solution was stupidly simple when presented that way. I still had some personal issues and the cargo was still hypothetical. We didn't have time to get in, unload, reload, and get out with enough time left. I had to admit the envelope of possibilities was certainly expanding.

"You'd be willing, the two of you?" I knew better than to ask that. They'd just set me up as neatly as any skipper was ever sandbagged by his crew.

They both shrugged and nodded. Mr. Wyatt added, "Why not?"

"Well, that's one problem solved, Mr. Wyatt." I looked between the two of them. "It's still hypothetical until that date gets to be April 11th or later, and I need to check with Chief Gerheart to find out if the ship is up to it before I can commit to it."

They both agreed and Mr. Wyatt removed himself from the bridge. Mr. Hill settled into his watch and I did the same. Breakfast was stone cold, but I didn't really taste it. The cargo list kept blinking on the console across the bridge while I ran the overnight logs and tried not to think of just how mad my wife would be when I got home a month late.

There was still the issue of whether the ship could handle the double. In my ponderations, I had overlooked one significant aspect. The *Agamemnon* had no kickers. Once we jumped between systems into the Deep Dark, we'd be down to maneuvering thrusters only. With no wind for the sails it would be like sailing into the doldrums with only oars to row with. I knew it was theoretically possible. The cargo waiting at the dock seemed to require it. Only the chief could tell me if we had the legs to get through a double jump. In theory, we only needed to be outside the burleson limit and oriented correctly in space. In practice, I knew we could spend a long, long time in the Deep Dark if we were sloppy.

I'd like to say the rest of the watch was routine, but it really wasn't. Routine is something that disappears. You do routine and three ticks later you wonder if you did it. Routine is not trying to clear overnight logs while watching a blinking red date on the screen across the bridge and wondering if it would flicker to something else while you were looking away. Self-discipline is a great thing. Mine got a workout for the rest of the watch, but it appeared to need more exercise because I couldn't stop watching. Finally I got up and shut the screen off.

Mr. Hill looked up when I moved and smiled when I shut it down. "Thank you, Captain."

"My pleasure, Mr. Hill."

After that, the watch was routine.

Mr. Pall relieved the watch promptly at 1145 and I took him aside while Mr. Hill headed for chow.

"Mr. Pall, I need two days."

He grinned. "Feel daring, do you, Skipper?"

"I'm feeling like I'm earning my princely wage on this trip, Mr. Pall. No lie." A thought suddenly occurred to me. "Have you ever actually jumped out into the Deep Dark and back?"

He grinned wider. "No, Captain, I never have. I've been on ships that did, but I've never tried to do it myself. In theory, it's no different, but ..." He shrugged and grinned even more broadly.

"What do you need to jump us back, Mr. Pall? If we get out there, can you plot us home?"

"I think you and I are the two most experienced astrogators on the ship, Skipper, and just between you, me and that stone deaf lamp post over there, Ms. Thomas ain't no slouch in her own right."

"Well, everything I know about it says jump out, do an alignment, and jump in. What's your understanding, Mr. Pall?"

"Skipper, if we know where we are and we know where we wanna be, folding space to get there only requires a heading and enough steerageway to move us through the fold."

"With no star, there's no wind. No wind, no sails, Mr. Pall."

"Long as we don't stop, Skipper. We should be able to scoot through on momentum."

"That word will bite us if we're not careful, Mr. Pall."

"Which one, Skipper? Stop?"

"No, Mr. Pall. Should."

He shrugged and kept grinning.

"Can you get me two days, Billy?"

"Lemme re-run some numbers this watch, Skipper. I'll tell you when you relieve me."

"That's good enough for me. Don't risk the ship, but five percent is plenty of cushion."

"Lemme see what I can do, Skipper."

"Thank you, Mr. Pall."

"Yo ho ho, Skipper."

I clattered down the ladder and headed for the cabin. I needed another few ticks to think about this. If Mr. Pall could shave two days, we had a chance of making that contract even with the current deadline. The sole remaining issue was whether or not it was viable from an engineering standpoint.

When I got to the mess deck, the crew had already gathered. They were in a festive mood and obviously the notion that we might be making the double was well received. The problem was that I really needed to talk to the chief about our jump capacity and I wanted to be subtle. I was pondering how exactly I would handle it. Perhaps after lunch mess, I'd follow her down to Engineering where we could talk.

I also wanted to talk to Ms. Thomas about her experience

jumping into the Deep Dark and back. I was focusing so much on my problem, and the lovely bit of braised chicken that Mr. Wyatt had done for luncheon, that I almost missed my cue.

Ms. Thomas leaned over to the chief. She lowered her voice to a level that was quiet for her although certainly loud enough to be heard in the passage outside, if not the bridge. "So, Chief? What about the drives, can they handle a double?"

The chief smiled up at her, the little girl voice on her lips. "Oh, pshaw, Ms. Thomas. Those bad boys are good for three or four big bends. Easy peasy." As she lowered her face to her plate again, she cast a brief look in my direction and I caught a distinct wink.

That wasn't so startling as it once might have been. I was getting used to her ways and it was exactly what I needed to know. I'd still chat her up about it later, but my unease over the ship's readiness was greatly reduced. At some point I'd have to sit down with folks and hash it all out in the open, but I really did like to have my water fowl all lined up before I started quacking.

There was something about Ms. Thomas, though. When she spoke, it reminded me of something. I tried to remember it, and couldn't. I had the feeling that it was something Mr. Pall had said, but that didn't seem right, either.

I sighed quietly to myself and finished off the last of the chicken on my plate. Mr. Wyatt had ice cream with syrup for afters. After that, I'd need a nap. It was shaping up to be a long evening.

By 1730 I was up, re-dressed, and even had time for a fast shower. I ran down to the mess deck and found Mr. Wyatt, as usual, bustling about and Mr. Hill waiting at the coffee urns. "What's for dinner, Mr. Wyatt?"

He smiled over to me but didn't stop moving. "Something called a 'beefy bean bake' on tap for tonight, Skipper. New recipe."

I took a good nose full. "Smells good, Mr. Wyatt."

"Have you talked to the chief, Skipper?"

"I have, Mr. Wyatt, and she assures me we don't have any technical issues." I turned to rest my rump on the counter edge beside Mr. Hill. The screen displayed the cargo list. Still. I noticed that a few more priority cans were showing up the closer we got. Nothing like that string of three at the top, but at least an alternative. "We still have a pesky timing issue, though."

He made a nonspecific noise of agreement and stuck his head into the oven to check on dinner.

I nodded to Mr. Hill. "Shall we head up to the penthouse, Mr. Hill?"

He grinned. "Yes, let's do, Captain."

We scampered up the ladders and found Mr. Ricks and Mr. Pall grinning at us as we popped up into the bridge.

"Let's relieve the watch and then you can show me, Mr. Pall."

"Aye, aye, Captain."

There was no sense to being coy around the crew at this point. It was an open secret with Mr. Ricks and Mr. Hill was no dummy. I had no doubt that most of the people assembling for breakfast would know what was happening before dinner mess was over.

"I'd calculated using the same five percent out and ten percent in we used for the jump here, but when I recalculate with the fiver on the inbound leg to Jett, we save three days, Captain." Mr. Pall brought up the calculator and I plunked into the seat to look it over.

It was a much more complicated plot with a jump to nowhere, a quick spin about the place, and then a jump to somewhere. Nowhere was a misnomer, of course. It was actually almost the midpoint between Welliver and Jett and about a burleson unit under Diurnia in the galactic down direction. Because there was no mass out there to speak of, safety margins weren't a meaningful construct because we were jumping in the flat of the weft of space-time. There simply was no gravity well to worry about.

"Any idea what's out there, Mr. Pall?"

"High Tortuga, Skipper."

"High Tortuga, Mr. Pall?"

"Oh, aye, Captain. It's where all the pirate captains meet to trade their booty and drink their rum between raids."

Mr. Ricks was still with us on the bridge and grinning broadly, and Mr. Hill snorted once in what could have been a very credibly muffled laugh.

"Thank you for that bit of space lore, Mr. Pall. I had no idea."

"Yo ho ho, Skipper." He turned to Mr. Ricks. "I'm feeling peckish, Mr. Ricks. Shall we dine?"

"Thank you, Mr. Pall. I think that sounds splendid."

They took their Chauncy and Edward routine down the ladder, presumably to the galley where they'd no doubt regale the crew with tales of great Ulysses.

"Mr. Hill? Has the crew gotten a bit–I'm not sure of the word? Space happy?"

"How do you mean, Skipper?" Mr. Hill was still focused on getting his watch in order and that reminded me that I needed to do the same. I brought up the logs before answering.

"Everybody seems a bit different from when I came aboard. Less tense."

"More twisted, Captain?"

"Well, that has such negative connotations, Mr. Hill, I hesitate to use that term exactly."

"Not in this context, Captain. Although I take your point."

"Your thoughts, Mr. Hill?"

"Well, Skipper, every ship I've ever been on, the crew's been a reflection of the captain."

"I was afraid you'd say that, Mr. Hill."

"You're welcome, Captain."

Just then Mr. Wyatt came up onto the bridge with our dinners. He sported an eye patch over his left eye, and had a very credible cutlass fashioned from aluminum foil thrust through a belt he'd strapped to the outside of his shipsuit. He delivered the trays without comment as was his habit and sailed back down into the ship.

Mr. Hill watched him come and go, and offered no additional comment until we were alone again. "Any time, Captain."

We managed to get the watch established and dinner eaten. Mr. Hill began to fidget in his seat before 1900.

"Problem, Mr. Hill?"

"Well, Skipper, unless I completely misunderstood, Mr. Pall just said we could deliver these cans on time."

"That he did, Mr. Pall."

"And we have no engineering issues, do we, sar?"

"It looks like a very viable route, if a bit nerve-wracking, Mr. Hill."

He turned to look at me. "Then why haven't you booked the cans yet, Skipper?"

"Call it a hunch, Mr. Hill."

"A hunch, sar?"

"Yes, Mr. Hill. A hunch."

He gave me the arched eyebrow, but subsided to his watch without additional comment.

I did have a hunch and we were still five days out. A lot could happen in five days, including having the cargo canceled, if it wasn't booked. As we ran the watch up to midnight, I kept thinking about the delay in getting home. In the end, I realized that I'd made up my mind some time back. This was a fat prize and it was my job to grab it. Given the chance, I would.

Toward the end of the watch I noticed Mr. Hill kept glancing in my direction.

"Something wrong, Mr. Hill?"

"No, Captain. Just..."

"Mr. Hill?"

"You're smiling, Captain."

"Is that unusual, Mr. Hill?"

"That smile, Skipper? Yes. It's a bit frightening, Captain."

"Thank you, Mr. Hill. I'll take that under advisement."

"You're welcome, Captain." He sounded amused as he settled back to his watch.

For three more days I waited. After the frenetic activity leading up to it, this waiting game seemed at once anticlimactic and agonizing. Each time I entered the mess deck, all heads turned to see if this were the moment. Even Chief Gerheart almost let her camouflage slip.

Mr. Hill and I had just come off morning watch on the twenty-fifth, and lunch mess was well underway, when all activity at the table, save my own, ceased. I glanced up to see them all staring at the screen.

In all honesty, I was a bit nervous about looking. One of two things had happened. I tried to be as nonchalant as I could as I turned to look. I was deliberate in my movements and returned to my plate and the succulent chop that waited me there. I took another small morsel and savored it almost as much as I savored–in a odd and twisted way–keeping my dining companions on edge.

I swallowed and, pretending not to see them all staring at me, took a languid sip of coffee. I dabbed my lips with napkin before speaking.

"If you'd book that at your earliest convenience, Mr. Wyatt?"

"Of course, Captain." He excused himself and headed for his cabin.

Nothing happened on the screen, but we were still running on data from the inner beacons and would need to wait a full stan for updates.

Ms. Thomas looked at me across the table. "Did you know it was going to go up, Captain?"

I shook my head. "No, Ms. Thomas. Just a hunch. We are the only tractor in the system that can take that load and have it de-livered in a reasonable amount of time. The shipper is undoubtedly aware of it. That last shift in date was a signal, I think. When we didn't jump on it, they were left with three courses of action–extend it again, pull the cargo, or raise the priority."

Mr. Schubert's eyes went round. "Pull the cargo, Skipper? You took a chance that we'd miss it altogether?"

I shrugged. "They had a lot riding on it and what are they going to do with it here if it needs to be in Jett?" I glanced up at the screen again. "It wasn't much of an increase, just enough of a wiggle to get us to bite on it. It worked."

Chief Gerheart raised her mug in toast and the rest of the crew followed. She didn't say anything out loud but her eyes congratu-lated me.

I made a little mock bow to the table at large and we settled down to a very credible granapple cobbler that Mr. Wyatt had prepared from scratch. It seemed we'd finally run out of frozen pies.

Chapter Thirty-five
Welliver Orbital: 2372-February-28

Rendezvous with the tug and docking was almost anticlimactic after the build up on the run in. We clamped on just before 1800 and I asked the crew to stay aboard until we got a solid handle on how long we'd stay. I knew they'd be disappointed so I'd asked Mr. Wyatt to do a little special arranging on the dinner menu while we were still a day out.

After docking, I went to the cabin and cleared the requisite paperwork to expedite unloading and reloading. That involved some relatively light lifting to clear local Customs, but since DST had a long standing relationship in Welliver, that amounted to dropping them a line to let them know we were in port.

Something after 1810, I joined them on the mess deck. I had to give them all a great deal of credit. There wasn't any where near the level of gray cloud I would have expected. Ms. Thomas, who had the duty anyway, held court on her corner of the table with great zeal while Mr. Wyatt looked like he was trying to think of what he should do next. We were so used to seeing him bustling about the galley that to see him at the table with a cup in front of him and nothing else going on was a bit odd. Even Mr. Ricks and Mr. Hill looked to be in good spirits.

When I stepped onto the mess deck, the general hubbub died down and all heads turned my way. "Thank you, all. I'll declare liberty as soon as we've had a chance to see where we stand in terms of resupply. This is going to be as short a stay as we can make it, because the deadline on the priority is already very close and I want to try to make sure everybody gets the same chance ashore. It's not going to work out that way, probably, but I'd like to be as fair as I can."

Ms. Thomas smiled at me. "What's for dinner, Skipper? Mr. Wyatt won't tell us."

Right on cue, I heard the visitor call buzzer from the main lock. "I think that's dinner now. I called ahead for take out."

When I arrived Mr. Schubert had just cracked open the lock. Outside two delivery people in white uniforms stood beside a grav pallet of goodies. I followed Mr. Schubert out and the shorter of the two turned to me. "Ishmael? You made captain since we met last!"

"Hello, Jimmy. I did indeed, and it's great to see you." We shook hands. I hadn't seen him in months, of course, but Jimmy Chin was one of the first people I met on Welliver. He ran three different restaurants on the orbital and the man knew food. "Thank you for doing this for us."

"No, thank *you*, Ishmael. You tip good and you like to eat. Two things any restaurateur appreciates." He grinned broadly. "Besides, this looks like a good racket! I may put this up as a regular service." He made a shooing motion with his hands, chasing us back into the ship. "Now, this dock is cold, the food is hot, and I bet you have hungry crew who want to celebrate! Go! Go!"

Mr. Schubert led the strange parade into the ship and Jimmy followed with his assistant sliding the grav pallet along behind. I followed them in and keyed the lock closed. Mr. Schubert had stopped at the duty station and Jimmy was looking around.

"First time on a ship, Jimmy?"

"Ah, no, but first time on a freighter! This is very..." Words failed him.

"Drab?" I supplied.

"No. Utilitarian. Something like that, Ishmael. Very useful."

I nodded at Mr. Schubert. "I think if you latch the lock for now, Mr. Schubert, we'll be able to hear if anybody rings the bell. Show Mr. Chin to the mess deck, if you would?"

The parade continued onto the mess deck and was greeted with curious looks. Jimmy knew his business though. His assistant slid the pallet up to the end of the table and popped the latch. Several bottles of wine and beer made appearance and everybody except the duty watch got a glass of beverage. I shrugged an apology to Ms. Thomas and Mr. Schubert. She toasted me with her mug. He just waved it off.

The food should have made up for any disparity in privilege as container after container appeared from the thermal carrier on the pallet. Piping hot, and redolent with spices and scents from far away, Jimmy Chen made the best Chinese food in the Western Annex as far as I was concerned. Purists can argue over whether this or that cuisine is authentic, but I judged by flavor and I always ate at Jimmy Chin's Chop Shop whenever I got to Welliver. In a matter of heartbeats Jimmy and his assistant had laid the table and part of the counter with tray after tray of goodness. With a flourish they stood back from setting up and the crew applauded.

Jimmy took a bow while his assistant closed up the now empty crate and pulled the grav pallet back toward the lock. I walked them back to the brow to let them off the ship.

"Thanks, Jimmy. I owe you one."

"Oh, yes, you do, Captain Wang!" He grinned and held out the tab.

I took it from him, added a sizable tip, thumbed it, and passed it back. "You know I mean more than the credits, you old reprobate. I appreciate this."

He shrugged and grinned. "You know we do take out on the station all the time, but this is a first even for Jimmy Chin." He watched the lock open up with some interest. "But I think this won't be the last."

"Well, I better get back in there before the chicken wings are gone." I shook his hand. "Thanks again, Jimmy."

He turned to wave from the dock and I slapped the latch to button up.

The food was a hit and the subsequent party was riotous. Luckily, we were surrounded by vacuum or the neighbors might have complained. It took us a couple of stans to chew through a large portion of Jimmy's fare and I could see Mr. Wyatt making mental notes as he contributed his share to the task of demolishing the mountain of food. Even Ms. Thomas sat back with a satisfied smile and a few morsels left on her plate when it was over.

As the feast ran down to the odd chuckle and desultory plate chasing, the conversation turned to the ship.

"Any word from the Orbital Cargo Master, Mr. Wyatt?"

"They'll be up in the morning to pull the cans, Skipper. They said around 0930 if that's convenient. The new shipment's being brought over from the marshalling yard and should be here by afternoon."

"How are we on tankage, Chief?"

She gave a little girl sideways nod. "We're down some, but not as much as normal, Captain. Flow meters say we should top out in another twenty-five stans or so. We should be ready to fly in two days."

"Mr. Pall? Is that enough time to get us to Jett before the deadline?"

"With a day to spare, Skipper."

I looked around the table. They all looked full and satisfied, eager even. "It's a short stay, but are you game to fly on?"

They took a moment to look around at each other, assessing themselves and their peers. It didn't take long before they all looked back at me, assent written on each face. I did a little math in my head, figured it was probably wrong, but made a decision anyway.

"Okay, then ladies and gentlemen, with that bit of planning and meager forethought, I'm going to declare liberty for the top of the stan." I glanced at the chronometer and realized it was already almost 2100. "If you'd make the announcement, Ms. Thomas?"

She grinned and leaned forward to look down the length of the table. "Liberty. 2100." Then she sat back with a grin. With the general level of mirth present, that set everybody off into a new gale of giggles.

Nobody appeared in any hurry to wander off. There was still wine and beer and the temporary permission to consume it. I had my limit so crossed to the urns to grab a fresh cup of coffee. I still had work of my own to do before the day was over. It felt good to stand and shake down the feast a bit so I took what was becoming a favored position and leaned my rump against the counter and looked over at the screen. It still showed the open cargo list and it was on live feed from the orbital. Our shipment was, of course, no longer in evidence, but the remaining cargoes were still updating.

I pondered the jump through the Deep Dark and remembered that I wanted to talk to Ms. Thomas about it. "So, Ms. Thomas? Have you ever pulled a double on a tractor before?"

The general level of conversation fell off, as it was wont to do when one of us raised a general question, and several heads turned to face Ms. Thomas.

She was still toying with a last spring roll and took a few heartbeats to notice that people were looking at her. She gave a little laugh and pawed down at the front of her shipsuit. "What? Did I spill?"

"No, Ms. Thomas, I asked if you'd ever done a double jump with a tractor before."

She continued to brush at her jumpsuit and looked around at the now nearly silent table. Her head came up and as she looked around she saw me standing behind her. "Oh, sorry, Skipper. You were talking to me. What was that again?" She turned around on the bench to face me.

"Have you ever jumped a tractor into the dark before, Ms. Thomas?"

"Oh, certainly, Captain. Dozens of times as third on the *Hector*."

"Any special techniques, Ms. Thomas?"

"Just ride the inertia, Skipper. The sails give us a lot of momentum and when we drop them to slip through the hole most of it goes with us. Unless we hit something pretty solid coming out the other side, fifty thousand metric tons moving even a bit carries a huge inertial load." She shrugged. "Just ride it till we get the fix. Use the thrusters to adjust the heading so we go through the next jump in good order and we're back in sunlight and ready to pop the sails up again."

Mr. Pall nodded from across the table. "Doesn't sound too tough, but that's a lot of vee to delta. How much thruster will we need?"

She turned her head to look at him. "How much thruster?"

He nodded. "Yes, that's gotta be a long burn to get that course shifted."

She shrugged. "It could take awhile if you're doing much in the way of line change, but a double is really just drawing a line from here to there, jumping to the middle, making sure we know where we are, and then continuing on. If it's more than a few points in any direction, that would be pretty surprising."

I could see the crew absorbing the information. I know it made me feel better to have it confirmed by somebody who'd done it. "Good to know, Ms. Thomas."

She turned to face me again. "Skipper?"

"Good to know, Ms. Thomas. Thanks."

She smiled and nodded. "My pleasure, Captain."

I focused on Mr. Wyatt next. "Any idea what's so all-fired important in those cans, Mr. Wyatt?"

He chuckled a little. "You're not going to believe this. The reason for the priority, and the reason it's so high, is that the shipper is under contract to a big glass works over on Jett. The contract is one of those that specifies quantity and delivery schedules and carries a very high penalty for failure to deliver to either quantity or schedule. If these cans don't make it, then the quarry operators here stand to lose a lot of money."

"Glass works? We're going to carry three cans of sand?"

He shook his head. "No, Skipper. Only one can is sand. One is a particularly fine clay they use for making rocket nozzle linings." He paused–waiting for the straight line.

Mr. Hill supplied it. "What's in the third can, Mr. Wyatt?"

His timing was impeccable. "Kitty litter."

The ambient mirth in the room ignited and burned for several ticks.

When the humor subsided a bit, I pressed him on it. "Seriously?

Kitty litter, Mr. Wyatt?"

He nodded, still smiling broadly. "Strictly speaking, Fuller's earth. A kind of crystallized clay that's a general absorbent. It's used a lot in industry. Apparently they have a good source here and it's part of the contract." He shrugged. "Quarry ran into some mechanical trouble and got behind on their production. This shipment should have left a month ago. Another few days and they're out of luck."

"If they're willing to pay this kind of premium, I'm betting they'd be out of business as well. Those penalty clauses can be nasty."

"Whatever the reason, Skipper, we stand to make a large pile of credits on this load of dirt. Long as they stay liquid long enough to pay the freight." Mr. Wyatt shrugged expressively. "I don't care if it's fifteen metric kilotons of *used* kitty litter. It'll be back there in the can and won't bother us one bit."

Mr. Ricks piped up. "I would not want to meet that cat."

Mr. Wyatt looked over his shoulder. "What cat?"

Mr. Ricks grinned. "The one that needs fifteen metric kilotons of litter."

The ambient mirth had reached critical levels once more and ignited anew. I left them there and, chuckling, took my coffee to the cabin. I still had ship's business to attend to, and then the difficult duty of telling my wife I'd be late to dinner.

By about six weeks.

I sighed and paused at the top of the ladder. I could hear Ms. Thomas clearly over the general hubbub, even from officer country and over the general thrumming of the ship. That woman had some pipes.

CHAPTER THIRTY-SIX
WELLIVER ORBITAL: 2372-MARCH-02

In the end we got caught in Welliver an extra day, not for tankage, but for food. Mr. Wyatt was almost beside himself over the delay. It was one of those can't-be-helped situations. We placed our replenishment order while we were still a few days out, and it was on schedule for delivery the morning of the first. Unfortunately, the carrier delivering to the ship got tangled up with a cargo handler and both units were slagged in the resulting fire. Luckily nobody was hurt and the losses were covered by insurance–except for the time we lost getting a new replenishment order filled and moved in from the warehouse.

The good news in the whole mix up was that the co-op got their first feel for flea market trading. I'd sent Mr. Schubert off in the morning of the twenty-ninth to secure a booth and they worked out a schedule for coverage that included the afternoons.

"Better deals in the afternoon," I muttered.

"Sar?" Mr. Pall looked up at me.

"Oh, nothing, Mr. Pall. Just something we used to say about going to the flea market."

He went back to his astrogation screens. "If we don't spend too much time in the Deep Dark, we'll be okay on this deadline, Skipper."

"Thank you, Mr. Pall. If you'd pass the word? I'll call the navigation detail at 1400."

"Aye, aye, Captain." He skinned up out of the seat and headed down to the galley. Most of the crew would be there. With the installation of the long table, the mess deck had become a kind of crew lounge. Mr. Wyatt's gentle humor and ready supply of samples encouraged people to hang out and "keep him company" while he puttered about.

I crossed the bridge to look out at the cans. The orbital's cargo people had been most expeditious in swapping out the loads. I sent a thank you note to their cargo master. His crews had done yeoman service in getting us set up to fly as soon as possible and I appreciated the extra effort. If they ribbed us about the cargo of 'platinum-plated kitty litter,' I was happy to laugh all the way to the bank.

I glanced up at the chrono. It was getting ready to click over to 1130 and I could hear Ms. Thomas holding forth on the mess deck.

I sighed.

I was on the bridge–granted, at the top of the ladder and there was a direct sound path down to the main deck–but she was two decks down, on the mess deck, and I could still hear her voice echoing clearly up through the ship. Other voices were indistinct mumbles but I could hear every word Ms. Thomas spoke. She reminded me of a colleague my mother had back at the University of Neris. He was a big, bluff professor of mathematics. He'd always claimed he developed his booming voice to reach the sleeping students in the back of the classroom. His colleagues accused him of learning to whisper in a steel foundry.

I snorted, thinking about my old life. I hardly ever thought about growing up any more–the dusty streets and languid heat of Neris, the small apartment I'd shared with my mother. I took another sip of cold coffee and tried to focus on the coming voyage, but my mind kept straying back to that math professor. *What the heck was his name?*

It was one of those irritating things that happens sometimes. I knew his name was in there somewhere, but I just couldn't dredge it up and I couldn't stop thinking about it. I remembered all kinds of things about him. Where he lived. His wife's name. There was even a joke going about that he made himself deaf from talking.

I closed my eyes and rested my forehead against the cold armor glass. Of course.

It was a matter of a few moments to scamper down to the mess deck. Everybody but Hill and the chief was gathered around the table engaged in making lunches. It looked like a good set up with Mr. Wyatt supervising.

"Mr. Wyatt, may I steal Ms. Thomas from your production line for a moment? I have a task that I need her to do for me before we get underway."

She'd glanced up as I entered the mess deck and looked startled when I singled her out.

Mr. Wyatt shrugged. "Of course, Captain."

I nodded Ms. Thomas out into the passage and she followed with a curious frown. "I need you to do something for me, Ms. Thomas." I kept my voice low and my head turned to the side. For good measure I rubbed the side of my face closest to her.

"I'm sorry, Captain. What was that?"

I turned to face her. "I need you to do something for me, Ms. Thomas."

"Of course, Skipper. How can I help?"

"Gwen, I want you to report to orbital medical right now. Go down and ask for a hearing examination."

"What?" Her voice–already quite loud–took on a note of alarm. It was loud enough that the general hubbub in the galley quieted.

I nodded in the direction of the lock. "This way, Ms. Thomas, if you please."

I led her out to the lock, and with a nod to Mr. Hill, cracked the lock and went out to the frigid docks beyond. It was loud enough and busy enough out there that we had a bit of privacy. I didn't want to embarrass her in front of the crew, but she needed help.

"What's this about, Captain?" By that point, she'd had enough time to process and was becoming angry.

I looked down at her. Our height differences never seemed to be that great until I stood next to her. "Gwen, I think you have a hearing loss. I want you to go get it checked out. That's all. If I'm wrong, then no harm, no foul, and I apologize for interfering, but if I'm right, then this is a matter regarding the safety of the crew, to say nothing of your health and well-being."

"But, Captain, I've been through this before. There's nothing wrong with my hearing!"

I smiled. "Prove it, Ms. Thomas. Bring me back the audiogram."

She started to screw up her face in that truculent frown I'd seen that first day aboard.

"Please, Gwen?"

"But we're getting underway this afternoon, Captain."

"I can spare you for the few ticks it'll take. Go now and you'll be back in time for mess." I pulled my face down closer to hers. "Please, Gwen. I need to know for the safety of the ship."

She looked like she might argue one last time, but she subsided. "Okay, Ishmael. You've been a square dealer so far. Take a bet?"

"What stakes?"

"Loser buys the winner a beer when we get to Jett."

"Agreed. Conditions?"

"I'll take the audiogram. If it's clean, you buy. If I have a loss, I'll buy."

"You have a bet, Ms. Thomas." I spit in my palm and held it out.

She spit in hers and took the grip. After a quick squeeze she headed off toward the lift and medical, and I headed back into the ship and out of the cold.

I went back to the mess deck and helped pack up the finished boxes to clear away for mess at noon. Mr. Wyatt had planned a hearty lunch and the smell from the ovens was delightful. I thought it was a spicy pork dish, but I'd stopped looking at the menus, trusting in Mr. Wyatt to surprise me with good food. With a couple notable exceptions, he'd lived up to that trust. I was more than willing to accept the exceptions as part of the price for training a first class chef.

The chronometer clicked over to 1200 and Mr. Wyatt opened the mess line. "Are we expecting Ms. Thomas back for lunch, Captain?"

"I was expecting her to be back by now, Mr. Wyatt, yes. I'm not sure what the delay is."

We didn't stand on much ceremony but continued through the serving. I did happen to notice that Mr. Wyatt set aside a plate with several choice cuts on it. We all got seated and I had several curious glances from the assembled crew and the odd look a the empty place across from me. Conversation lagged until Mr. Pall offered the first salvo.

"So, what do you think is really in the cans, Skipper?"

"My initial hunch is that it's probably kitty litter, sand, and clay, Mr. Pall. Why?"

"Sar, nobody pays that much to ship kitty litter." He looked like it was so obvious.

I turned to our cargo expert. "Mr. Wyatt? Your thoughts?"

He took a moment to finish the bite in his mouth before speaking. "Interesting question, Captain. I'll admit that I wondered myself."

"Any idea on the actual commercial value of the cargo, Mr. Wyatt?"

He shrugged. "Not really, Skipper. I don't really follow the futures market in kitty litter."

Mr. Hill surprised us. "Actually, sars, the valuable can in the three is the sand, then the clay, then the Fuller's Earth."

"Fascinating, Mr. Hill. Do you have an approximate value on the worth of the three cans?"

"It's hard to say, Captain, because it's part of a long term contractual agreement between Welliver Mining and Extraction here and Jett Ceramic Components. The details of that contract are not on public record. Going rates on the open market for the three components would place the value of the shipment at something like three times what they're paying in priority shipping."

Mr. Pall whistled appreciatively. "That's a lot of money for freight."

Mr. Ricks shrugged and tossed a few tidbits of his own onto the table. "Contracts are funny things, sar. These bigger players out here toss them around like confetti and everybody's trying to do in everybody else while they're trying to make it look like they're cooperating."

That struck a chord with me. "How so, Mr. Ricks."

"Well, take this WME and JCC contract, Skipper. Nobody knows for sure, but rumor is the two got into a kind of brinkmanship game over it. They couldn't really play too fast and loose in the primary conditions of cost and schedule, but they knifed each other pretty badly on the penalty clauses."

Mr. Pall's eyes glittered. "How badly, Mr. Ricks? Do you know?"

He shook his head. "Not in detail, but I'm guessing this priority they're paying is a drop in the bucket. Apparently JCC was late in payment sometime last stanyer. The late fees were reported to be record-breaking in the local press here."

"I knew it." Mr. Pall looked jubilant. "They're all pirates!"

Mr. Wyatt turned to Mr. Ricks. "That's a lot of information for a private contract, Mr. Ricks."

Mr. Ricks shrugged. "I think it's as much about claiming the win as getting the money. WME couldn't help crowing."

Mr. Wyatt smiled. "I wonder if the JCC did the same on the other side but with a slightly different twist."

Schubert grinned. "I can see the headline. 'JCC Victim of Corporate Greed'."

We shared a chuckle and I saw the chief stiffen and look over my shoulder.

"What's–" Ms. Thomas's voice came from behind me but stopped suddenly before resuming at a more normal volume. "What's all the funny?"

Conversation, laughter, all of it stopped and all heads turned to where Ms. Thomas stood in the entrance to the mess deck.

I smiled at her. "We're just laughing over corporate greed, Ms. Thomas. And wondering how we can take better advantage of it."

She crossed to the galley and started looking over the serving area.

Mr. Wyatt rose. "I saved you a plate, Gwen. I wasn't sure how long you'd be, and I wanted to protect some small portion from these scavengers." He grinned and looked at us all in mock fierceness.

She beamed at him. "Thank–" She stopped and thought for a moment before resuming in a more normal tone. "Thank you, Avery. That was thoughtful."

He used an oven mitt to pull the warm plate from the oven and slip it onto Ms. Thomas's place.

I turned to the chief. "Any problems with getting underway in a few stans, Chief?"

"Oh, no, Captain. We're topped off and ready to sail off into the night." She smiled her little girl smile.

Ms. Thomas tucked into her lunch with a will, and I turned to Mr. Hill. "If you'd take a moment to hang out the sign, Mr. Hill? We'll make the orbital happy by locking down now."

He scraped the last bit of dinner from his plate and stood. "Aye, aye, Captain. Securing ship for scheduled pull out at 1400." He took his empties and slotted them in the cleaner before heading back to his watch.

Mr. Wyatt eyed the clock and mumbled, "We'd probably better serve dessert if we're going to get done before 1300."

Ms. Thomas turned to him, leaning in to see around the chief who sat between them. "I'm the late one here, Avery. Don't wait on me. Please, serve dessert."

It was a little unnerving to hear her speak at a near normal tone and she seemed to sense it.

She sighed once and looked around the table. She seemed to be trying to make up her mind about something. She looked at me and that decided her. "I owe ya a beer, Skipper." Her voice was that rough burled alto that I associated with heavy worlders. Clear of the volume artifacts, it had a richness to it that was completely at odds with the sharp voice we'd all come to associate with her.

"I'll collect with pleasure when we get to Jett, Ms. Thomas."

She turned to the table at large and took a deep breath. "The captain sent me to medical. I had a hearing check." She turned her head little to show a small button of flesh colored material in her ear. "The test itself was very fast. It took a little longer for them to install my new ears."

Chief Gerheart was closest to her and leaned in to look. "That's cute!" She grinned happily. "And you can hear better?"

Ms. Thomas nodded. "Yes, Chief. I can hear better, and I shouldn't have to shout as much."

The Chief clapped her hands happily. "That's wonderful!" She offered a quick, seated hug. "I'm so pleased."

Ms. Thomas looked a little taken aback by the hug but as

everybody around the table offered congratulations and good wishes she soon relaxed and finished off her lunch while Mr. Wyatt doled out pie and ice cream.

CHAPTER THIRTY-SEVEN
WELLIVER SYSTEM: 2372-MARCH-20

We were only eighteen days out of Welliver when we went to navigation stations for our jump into the Deep Dark. The ship and crew functioned smoothly. Ms. Thomas was adjusting to her new levels of sensory input and she seemed younger. It was something about her eyes. She didn't seem as haunted. The Chief was relaxing a little as well. Her mask didn't exactly come off, but she appeared more at ease. The little girl was still there, but maybe she was growing up a bit. Mr. Wyatt had obtained some new spices and he treated us to some wonderful curries on the way out. Even the bad boys seemed happy. Their first try at doing a flea market booth had yielded good, if not great returns, and somebody had taken my advice on finding new trade goods there. The guest locker still contained a number of items that I thought might not sell well at the flea, but they'd also picked up some bolts of fabric and a few pieces of flat artwork from a local artist.

Mr. Pall, however, still insisted that something else must be in the containers. His speculations went from toxic waste to dead bodies to the inevitable pirate horde. I found him with an ear pressed up against the aft bulkhead as we were preparing the ship to jump.

"What are you doing, Mr. Pall?"

"Listening, Skipper."

"I see. And what are you listening to?"

"Nothing at the moment, Captain."

"We are surrounded by vacuum, you know, Mr. Pall."

"Yes, Skipper, but any vibrations in those cans would be transmitted to the hull."

I considered that for a moment. "Actually, I don't think they would, Mr. Pall."

He looked surprised. "Why not, Skipper?"

"The pads on the edges of the cans are built to damp out vibrations. It keeps the ship's vibrations from being transmitted into the cans and stirring any volatiles that might be in a cargo."

He looked crestfallen. "Then I wouldn't be able to hear if there was, like, a fusactor back there supplying power?"

I shrugged. "You might, Mr. Pall, but it would have to be back there, for starters, and it would have to be vibrating more than ours for you to pick it out of the hum."

"Excellent points, Captain. Thank you."

"You're welcome, Mr. Pall. Do you think we might get the course plots laid in for the jump?"

"All done, Skipper. I did it earlier, and then came down here to listen. Timing is everything."

"Timing, Mr. Pall?"

"Yes, sar, the pirates won't want to act too soon. They'll wait until we jump into the Deep Dark before they strike, and we'll just be another statistic on the lost ships roll." He looked positively gleeful at the prospect.

"Are there any precautions you think we should take, Mr. Pall?"

"Just keep an eye open for the murthering scum, Skipper."

"Murthering scum, Mr. Pall?"

"Yea, it means like cold blooded killers but meaner, Captain."

"I'm familiar with the term, Mr. Pall. I was just surprised you used it."

"I've been working on my vocabulary." He looked down shyly. "Never know when you might hear a word you don't understand and feel like a ninny-come-pooper, know what I mean, Skipper?"

"Yes, I can see where that might be embarrassing. Well done, Mr. Pall. Now? If we could secure the pirate patrol and adjourn to the bridge, I've a mind to see the Deep Dark this afternoon."

"Capital idea, Skipper." He raised a hand dramatically. "High Tortuga bound!" He scampered off up the ladders and I could hear his eager footfalls all the way up to the bridge.

It was a bit distressing. I kept remembering the comment that Mr. Hill had made on our way into Welliver about the crew being a reflection of the captain. The thought gave me a few moments' pause. I slipped into the galley for a fresh mug of coffee before following Mr. Pall to the bridge. The rest of the crew was waiting when I got there and I nodded to Ms. Thomas to call us officially to stations.

The swap over was seamless since Ms. Thomas and Mr. Schubert had the watch already. I took my seat as her now mellifluous tones echoed through the ship. Ms. Thomas appeared to enjoy the effect her heavy worlder's growly voice had on the male of the species and I suspected she practiced in her stateroom.

"Do we have enough way on the boat, Ms. Thomas?"

"I should think so, Skipper." She took a few moments to look at some data. "It looks good to me. When we furl the sails, we'll go ballistic at something over twenty kilometers per second. We really only need a meter per second to jump through the hole, Captain."

Mr. Pall added a macabre thought. "We'd have to hit something pretty big awfully hard to lose that much momentum, Captain. If we did, I suspect our vectors after that would be in the hands of a higher power."

"Well, now that you two have done such a good job of calming my fears, perhaps we might actually go somewhere else?"

"Did you have any place in mind, Skipper?" Ms. Thomas practically purred.

"What do you think, Mr. Pall?"

"High Tortuga, Skipper. We're plotted and locked."

Ms. Thomas consulted her console. "Ship reports ready to jump, Skipper." I glanced over and saw her board all in green.

"Ready about, Mr. Pall. Hard a-lee."

He mashed a key and we jumped.

When a ship jumps, usually the view through the forward screen changes. Typically, a bright pinpoint of light appears in what was near blackness before and the background spatter of lights shifts position, sometimes radically. When we jumped into the Deep Dark, there was no central star, just more of the same scatter-shot pin points as when we left. If I hadn't been watching, it would have been easy to miss.

"Did we go anywhere, Ms. Thomas?"

"We did indeed, Skipper. We are out of range of any beacons and somewhere in the limbo between the lanes."

"Do you know where we are, Mr. Pall?"

"High Tortuga, Skipper. I'll have a more precise answer shortly." His fingers flew and the screen in front of him exploded in data.

I tried to hide the uneasiness in my coffee cup.

Ms. Thomas broke into my pretended reverie. "I've got a contact on the long range, Skipper."

"Ship, Ms. Thomas?"

She was staring at a plot on her screen. "Looks more like a collection of ships, Captain."

Mr. Pall looked up from his screen, for all the world like some kind of ground squirrel sticking his head out of a hole. "High Tortuga." He went back down the hole.

Ms. Thomas leaned over to look around the end of her console in Mr. Pall's direction. She cast me a look and gave her head a little shake, before refocusing her attention on the plot. After a few ticks of fiddling, she grunted. "Hmmph. I really hate to say this, Captain, but it looks like someplace that might be called High Tortuga."

I got out of the chair and went to look over her shoulder. It looked like a collection of ships, cans, and assorted other metal arranged in a haphazard pattern. As we watched, one small blip split out from the mass and began accelerating away.

"Any idea what that is, Ms. Thomas?"

"Yes, Captain. I believe that's Odin's Outpost. It's grown a bit since I saw it last."

I leaned in to look at the display. At our range there wasn't a lot of resolution but it was enough to see what looked a lot like a freight marshaling yard when viewed from a hundred-thousand kilometers out. "What pray tell is an Odin's Outpost, Ms. Thomas?"

"It's kind of a way station, Skipper. It's not really much of anything. Officially, it's not there. It's been so long since I jumped out here, I'd practically forgotten it. We skimmed by it on some of the doubles we did back on the *Hector*. We got close enough to give it a good scan on short range, but I've never been close enough to get a direct look."

"Looks like a collection of cans and some small ships, Ms. Thomas."

"I think there's a ship at the heart of it, Captain. The story on the *Hector* was that this guy, Odin, jumped in and his burleson drives went out on him. He couldn't jump back. He flew around out here for awhile and the next ship through rendered assistance, so he was able to get out eventually. The story goes that when it was over, he took it into his head to come back out and set up this way station. Started as a shipload of food, fuel, and spare parts." She nodded at the screen. "It's more now."

"He just sits out here in the Deep Dark, Ms. Thomas?"

She shrugged. "It appears so, Skipper, but he's really near the crossroads between the Breakall-to-Dree run and the course from Welliver-to-Jett. Those four systems are almost on the same plane so if you've jumped clean, you'll go through this relatively small volume of space no matter which direction or which pair you're jumping to." She eyed me with a frown. "The *Tinker* never pulled a double jump through here?"

"No, Ms. Thomas. We almost always ended where we began. Diurnia to Jett and back. Diurnia to Welliver and back. Once in a great while we ran a triangle route, but that was rare."

"This is the first one we've pulled on the *Agamemnon* since I've been aboard," she said.

"Having the only bar in a billion klicks must be handy for Odin," I said.

She snickered. "Yes, sar. That it is. He's been out here something like thirty stanyers. Nobody's quite sure how he's making a go of it, but apparently enough ships come through that need spare parts or forgot the toothpaste to make it worth his while."

"Blackmarket, Ms. Thomas?"

"I don't know, Captain. With plenty of time, the right incentives, and a twisted mind, anything is possible."

Mr. Pall's voice came over the top of the console. "Location fix verified. I know where we are, Captain."

I straightened from the screen and looked over to where he was still pattering on the keys. "Do you have a course correction, Mr. Pall?"

"I do, indeed, Skipper. Programming thrusters now." He slammed a few more keys. "Estimated total elapsed burn time—" He leaned in to look at his screen. "Twenty-two stans, Captain."

"Did you say twenty-two stans, Mr. Pall?"

His fingers rested unmoving on the keys. He turned to look at me. "Yes, Skipper. Twenty-two stans." He looked apologetic.

"Comment, Ms. Thomas?"

She shrugged. "A little on the long side, but not out of bounds from what I remember from the *Hector*. Seems to me, was pretty common for us to jump in one day and out the next."

I turned back to where Mr. Pall waited, his eyes on me "Initiate burn sequences, Mr. Pall."

Without turning his head, one finger twitched and a key clicked. "Initiate burn sequences, aye, Skipper."

"Does this change our ETA in Jett significantly, Mr. Pall?"

"I'll have to re-run the numbers, Captain, but I was planning on twelve, not twenty-two. A lot will depend on where we jump to in Jett and the condition of the winds."

"Thank you, Mr. Pall. Ms. Thomas, if you'd secure from navigation stations and resume normal watch rotation?"

"Securing navigation stations and resuming normal watch, aye, aye, Captain."

I glanced at the chronometer just as it clicked over to 1103. I had less than a stan before I took over the watch again myself. When Ms. Thomas had finished the announcement, I went to the cabin intending to work on the reports, but spent half a stan just gazing out into the Deep Dark ahead, and wondering if I'd made a horrible mistake.

Chapter Thirty-eight
The Deep Dark: 2372-March-21

For me, the twenty-odd stans of programmed burn passed in nail-biting uncertainty. I tried not to look nervous in front of the crew. Lucky for me, being on watch meant the only one exposed to me for any serious amounts of time was Mr. Hill. While we were maneuvering under programmed thrust on a ballistic trajectory, there wasn't really much for helm to do but the regs said he needed to be on the bridge, so he kept me company and worked on his cargo exam.

We did keep an extra screen open for long range scan. It wasn't likely that we'd meet another ship head on, or even be t-boned by a ship coming across our course on a doublejump to the other pair of ports, but it didn't hurt to watch. It's rare to see even one other ship on long range once you're out of port more than a week or so. We saw two in the short time it took to slide past Odin's Outpost, not including the smaller craft that seemed to be coming and going from the Outpost itself.

"What do you suppose they're doing, Mr. Hill?"

"Mr. Pall thinks they're pirates, Skipper."

"What do you think, Mr. Hill?"

"They look like fast packets, Skipper. I'd bet on casino junkets."

"Why casinos, Mr. Hill? Gambling's legal in all of the systems around here."

"Yes, Skipper but not in Grail or Fischer. Those are both in range of a fast packet."

"Yes, but why jump way out here?"

He shrugged. "Exotic destination for people with disposable income. I bet there's a lot of people who are in it for the adventure. They run these junkets on the quiet, even out of Diurnia. And I'd bet he has a pleasure dome in there, too, fully stocked with hot and cold running pleasures. All untaxed and unregulated by the Confederated Planets Joint Committee on Everything."

"And plenty of room to dispose of the bodies, eh, Mr. Hill?"

"Can't be too many or the authorities would begin to notice, but who's to say, Skipper."

"The ultimate free port, eh, Mr. Hill?"

"So it would seem, Captain, but free is a matter of opinion."

"Interesting observation, Mr. Hill."

He shrugged. "Some see fences as keeping dangers out. Others see the same fences keeping them in."

"And you, Mr. Hill?"

He grinned up at me. "Yo ho ho, Skipper."

I chuckled. "Indeed, Mr. Hill." I straightened from the screens and looked out at the ice cold sheets of darkness all around. Odin's Outpost was too far away to pick up with the naked eye, but there were plenty of glittery lights to look at. "How's Mr. Ricks doing as morale officer, Mr. Hill?"

"Fine I guess, sar. He hasn't had a lot of opportunity to do much."

"How's morale holding up? We had a short stay and liberty was cut short on both ends."

He looked up at me under an upraised brow. "Not as bad as it might have been if we didn't have so many credits stapled to the aft bulkhead, sar. And the shares we got in Welliver were the biggest I think we've ever had."

I turned to look aft at the rounded tops of the cans glittering dully in the reflection of our running lights. "The shares on these should be two or three times that, Mr. Hill."

He got a kind of sideways smile on his face. "Trust me, Skipper. Every single one of us is aware of that. You primed the pump with that first one. The biggest problem you're gonna have after this one is how to top it."

We rode along in companionable silence for a time. Watching the dark. Letting the chrono click over. The programmed burns of the thrusters flashed periodically as the repeated, small kicks curved our course the few points we needed to open a hole in the direction we needed to go.

"So, how did it really go with the co-op, Mr. Hill?"

He laughed. "If I'm gonna be your spy, Skipper, I wanna raise."

"You're right, Mr. Hill. It's unfair of me to put you in that position. We have the coincidence of propinquity and I used that unfairly. I withdraw the question, Mr. Hill, with respect. Thank you for calling me on it."

He was right. It was unfair of me to lean on the power relationship and the forced contact that we shared as a watch section. The chrono clicked over a few more times.

"You know, Skipper, that co-op thing was a good idea."

"The settlement to the Agamemnon account looked reasonable. Did you all do as well personally?"

"I can't speak for the others, Captain, but I did pretty well. I think we need to look at our cargo mix. We got a lot of things that aren't really suited to the flea. We'll need to cut our losses on those and turn them over for goods that work better."

"Understandable, Mr. Hill. Different markets move different goods."

Eventually the chronometer ticked around enough to chew through the twenty-two stan course adjustment. I called for navigation stations at 0830 and the crew responded with a will.

When we were all settled in our stations, I turned to Mr. Pall. "Double check on location and velocity, if you please, Mr. Pall."

"Double checking now, Captain."

Ms. Thomas was scanning the immediate locale to make sure we were clear. We'd crossed the main east-west lane sometime in the night. That fell off astern, along with Odin's Outpost.

"Location verified, Captain. Vector adjustment still needs two more bursts to finish the cycle."

"Time to completion, Mr. Pall?"

"About seventeen ticks, Skipper. Should be on track to jump at 0852."

"Set it up, Mr. Pall. I'm getting a hankerin' to see someplace else."

Ms. Thomas added her part to what was becoming our little ritual. "Did you have any place in mind, Captain?"

"I'm thinking I'd like to drop these cans in Jett, Ms. Thomas."

"Mr. Pall? Did you hear the captain?"

"I did, Ms. Thomas. I think I can help with that." He stopped tapping. "Jump locked and ready, Ms. Thomas."

"Thank you, Mr. Pall. Please let me know when the thruster sequence has completed."

"Aye, aye, sar."

"Captain, the chief reports we are ready to jump on your signal. Burleson drives are online and ready."

"Thank you, Ms. Thomas. There are no pirates crawling up over the cans at the moment, are there?"

She actually turned to look and I had to suppress a chuckle. "Not that I can see from this vantage point, Captain."

"We seem to be clear of pirates, Mr. Pall."

"Thank you, Captain, and I appreciate you checking. You can't be too careful."

We canned the jocularity as the chrono clicked closer. I could hear the vibration of the thruster motor in the frame of the ship–not so much as a sound but a feeling. There wasn't really anything to hear in the vacuum of space, but the mechanisms were mounted solidly to the ship's skeleton and the movement of the plasma through the nozzle produced a vibration that I could hear. Suddenly, it was gone.

"Programmed thruster sequence completed, Ms. Thomas."

"Thank you, Mr. Pall. I see the board is green for jump, Captain. Ship is ready."

"Ready about, Mr. Pall. Hard a-lee."

He mashed the key and the ship jumped.

I was gratified to see the view in the forward armor glass change to include a very bright point of light almost dead center ahead.

Ms. Thomas called it as soon as the screens registered. "Welcome to Jett, Captain."

Mr. Pall was silent but he was hammering on his keys. I didn't like the look on his face, but I didn't joggle his elbow.

Ms. Thomas finished her scan. "No proximity alarms, Captain. Nothing unusual on long range."

"Thank you, Ms. Thomas."

Mr. Pall stopped hammering. "Location locked and verified, Captain." He looked up at me with a stricken expression. "I'm sorry, Skipper. We jumped long by eight per cent."

Ms. Thomas stepped out from behind her console so she could see Mr. Pall directly. "What's that do to transit time, Mr. Pall?"

"Our current ETA is April 12th, Ms. Thomas."

"How much over will we be, Mr. Pall?" I asked.

"Thirty-three standard hours, Skipper."

I sat back in my chair and closed my eyes to think. A day and a half on a twenty-one day run.

"Ms. Thomas? My compliments to the chief and would she come to the bridge as soon as she has the sails up and the keel out?"

"Aye, aye, Captain." She tapped a few keys and waited. "Five ticks, Skipper. She's on final spin up now."

The first sails came up almost instantly and the keel extended shortly after. "Helm, report steerageway."

Mr. Schubert answered almost immediately. "Ship responding to helm, Captain."

I turned to Ms. Thomas. "Anything else we need to do, Ms. Thomas?"

"Nothing I can think of, Skipper."

"Secure from navigation stations, Ms. Thomas. Resume normal watch."

"Secure from navigation stations and resume normal watch, aye, aye, Captain."

The word went out and within a tick Mr. Hill came bounding up the ladder. We traded watches off once more. Mr. Hill and I had the watch until noon, when first section would take over.

I glanced at the chrono–0943. "You've got two stans if you'd like to grab a quick nap, Ms. Thomas."

"I'd rather hear what the chief has to say, Skipper."

"I'd rather you did, too, Gwen. Thanks."

As if on cue, Chief Gerheart came scampering up the stairs. "You rang, Skipper?" It was the little girl, but there was sapphire just under the surface.

"We jumped long, chief. Deceleration and alignment needs a day and a half more than we have. We need to cut down the run time to Jett."

The news registered with a brief flickering in the eyes, but her mask stayed on. "Sure thing, Captain."

"Mr. Pall, can you put our projected course on the drop down so we can all see it please?"

A repeater screen hanging from the overhead immediately lit up with a schematic of the system and a projected plot.

All eyes went to it.

"Gimme the two credit tour, Mr. Pall. What are we looking at?"

"Least distance path from here to there, Skipper." He swung in his seat to look up with the rest of us.

It wasn't a smooth curve, but had a few bumps and corrections in it. "Run the plot timeline for us, Mr. Pall."

A small blip appeared on the screen. As it moved along the projected line, the reasons for some of the bumps became obvious as planets or sometimes just moons slipped into the pathway.

The time stamp at the top became a counter as we watched the days melt away ending with the ship and orbital in the same place at the same time on the afternoon of April 12th.

"We need that date to be April 10th, people." I looked around. "How do we do it?"

The chief walked up to peer into the screen and even Ms. Thomas stared at it.

I was startled to hear the chief speak. It wasn't the little girl. "Deceleration is multiplicative. If we can get even five percent more now, it'll pay big dividends at the end."

Mr. Pall jerked in his chair and stared at her for a heartbeat and a half before diving into his screen again.

Ms. Thomas seemed not to have noticed. "Can you give us more sail, Chief?"

I saw the back of the chief's head move as she nodded. "Yes, Ms. Thomas, I can and that'll help a bit. The girls have some governors on them that I can override if I need to. We can't run them for long like that, but maybe as much as a couple of days here where every meter per second matters. It'll help, but I don't think it'll be enough."

I grabbed at the straw. "Parameters, Chief?"

"Maybe ten percent more sail for forty-eight stans. It'll depend on sailing conditions of course, but all other things being equal it should be something on that order of magnitude, Skipper."

"Factor that in, if you would, Mr. Pall."

"Plotting now, Captain." He punched a few more keys and the plot on the overhead shifted.

"Run it, please, Mr. Pall."

He punched it and the clock ran up again. The course took slightly different curves but the same objects offered similar obstacle to our path. The icon reached the orbital and the clock read April 11th, near the end of the day.

"Better but not enough."

Ms. Thomas turned to look at me. "That's least distance. Can we do a least time?"

Mr. Pall looked over at her. "They should be almost the same thing."

She shrugged. "Should be and would be in an empty system, Billy, but this one isn't empty. If we can find a longer path that gives us better wind or take advantage of a gravity well to slow us, we might go farther but arrive sooner."

The Chief cocked her head slightly. "We're coming in awfully close to the ecliptic. If we could get above it even a few hundred thousand klicks, we'd get a more stable flow."

"Changing vectors will be tough sledding until the sails get a little more wind to work with," Ms. Thomas said.

The chief turned to look at me. The little girl was gone and Chief Gerheart stood revealed in the middle of the bridge. Excitement danced in sapphire flames and a lean, eagerness in her stance banished all thoughts of little girls. "Or below it, Captain," she said.

She stretched up an arm and pointed at an object that was coming toward us in one of the outer orbital bands. It was close, but the plot took us clear before it would cross our path. A small label identified it as a planetoid named "Last Chance."

"Can we alter course enough to intercept this rock? We might
be able to slingshot on the gravity well and drop under the ecliptic."

Mr. Pall had turned his head to look at what she was pointing
to. From my angle I couldn't see his face but he stiffened in his
seat. "You've got to be kidding me."

She turned to look at him. "No, Mr. Pall, if we can graze it
right, it should slow us a bit but it'll change our vector and have
us heading down. When we reach better wind, we should be able
to shed even more velocity because the sails will have better bite."

"But that's going to add a huge amount of distance to the track,
Chief."

I interrupted. "Plot it, Mr. Pall. Let's see what she's got."

He shrugged and turned to hammer his keys a bit. A bit turned
into rather a long time. "Sorry, Captain, this isn't the normal
course. It's taking me a bit."

"Take your time, Mr. Pall."

We were so used to having things done immediately, that even
a few ticks delay seemed long. Eventually the plot refreshed and
the corkscrew pattern was revealed. Ms. Thomas whistled in ap-
preciation. "That's a long way to the barn, isn't it."

The projected distance on the plot was almost half again longer.
"Run it, Mr. Pall."

He mashed a key and the icon representing the ship skewed
around until it was running almost at the planetoid. It passed
very close and looped down sharply. A wide curve back toward the
primary and a very smooth curve deposited the ship and orbital
together at April 11th at mid day.

Ms. Thomas shook her head. "So close."

I saw the chief's head tilt just a couple of degrees to one side.
"Mr. Pall, if you'd rerun it and zoom in on this flyby, please?"

He did it without my having to tell him and I watched closely
to see what the chief was looking at.

The view focused on the curve and, as the icon passed the planetoid, the chief barked, "Freeze it!'

Mr. Pall's hand twitched and the frame stopped. "What's our
closest approach, Mr. Pall?"

"Four diameters, Chief."

She stepped back from the screen and folded her arms across
her chest, still staring at the screen. She stood that way for a full
tick.

She finally turned, just her head to look at him. "Can we get
any closer, Billy?"

He grimaced. "Sails that close to the planet? If there's enough iron in it and we drag a sail across it ..."

She winced and turned her face back to the plot.

"What if we didn't have sails, Skipper?" It was Mr. Schubert. His voice startled me. I had overlooked the fact that he'd stayed on the bridge after the watch at been relieved. All heads snapped to face him where he leaned against the ladder railing.

"No sails, Mr. Schubert?"

"Yes, Captain. If we want to get closer, the turbulence around that rock is going to be pretty ugly anyway. I'm not sure I'd like to try to sail it, even at four diameters. If we go ballistic four diameters out, then graze the shell..." he shrugged. "Thrusters give us a little steerage but even the sails won't actually be dragging us around in that sharp a turn. We'd be relying on the gravity to turn us, and it'll turn us a lot faster if we can get closer."

Behind me I heard the chief speak the word that had surfaced in my brain. "Brilliant."

I turned to look at Mr. Pall. "Can you thread that needle, Billy?"

His hands were moving before I got the sentence out. "Yo ho ho, Skipper. And a bottle of rum."

The wait was shorter this time. He only had some minor adjustments to make to the plot. In three ticks it was on the screen. This time the green line was interrupted by two yellow segments with an angry red bit in between where the bend in the course was the sharpest.

"Run it, Mr. Pall."

We watched and even though it was only a simulation plot, I held my breath as the ship made the loop and shot out the other side. I think we all breathed a sigh when the corkscrew flattened out and the ship made the turn to run inward. The plot was longer again. The sling shot threw us downward a long way that had to be made up. When icon and orbital met this time, the date was April 10th around 2200.

There was a general intake of breath before anybody spoke. I broke the silence. "Closer."

They all turned to look at me. Mr. Pall spoke. "It's the 10th, Skipper."

"Just barely, Mr. Pall, and I'd bet those parameters you're trusting are just estimates. Good estimates but still guesses."

I could see Ms. Thomas nodding. She suddenly frowned and turned to Mr. Pall. "Where are we meeting the planetoid, Mr. Pall? Are you plotting us over the pole?"

It wasn't precise language but we all knew what she meant. "Yes, the chord is angled to give us the most push down."

"Can you shave it? We don't want the same plane as the ecliptic because that'll just throw us inward through the junk, but can you carve it maybe halfway between? Say forty-five degrees?"

He frowned and stared at the plot on the overhead, but I knew he was thinking about the course. "Lemme see."

A few ticks later and a slightly different corkscrew pattern flashed up on the screen. It still had red and yellow bands, but the downward leg wasn't as pronounced. The running plot gave us April 9, at 2100.

Several grins broke out around the bridge. The Chief's wasn't one of them.

"What's the problem, Chief?"

"That red band, Skipper. That's red for a reason and I'm not sure we're going to like finding out what it is."

"Mr. Pall? Parameters on the warnings?"

He turned back to his screen. "Inertial dampeners, Skipper. Yellow is within ten percent of safety margin. Red exceeds it. Maximum value shows eight percent over maximum rating."

I turned to the chief. "Recommendations?"

She ran a hand across her mouth and I could see the wheels spinning. "That's cutting it very, very fine, Skipper. If we get away with it, the ship gets a good work out."

"If we don't, Chief?"

"Then best case is that dampeners fail and we all become spacer paste on the nearest hard surface."

Mr. Schubert barked a laugh. "That's best case, Chief?"

She nodded. "Yeah. It'd be fast and over."

I hated to ask but morbid curiosity won out. "Worst case, Chief?"

"The ship breaks up without killing us outright and we get to experience dying in a vacuum."

Mr. Pall broke the silence. "That seems a bit extreme, Captain."

"Your gift for understatement hasn't failed you, Mr. Pall." I looked at the plot. "Pull back from the planet a bit. See if you can find a trajectory that doesn't have any red in it."

The chief nodded in approval.

Mr. Pall turned back to his screen. "This could take awhile, ladies and gents, and I don't really work that well with an audience."

"Okay, Mr. Pall, we really don't want to joggle your elbow on this one. I think we can clear the bridge except for the watch. I'll call you all when I know something." I looked at Ms. Thomas. "You're going to be back here soon enough to take the watch anyway. With luck he'll have something we can–pardon the expression–live with."

They took the hint. Which was good because, as a rule, Captain generated hints carried the force of orders. The bridge cleared out and I took my seat at the console. Mr. Pall continued to hammer keys and I forced myself not to watch.

I'll give him credit. It took him almost until the watch change, but he never wavered. Tappity-tappity-tappity-tap. Wait. Curse. Repeat. The first few took him a while to plot up, but he soon had the process down and the periods between curses grew quicker if less vehement as the watch wore on. In the end, there was a wait, but no curse. I heard a few more keys, and another pause. A few more.

"Okay, Captain, you can look now."

"Thank you, Mr. Pall. You were doing those last few just to torture me, weren't you."

He looked startled when I stood up from behind the console. "No, Skipper. I would have if I'd thought of it, though, if that's any consolation."

I laughed. "Run it, Mr. Pall. Let's see what you got."

The path was twisty but free of red. When icon and orbital met, the date read April 10th, 0200.

"Best I got, Skipper."

"Lay it in but hold it until I can get the chief up here."

"On it, Skipper."

I called the chief and Ms. Thomas. My finger had barely cleared the keypad when they both bounded onto the bridge.

The plot was on the overhead. It took three runs before the chief nodded. Ms. Thomas gave a shrug. "If the chief says 'good' that's good enough for me, Skipper."

The chief said. "If you'd run it once more, Mr. Pall."

He did and she stood up close. When it was over, she didn't look at him when she spoke. "And if you'd zoom in on the flyby, Mr. Pall, and freeze it at closest approach?"

He did so.

She stepped back from the screen. "Good."

"Lock it in, Mr. Pall. When's our flyby?"

"It's on the screen, Skipper."

The date and time readout read March 25th at 0200.

"That's gonna be a long night, I'm afraid."

The chief looked up at me and snorted. "Long is good, Captain. On that course, short is not an option we want to explore."

There was no sign of the little girl on her face at all.

Chapter Thirty-nine
Jett System: 2372-March-24

I wasn't sure if the crew really understood the reality of what we were about to do. I wasn't sure I did, for that matter. Every time I tried to visualize it I got the image of our relatively small ship playing chicken with a planet. We were going to actually fly at a rock that was two thousand kilometers in radius, try to miss it by a distance that threatened to scrape paint off the hull, and at a precise angle to the limb while closing at way over ten kilometers per second. The trick was going to be to fly at the correct velocity and to catch the correct angle. Too slow and instead of shooting us out the far side, we'd be grabbed by the planetoid. Too close and we'd just be ripped apart by the stresses on the ship. Too far and we'd be off course, out of position, and late to deliver.

Assuming, of course, that we didn't just smack headlong into the surface. I didn't know which was worse. The idea of crashing my first command into a rock that I shouldn't be flying near or that the last thing that would flash through my brain would be fifteen metric kilotons of kitty litter.

In spite of the potential pending doom, the crew seemed in high spirits at the prospect of a thrill ride. On the twenty-fourth I had all three of the ratings wanting to take the exams. Ratings exams happen at the same time across the Western Annex. Every ninety days, training officers on ships underway, and union halls on orbitals offered promotional ratings exams to anybody who wanted to take one. I'd had more than my share of them back on the *Lois McKendrick* and I'd administered many more in the stanyers since.

Mr. Hill and I had the morning watch, so I used the spare console on the bridge to administer the exams. Mr. Ricks reported first. He took, and passed, the exam for Able Spacer. As I made the appropriate notations on his record, I noted that it was the fourth time he'd taken and passed the exam.

"Try to hold on to it, Mr. Ricks?"

He grinned a lopsided grin. "I'm thinking of moving up instead of down next time, Skipper."

"While I've got you here, Mr. Ricks, I realize we've been on a dead run ever since I came aboard, but what do you think we should do to improve morale aboard?"

"Making lots of money has certainly improved my morale, Captain. And things have certainly been interesting since you came aboard. My problem is I haven't a clue as to what might be possible."

I pondered for a couple of heartbeats. "Well, on other ships, I've seen morale officers work to improve the recreation facilities of the ship, and intercede when some individual member of the crew was having a particularly hard time."

He took his time replying to that one. "You're doing a good job looking out for us, Captain. Everybody in crew quarters seems pretty upbeat." He thought some more. "As for recreational facilities aboard, the work out room is about the only thing and other than the hot tub idea, I can't think of what else to add to it. The weight machine, treadmill, and rower are all first rate. The only thing it's really missing is a stationary bicycle and I'm not sure if anybody noticed."

"Thank you, Mr. Ricks. If you think of anything, please let me know. Put your heads together in crew berthing there and check with Mr. Wyatt. See if he has any ideas."

He seemed a bit startled by the notion, but nodded in agreement. "Aye, aye, Captain. I can do that."

Mr. Schubert came up and took his exam next. It was no surprise to me that he was going for his specialization in ship handling, but it did surprise me that he was going for spec one. In the earlier and admittedly hurried review of crew records, I'd overlooked the fact that he held spec two shiphandler already.

I asked him about it when he came up to the bridge. "So, why are you still on the *Agamemnon*, Mr. Schubert? With a spec two rating, you could have found another berth."

"It's not as easy as it sounds, Skipper. When you're from the *Agamemnon*, well, let's just say our reputation precedes us." He looked chagrined.

Thinking back to my own reaction when offered command of the ship, I had to nod in agreement if not in total sympathy. There's a certain justice in having to sleep in the bed you made, and the three of them had certainly had a big hand in rumpling the coverlet.

Still, it wasn't solely their fault. Bad management and a cascade of errors certainly added a lot of extenuating circumstances.

"We'll have to try to reverse that, eh, Mr. Schubert?"

"I don't know, Skipper. The way things are going here lately, seems like I might already be in a sweet berth." He gave me a cheeky grin.

I had to laugh at that. "Well, we'll see if you feel that way after tonight."

We got down to it and he worked very methodically through the exam. It took him the better part of two stans and in the end, he missed it. Not by much, but enough.

I sat with him at the console and we went through the sections. "The math skunked you, Mr. Schubert." I pointed out the questions where he'd missed the most points.

He sucked air through his teeth and shook his head slowly. "Always been my problem, Captain. I thought I'd done enough studying to beat it."

"Well, no harm, no foul on this one. When we get to Jett, remind me. I'll see if I can find some supplemental math work to help you." Some of the questions didn't really seem that tough to me, but I was looking at it from the perspective of four stanyers of Academy math, and decades of practice since.

"Thanks, Skipper."

We had to wait until Mr. Pall and Mr. Ricks relieved us and lunch was over before Mr. Hill could take his cargo exam. He took the third class test and passed it with flying colors. By 1400 we'd finished the testing, and I had a few stans before we went back on watch. Mr. Hill and I had the evening watch, and we'd be going to navigation stations with the watch change at midnight. The fly-by was expected around 0145 and I wanted everybody in place well in advance. Things were going to happen pretty quickly when they started, and I wanted my people up and awake when they did.

I headed down to the cabin after the last exam and found Chief Gerheart waiting for me outside my door. "Gotta tick, Skipper?" The little girl had disappeared altogether after the performance on the bridge. The mask was, apparently, gone for good. Having been exposed to a large number of the crew, there was little point in continuing. Nobody made any comment that I'd heard, which was interesting in itself.

"Sure, Chief, come on in." I led the way into the cabin and indicated the chair.

We sat and she looked at me with an oddly appraising look across the desk. "This is going to sound funny coming from me, Skipper, but are you mad?"

"I don't think so. Mad about what, Chief?"

"Not angry. Crazy."

"Quite likely. Do you have anything in particular in mind?"

"Why did you agree to this hair brained plan? Captain Health-n-Safety is gonna fly his ship into a rock in pursuit of a few credits?"

"Well, it was your idea, Chief."

"I know, Skipper, that's why I said it's going to sound funny coming from me. Have you thought about this? Really thought about it?"

I snorted a small laugh. "I've had a hard time thinking of anything else."

"So why are you risking the ship? New captain's stars choking the blood supply to the brain?" She said it kindly, but there was a look of concern.

"Do you think it's too risky? Can the ship take it?"

"It's a tractor, Skipper, not a battleship. We just don't have hard data on that kind of stress on the hull. The manufacturer's tests are almost twenty-five stanyers old. There's been a lot of Deep Dark sucking on this hull for a long time and who knows how she's aged."

"Do we have any safety margins at all, Chief? We're in the yellow all the way in terms of the inertial dampeners. The physics check out as far as we know them."

"It's the 'as far as we know them' part that gives me pause, Skipper."

"Me, too, Chief."

"Then why?"

I sat back in my chair and thought about it. I'd been worrying ever since we decided to take the chance. Ever since *I* decided to take the chance. I swiveled my chair so I could look out through the armor glass. The planetoid was still too far away to see, but I knew it rushed towards us on a near collision course, closing the gap at over ten kilometers per second.

Without turning back to her, I asked a question in reply. "Why did you suggest it?"

I heard her sigh. "I got caught up in the moment, Skipper. I could see it in my mind's eye, the solution, and in the excitement of seeing what this old girl can actually do at the hands of good crew, I just let it all go."

I did turn back to her then. "What's changed your mind?"

"Call it second thoughts. Even cold feet, if you like. I'm just trying to get a grip on the balance between risk and reward. If we do this and fail, we could all die. The cargo could be lost and the ship with it. That's a whole lot worse than losing money on a tight priority gone bad. The company has insurance to cover both those eventualities, but the immediate implications for us are considerably different."

That sobering thought gave me serious pause. I let out a long breath and turned to look out the port again. "They pay me to make a profit."

"They pay you to bring the ship back in one piece." Her voice sounded quiet in the hush.

"This is crazy, isn't it." I said it without looking back at her.

"Weathering a storm that's caught you is one thing, Skipper. Flying into a storm on purpose is another."

I stood and crossed to stand next to the port. That rock was coming at us very, very fast. Our margins for error were slim and the downside risks were catastrophic. The upside gain was money, a lot of money, but just money. After a couple of ticks, I realized she was still sitting in the chair. "Thank you, Chief. I needed to hear that."

"Thanks for listening, Skipper." She stood and I heard her walk across the cabin to the door. "I need to get back to the girls and make sure they're okay."

"Give them a pat for me, Chief."

"Aye, aye, Skipper." There was a note of amusement in her voice.

I stood looking out at the darkness but I'm not sure what I saw. After a couple of ticks, I crossed to the terminal on my desk and started running numbers. Time was short, and I needed answers fast. Half a stan later, I climbed up to the bridge. Mr. Pall and I had some work to do.

Somewhere in there, I realized that what they really paid me for was to make the hard decisions. This one wasn't very hard to make, but it was going to be hell to follow through with.

Chapter Forty
Jett System: 2372-March-24

I sat on the bridge for what was left of the afternoon. Mr. Pall was very helpful in fine tuning my rough calculations, and even Mr. Ricks offered some suggestions that made the outcome slightly better. Not good enough, but better.

At 1745 Mr. Hill came up to the bridge to relieve the watch but I forestalled him. "Mr. Pall, if you and Mr. Schubert would hold the bridge for a few more ticks. I need to go let everybody else know what's going on."

Mr. Pall was subdued but smiled. "Certainly, Skipper."

Mr. Hill looked around confused and then he saw the new plot on the drop down.

"Let's go spread the glad tidings, Mr. Hill." He followed me down to the mess deck and we found everybody but Chief Gerheart already there and waiting for dinner mess to begin. Every head turned as we entered and the look on my face was apparently enough to halt conversation. Mr. Wyatt who was setting out dishes on the serving counter noticed and stopped his bustling. I reached for my tablet to bip the chief when she came skidding around the corner and into the mess deck.

I took a deep breath and then began. "Folks. It's crazy. I was reminded of just how crazy it was this afternoon and I apologize for getting everybody's hopes up. We aren't going to make it to port on time."

There was a moment of stunned disbelief as everybody but the chief responded to the news. I picked up the portable keyboard and routed the course plot from the bridge onto the repeater screen and all eyes turned to look at it. A green snake ran around the oncoming planet but skirted it at a safe distance. Regulations called for a minimum of three diameters when passing near a large-body astronomical artifact. We would skirt it at four, well within the safety margins. The snake was green all the way. I triggered the play back and when the ship's icon finally met the orbital at the end of the animation, the date at the top said April 12th, 0300.

Nobody offered any comment so I filled it in. "We're too close to miss it altogether at this point so the best course is use what we can of it but stay a good distance out. Mr. Pall has given us a good balance between sling shot and getting below the plane of the ecliptic and into a nice clear wind stream. It's going to cost us the two days we need. That means we'll miss the priority and sacrifice the cargo. They're basically getting a free ride and our shares will be effectively zero. The alternative carried a level of risk that we—*I*—just could not accept."

A couple of ticks went by before Ms. Thomas spoke up. "Do you think they did it on purpose, Skipper?"

I shook my head. "No, I think it was just luck of the draw on a razor thin deck. If we'd jumped short instead of long, we'd be in the money. We didn't. It happens. Every jump has a chance of being off and there's nothing you can really do about it. It's why we add margin errors to the jump on both ends. This one went the wrong way and we're left holding the bag."

Nobody had anything else to say.

I looked around at them. They all stared at the plot with various looks of disbelief and disappointment. "I'm sorry, people. Really."

I nodded to Mr. Hill who followed me up to the bridge where we did the needful just before 1800.

It was a long watch. The drop down tracked a shorter range view of our course showing the rapidly approaching planetoid. We were still going to be flying very close to it, but the margins of error were much bigger and the probability that we'd actually hit the rock, or damage the ship in transit were negligible.

At 2345, Ms. Thomas and Mr. Schubert joined us on the bridge to relieve the watch. "Chief Gerheart is standing by in Engineering, Skipper."

"Thanks, Ms. Thomas. I trust that we won't need her for this but good to know she's there if we do."

I sat at the engineering console on the bridge and fired up the engineering displays. The status showed green on all systems. There wasn't a lot of draw on the system as a whole. Sails were at near maximum but this far out from the primary there was little strain on them. The keel was likewise extended but we weren't very far into the gravity well so there was only moderate bite. As we got deeper, we'd be able to sail closer to the wind. We were still moving at a pretty good clip. The planetoid coming at us was moving faster and the closing vector was a surprisingly large number.

The chrono ticked over and the mass of the planetoid ahead of us began to show in the occlusion of the brighter objects behind it. The albedo of the surface wasn't high and the light cast this far out from the primary was pretty low. Looking forward, the suddenly looming object was, for all the world like a huge cloud blowing up ahead of us.

Ms. Thomas sat at her console and looked out the armor glass ahead. "Helm? You ready?"

"Ready, sar. Course plot locked and ready for execution."

She looked at me.

"You're the OD, Ms. Thomas. At your discretion," I said.

"Thank you, Skipper." She turned to Mr. Schubert. "Chooch? Try not to hit the planet?"

"No hitting the planet, aye, sar." He grinned.

"Helm, execute transit plan."

"Execute transit plan, aye, sar."

His hands were already on the handles and the only real indicator was a slight twist of his wrists. Ahead of us the darkened mass that had been about to slide by to our starboard side rotated around the forward view until it looked like we were going to fly directly under it. The sensation was uncanny. Intellectually, I knew that Mr. Schubert had just rolled the ship onto its back relative to the surface of the planetoid that was now growing visibly ahead. It was obvious that we were going to miss it although four diameters seemed like it might still be close enough to scratch the paint. I shuddered to think of what it might have looked like if we'd been shooting for half the distance or less. As it was, I found my jaw clenched as we bore down and the cloud grew from a circle of darkness to a grayish mass in the distance to a solid curved ceiling over our heads.

At the helm, Mr. Schubert was grinning, his hands firm on the maneuvering handles, as he guided us around. At ten diameters there was a slight juddering in the ship and I saw the load on the inertial dampeners jump up a bit. Mr. Schubert murmured softly. "Easy, baby. Daddy's got you." The juddering didn't stop but it did smooth out.

At five diameters, Ms. Thomas slapped a key and the sails dropped to standby. We were on a ballistic trajectory, but not any where near as extreme as the one we'd planned originally. We were flying a sixty metric kiloton rock through space and Mr. Schubert looked elated.

We coasted into the planetoid's gravity well and the attraction between ship and planet started having an effect. It wasn't enough to be felt by humans inside the vessel but the gravitational force was enough to begin tugging the ship. At a prescribed time, the bow thrusters fired to slow us a bit, to give gravity a chance to pull us down toward it even faster, and shortly afterward the heavy thrusters along the bottom of the ship kicked in to aid in that curving arch around. I watched the load on the inertial dampeners rise. It kept rising as our arc around the night time sky became more extreme until suddenly we were out from under. The planetoid continued on its long, dark journey imparting a small bit of its momentum to us as the changes in delta-velocity changed vector and tossed us free again. By then the forward port was open sky and when I turned to look out the after windows, I could make out the curve of the planetoid falling away. At five diameters out, the sails came back on line and our plot showed us slightly below the plane of the ecliptic and dropping. The course called for us to follow this line until we came to almost ten degrees below the plane and then we'd start the long climb down the well.

"Well done, Mr. Schubert."

"Thank you, Skipper."

I stood up and stretched. It had been a long, long day.

"Thank you, Ms. Thomas. Carry on."

She smiled sympathetically. "Thank you, Captain. Sleep well. I think you earned it today."

I chuckled, although there may have been more bitterness than humor in it. "Thank you, Ms. Thomas."

Mr. Hill followed me off the bridge and I headed for the cabin. I'd planned to just crawl into bed and let the universe unfold without me for a bit. It was the start of my twenty-four and I didn't have to be on until the next mid watch. It was approaching 0300 already and I felt completely wrung out. When I stepped into the cabin, though, I only made is far as the desk chair. I sat there with my hands flat on the surface and just felt numb. The port behind me drew me around. In the darkness ahead the bright point that was Jett gleamed in the soft black.

I watched it for a time and pictured the system's movements in my head as I imagined us flying under the surface of the system, sails wide and beating against the gale to bleed off our velocity, moving ever closer to the point where the orbital would be when we got there. At 0430 I dragged myself to bed and slept soundly.

Chapter Forty-one
Jett System: 2372-March-30

The long climb down into the well seemed particularly onerous after that. I think Mr. Pall may have felt almost as bad as I did, and probably blamed himself for the long jump. It was not his fault. You just can't predict it to a sufficient degree of accuracy. Sometimes jumps run a few points long, sometimes a few points short. We rolled the dice, took a chance and lost. It wouldn't have been critical if we'd not tried to get greedy and cut the run times too close. I won't say the life went out of the ship, but the spark of excitement certainly sputtered.

Mr. Hill and I had the morning watch and I was trying for the hundredth time to convince myself that I'd made the right decision. I was almost through with the overnight logs when Mr. Hill made a noise.

"Everything all right, Mr. Hill?"

"We just took a gust on the portside, Skipper. A good one."

I pulled up the system navigational reporting and saw no issued warnings. "Nothing on SNR, Mr. Hill."

"It was just the one, apparently, but flux rates are up about five percent over the last half stan, Skipper."

Flux rates are a measure of the solar wind. We always talked about it as if the star was actually putting out a breeze, but wind is the movement of gas on a planet. The solar wind is plasma of atomic components that's ejected from the upper regions of any star. Flux rate measures the density of the particles and provides a kind of strength metric analogous to a wind gauge.

"Can we use that to bleed off a little more speed, Mr. Hill?"

"I'm working on it, Skipper. Can we have a little more sail?"

I pulled up the sail configurations and we were running close to maximum. In the outer reaches of the system we carried as much sail as we had most of the time because the wind density was so much weaker out that far. As we got closer to the primary, the wind would become much stronger and we'd have to pull in area to maintain strength. So far the field sensors were saying we had plenty of strength for the current flux density but there really wasn't more sail to put up.

I bipped the chief to the bridge and she arrived almost immediately. "We've gotta stop meeting like this skipper. Mr. Wyatt's getting suspicious."

Mr. Hill snorted a laugh and I admit it hit me funny, too. Funny felt good after the few days we'd been through.

"I'll take that under advisement, Chief." I beckoned her to look at the displays. "We're getting increased flux rates out here. Mr. Hill reports they've gone up five points in the last half stan."

"Seven now, Skipper, and I think it's still climbing."

The Chief's eyebrows shot up. "I suspected we'd pick up some better quality wind off the ecliptic but that seems a lot."

"Seemed it to me, too, Chief. The girls are all but maxed out here in terms of area, and we're still in the green on strength. Do we have another wee rag or two to hang off the mizzen mast? I'd like to take advantage of this if we can." I looked up at her. She leaned over my shoulder, looking at the display. "I thought I remembered you said something about a bit of reserve."

"I did, indeed, Skipper. I did, indeed." She crossed to the engineering station and took a seat. She brought up the system configurations for power, sail, and keel. I saw her give a little extra kick to the fusactors and siphon the extra power into keel and sail generators. She opened a maintenance display and unchecked a few settings there. "Try it now, Skipper. Ease it up."

I used my sail control to boost the area and the needle indicating sail size slipped right past the mark that indicated maximum sails on the display. Mr. Hill braced a bit. I knew there wasn't really any feedback from the controls but his course plot reacted to the increased sail. The strain gauge climbed but stayed short of the yellow.

"How's she handling, Mr. Hill?"

His focus was on his helm but his face was alight. "She's doing great, Skipper. That was a nice little kick in the pants there."

"Flux rates, Mr. Hill?"

"Flux holding steady, sar. About seven or eight points higher than we've been seeing. Smooth sailing. I'm not getting any flutter."

The chief made a few small adjustments to the keel generator.

"You've got a bit more bite on the keel, Mr. Hill. You might be able to use that as well."

I looked over at her.

She gave a little shrug. "Can't let the girls have all the fun, Skipper. We can't keep it up too long, but as long as we're not stressing the systems on strength, there's a bit of advantage to be had here."

"See if she'll come another point or two into the wind, Mr. Hill."

"I've got two points more now, Skipper. I think that's all we can get."

"Two points on a million kilometers is a nice savings, Mr. Hill. We'll take it."

I looked over to see the chief grinning back. "That'll help a little, Skipper. At least keep the suffering to a minimum."

"All gifts are gratefully received, Chief. How long can the girls keep this up?"

"At these flux rates, probably a couple days."

"After that?"

"We'll need to pull back a bit. Depends on how much they overheat and how stable the flux. If we get much more we're going to start running into field integrity issues and we'll have to reef up anyway."

"We should have these talks more often, Chief. Mr. Wyatt can tend his pies."

She grinned and headed back to engineering. "Lemme just check on the girls and I'll see you at lunch, Skipper."

I won't say I wasn't a little more hopeful. Getting a good wind this far out in the system when we were typically moving the fastest meant leverage on our arrival time. Whether it would be enough to shave twenty-six stans from the deceleration plot, only time would tell.

The rest of the watch went by pretty normally given the circumstances. The higher than normal winds and larger sails gave Mr. Hill something more to do than he was used to. There was just enough turbulence in it to keep him on his toes and the plot showed him doing an excellent job in carving the line.

Ms. Thomas scampered up onto the bridge at 1140 with an odd look of curiosity on her face. "The chief has a very odd smile, Captain. You know anything about that?"

I nodded her over to the display. She saw the gauges run off the ends of the scales for sail and keel and gawked. "I've never seen anything like that, Skipper."

"Me, either, but apparently it's one of those little hidden functions on the generators. Normally we don't need more than we got because we're operating in the inner system. Integrity wins over area there." I stood up and looked out the armor glass. "Out here, we need as much area as we can get, but we need to be careful not to overstress the generators and burn one out. The governors make sense on the average run."

"We're sailing a fine line then, Skipper." Her face took on a smile as well. "Anything I need to watch?"

"Just keep an eye on sail integrity. If it starts to climb, reef up. The overrides are off so be careful in how hard you drive her. It's too far to get out and push if something goes wrong."

Mr. Schubert joined us on the bridge and we relieved the watch at 1145.

As I headed down the ladder, I couldn't help but notice the beatific smile plastered across Mr. Schubert's face as he caressed the helm and the ship surged against the dark.

Lunch was a nicely done casserole of beans and ground meat. Mr. Wyatt was still experimenting with curries and had developed a fine hand with the spice rack. I made a note to track down some of the more exotic ones when we got back to Diurnia. With his awakening skills, I thought he might find them useful.

The lunch mess was subdued but obviously the word about the higher than normal flux rate had made its way through the crew. There were quiet, hopeful smiles around the mess as the meal progressed and polite applause as Mr. Wyatt pulled out a simple tray of brownies and a gallon of vanilla ice cream for dessert.

About halfway through the brownies, the chief sat upright on the bench and cocked her head as if listening. I didn't hear it at first, but then as the general hubbub died down I caught the shift in sound as well. The ship sounded different.

She jumped from the table and raced for the engine room just as Ms. Thomas's voice came on the ship's announcer. "Captain to the bridge."

I ran. It probably wasn't dignified and certainly did little for assuring the crew but I wasn't really thinking of appearances at the moment. One tick and what felt like several hundred heartbeats later I was on the bridge. "What'd you have, Ms. Thomas?"

"Flux rates are twelve points above normal and climbing, Skipper. I've reefed up. We're down to sixty percent of normal, and still having trouble with integrity."

I looked at the strain gauges and saw they were well up into the yellow and ticking up toward red.

"With this level of flux we shouldn't be seeing this kind of strain, Skipper."

I glanced over to where the chief had left the Engineering console fired up. The keel was still extended and I slipped into the seat there just as the display showed the keel coming back in to normal levels. The chief beat me to it from engineering.

"Did that help, Ms. Thomas?"

She looked down at the telltales and nodded slowly. "Yes, Skipper, I think it did. Integrity's coming back toward nominal levels."

"How's she handling, Mr. Schubert?"

He was grinning like a madman. "Thrilling, Skipper! Thrilling!"

I snorted. "Thrilling is just a heartbeat from terror, Mr. Schubert. Try to stay on this side of the line if you please?"

"Aye, aye, Skipper."

I looked at the flux rate over his shoulder. "Did this just blow up suddenly, Ms. Thomas?"

"Yes, Skipper. We were finishing up our lunch here and the flux rate was sliding down the scale just ever so slowly. Then wham. In a matter of less than a tick it jumped from around six points above average to near twelve. It was like we hit a wall."

I looked at the ship's estimated velocity and was impressed with the decrease in speed. "Ride it as long as you can, Ms. Thomas. We may see these cans delivered yet."

"Aye, aye, Skipper. We'll do our best."

"I know you will, Ms. Thomas."

I met the chief in the passage outside of the mess deck. She stepped off the ladder from Engineering as I came down from the bridge.

She chuckled when she saw me. "That is why we have the governors in place, Skipper."

"Any damage to the ship, Chief?"

She shook her head. "Naw. She's rugged and we got to it right away. Did the wind come up?"

"Yeah, we're up about twelve points now and it came up pretty sudden."

The Chief's eyes widened with surprise. "Stiff wind for these parts. Ms. Thomas did the right thing by dropping the sails like that, but it was the extra drag from the keel that caused the integrity issues. She had no way of knowing."

"Are the governors back in place?"

"Yeah. I doubt we'll need them much now."

"You think this is just the effect of a more laminar flow, Chief?"

She screwed up her mouth in concentration. "Not likely, Captain. The transition would be smoother. I'd guess it's a solar storm. We just came through the gust front."

"That's what I thought, too, but I needed a reality check. Shall we finish dessert?"

"Lovely idea, Captain." She smiled happily as we reentered the mess deck and four anxious faces turned in our direction.

I held up a hand. "It's okay. Wind came up. We're making exceptional time. We were pushing the integrity limits. Nothing to be alarmed about."

They looked at each other and a general rumble of relief went around the room. As for me, I was wondering how long the storm would last and whether or not we'd find another, more violent gust.

Chapter Forty-two
Jett System: 2372-April-06

The storm blew out late in the day on April third. We'd had to reef down to as little as twenty percent on the sails in order to maintain integrity, but the good news was that we had a substantial reduction in our velocity. Mr. Pall ran continuous updates on arrival time and after watching the date go from early in the day of April 12 to early in the day on April 11, there was some hope in the ship that we'd carve enough off to make it. Then the storm blew past and we were back on a normal model for our estimated course and speed. We only needed to dock by the end of day on April 10th to make the deadline. The current projection showed us four stans short. We'd be there, the tug would be pushing us in, but we'd miss by a hair unless we could pull a few more stans out of the course.

It wasn't really likely, but we had hope.

Mr. Pall had the morning duty and managed to pick off the inner markers. We roused ourselves collectively to pay attention. We'd had the outer markers for days but the cargo list was nondescript and uninspiring after our experience on Welliver. Of course, the fact that all that excitement appeared to be a forty-five metric kiloton liability strapped to our butts contributed to the general lackluster air.

I was tempted to hide in the cabin when not on watch. It killed me to see the crew so dejected. We were so close. If I'd only risked a little more, could we have made it? We got lucky with the storm. It let us get even that much more tantalized by the date and what we were going to miss. I fought my temptation and went to the mess deck to sit with the rest of the crew. We were all in the same boat. If we were gonna be miserable, we'd be miserable together.

After lunch I hung around the mess deck to talk to Mr. Ricks and Mr. Wyatt about morale and what we might do once we got to Jett.

"How about movies?" Mr. Wyatt was leaning against the deep sink and looking at the big repeater screen over my head.

Mr. Ricks perked up. "Can we get the equipment, sar?" He was looking back and forth between Mr. Wyatt and me.

Mr. Wyatt nodded at the repeater behind me. "We've got the screen. Just need a cube player."

Chief Gerheart came onto the mess deck in time to hear that. "Already got it, Mr. Wyatt." She crossed to the unit on the bulkhead and pointed to a spot on the lower left edge. "Socket's there. This is really just an entertainment screen that's got the interface to be used as console repeater built into it. Plug in a cube and it'll play it."

I spun in my seat and leaned back against the table to consider it. "When I first made the run out from Port Newmar to Diurnia, the packet had movie nights after mess. As a passenger, I found it to be a rather pleasant way to spend an evening."

Mr. Wyatt piped up. "I can lay in some popcorn when we get to Jett."

"Where do we get the movies?" Mr. Ricks asked. "I mean I have some loaded in my personal player." He colored slightly. "I doubt that they'd be of general interest."

I looked around at them. "Any cinema fans in the crew?"

I got shrugs back.

"Well, let's take it under advisement. Some opportunity will present itself, I'm sure."

My tablet bipped and I looked down to see a message from Ms. Thomas on the bridge.

"This is a good idea. Do we have a chess set? Bridge deck? Any pinochle players? That's a nice table. Can we play games on it?" I let that sit for a heartbeat to distract them a bit. "If you'll excuse me, I need to check on something."

I left the mess deck in good order. After abandoning all decorum and bolting before, I'd vowed to never scare the crew that badly again so I forced myself to a sedate jog up the ladders and onto the bridge.

"Whadda ya got, Ms. Thomas?"

She turned as I popped up onto the bridge and pointed to her screen where I could see a red flashing blob and I got a sinking feeling.

"Mayday, Skipper. We got a problem."

I sighed. "Never rains but it pours."

Mayday is the distress call for ships in trouble. It was an old, old signal that followed mankind off old Earth and into the stars. My mother used to celebrate May Day as a kind of holiday of a more fecund nature, but this was apparently a corruption of a French phrase meaning "Help Me."

"The *Sarcastic Voice* out of Fischer has an environmental issue. Her scrubbers are all off line with bad cartridges and twenty-eight people aboard. It's a fast packet. Looks like another Damien hull."

I frowned. "That was sloppy. No spares?"

She shrugged. "Report says all the spares are contaminated. CO_2 is building up and they can't get rid of it."

"And we're the only ship in range?"

Ms. Thomas shrugged. "We're the closest, but can we help them?"

"Let's find out. Call the chief, would you, Ms. Thomas?"

"I'm right behind you, Skipper." I turned and saw she'd followed me up to the bridge. She shrugged a apologetically. "I had a feeling when you bailed on the movie discussion."

"You heard, Chief?"

She shrugged. "Enough. Damien's have good scrubbers. We use cartridge based scrubbers, too, but our cartridges aren't interchangeable." She turned to Ms. Thomas. "Did you say twenty-eight people aboard?"

She shrugged. "That's what's in the Mayday message, Chief."

"No wonder they have scrubber problems. I thought they were only rated for a crew of four and sixteen passengers."

"Can we help them, Chief?"

"If we get there before they all suffocate, probably we could do something. We got more than enough environmental capacity to handle them all, although where we'd stack them, that's another question."

I turned back to Ms. Thomas. "Are we nearest responder?"

"We'd need Mr. Pall to tell us that, Skipper. We're on parallel tracks but I don't know if anybody else is on a closing course with us. They might be able to reach her sooner. No other ship has responded yet."

"Page Mr. Pall to the bridge, please, Ms. Thomas."

She rang his stateroom directly. "Sorry, Mr. Pall, but could you come up to the bridge? We need your help here."

She hung up and less than a tick later, Mr. Pall belted up the ladder, shipsuit half zipped, and with a serious case of 'I just woke up' on his face.

Ms. Thomas filled him in on the situation and he sat down to plot, while I brought up the long range scanner.

"Six stans plus or minus, Skipper. Less if they can speed up a little to match us."

I found the ship on long range. There didn't seem to be anybody else in the immediate vicinity.

"Can you raise them on a voice channel, Mr. Pall? I think we'd like to chat them up."

"I can try, Skipper." He burrowed into his console. A few ticks later, he looked up at me. "I have Captain Allison, Skipper."

"On the speaker, if you please, Mr. Pall."

"Circuit is live, now, Skipper." He snapped a key down.

"Captain Allison? Captain Ishmael Wang of the *Agamemnon* here. How can we help?"

A woman's voice came from the overhead speakers. "Thank you, Captain Wang. We've got a right mess here with too many lungs and not enough scrubbers. Anything you can do to help with one or the other, or both, would be greatly appreciated."

"We're at least six stans behind you, Captain. Can you last that long?"

"We're good for maybe ten more stans." She coughed a little and when her voice returned I could hear the stress in it. "We're getting people into suits now to try to relieve the load on the scrubbers. It might buy us some time."

"Is your engineering officer available, Captain? Chief Gerheart is with me on the bridge. It might be useful if they could chat a moment."

"One tick, Captain. I'll get him." The circuit went quiet for a moment.

Then a man's voice came on. "Chief Green, here." If the captain's voice carried a bit of stress, then Chief Green's stress was packed in a can and mounted on his back.

I nodded at Chief Gerheart and the two engineers talked technical for a bit, while I conversed with Mr. Pall over matching course and speed.

They came to a break point and she nodded to me that she was done.

"Captain Allison? I've been talking to our astrogator and we can match velocities much quicker if you can add a little velocity to facilitate matching course. We can probably be there in a couple of stans."

"Of course, Captain Wang. We'll open a telemetry channel now and coordinate the rendezvous." There was a catch in her voice. "Thank you, Captain."

"Don't thank me, yet, Skipper, but I'll take a rain check when we all get to the orbital."

"Done and done, Captain. *Sarcastic Voice*, out."

"*Agamemnon*, out."

"Circuit is closed, Captain." Mr. Pall turned to me, his eyes glittering with excitement. "So you think they're pirates, Skipper?"

"Pirates, Mr. Pall?"

"Yes, Captain. Running the bad scrubbers trick to get us to dock with them, then they hijack us, kill the men, rape the women, and steal the cargo?"

I looked to Chief Gerheart who shrugged in return.

"It's a fair question, Skipper," she said.

"You think they'd hijack a cargo of kitty litter, Mr. Pall?"

"The ship would be worth something, even if it's just for parts, Captain," he said.

"I'm not sure we live in the same universe, Mr. Pall. What do you think, Chief? Were they good enough actors to make you believe they were really in trouble?"

She ran both hands up over her head and scratched her fingers along the scalp. "Well, the chief talked a good story. It made sense and hung together, but then, it would if it were fake. He sounded worried enough and so did that captain. They *did* put out a public Mayday and anybody could answer, including a patrol craft. They're on an inbound track so it's not like they've been lurking in here in wait, unless they've been really clever. Which I suppose they might be." She was thinking out loud for Mr. Pall's benefit as much as mine, I think. "It's a dangerous universe, Captain. He could be right. They might be pirates."

"Do you think so, Chief?"

"No, but I could be wrong, too, Captain."

"Okay, then I think I know how to handle it." I turned to Mr. Pall. "Please make a least time rendezvous with the *Sarcastic Voice*. We'll use the emergency collar and link up nose to nose. We can use the locks to keep the bad air out of our ship and let a few people at a time through. First few should tell the tale. Does that meet with your approval, Mr. Pall?"

"Yes, Captain, I think that would be secure enough."

"Chief?"

"Good idea, actually. If we can get them off the ship and give their scrubbers a chance to recover, we may be able to get them stable enough to finish on their own."

"Can our scrubbers handle the load?"

"At least that number, Skipper. I've got half our scrubbers shut down at the moment to save power."

"Can the girls handle the extra mass, Chief?"

"Docked up we won't be able to have the sails up, but we'll be moving inward."

I took one more wistful glance at the priority delivery plot on the drop down above my head. "Well, it wasn't meant to be, I guess. At least it won't be a total loss."

"Why's that, Captain?" Mr. Pall was looking up.

"We weren't going to make any money anyway, Mr. Pall. The least we can do is save their lives on the way."

"Unless they're pirates, Skipper."

"True, but maybe we'll capture them and there'll be a reward, Mr. Pall. Try to look on the bright side."

"Excellent point, Captain."

"That telemetry channel, Mr. Pall?"

"Yes, Skipper, we're already linked and adjusting courses now. The new plot should be on the helm as we speak."

Ms. Thomas turned to Mr. Schubert. "Helm?"

"New course loaded, and ready for execution, sar."

"Execute new course, Helm."

"Execute new course, aye, aye, sar."

I watched for a bit as we shifted course and trimmed sails to begin matching velocity with the crippled ship. "Well, I should go tell Mr. Wyatt we'll be having guests for dinner."

Chief Gerheart followed me off the bridge. When we got to officer country, I turned to look at her over my shoulder. "You don't really think they're pirates, do you?"

She grinned. "No, I don't. We're too close in and the story was just ragged enough to be real." She paused and rubbed one finger along her nose. "He did raise a good point, though. Just because I've never heard of a ship being successfully hijacked, doesn't mean there hasn't been one."

"Absence of evidence is not evidence of absence, eh, Chief?"

"That's what my daddy used to say, Captain."

We'd made it down to the mess deck by then, and I headed in to share the news with Mr. Wyatt. The chief headed to engineering to crank up our extra scrubber capacity. We were going to need it.

Chapter Forty-three
Jett System: 2372-April-06

It took us closer to four stans to match velocities. I called the crew to stations at 1700 and briefed them on the ship's announcer. Mr. Ricks was stationed at the lock, and Chief Gerheart had prepped and run up the emergency coupling that would allow us to lock nose to nose.

Between Mr. Pall's astrogation and Mr. Schubert's delicate hand on the helm we came into position with zero delta velocity between the two ships, lined up at just over twenty meters. We'd hold, and the *Sarcastic Voice* would nudge in. While we had better air, they had less mass and more responsive thrusters. They'd have the better chance for a good first lock.

Ms. Thomas turned from her station. "We have zero delta-v, Captain. Ready to commence docking."

"Signal our partner, Ms. Thomas, and let's start the dance."

"Aye, aye, Captain. Signaling now." She hit a key. "Signal sent and acknowledged, Captain."

I sat back in my chair and tried to look nonchalant. "Nobody sneeze."

Mr. Pall chuckled and I heard Mr. Schubert sniff back a laugh.

Ms. Thomas announced. "They're coming now. Delta-v of negative one meter per second."

We watched as the smaller craft moved closer to us. "Minus half a meter per second."

The helm on the other ship did an excellent job in cutting their relative motion just as the two ships bumped. We felt the nudge, but it was barely more than we got on docking. Ms. Thomas reported. "Locks engaged." She paused. "Seal is good."

On the run in, we'd explained that we wanted to keep as much of the bad air on their ship as possible and that we'd be using the locks to isolate the two ships to minimize the load on our scrubbers by not bringing a lot of bad air with them.

I got up from my chair. "Steady as she goes, people. I'm gonna go greet our guests."

I scampered down the two ladders and jogged to the brow just as the first of the party was entering our lock. I peeked through the view port and saw three older couples each pair with one of the smaller ship's mattresses. They were in light duty emergency ship suits and their skin looked a little gray through the nearly transparent material.

Chief Gerheart sidled up and peeked through beside me. "Think they've got assault weapons in those mattresses?" Her voice was almost a whisper and I choked back a laugh.

"Air has been replaced, Skipper."

"Open it up, Mr. Ricks."

"Opening the lock, aye, aye, Captain."

The latches clanked slightly and the inner doors swung up. Our guests shuffled tiredly aboard and stood looking a bit lost and bewildered. "Come in, ladies and gentlemen. Just follow this passageway and Mr. Wyatt will take care of you." I pointed down the passage and Mr. Wyatt waved from the door of the mess deck.

They shuffled on down the passage and Mr. Ricks cycled the lock closed again. Two more groups of passengers came through. The next were younger and a bit more fit looking, but still not very lively as they shuffled off, each pair dragging a mattress with them. They all got sent down the passage where Mr. Wyatt was serving a light meal and plenty of fluids. The noise grew as each new group joined the gathering throng.

The last group through consisted of five officers including a very tired looking woman wearing gold stars on her collar. The inner lock opened and they stepped through in good order. The captain saluted the ship and then me. I returned the honor before taking her hand. "Welcome aboard, Captain."

She smiled tiredly. "Thank you, Captain. I don't think words are enough to express just how grateful we all are for your assistance."

"Timing is everything, Skipper. We happened to be in the right place at the right time." I held a hand out to indicate the passage. "Your passengers should be getting something to eat and drink. Shall we join them?"

I led the way with Captain Allison beside me. Chief Gerheart fell in beside a stocky man with engineering flashes on his collar.

Mr. Ricks cycled the lock closed and secured it as we headed toward the gathered party.

Mr. Wyatt had lined up the mattresses on the deck and against the bulkheads so the visitors could sit and lean on something. The table itself served as a combination buffet and work station with several of the more lively looking passengers helping to make more sandwiches and ladle soup into china mugs.

As Captain Allison took in the scene, I could see the tension begin to seep out of her frame. I turned to the group behind me. "Please, help yourselves. Get something to eat and drink. Breathe a little bit and then we'll get our heads together to see what the next step is."

I put a hand on Captain Allison's arm to get her attention. "Why don't you and I and our Engineering betters grab some food and adjourn to the cabin. We can put our heads together there."

She nodded. I saw the two Engineers already had their heads together. I headed for the soup line myself but Mr. Wyatt caught my eye and nodded to two covered trays on the sideboard. "I thought you might like to leave this little operation to us, Skipper."

"Thank you, Mr. Wyatt. Very thoughtful of you."

I grabbed one tray, Chief Gerheart grabbed the other, and we led the way back out of the hubbub and up the ladder to the cabin. I popped open the door and deposited my tray on the head of the small conference table. Captain Allison followed me in but the view of her ship just outside the port drew her like a magnet. The packet had a much lower keel to dorsal profile so her bridge was right outside the armor glass and not more than ten meters away above a gently curving bow.

She smiled and, if there was a glitter in the corner of her eye, I didn't see it. I got busy with the two chiefs to make sure they didn't either. In just a few heartbeats we had plates of sandwiches, mugs of soup, and even a carafe of coffee distributed.

Captain Allison turned back to us. "I don't get to see her from this view very often, Captain."

"One of the oddities of shipboard life," I said. "You see everybody else in action, but seldom see yourself unless you're tied up someplace and not doing anything." I remembered my manners then and indicated Chief Gerheart. "Captain Allison, let me formally introduce my Chief Engineer, Gretchen Gerheart..." The two women shook hands briefly.

"Call me Allie, Chief."

"Greta."

Captain Allison turned to me. "And let me introduce you to my chief, Richard Green."

I offered my hand and he took it in a business like grip and a nodded politely. "Chuck works for me, Skipper."

"Call me Ishmael." I grinned at their reactions and some memories from my youth.

I realized they were waiting for me to sit. I hurriedly took a seat at the head of the table and helped myself to a bite of sandwich so they'd not feel constrained by protocol.

The short flurry of replenishment ended rather quickly. "So, let's open up this can of worms, shall we?" Seeing general nods around the table I turned to Captain Allison. "What's the condition over there?"

"Scrubbers at ten percent and failing. CO_2 approaching critical levels. You can breathe it still, but for some of those people–like the Carrolls and Wassinks–they weren't doing all that well when we picked them up." She shrugged. "The scrubbers just aren't engineered for that level of abuse, and we burned through our filter cartridges in nothing flat. We even picked up a few more at the Outpost, but they weren't exactly in first rate condition and they failed within a day or two."

I could almost see Chief Gerheart's wheels turning as the sapphire flashes of her eyes went back and forth between watching what the captain was saying and the expression on her chief's face. When the captain finished her report, Greta looked up at me with a small nod.

I turned to our guests. "Okay, then, it seems to me that our first priority is to clear that CO_2 load out of your ship. We don't want to add cleaning your bad air to the load already on our scrubbers. Can you vent most or all of your bad air now that the ship's not full of people? Replenish with a good air mix?"

The captain looked to her chief who nodded in return. "Should be easy enough now that we don't have to work around passengers, Captain, but what then?"

"Then we can open the locks between the ships and your people can go sleep in their own beds. We can set up some blowers to move the air between us, and send to the Orbital for some replacement cartridges."

Chief Green blinked. "Can your scrubbers handle us?"

Greta smirked. "We're a tad over-engineered for a crew of eight, Chief. I think when they built this hull they expected a crew of forty and built scrubbers for all of them."

"What they didn't build was bunks," I said. "We're going to get awfully cramped in here with all of your people on mattresses in the passages and mess deck."

Captain Allison looked down at her hands where they cradled the almost empty mug of soup. "As crowded as we all were on the

Voice, I'm not sure they don't see this as a step up, Captain, but you're right. One step at a time." She started to rise.

"Take a break for a minute, Allie." She looked at me. "We'll be all better off if we do this right and carefully the first time. Too much haste gets in the way of making good speed."

Chief Gerheart snorted but hid her face in her coffee mug.

"Chief, can we maneuver with the ships tied together? How solid is that coupling?" I asked.

The two chiefs looked at each other, obviously trading secret engineering wisdom telepathically. They got the same pained grimace almost at the same moment.

They broke their mind meld and Chief Gerheart turned to me. "It's about what you'd expect if we were docked, Captain. It'll hold us against minor jolts and stresses, but ..."

Chief Green added a bucket of cold water to my already sopping blanket. "And if we've got to keep the locks open to keep the air moving, then you won't want to risk breaking the seal. We could both lose a lot of air before they closed."

I leaned over in my chair to get a better look at the bridge repeater on the top of my desk. "Well, we're basically on a ballistic trajectory now with a decent delta-v against the orbital. We can coast along for awhile."

Chief Gerheart turned to her counterpart. "How long would it take you to vent and replenish your air?"

"Three or four stans. As long as we're suited up, we can flush it with nitrogen and keep hull pressure without having to worry about vacuum damage."

Greta grinned. "The Verminator Protocol."

Green grinned back. "Exactly."

Periodically ships needed to do a complete fumigation to rid themselves of the odd stowaway vermin that had followed man into space. That was usually done by flushing all the breathable air from the ship and filling it with nitrogen gas, sometimes laced with a fungicide. It was usually done with the ship docked and the crew safely ashore. There wasn't anything that would prevent it from being used in this situation, so long as the people aboard were suited and supplied with oxygen. The nitrogen would push all the carbon dioxide laden air out and would, in turn, be replaced with a clean mixture.

I glanced at the chronometer and nodded. "Okay, well, if you two chiefs would get on that? I think we can have these people in their own beds before midnight."

Chief Gerheart stood with a nod and an "Aye, aye, Skipper." Chief Green followed her.

Captain Allison settled back into her chair as they filed out and closed the door gently behind them. She sighed. "Now, we wait."

"No, now, we do paperwork" I grinned. "Do you need to send any messages?"

She shook her head. "I notified the owners already, and I've actually got a shipment of scrubber cartridges on their way out by courier." She grimaced. "It'll be expensive but cheaper than the alternatives."

"Yeah, dying is expensive and there are so many unfortunate forms to fill out."

She laughed a little tiredly. "Amen to that, Captain."

"Well, I need to send some signals to the owner and our agent on Jett. We're going to be a little late to dinner."

"Sorry about that, Captain, but thanks."

"Glad we could help."

I crossed to the desk and started putting together reports to DST's office on Jett for forwarding back to home office in Diurnia. Captain Allison helped herself to another mug of coffee and chewed half-heartedly on the end of a sandwich. I attached a copy of the distress call to my messages and sent them off with a priority routing.

"It was greed." I looked over to where Captain Allison stared into her coffee mug.

"Captain?"

"We got greedy. Or perhaps it's that no good deed goes unpunished."

I nodded sympathetically. "The number of passengers?"

She grimaced. "Yeah. We run this junket out to the Outpost on a three-legged course. It makes for a nice run with some usually polite passengers. Most of them aren't really high rollers. They just want to think they are."

"Really?"

"Oh, yeah. The real high rollers fly their own yachts. We get the people who are just looking for a little adventure. They work all stanyer and save for an exotic holiday. Some of them, it takes more than a stanyer." She sighed. "Me? I'd like a nice vacation on a desert island with no clock and my Chuck on call."

I must have looked surprised. She chuckled. "Oh, yeah. I'm sleeping with my engineer." She paused for effect. "We got married about twenty stanyers ago when I made captain. I tell him it's because I know how hard it is to keep good help."

We shared a quiet laugh, then she continued. "We had a group ready to head home. Almost a full load, but they'd met friends and they all wanted to come home together. One-Eye was just about fed up with them, too. They'd run out of funds and were just taking up spaces at his tables. All they had was their return tickets. One of our sister ships was supposed to pick them off in a few days but they were in a hurry and the owner said to take them." She stared dreamily into her coffee mug, riding the course of her memory. "It started out as just a couple over. By the time we pushed off, it was eight."

"They must have been very friendly to get extras into the ship. Where'd they all sleep?"

"With each other, I think. They weren't too concerned by it, and I didn't pry." She shook her head. "We'd gone as high as twenty-four before. It was a little close, but not dangerous. The models said we should have been able to make it, and we probably would have but for the contaminated cartridges we got from the Outpost. Odin said they'd been slightly used. I should have asked by what."

She sighed and stood to gaze out the port at her abandoned bridge.

"He didn't charge me much, and I should have known I got what I pay for out there."

I snorted. "Not just out there."

She huffed a quiet laugh in agreement. "Too true."

Conversation lapsed for a time. "How soon before the spare cartridges get here from the station?"

"Day after tomorrow." She looked haunted.

"Ouch."

"It was not looking pretty, Ishmael." She looked at me. "Thanks."

"I'm glad we could help."

She sighed. "Well, I need to go show the flag. Let them know what's happening." She put her mug back on the tray.

"I need to check on my bridge crew and see how we're doing."

We split up at the cabin door, she headed down, and I headed up to set the normal watch.

Chapter Forty-four
Jett Orbital: 2372-April-15

We finally docked at Jett around noon on the fifteenth–five days late and two full days behind the *Sarcastic Voice*. The courier rendezvous had gone without a hitch. With new cartridges, they were able to get their scrubbers back up and running long enough for the short run into the station. They'd been considerate guests but it felt good to get our ship back. The longer we drifted along with those locks open, the more likely it was that something would go wrong. I breathed a sigh of relief when we were finally able to secure it and get some sails up.

We needed a little more time to get turned around and catch up. We were just less lively at maneuvering than the lightweight fast packet. We'd already missed the deadline so it didn't cost us any more, except for a few more days of operational expense.

As per my agreement with Mr. Hill, I'd picked a can from the available cargoes list while we were still a couple days out. It wasn't anything to write home about, but a good solid cargo of ceramic heat tiles heading back to Diurnia. No priority or bonuses, but no deadline to miss and a good base rate. The next day Mr. Hill snagged a nice little priority can of thruster nozzle liners going the same direction. Their delivery deadline was nine weeks out, so we had plenty of time on it. Mr. Wyatt was holding out for something decent and he had some time. Being docked gave us the best data feeds and the highest probability that he'd be able to grab a hot cargo. We agreed that we'd not take anything with a deadline closer than the middle of June, which gave us about eight weeks to get from Jett back to Diurnia.

I had Ms. Thomas declare liberty as soon as we were tied down and cleared customs. First section took the watch and we settled down to a solid, four day stay. I planned to pull out on the morning of the 21st to give everybody a little break before we headed back to Diurnia. After the run we'd had, we all had earned a little down time.

Around 1400 I got a message from Captain Allison inviting Chief Gerheart and me to dinner, their treat. I found the chief in her office in Engineering finalizing the tankage operations and getting ready to swap out our own scrubber cartridges.

"Hey, Chief. Captain Allison invited us to dinner tonight. Feel like a little shore food?"

She looked up from her terminal and her sapphire-laced smile beamed over the top. "Oh, yes. I'm more than ready for a little shore food, Skipper." She pointed to the scrubbers. "And after swapping out these, I'm sure I'm going to have a healthy appetite. What time?"

"1900 at Adam's on the Eight."

"Oh, ritzy. I'll have to dress."

I chuckled. "I should probably find something to wear other than a ship suit, myself."

She squinted at me. "I don't know if I'd recognize you in civvies, Captain."

I laughed again. "I look pretty much the same, but I take your point." I tried to think back and was pretty sure that I had been in uniform since the day I first stepped onto the ship, barring a few stans when we were still docked at Diurnia or when I was asleep.

She grabbed the handle on the pallet load of scrubber cartridges and headed over to the scrubbers.

"Need a hand with that, Chief?"

"Why? We have an extra crewman who needs work?" She looked at me over her shoulder. "I didn't think we had anybody on punishment lately."

I shrugged and held up my own hands to show her. "I was thinking of these. Been a while since I got 'em dirty, and I feel the need for a little penance after missing that priority."

"Not your fault, Skipper. You and I both know that, but I'm glad for the help." She nodded toward the nearest scrubber. "This is the one that's due."

I started rolling up my sleeves and watched as she opened up the scrubber's cover and began rummaging around in the innards. "Yeah, maybe. But I still feel bad. The insurance will cover the operational costs, but the shares are worth zero on that trip and everybody worked hard. Doesn't seem fair."

She snorted and pointed. "If you'd strip the packing material off three of those for me, Skipper, I'll haul these old ones out." She stuck her head back into the case before waiting to see if I did it. "Besides, who said the universe is fair?" Her voice echoed inside the scrubber.

She had a point and I set to with a will. The new cartridges were easy to handle and relatively light. The used ones had a slimy texture and were a lot heavier. I laughed when I saw what it had done to my shipsuit.

She noticed the sludgy smear across my chest and arms and smiled. "It'll wash out, Skipper. It's all water soluable."

"Yeah, I figured as much. I was just remembering how messy the algae matrices were to change out back on the *Lois McKendrick*. Now that was a dirty job."

"You actually changed matrices, Skipper?"

"I was assigned to environmental for a time. I'm not much of an engineman any more, but I did my share of getting mucky back in my misspent youth."

"You're just full of surprises, Skipper." She said it with a smile and a little laugh. She stepped back from the scrubber and latched the case closed again. "That should hold her for a month or so."

I looked around Engineering. "How's she holding together in general? Any problems on the horizon?"

The chief grabbed a rag off the pallet and wiped her hands down as she considered. "Nothing I can think of, Captain. She's none the worse for wear on the docking and even the extra load of having twenty-eight extra people aboard for a couple of days didn't change much. The girls are in good shape. I think they liked the workout, frankly." She finished her mental inventory with a shake of her head. "Nope. She's going good at the moment."

"Okay, well, I'm going to go get cleaned up and maybe take a nap before dinner." I grinned. "Thanks for the exercise."

She snickered. "Any time, Skipper. Any time."

At 1845 I met Chief Gerheart at the lock. I'd dug out my civvies. It felt great to be out of a shipsuit and in a set of clothes that actually looked like clothing. Chief Gerheart came down the passage in a stunning black pantsuit with a ruby red silk blouse and matching pumps. Small sparkles of ruby glinted on her lobes. I heard Mr. Ricks stop breathing which reminded me to breathe myself.

She had a small smile and the sapphire eyes were as dazzling as the rubies at her ears. "Well, I'm glad to see I haven't completely lost my touch."

Mr. Ricks coughed and tried to pay attention to his console. I just smiled back. "No, Chief, I'd say, you hadn't lost your touch." I turned to Mr. Ricks. "The Chief and I will be guests of Captain

Allison up at Adam's on the Eight, Mr. Ricks. If you'd log us out? We should be back in a couple of stans."

"Aye, aye, Captain." He winked at me, and I had a bad feeling.

Chief Gerheart apparently saw it, too. She snickered.

Mr. Ricks keyed the lock for us and we stepped down onto the dock together. The crisp air of the docks bit into my sinuses and felt wonderful after the weeks of canned air on the ship.

Chief Gerheart looked over at me with a grin. "What? You don't like my air?"

I laughed. "We don't usually keep the ship's temperature this low, Chief." I took a deep breath. "It's bracing."

Behind us the lock started to swing closed. "We could, Captain. I think some of the crew might complain, but we could." She was laughing at me and I didn't care.

"I like your air just fine, Chief."

"Please, could you call me Greta or Gretchen? We're off the ship. Can we be people tonight?" Her eyes stabbed me with their intensity.

I thought about it and took a deep breath. I had to confess to myself, if not out loud, that the idea scared me. "Of course. Greta."

"Thank you..." There was a question in her voice.

I answered it. "Ishmael."

She gave me a kind of sideways smile and headed on down the docks to the lift. "Well, then, Ishmael, let's find Allie and Richard. I'm hungry enough to eat one of those scrubber cartridges."

"One of the new ones? Or one of the used?"

She looked over at me out of the corner of her sparkly eyes. "You're a sick man, Ishmael."

"Don't look at me! You're the one willing to chew on a scrubber cartridge."

She laughed and we walked a little faster toward the lift. Refreshing or not, the docks were cold.

Dinner with Allie and Richard was a comfortable affair and they treated us to a wonderful meal with wine and postprandial cordials. It was the first time since taking over the ship I had really let my hair down. Longer than I cared to remember, if I was going to be honest with myself. Being in the company of good hosts and intelligent companions made the evening very lively.

We lingered over our drinks until the staff began to look pointedly at the table. In their defense there was a line at the door and we occupied a prime spot. Adam's was a popular place for good reason. In the evening rush they needed to keep the tables turning and we had been camped for a couple of stans.

Allie bowed under the pressure of a rather pointed sniff from the *maitre d'* and thumbed the tab, signaling our departure. We trooped out into the curved orbital passage past a surprisingly long line of diners waiting to enter.

Outside, we shook hands all around and Greta and I bid them good night.

As we turned toward the lift, Captain Allison stopped me with a hand on my arm. "Thank you isn't enough, but thank you, Ishmael. I know you were late on your priority already and all that, but you came to our rescue and I can't bear to think about what would have happened to us if you hadn't."

I forced a smile. The memory of the bloated horrors on the *Chernyakova* came back to me unbidden and I tried to put them out of my mind. "I certainly couldn't sail by you, knowing you were in that kind of danger. Even if we'd still been in time. I'm just glad we could help. If we'd managed to get on the course we needed to make that delivery, we'd never have been in the position to help." I shrugged. "Guess it was the right course after all."

"Still." She looked a bit moist around the edges. "Thank you. If you ever need anything, get in touch, okay?"

Richard stood behind her and nodded along with each of her words.

"I will, and you're welcome."

Richard led his captain away going one direction and we headed toward the lift in the other.

After a few meters I looked at Greta. "That makes me uncomfortable. I just did what anybody would do."

Her breath puffed out in a quiet laugh. "You think so? I don't."

"You would have."

She looked over at me and shook her head. "I'm not a Deck officer. It wouldn't be my decision."

"Okay, hypothetically then, You would have."

She considered it for a moment before conceding the point. "Yes, all right. I would have." She paused for a heartbeat before continuing. "Captain Delman wouldn't have."

"You really think so?"

She nodded. "I do."

I considered that and wondered how any skipper in his right mind would have been able to sail past. Memories of the *Chernyakova* would not stay away.

We were almost to the lift when I remembered to ask a question that I didn't really feel right about asking while aboard. "So, what happened to the protective coloration?"

She gave me one of her crooked smiles and her eyes flashed at me. "You were right. I didn't need it anymore."

"Did anybody say anything?"

"What? When I stopped?"

"Yeah. It's rather a striking change."

She gave a half shrug. "With all the changes on the ship, especially with Gwennie not shouting and actually relaxed for the first time since I've known her, and Avery bustling about like a mother hen in the galley..." She shrugged again. "I think the only one who really was hit hard by it was Billy."

"Has it been a problem?"

She wrinkled her nose in contemplation. "No, he's just being a bit–I'm not sure what the term is. Maybe shy. He gets a bit tongue tied and nervous."

"You're a pretty imposing figure, in case you hadn't noticed." I smiled over at her.

She laughed. "That's funny coming from you, Captain, my Captain."

"Me?" I snorted. "I probably would have killed us all flying too close to that planet, if it weren't for you."

She shook her head. "You wouldn't have considered it at all, if not for me. I'm just glad I had second thoughts."

I pressed the call button for the lift. "Do you think we could have made it?"

"I don't know." She took a deep breath and let it out before looking me in the face with those sapphire stilettos. "I do know that you made the right choice. The downside risk was just too big and there aren't any do-overs out there. You miss once and you're dead." She shuddered and licked her lips. "Allie and Richard got lucky because you made the right choice."

She stood way too close to me at that moment, but luckily the lift dinged and the doors slid open. We stepped aside and let a laughing party of spacers troop out. Several of them smiled at us as they passed. One nodded his head and offered a jaunty, "Evenin' Captain," as he passed.

I stepped into the lift after Gretchen. "I wonder who that was."

"Who?"

"That spacer. He said, 'Evenin' Captain' but I don't recognize him and I'm not in uniform. How did he know?"

She started to laugh and held a hand up to her mouth. "You really don't know?"

I thought about it for a tick as the lift dropped us quickly back to the docks. "It shows already?"

She laughed again. "You're a funny man, Ishmael Wang." She looked me in the eye then. "It showed that first time you stepped aboard."

"But I wasn't Captain then. Just a jumped-up first mate."

She just shook her head and laughed some more as the lift dinged again and the opening doors flooded the car with icy air. I think she laughed all the way back to the ship.

CHAPTER FORTY-FIVE
JETT ORBITAL: 2372-APRIL-20

Part of my mind nagged me about staying too long in port. My bad boys hadn't been in trouble since we'd left Diurnia. It's not like they'd really had much of a chance on Welliver, but I was a bit leery about giving them new opportunities on Jett. On the other hand, they were my crew, and having spent quite a lot of time with Mr. Hill over the previous months, I knew he really wasn't the thug-like hard case his service jacket portrayed. Mr. Schubert was shaping up to be a rather impressive entrepreneur. The extended stay gave the co-op a chance to shake out their procedures and, if the snippets of conversation I'd overheard were any indication, the results from the port stay would be rather good. Mr. Ricks was still working into the role of morale officer, and spent his off-duty mornings scouring the flea market for games and amusements that the crew might take advantage of while underway. Mr. Wyatt had provided a small cupboard on the mess deck for storage and the flea market had already yielded a chess set, a backgammon board, and a clever deck of playing cards made of thin sheets of plastic to cut down on the wear and tear of many hands and stanyers of use.

The company's insurance examiner visited soon after docking. I had to file a full report on how we happened to be late on the priority, including plots of the fly-by and a full debrief on the encounter with the *Sarcastic Voice*. There was rather a lot of attention paid to the fly-by and why we didn't skim closer and try a little harder to make the time, particularly in light of the improved wind conditions. I confess I was feeling a little defensive on that score, and I suspect the examiner picked up on it. By comparison, he paid little attention to our rescue of the *Sarcastic Voice*. When he was done, he held out his report for me to sign, and then credited the ship for a flat rate per diem for operations. It was actually a pretty generous rate when compared to our actual expenses, so I thanked him and showed him off the ship.

The extended stay also gave me time to hunt down the advanced mathematics courses that I'd promised Mr. Schubert. The Union Hall had a complete set of study aids in a variety of ancillary disciplines including biology, accounting, engineering, and astronomy in addition to an extensive collection of maths. They weren't free, but they also weren't expensive. I grabbed the whole set for the ship. Math messed up everybody working up through the ratings and I could envision the material being very useful.

By noon on the fourth day, we were ready to get underway again. Mr. Wyatt had picked his can—another priority, which would put the two of them neck and neck in terms of the contest. When we'd come out of Welliver, Mr. Wyatt had a very small lead. The run to Diurnia should see that reversed. In neither case was the lead more than a few hundred credits. The Jett run earned us nothing in terms of share because of the penalty clauses built into the contract. At least we didn't lose any either, thanks to the insurance payment.

Mr. Wyatt had planned a rather extensive last-day luncheon at my request. Second watch had the duty and I had a little surprise for them. I passed the word among the officers and so we had the whole crew, such as it was, on hand.

Just before the lunch mess opened, Mr. Wyatt gave me the nod and I stuck my head out into the passage and called to Mr. Ricks at the lock. "If you'd hang out the Do No Disturb sign, Mr. Ricks? Lunch is about ready."

"Aye, aye, Captain."

In a tick he walked onto the mess deck and skidded to a stop when he saw the whole ship's company lined up in formation there.

Ms. Thomas gave the command. "Company, ah-ten-HUT! Ordinary Spacer Zachary Ricks, front and center."

He looked a little confused as to where he was supposed to go until Ms. Thomas looked pointedly at a spot on the deck in front of me.

He nervously took his post and after a moment stood at a passable attention.

I smiled at him and raised my voice. "Ladies and gentlemen of the *Agamemnon*, it gives me great pleasure to announce the promotion of Ordinary Spacer Zachary Ricks to the rank of Able Spacer." I held out the shoulder patches that indicated his new rank and he took them with a smile. "Congratulations, Mr. Ricks. Try to hold onto them this time."

He grinned back at me. "Thank you, Captain. I'll do my best."

He snapped a very tight salute and held it until I returned the honor.

"Dismiss the company, Ms. Thomas."

"Company, dis-MISSED!"

Lunch was a joyous occasion and if nobody was on the lock for a stan or so, I don't think anybody on the docks noticed. Even with the happy hubbub, we'd have heard the call bell. As it was the last afternoon in port, Mr. Hill and Mr. Schubert left very shortly after the lunch mess and headed for one last pass at the flea market. I was pleased to see Mr. Pall organizing an outing for later in the evening. Mr. Hill and I would have the duty and would miss it. I liked the idea that Mr. Ricks and Mr. Schubert would be engaged in activities which–if not strictly speaking, controlled–were not entirely on their own for at least part of the evening. My experience in bailing them out of security in Diurnia wasn't one I wanted to repeat, even though they'd paid off their fines on that first run to Welliver.

After we secured the mess deck, I took Mr. Wyatt aside. "Avery, don't bother with making dinner tonight. Take the afternoon and evening off. Enjoy it."

He looked startled. "Skipper?"

I chuckled. "You've made every meal on this ship for weeks. Mr. Hill and I will be the only ones aboard at dinner time and we can certainly fend for ourselves for one meal. In fact, let me handle breakfast for you, too. You sleep in tomorrow. I'm going to be up all night on OD watch anyway so why not?"

He seemed somewhat distressed. "Are you sure, Captain? I don't mind. Really."

I smiled at him. "I'll make it an order if I have to. Go eat somebody else's cooking for once and have a nice sleep in tomorrow. You'll feel better for it."

He adjusted to the idea, if slowly, and I left him to ruminate while I went to grab a nap. Port duty midwatches weren't difficult. I was almost caught up on my reports so I really didn't have a lot to do. I had a suspicion that staying awake might be a problem.

Around 1730 I woke up ahead of my alarm and felt refreshed. I'd apparently made peace with myself over missing the priority shipment. The greater good of saving lives and influencing people helped, I think. There's always the possibility of profit on the next run as long as we don't die on the current one. It was rather a morbid thought, but I took comfort in it.

I snagged a quick shower to freshen up, slipped into a clean shipsuit, and headed to the mess deck. I found Mr. Schubert going over the co-op's books and Mr. Hill looking at a block of perforated plastic on the table.

"What do you have there, Mr. Hill?" When I got closer, I saw what it was. A wave of nostalgia washed over me.

"It's a game, Captain. I found it up at the flea market this afternoon. The guy in the next booth was selling them and it looked interesting. He called it a Crib-batch board." His brow furled. "Crib-something."

"Cribbage, Mr. Hill. Cribbage." I pronounced it distinctly for him.

"You know this game, Skipper?"

My mind flashed back to long evenings across the board from my mother back on Neris. "I haven't seen a board in decades, Mr. Hill, but I think I remember how to play. Does it have pegs?"

"Pegs, Skipper?" He looked down at the board with a frown. "The ones he had on display did."

I picked up the block and turned it over. A small metal door slid open and revealed four small pegs molded from some kind of plastic or resin with the shape of a tiny stylized rocket on the top as a knob. I held the board so Mr. Hill could look in. "Pegs, Mr. Hill."

I glanced up at the chrono on the bulkhead just as it clicked to 1744. "We need to relieve the watch, Mr. Hill, but I suspect we'll have a chance this evening to explore this more." I latched the door shut and handed him the board. "Nice find, Mr. Hill."

"Thank you, Captain."

The change over went smoothly enough and by 1815 the shore party began gathering on the mess deck. Ms. Thomas showed up first in a natty denim jacket and jeans with a very attractive peasant style blouse under. "Nice outfit, Ms. Thomas. I think this is the first time I've seen you in civvies."

"Thanks, Skipper. I don't go out much." She stopped herself. "I didn't go out much. I think I might do it a little more often now." She smiled. It was a good look for her.

Mr. Ricks showed up next with Mr. Schubert close behind. They were in standard slacks and jersey garb. Enough pockets for money, tablet, ID, and not enough loose fabric to provide handles should the need arise. I eyed them warily. "You gentlemen aren't going out looking for trouble, are you?"

Mr. Ricks shook his head. "No, Captain, but trouble sometimes finds us."

Mr. Schubert added. "It's all we have, Skipper, and like he said. Trouble sometimes finds us."

I gave him a stern look. I'm not sure he bought it.

Mr. Wyatt joined the party in a non-descript pair of slacks and a jacket that was a little short at the cuff and a little long on wear. "Good evening, all."

Ms. Thomas beamed at him. "I wouldn't have recognized you out of your shipsuit, Avery!"

Mr. Wyatt grinned and nodded as Chief Gerheart entered the mess deck looking radiant in a gorgeously tailored jacket and slacks suit embroidered with a deep red flower pattern. She was accompanied by Mr. Pall in an outfit that convinced me that I really needed to take the men folk from the ship out to visit a good men's shop at the next port.

I took them all in. "Looks like the gang's all here. Try to stay out of trouble tonight, huh?"

Ms. Thomas grinned. "I'll keep any eye on 'em, Skipper."

"See that you do, Ms. Thomas. They're a rum lot but the best in the fleet."

She did a little mock salute with one finger to her brow. "Aye, aye, Skipper, and yo ho ho!"

They all laughed and headed for the lock. I followed in their wake. Mr. Hill and I watched them parade off the ship, Mr. Pall leading the way and Mr. Wyatt and the chief in the rear.

Mr. Hill chuckled as the lock closed behind them. "That looks like trouble on the hoof, there, Captain. Are you sure they're safe?"

"Who, the crew?"

"No, Skipper. The station."

We shared a laugh at that. "What would you like for dinner, Mr. Hill. I'm cooking tonight."

"I'm open, Skipper. Although I am getting a bit hungry so fast is better than long."

"I know what you mean, Mr. Hill. I feel the same way." I pondered for a tick. "How about I raid the galley and see what leftovers Mr. Wyatt has tucked?"

"I'd settle for a ham sandwich skipper. Seriously." He grinned at me.

In the end, I managed to rummage up a few ham sandwiches, some pickles, and assorted other small foods including some fresh fruit. We even had cookies and ice cream for dessert.

After dinner and the subsequent cleanup, I rummaged in the games locker for a pack of playing cards and took the cribbage board out to the lock along with one of the work stools from the galley. "Mr. Hill? If you've a mind to, perhaps we can see if I remember how to play after all these stanyers?"

"You really know how to play this game, Captain?"

I shrugged. "I'm pretty sure. It's an old, old game, but my mother loved to play. Until you brought this aboard, I'd forgotten all about it, so I'm probably a little rusty, but I think so, yes."

We set up the board and settled in to pass the time while waiting out the crew's return. The sounds echoed down the passage in the quiet of the docked ship. The snapping of the cards on the desk, the rhythmic call and response as we added our pips and counted our scores took me back to another place, another time.

Around 2200, Chief Gerheart returned alone and found us still playing. "I've had enough merriment for one night. What are you two up to?"

I smiled at her. "I'm just teaching Mr. Hill how to beat me at cribbage. He's an apt student."

"It seems pretty even to me, Skipper. I'm only up by two games."

I turned to the chief. "Gave up on the party?"

"Dinner was good. Mr. Wyatt has a rather dry wit when left to his own devices, but they were heading out for some music and dancing. I'm thinking I'd rather not get underway with a hangover."

"Probably wise, Chief."

Mr. Hill grinned. "It's not a fun way to get underway, Chief."

She grinned back at him. "Bitter voice of experience, Mr. Hill?"

He nodded.

She chuckled. "Well, I'll let you gentlemen get back to your game. I need to get some sleep. Morning comes before breakfast and I'll need to get the fusactors back online before that."

We both bid her good night and she sauntered down the hall and we could clearly hear her walk up the ladder and the faint sound of her stateroom door close.

"I had no idea sound carried that well in a quiet ship, did you, Mr. Hill?"

"You can't hear that much with all the equipment running, Skipper, but when we're docked, and in the middle of the night? Yeah, you can hear an awful lot."

We finished off the game in progress, but packed up the board after that with Mr. Hill up seven games to four and demonstrating a fine understanding of the mechanics of pegging. I left him to study his Cargoman Two exam and I returned to the cabin to discover the 'almost caught up' pile of reports had multiplied while I wasn't looking.

I sighed and dug into the pile.

Around 0100 I realized that the ship was still quiet and that I hadn't heard the lock open since I'd returned to the cabin. It was about time for me to stand up and walk around a little anyway so I headed down to the brow to check with Mr. Hill.

He shook his head. "No, Captain, nobody's back yet."

I thanked him and headed into the galley to make up a fresh pot of coffee. It was too early to think about organizing breakfast, and I'd already decided that I'd make pancakes with fruit for the morning meal. If the hour were any indication, I suspected that breakfast might be somewhat sparsely attended.

The ready light had just blinked on the pot and I was reaching for a mug when Mr. Hill called from the brow. "Skipper? You might want to–"

The call buzzer rang, interrupting him.

"–come out here."

I heard the lock start to cycle and hot-footed to the lock, arriving just as the big doors latched into the open position. A burly Orbital Security man stood at the foot of the ramp. Behind him, in a more or less straight line, stood my crew.

I spared a glance at Mr. Hill who shrugged in return before heading out to see what was going on.

It didn't take long for me to take in some of the more prurient details. The two ratings looked like they'd escaped the worse of it, whatever it had been. Mr. Schubert had a bruise beginning to form on his right cheek and Mr. Ricks kept licking at a small cut on his upper lip. Mr. Pall's ensemble was improved greatly by having the jacket torn in several places and one sleeve actually missing. He didn't seem to have any obvious wounds but he was standing oddly. Mr. Wyatt had one eye swollen nearly shut and his rather nondescript outfit would have to be destroyed because I doubted that much blood would come out. I assumed the blood wasn't his, at least in its entirety, or security would have had him in medical. Astonishingly, it was Ms. Thomas who looked the worst. Her jacket hung in actual tatters and she looked like she'd lost a fight with a revolving door. The effect was exacerbated by the fact that she was missing one shoe. I almost winced to think of how cold that deck must be on her foot.

A small squad of officers stood in loose formation behind my line up of crew. The lead officer gave me a chance to finish my once-over before speaking.

"Good morning, Captain. I believe these belong to you?"

I glanced at his name plate. "Yes, Officer Henry. They bear an uncanny resemblance to my ship's company. They seem a bit more worn than when last I saw them. Wherever did you find them?"

"Well, Captain, some of them were under a pile of angry, drunken spacers. Those two on the end seemed to be trying to dig them out when we arrived." To my surprise, he nodded at Ricks and Schubert.

Schubert shrugged in response to my surprised look.

"I see. And what do I owe for this rather unfortunate delivery?" I swept a hand down the line. "Fines? Damages? Medical bills?"

Officer Henry shrugged. "The owner isn't claiming damages and we couldn't really get a clear handle on who started it. Medical says there was no permanent damage to this lot, although there are a couple of other crews that might be on light duty for a day or so." He shrugged again. "We won't charge 'em if you'll promise to keep them aboard until you leave." He looked somewhat apologetic. "Between you and me, Captain, I just don't want to do the paperwork. It's too close to the end of shift."

I chuckled. "You have my sympathy and complete understanding, Officer Henry. May I take them off your hands now?"

"Oh, please do, Captain."

I turned to them. "Ms. Thomas, if you'd gather your little damage control party on the mess deck, I'll be along shortly."

"Aye, aye, Captain." She led the way and the rest followed with Mr. Ricks bringing up the rear, ambling along with a slight limp.

The security man just watched them go and when they were safely aboard turned back to me. "You're getting underway later this morning, aren't you, Captain?"

"That's my plan. I'm assuming the crew will be actually fit enough to stand to for a few stans."

"They're a spunky bunch, Skipper. Gotta give 'em that." He chuckled. "What's the phrase? You should see the other guy."

I couldn't help but chuckle a bit in return. "Well. They'll have plenty of time to heal up on the ride home, and that should give me a chance to order leashes and muzzles for them before we arrive."

He laughed at that and gave me a little salute. "Good luck, Captain, and safe voyage."

"Thank you, Officer Henry. And thanks for bringing them back to me. They're a disreputable lot, but they're all I've got."

He chuckled again and turned, waving to his squad, headed back down the docks toward the lift.

I shook my head and climbed back up the ramp into the ship and Mr. Hill keyed the lock closed behind me. I could hear faint murmurs from the direction of the mess deck and Mr. Hill regarded me with an almost incredulous smile. "Aren't you glad you had the duty tonight, Mr. Hill?"

He laughed and shook his head. "Actually, no, Skipper. I have a feeling that when we find out what happened out there tonight, I'm gonna wish I'd been there to see it!"

He caught me funny with that one and I barked a soft laugh. "Good point, Mr. Hill." I sighed and shook my head as I walked down the passage and toward the brightly lit mess deck.

Their murmuring died out as I got closer to the mess deck. By the time I got there it died out completely. The crew stood lined up and braced more or less at attention. Given the nature of their injuries, I didn't press it.

Ricks and Schubert looked resigned. Mr. Pall looked the most ill at ease, but I'd look uncomfortable too if I were wearing those clothes. Mr. Wyatt looked apologetic, but Ms. Thomas looked almost radiant. Inwardly, I shrank. Somehow I knew I wasn't going to like this story, but I needed to find out what it was.

I sighed loudly. "Anybody have anything to say? Mr. Ricks? You're junior man here. Comments?"

"I told you, Captain. Sometimes trouble just finds us."

"So you did, Mr. Ricks. Somehow I thought you might avoid it tonight."

"So did I, Captain. But we didn't start it. Exactly."

Mr. Wyatt started to say something, but apparently thought better of it and closed his mouth.

"Mr. Schubert? Any comments?"

"No, Captain. We did our best, but security showed up and broke it up."

"Broke it up, Mr. Schubert?"

"Yes, Captain. We'd almost gotten Ms. Thomas and Mr. Wyatt out of the pile when they arrived. Another five ticks and we might have gotten away."

I glanced down the line at my first mate and cargo officer. Ms. Thomas continued to gaze straight ahead, but Mr. Wyatt was beginning to look a little more abashed.

"Mr. Pall? Comments?"

"Well, Skipper, they started it. After dinner we went down to the Gravity Well for a few drinks and maybe some dancing. We got to talking with a couple of the other crews."

I waved a hand to indicate his sartorial disarray. "That must have been rather an interesting talk, Mr. Pall."

He glanced down at himself. "Yes, Captain. After a few getting acquainted drinks, they started talking about the ship."

"Which ship, Mr. Pall?"

"This ship, Captain. The *Agamemnon.*"

"Curiouser and curiouser." I stepped down the line to where Mr. Wyatt was beginning to fidget. "You were privy to this conversation about the ship, Mr. Wyatt?"

"Well, yes, Captain. We all were."

"And what were these comments that caused such damage to your clothing and bodies? And I trust all this blood isn't yours,

Mr. Wyatt."

He looked down and took in the dark shambles of his coat and shirt. "I can't be sure, Skipper. Some of it's mine. I had a nosebleed for a while."

"Go on, Mr. Wyatt."

"Well, we got to talking about the ship, running the double in from Welliver, missing the priority, but rescuing the *Voice*. Unfortunately, the *Agamemnon* has something of a bad reputation, Captain."

"I'm aware of that, Mr. Wyatt. I thought we were working to turn that around."

He looked more than a bit abashed at that. "Yes, well, the news hasn't spread." I noticed that his eyes kept being drawn to Ms. Thomas, but he kept bringing them back to front. It was almost as if he was trying not to look at her.

"I see." I let him off the hook and moved down to Ms. Thomas. "Ms. Thomas? Comments? I thought you were going to keep an eye on them."

"I did, Captain. When they started talking about what a bad ship the *Agamemnon* was, I kept Mr. Pall from starting anything more rash. Sticks and stones, Captain."

I glanced down at Mr. Pall.

He looked at his feet.

"Something else happened?"

"Well, they were bad-mouthing the company, too, Captain, and at one point I thought Mr. Wyatt might take serious offense."

I looked to Mr. Wyatt.

"DST is no more a corporate vulture than any other freight hauler, Skipper. They had no right–" He cut himself off as I raised an eyebrow.

"Corporate vulture, Ms. Thomas?"

She shrugged. "They had some stronger words–nasty words like unreliable, untrustworthy–that sort of thing."

I nodded. "I see, Ms. Thomas, but that apparently didn't start the fight."

"Well, no, Captain but it was sort of the prelude."

"And judging from the smell, I'm guessing that the drinks kept flowing during this friendly discussion of the relative merits of ship and company?"

"Yes, Captain. Although I think most of the smell is coming from the spilled drinks. The waiter had just brought the next round when..." Her voice trailed off.

Suddenly, the rest of them looked like perhaps that would be a good time for a hull breach.

"When what, Ms. Thomas?"

"When it started, Captain."

"I see. And what was the trigger?"

She mumbled something that I couldn't quite understand.

"Ms. Thomas in all the weeks I've known you, I have never heard you mumble."

That got a short snicker from Mr. Schubert that he quickly squelched.

"He started talking about the captain, Captain."

"Me?" I was so surprised that I just blurted the word.

"Yes, Captain. We'd had rather a lengthy discussion of the fly-by. How we'd planned to try to graze the planet but were concerned for the safety of the ship and all."

"And that led to a discussion of me, Ms. Thomas?"

"Yes, Captain." She forgot herself and focused on my face for a heartbeat before resuming the approved stare-into-nothing required by being at attention. "They seemed to know you from before."

"I've been here many times."

"They said that, Captain. They made some comments about how you never go out carousing with the crews."

"And that's what started it?"

"No, Captain. They also had some unkind words about your parents and their marital status."

"And that's what started it?"

She shook her head slightly. "No, Captain. They got going on that fly-by thing again."

"What about the fly-by, Ms. Thomas?"

"Well, Captain, they thought we should have taken the first course and delivered the priority on time."

"That's as may be, Ms. Thomas. Dockside piloting is always easier than doing it with the sails up in the Deep Dark." I looked at her with a frown. "That wasn't what started it, was it?"

For the first time she looked uneasy. "No, Captain."

"Then what did start it, Ms. Thomas?"

She mumbled something.

"You're mumbling again, Ms. Thomas."

She mumbled the same thing again. I could just make out a phrase. "He called you..." and then it petered off.

Mr. Wyatt supplied the offending words. "He called you a chicken, Captain."

I almost laughed aloud. Ms. Thomas stiffened. "Yes, Captain. He called you a chicken and then he started putting his thumbs in his armpits and flapping his elbows making squawky, chicken noises. It was intolerable, Skipper."

"Then what happened, Ms. Thomas?"

She shrugged. "I slugged him."

I had the unnerving experience of hearing Mr. Hill's barked laugh echo down the passage and remembered how well sound carried. To his credit, he choked it off after the single explosion.

"His friends didn't take kindly to this, I take it?"

She shrugged again. "No, Captain. About half a dozen of them came over the table after me."

"More like ten," Mr. Ricks said.

"Was that when you got dragged into the melee, Mr. Ricks?"

He shook his head. "No, Skipper. She was doing pretty well on her own. Chooch and I just kinda hung back and watched the floor show." He nodded at Mr. Schubert.

"On her own?"

"Well, Mr. Pall tried to help, Skipper."

I looked at Mr. Pall. "It doesn't sound like you were that effective, Mr. Pall."

"No, Skipper. I was never very good in bar fights, but I managed to absorb some of the damage."

"Mr. Wyatt? You were just standing by?"

"Not at all, Captain, but do you know how hard it is to restrain a heavy worlder?"

"You were trying to restrain Ms. Thomas?"

"Well, at least get her out of the bar and into the passage, Skipper, yes."

She glared at him. "Yes, and if you'd have given that one dock monkey as much attention as you were giving me, we'd have beaten those..." She remembered herself and went back to attention.

I felt the unreasonable and almost irrepressible urge to laugh. It would have set a bad example and I managed to stifle it. Hearing Mr. Hill's not quite stifled giggles from the brow did nothing for my self control.

I sighed. "Well, you're home now and in more or less one piece. We'll be getting underway soon, and Ms. Thomas, you have the watch in a few stans. You might wanna grab a snack and a few ticks of shut-eye before you relieve me at six." I glanced at the chrono. It seemed much later, but it was just going on 0200.

"Yes, Captain."

I stepped back from the line-up. "Dismissed."

Mr. Pall led the way off the mess deck, followed closely by Mr. Schubert and Mr. Ricks. Mr. Wyatt helped Ms. Thomas find a couple of sandwiches in the cooler before they followed in the wake.

I sat at the table and held my breath until I heard them get to the top of the ladder. Ms. Thomas was practicing her low alto growl on Mr. Wyatt and even though I couldn't hear what she said, the effect of that heavy world voice was intoxicating. I could hear their footfalls on the way up the ladder and a moment of silence at the top.

One door opened. One door closed. Other than a short and muffled giggle, I didn't hear anything else.

I put my head down on the table and laughed quietly to myself for a few heartbeats and then crossed to the coffee pot and drew two mugs. I took them out to the brow and Mr. Hill and I settled in for a few more games of cribbage as we counted down the ticks left to the watch. If there were any other sounds in the ship, they were drowned out by the slapping of the cards and the counting of the points as we played.

Chapter Forty-six
Jett Orbital: 2372-April-21

Ms. Thomas and Mr. Schubert showed up to relieve the watch right on time. I had pancake batter and several kinds of fruit ready. The oven kept the bacon warm but lent its aroma to the festivities.

"Good morning. What kind of pancakes would you like this morning?"

"Granapple for me, if you have it, Captain." Ms. Thomas seemed none the worse for wear after her excursions of the night before, not counting the bruising on her forehead, left eye, and along the right side of her jaw. I wasn't sure what the swollen looking lip was from.

"Just plain batter for me, sar." Mr. Schubert looked a bit rumpled and his bruised cheek looked rather painful. He appeared in good humor, though. "I like mine with just lots of syrup and butter."

"Of course. Coming right up." The nice thing about pancakes is that, with a hot griddle and the right mix, it really takes next to no time to make up fresh cakes. By the time they had retrieved coffee and settled at the table, I had plates of hot food ready.

Mr. Schubert excused himself to relieve the brow watch and returned with Mr. Hill. I had Mr. Hill's blueberry pancakes all ready and was still trying to decide what kind I wanted when Chief Gerheart sauntered onto the mess deck to join our merry band. Her eyes widened when she saw Ms. Thomas's face and she slowed for a step but offered no comment.

"Morning, Chief, what kind of pancakes would you like?"

"Good morning, Captain. If I could have mine plain with some sliced apple on the side?"

"Coming up, Chief."

She crossed to the pot and pulled a mug of her own before taking a seat. It took me a tick to realize that she'd left a space beside Ms. Thomas instead of taking her usual position immediately to her left.

"How are the girls this morning, Chief?"

"They're waking up, Skipper. They had a nice sleep and they're just puttin' on their makeup now." She eyed Mr. Schubert's bruised face and then turned to look at Ms. Thomas.

Ms. Thomas saw the look and grinned. "You missed the party, Chief. Things really started jumping after you left."

"So it would seem. Did you win, lose, or draw?"

Ms. Thomas shrugged. "I think we have to call it a draw."

Across the table Mr. Schubert nodded in agreement. "Orbital security showed up before we could get Ms. Thomas and Mr. Wyatt out of the pile up, sar. I think if we'd had five more ticks, we might have claimed a win."

The chief turned to look at Mr. Schubert when he spoke but then turned back to Ms. Thomas. "For somebody who doesn't go ashore much, Gwen, you sure know how to have a good time."

Ms. Thomas chuckled a little.

I slipped a hot plate of griddle cakes onto the table in front of the chief and she turned to on them with a will while I settled into a pile of granapple pancakes of my own. Mr. Schubert made short work of his and excused himself to go to the brow. Mr. Hill left a few ticks behind him, probably headed for a short nap. We had about three stans before the tugs showed up and I intended to follow his example myself.

Around 0630 Mr. Wyatt joined us, looking like two kilometers of corrugated metal. He appeared both a bit sheepish and proud of himself. I found it a most astonishing expression. I'd finished my pancakes and was fighting the urge to make another stack so I took the excuse to get up and cross to the griddle. "What kind of pancakes would you like this morning, Mr. Wyatt?"

He pulled his eyes away from Ms. Thomas who beamed back at him and turned to me with concern splashed across his face. "Oh, I can fix my own pancakes, Skipper." He started to head toward the griddle but I waved him off.

"Grab some coffee, Avery. Have a seat. I can handle a few pancakes." He looked uncertain. "I can make it an order if need be, Mr. Wyatt." I grinned at him.

He smiled back. "Well, thank you, Captain. Any blueberries left?"

"Coming up."

He crossed to the urns and drew a mug of coffee. Out of the

corner of my eye, I saw him start to take his usual seat to the left of the chief before he registered that the chief was sitting in the spot he usually claimed as his own, leaving a space for him beside Ms. Thomas. He hesitated for a heartbeat and the chief leaned sideways giving him extra room to take the spot she'd left. It was a clear indication. He gave a little shrug and sat with a little smile in the chief's direction and a shy nod in Ms. Thomas's.

The chief leaned forward over her almost empty plate to get a good look at Mr. Wyatt's face. "You look like you had a little fun last night, too, Avery. Don't you know officers are supposed to set an example?" She was grinning.

He laughed a little ruefully in return. "Well, Mr. Ricks and Mr. Schubert were observing and it wasn't until the second crew started to help the first that they stopped laughing long enough to try to help."

She chuckled. "I'm almost sorry I missed it."

Mr. Wyatt shook his head but winced. "Don't be."

"I said almost."

I slipped a plate of pancakes in front of Mr. Wyatt and started to clean up the galley a bit while they shared some good-humored table conversation on the relative merits of various bar fights they had known. The chief's depth of knowledge on the subject surprised me, while Mr. Wyatt seemed to be lacking a ready supply of war stories. I pondered my own limited experience in that regard. Not that I hadn't occasionally been around when they broke out, but I was usually close enough to the periphery to slip out without much damage.

The clock ticked up to 0700 and I started to secure the griddle and dispose of the left over batter, when Mr. Pall dragged onto the mess deck. His face wasn't too badly marked if you didn't count the bloodshot eyes and the pinched hangover look. "Good morning, Mr. Pall. I've just secured the griddle but if you'd like some pancakes...?"

He moaned a little. "No, thank you, Captain. I don't think I can eat just now." He shuffled to the coffee pot and drew a mug. He settled gingerly onto his usual seat and leaned forward onto the table, his head hanging forward on his neck.

The Chief smiled sympathetically. "Looks like you had fun last night, too, Mr. Pall."

He snorted and winced. "Bloody pirates." He tried a tentative sip of his coffee.

I finished securing the galley and, out of respect for Mr. Pall's condition, didn't rattle things any more than absolutely necessary. Hangovers were not something I had a lot of experience with either, but I knew how debilitating it was to have people making fun of you by making unnecessary noise while you suffered one. I refilled my mug and took my seat.

"Since we're all here, are we ready to go?"

"Cans have been locked down since yesterday, Captain. Stores are topped off."

"Engineering is ready. Fusactors came up nicely and the sail generators are on safety standby. We restocked on cartridges for environmental. I even picked up a couple of extras." She shrugged. "Won't hurt and they've got a real long shelf life."

"Astrogation is updated as of yesterday, Captain. I put a tentative plot up but I'll need to refine for actual pull out time. Should be in Diurnia in about six weeks."

I turned to Ms. Thomas. "Sounds like we're ready to go to me, Ms. Thomas."

She nodded. "I think so, too, Skipper. Ship's in good order and crew is present or accounted for."

"All right, then. I'm going to go grab a couple stans of rack time. I should be up at 0900 to get ready for a 1000 pull out. Mr. Wyatt if you'd organize some box lunches?"

"Already on it, Skipper. Boxes are staged in the ready cooler."

"Thank you, Mr. Wyatt." I rose to leave the mess deck and the chief followed me, slotting her dishes into the cleaner.

"I need to check on the girls and get stuff secured myself. I'll be back up to help with the lunches in a bit, Avery."

"Thanks, Chief. More the merrier."

I fell into a dreamless sleep almost as soon as my head hit pillow. I had to fight my way back up when my tablet bipped me awake. I took a longer shower than normal, and used a little colder water than I was comfortable with to try to shake some of the cobwebs out. I'd been pushing too hard and needed to get more rest while underway. I chuckled at that thought as I shut off the water and toweled off.

On the mess deck I found the lunch box brigade just finishing a small mountain of lunches. Ms. Thomas smiled and said, "A courier came for you while you were sacked, Skipper." She nodded to a middling-sized package on the end of the table.

I grabbed a cup of coffee and then went to look at it. The label indicated it was from "Plunkett's Junkets" and showed an office address up on three-deck. I pulled the tab and opened it up. Inside I found a note and a rather large folio.

I scanned the note before looking over at the curious eyes doing their best not to stare. "It's from the company that owns the *Voice*." I held up the note and read it aloud. "Dear Captain Wang.

Words alone cannot express my gratitude for your help in rescuing Captain Allison and the passengers and crew of the *Sarcastic Voice*. Your selfless action and the hospitality offered by your ship and crew can never be repaid, but permit me to offer you these small tokens of our esteem and the assurance that, should there ever be anything we can do to help you, you need only to ask. Sincerely, Jacob J. Plunkett, CEO Plunkett's Junkets."

I looked up at beaming faces. Ms. Thomas came over and looked in the package curiously. "What'd they send, Skipper?"

I pulled out the folio and held it up so all could see. The cover read, "A Hundred Stanyers of Cinema, 2270-2370." Inside were hundreds of entertainment cubes cleverly slotted into pages labeled with decades.

Mr. Wyatt laughed. "That should hold us for a while."

Ms. Thomas smiled. "That's a nice touch. How thoughtful!"

I handed her the folio to thumb through and reached down to pick up the loose packaging when I spotted another slip in the bottom of the box. Curious, I pulled it out and stared at it. The shock on my face must have showed because everybody froze in place and looked at me.

Mr. Wyatt asked. "What is it, Skipper?"

I had to blink a couple of times to get time to actually process it. "It's a receipt for shipment delivery on our last load."

They looked at each other and then back at me.

I tried to explain. "Plunkett paid the freight on the cans from Welliver."

Mr. Wyatt focused first. "Plunkett paid? At what rate, Captain?"

I looked up at them. I couldn't believe it myself and I held the slip in my hands. "Full priority."

There was stunned silence for a heartbeat.

Ms. Thomas cocked her head. "Full priority as in what, Skipper?"

"As in the priority rate we contracted for in Welliver. They paid it in full." I held up the receipt so they could see it.

A single line was scrawled across the bottom in a black stylus. "It's the least we could do. JP"

There was a moment or two of silence before Mr. Pall raised his head and blinked back his headache. "Can we keep it, Captain?"

He winced as we all laughed and I assured him that it was already a done deal. The funds were already in the ship's accounts. "I'll do the accounting and distribute the shares on the way back to Diurnia."

Chapter Forty-seven
Diurnia System: 2372-June-01

The run back into Diurnia from Jett was strictly routine. It didn't seem possible that we'd been gone almost six months. Mr. Pall threaded the needle for us quite nicely and in something under seven weeks, the tug nudged us toward Diurnia Orbital and home port. We experimented a bit with the jump, shooting for a point somewhat higher in relation to the plane of the ecliptic to see if the winds there were more stable. Diurnia has less in the way of orbital real estate than Jett does and several of the larger bodies were on the far side of Diurnia's primary which cut down on the local disturbances.

The only thing out of the ordinary–and it rapidly became normal–was the relationship between Ms. Thomas and Mr. Wyatt. Nobody said anything, just accepted it. Perhaps there'd been more there than I'd been aware of before, based on a mumbled "About time," that I overheard from one of the ratings.

I had no complaints personally. They both reported to me and it created no conflicts in the chain of command. If anything, I found that Ms. Thomas was much more diligent than before in terms of her relationships with the ratings and Mr. Wyatt was especially careful of her dietary requirements.

We also instituted "movie night on the mess deck" and Mr. Ricks proved to be an amusing and erudite critic of film. I don't know if he had a secret encyclopedia of movie trivia on his tablet or if he really did know a lot. Perhaps some of each because the films jumped around from night to night, never any two films in a row in the same decade or genre. We got around the "who's on watch" problem by showing the same film for three nights, which gave everybody a chance to watch it twice, rather than shorting somebody who didn't get to see it at all. It worked out surprisingly well.

One other thing marked the return home. I started practicing my tai chi for the first time since taking over the ship. It was a discipline that I'd picked up at the academy and carried with me for all the stanyers I'd been aboard the *Tinker*. The gym there had a small floor for those members of the crew who practiced one of the martial arts and I'd taken full advantage of it. The *Agamemnon*, by comparison, had no room in the workout room to do anything like tai chi. It didn't require a huge amount of space but it needed more than was available. It occurred to me as I was getting off the treadmill one day that the main passageway provided more than enough room. We tended to ignore it as a ship's space since it really was a transitional area but it was the single largest uninterrupted deck space aboard. I found that it offered more than enough space for me to do a full Jung Long Form without having to worry about bumping into a bulkhead or cramping a movement. I was very rusty after so long without practice, but within a few days it evened out, and by the time we got to Diurnia, it felt smooth and fluid again. The moving meditation worked its magic and I found myself relaxing into it, carrying that sense of being in the moment with me after the session was over.

By the time we nuzzled into the lock at Diurnia, we already had our cans lined up for the next trip. I'd snagged a low level priority shipment of machine parts going to Dree which set our course up. Very shortly thereafter, Mr. Hill managed to grab the contract on a middle priority can of pharmaceuticals and Mr. Wyatt got a container of unprocessed silicon wafers that also had a middle level priority. I was waiting on the final tally from the shipments from Jett, but it looked like the two of them were still neck-and-neck.

Frankly, I was about ready to spend a night or two ashore. The *Tinker* was not a long hauler, and had a pretty regular route. Sometimes it was Jett, other times Welliver, but wherever we went, we always jumped back home. I'd never been gone more than two and half months in all the time we'd been married and I was ready for a warm homecoming.

We docked just before noon and first section had the watch. It didn't take long for us to clear customs and get settled in. I had Ms. Thomas declare liberty just past 1300. While I wasn't the first one off the ship, nobody seemed to begrudge me not being the last either. I had packed a kit already and only needed to grab and go. By 1305 I was walking down the passage toward our apartment.

I have to confess to a bit of nervousness. If Jen were still on the same schedule, she'd be home. She normally reported to work around 1600 and then worked until 0100 or so. There were more people around in the afternoon and I met several of them as I headed toward home. I met my cross-the-hall neighbor heading for the ice machine in his stocking feet. He seemed almost embarrassed to be caught out without his shoes. I'm not sure why. I often made the same trip myself. I nodded and smiled as we passed.

When I slipped into the apartment, it was still dark although I heard rustling in the bedroom as I crossed the kitchen. Before I got to the door, I spoke. "Honey, I'm home."

I stepped around the corner and she sat bolt upright in bed. She took my breath away. "Ishmael?"

"You were expecting the plumber?" I smiled.

"No!" She caught herself. "I just didn't expect you until tonight!"

"We docked before noon. Customs cleared us right away and I came right home. I don't need to be back until 0600."

I crossed to the bed, dropping my kit at the foot and crossing over to my side to start stripping down. Boots, shipsuit, boxers and tee all went flying as she launched herself at me dragging me down so strongly that we both rolled over to her side in a giggling mass of limbs and skin. She was quite vocal and I was glad we were there in the afternoon and not when the neighbors might be around. It didn't take too long for me to not be thinking at all.

Around 1500 she extricated herself and climbed into the shower. I must have been exhausted because I fell right back asleep again and slept through until almost 2200. It's one of the side effects of the watchstanding merry-go-round. When you finally get a chance to sleep, it all hits at once. The release of being off the ship and home, to say nothing of the vigorous homecoming, served to tell my mind and body that it was time to rest. I slept like a log.

My bladder finally drove me to crawl out and once up, I slipped on my boxers and padded out into the kitchen. I wasn't in the mood for big food or major productions, so I just made a sandwich and washed it down with some fruit juice before thinking that bed was a good place to wait. I could feel more sleep in my immediate future and I expected I wouldn't get much between her homecoming and my having to leave to take over the watch at 0600.

I was right.

I didn't get much but my tablet had to bip me to get me moving at 0500. I was muscle sore, and a bit raw in places, but I felt great as I got into the shower and sluiced off the accumulated slime. The scent of her soap and shampoo tickled my nose. It made me feel warm and at home all over again.

Time was ticking and I couldn't linger, so I toweled off quickly and padded naked out to the dimly lit bed room. My kit was where I'd tossed it, and I fished out fresh boxers, tee, socks, and a rolled up shipsuit. It was a matter of just a few ticks to get the fresh clothes on, gather up the dirty and stuff them into my bag. I crossed to my side of the bed and sat down on it, leaning over for a good morning, good-bye kiss and was rewarded with a warm snuggle that threatened to make me late.

"See you tonight, hon."

She mumbled something but was asleep again before she finished the thought. I grinned and reached down for my boot. The chrono on the side table said 0525 and I had plenty of time.

It occurred to me suddenly that my boot was not going on. I had it by the top and was stuffing my foot into it, but it wasn't going. I pulled it off to see if I'd dropped something into it and it wasn't until that moment that I realized it wasn't my boot. For a few heartbeats I thought it might be Jen's, but I leaned over and pulled out the mate from under the edge of the bed. Not Jen's. They were a very serviceable, station-style work boot. Almost every stationer had a pair like them. These were scuffed about the toe a bit and a tad run down at the heel. About three sizes too big for Jen and at least one size too small for me.

There are moments in one's life where things become at once crystal clear and very dark. As I sat there on the bed I remembered the day Neris Security knocked on the door to tell me that my mother had died. I realized I was holding my breath. I tried to breathe out and in, and out and in. It seemed to work. Sort of. I leaned down and put them back on the floor. A little to one side, I found my own boots and I realized that I'd stopped breathing again as I slipped them on. So I focused on breathing in, breathing out. I remembered the way my brain would vapor lock when we had our "getting underway fights" back before I was a captain. That's what it was doing. It had shut off. I had to remember to breathe.

I wanted to scream. I wanted to rail against the unfairness.

But I had to admit to myself that the unfairness was being away too long. Being gone when I should have been here. I had to force myself to breathe in, breathe out.

The chrono clicked to 0530 and I had to move. My ship needed me. I needed my ship.

I stood and grabbed the strap on my kit. The pair of boots was still there on the deck. I could see the darker shape of them against the floor covering. Without thinking, I stooped and grabbed one, stuffing it into my kit as I left the apartment for what I knew would be my last time.

The path to the docks was clear at 0530. Most of the people who needed to be there were already there and those who didn't were still closeted. I don't think I met a single soul on the way. I'm not really sure, but I did breathe in and breathe out. The lift doors opened onto the docks and the frigid air tingled into my nose and down to my lungs. I breathed it out, hot and moist. One step at a time and the lock opened on my key. Mr. Ricks was on duty and I tried to smile a little but it was a brittle thing that wasn't working. I could see it in his eyes. I shrugged and nodded and escaped down the passage.

In the cabin the wide port showed the scarred white metal of the orbital and that seemed appropriate. I didn't need to focus on breathing any more. It seemed to be coming more naturally. The lock was closed, my shore tie was cut. I could focus on the ship, on the next watch.

Watch. Yes.

I tossed the kit onto my bunk and used the sink in the head to splash some water on my face. I needed to get a bit more control before I faced any more of the crew. I was the captain. I could do it.

At 0545 I found Mr. Pall on the mess deck and managed to hide behind a mug of coffee. He wasn't very much awake and I managed to fool him long enough to relieve the watch and send him off to wash up a bit before breakfast.

Mr. Wyatt, however, gave me a very concerned sideways glance. "Good morning, Skipper."

"Good morning, Avery. What's for breakfast? I'm starved." I sounded okay to me. Good solid voice. The right level of volume and intonation. I just pretended I was me being captain. I knew what I was supposed to sound like. I just did that.

He didn't seem fooled, but he played along with me. In my heart I thanked him profusely. "Omelets this morning, Captain. Can I make you one?"

I glanced at the chrono on the bulkhead. "Mess isn't for another few ticks, Mr. Wyatt, but if you'd like to test the pans, I'd be happy to help out." I tried the smile again. I don't think it actually worked that time either, but at least Mr. Wyatt didn't seem frightened by it as Mr. Ricks had earlier.

"Anything in particular you'd like to have in it, Skipper?"

I crossed to the table and took my seat. "Surprise me, Avery. You've never made a bad omelet for me and I'm sure you won't start now." The smile came more easily. The familiar surroundings helped. There was enough oxygen in the air. Chief Gerheart saw to that with the utmost diligence.

It seemed like I had just seated myself when he slipped the plate in front of me and I tucked in. "This is delicious, Avery. What all did you put in here?"

"Oh, a little of this and that. Some sweepings from the meat cooler, and a bit of grit from the lock. Mr. Ricks found a bit of mildew that was a particularly poignant color, as well."

"It really is wonderful, Mr. Wyatt. You've outdone yourself again."

"Thank you, Captain. I knew you'd like it."

The rest of the crew gathered and I thought I did fairly well at pretending to be me. Ms. Thomas and Mr. Wyatt had a quiet conversation at the stove top and I thought they looked remarkably domestic. They really did make a good couple.

None of the ratings lingered over breakfast. Mr. Hill went back to the lock and the other two headed up to the flea market. They'd picked up some nice items during the stay at Jett.

Mr. Pall seemed barely awake and ate mechanically, almost falling asleep in his plate.

The chief on the other hand sat across from me and looked at me with those sapphire daggers. Once she arched an eyebrow, but she made small talk without asking questions.

Ms. Thomas and Mr. Wyatt sat beside each other and talked shop and ship, odds and ends. They glanced in my direction occasionally, but offered no pointed questions.

The food helped and before I really knew it I'd polished off the omelet, a couple slices of toast, and even a pastry. I sat back in my chair, and looked across the table at them.

Bless them, every one. They didn't say a word.

I took a deep breath and let it out slowly. "No, I'm not all right."

The chief choked on a laugh. "Really? You seem perfectly fine to me. Doesn't he seem fine to you, Avery?"

"Never better, Chief. Just marvelous." They were twitting me but they had soft eyes and softer smiles.

"Thank you. I'll be in the cabin if anybody needs me. I've got reports to finish."

Ms. Thomas nodded. "Of course, Skipper."

I got up and slotted the dirties out of habit before pulling a fresh mug of coffee from the urn. I took several sips from it as I headed for the ladder.

Mr. Wyatt stopped me. "Captain? Is that coffee okay?"

"Yes, Avery. Why?"

"Captain, that's the cold pot. I haven't had a chance to rinse it out yet. You might want to warm that up a bit..."

I stopped and looked into the cup. Yes. It was stone cold, the mug ice in my hand. "I thought it seemed a bit cooler than normal,

Avery. Thanks." They didn't say anything as I emptied the cold coffee into the sink and refilled the mug with hot. The china warmed to my touch and the heat sunk into me in some fundamental way. I took a sip of the dark, aromatic brew, drawing the scent of it into my lungs as the warm liquid fell down my throat. "Yes, much better. Thanks."

I managed to make it to the cabin without further mishap and settled at my desk. The reports needed to be reviewed and the overnight logs approved. I forced myself to read carefully. I focused on the words and the meanings. A mistake here and somebody might die. I got through several of them and as I worked I felt the spinning in my head begin to ease. At noon, I went down to the mess deck and had a light lunch before returning–with hot coffee the first time–to the cabin to complete the reports. The routine soothed me and by 1500 I had finished off the paperwork. I had three more stans of watch and then I'd be off duty.

The thought hit me hard. Off duty, but then what?

I went into the sleeping cabin and began to unpack my kit, dropping the dirty clothing into the cleaner and stowing the toiletries back in the head. I had almost forgotten the boot—blocked it from my mind, more like—and when I pulled it out of the bag I had a moment of befuddlement before it all came back and I felt foolish.

I took the boot back to my desk and sat it down in the middle. I looked at it for a long time.

At 1730 I got up, stripped off my clothes, and took a shower. When I got out, I put on an undress uniform and fastened the gold stars to my collar. I grabbed the empty kit bag and stuffed the boot into it before slinging the strap over my shoulder and heading for the mess deck.

Ms. Thomas and Mr. Wyatt were waiting for me there and at 1745 we relieved the watch. With the formalities served, I smiled. Really smiled for maybe the first time all day. They looked relieved but not yet relaxed.

Mr. Wyatt asked, "Will you be staying aboard for dinner, Captain?"

"No, Avery, I have some business I need to deal with ashore, and then I'll grab a bite there. I should be back within two or three stans."

I left them getting ready to open the dinner mess and headed for the lock. I met Mr. Schubert coming in with a bundle of goods from the flea market and stood aside while he wrestled it into the locker. "Good day at the flea, Mr. Schubert?"

"Very good, Skipper. We're getting the hang of it now, I think."

"Carry on, then." I smiled and nodded as I left the ship and keyed the lock closed behind me.

The oh-one deck on the orbital is where all the offices and support staff for the docks are located. One level down from the docks, it was open for business around the clock. Ships and their crews were often at the mercy of schedules that knew no day, no night, just now. By 1830 I was wrapping up my business with Ms. Audrey Pacquette, Solicitor.

"Are you sure about this, Captain?"

I sat there for a full tick. Was I sure? "No, but it's what has to happen."

"But you haven't talked this over with your wife? It's normally done with the two parties in the same room at the same time. It cuts down on–how do I put this–ambiguity? She'll have to sign the agreement and if she's never seen it how can you be sure she'll agree to dissolving the marriage on the grounds of irreconcilable differences?"

I fished in my kit and pulled out the boot. I reached over and, to Ms. Pacquette's horror, placed it on the center of her blotter topped desk. "Deliver the papers in that."

Leaving the lawyer's office, I felt empty. I had almost a full day before I went back on duty and normally when in home port, I'd spend the time at the apartment. I must have stood there in the passageway for a full tick trying to think of what to do, where to go. My stomach growled to let me know that it had been a long time since lunch, and my feet took their cue without my having to think about it.

The lift dropped me down one deck and opened up to the familiar smell of Over Easy. I wondered how much business they must get just from that one factor. Spacers coming in from the cold of the Deep Dark, walking out of their ships filled with canned air, crossing the frigidly cold and mechanically freighted dock, getting into the lift and dropping down to the oh-two deck for a little R&R and when the lift opens, they're hit, quite literally, between the eyes with the warm aromas of coffee, bacon, and toast.

I followed my nose and found myself sitting at my favorite stool at the long counter. The guy behind the counter was a new one I hadn't seen before, or maybe having been absent so long, I just didn't remember. His badge said "Phil" and he waited for my order with that little chin up look they all seemed to have. A posture that said, "What can I get ya?" without actually speaking.

"Coffee, high test, Frank's finest, three rashers, three over easy, double toast."

He smiled a little smile and nodded once as he reached for the metal clad pot under the counter. "Welcome back."

"Thanks."

He finished scribbling the order and tore it off the anachronistic pad of paper, slotting it into the wheel at the pass through. "Order up, Sammy."

He moved on down the counter–filling cups, clearing dishes, keeping the customers happy and moving. More than a few eyes watched him go, male and female. I took a moment to look around the place. It wasn't as full as normal. Not too surprisingly, the dinner hour was one hour that Over Easy didn't really have a lot of draw. A few tables were full and about half the stools at the counter. One other waiter worked the floor and Phil was alone behind the counter. It would fill up later as late night revelers looked for sustenance, or maybe one last chance at a decision on who to take home.

It wasn't too long before Phil got back down to my end again and slid a plate of hot food in front of me.

I dug in with a will and, if the familiar home-spun fare didn't fill the hole inside me, at least it helped warm the chill a bit. As I worked down to the plate I think my mind started catching up with me. I started thinking again, instead of just reacting.

I wanted to feel hurt and angry and betrayed, something hot and passionate. What I felt was numb and cold. For seven stanyers I'd asked her to wait for me while I went haring across the quadrant and in return, I paid her rent and visited her a few days every few months. If I were going to be brutally honest with myself–and sitting there in Over Easy with the empty plate staring up at me from the counter, I couldn't help but rub the salt in my own wounds–aside from the coming home part, it hadn't really been all that great for me, either, and I really couldn't find it in me to blame her for finding what she needed somewhere else. It's cold in the Deep Dark, and if life on the orbital wasn't exactly Deep Dark, in a certain sense, we all carry a bit of the Deep Dark inside.

I sighed and ran the last corner of toast around the plate before popping into my mouth and washing it down with coffee.

Phil brought the tab and I thumbed it, before heading back out into the passage. I wasn't quite ready to go back to the ship so I took a spin around the oh-two deck, strolling past the shops, restaurants, pubs, and clubs. Down here was the antithesis of the cold of the docks. All the extra bodies gave the air a moist texture that the environmental systems never caught up with. There was a constant hubbub of coming and going, of greetings and farewells. I looked at the faces going by me and noted the various looks–some smiling, some frowning, some thoughtful as if trying to decide something, and others jovially unfocused from having perhaps one or four too many drinks. A cross-section of the universe strolled the deck beside and around me, thickening and becoming more active as the chrono clicked toward the later evening hours in station time.

I'd forgotten–or perhaps blocked–that The Miller Moth was on the oh-two deck and my circumnavigation of the passageway would take me past the open door. It was coming up on prime time for the pub and a quiet cascade of voices came from inside. I couldn't help but look in as I walked past and caught sight of Jen behind the bar, smiling and laughing at a customer as she drew him a beer. She didn't look up and I kept walking steadily.

Something in that glimpse gave me a certain peace. I couldn't explain it, but it was as if, peeking into her life from the passage outside underscored what our relationship had been. I really didn't know what her life was like, day in and day out. Stanyers ago I'd had some romantic notions about how we'd make it work and what life would be like together, but we'd never really been together. We only had these little glimpses into each other's lives before I left again, leaving her to live her life alone.

That feeling of being alone crashed over me and made me stumble once as I realized that she wasn't the only one who'd been lonely. Over the stanyers, my shipmates had become, in a very real sense, my family, but like a family, some part of me was always reserved from them. They were my brothers and sisters, or perhaps cousins, aunts, and uncles, but they were never my wife, never my lover. They offered the companionship against the Dark but never really took away the cold and I realized that I'd been cold for a very, very long time.

Ahead of me, Over Easy and the lift came into view again around the curve of the passage and I closed the loop on my circuit of the orbital. I felt suddenly very tired. Some part of my brain worked at solving the equation of how much I wanted anything that might be left in the apartment, the function of a desire to just walk away balanced against the salvage rights for an abandoned life. As the lift doors closed behind me, my hand wavered over the button pad.

I realized that I couldn't really remember what I might have left in the apartment and I'd be unlikely to miss any of it. Everything that meant anything to me was already aboard ship. The realization saddened me, but also provided a solution to my emotional calculus. I punched the button for the docks and headed for the ship.

Mr. Schubert logged me back aboard with a sympathetic smile. "Good evening, Skipper."

"Hello, Mr. Schubert. How did the co-op do today?"

"Very well, Captain. We unloaded the last of the leftovers from before and Zack found some really nice tapestries late in the afternoon. We were able to pick up several at a bargain price."

I smiled. "There are always better deals in the afternoon, Mr. Schubert."

He grinned in return. "So we're learning, Captain."

I headed into the ship and stopped at the door to the mess deck. Ms. Thomas and Mr. Wyatt played chess at the table and Ms. Thomas looked up as I stopped. "Good evening, Skipper. How are you doing this evening?"

Mr. Wyatt sat in my spot so they could play across the table and be comfortable. When he saw me, he started to get up but I waved him back down. "I'm feeling a little better this evening, thank you, Ms. Thomas, but I think I'm just going to go up to the cabin and get a good night's sleep."

They both smiled sympathetically but offered no words, for which I was grateful.

I nodded at them and bid them good night before heading up the ladder and stepping into the cabin. The reflection from the side of the orbital just outside the armor glass filled the room with cold, white light and cast the main objects in the room in bold relief. The glare on the pastel yellow walls lent a sickly glow to the room that I'd never really noticed before. I flicked on the overheads, but the added brilliance stabbed my eyes and I shut them off again. My body said it was night-time and I needed less light, not more. I crossed to the sleeping cabin and pulled the slider shut, throwing the room into near total darkness with only the glow from a bridge repeater on the bulkhead to offer enough light to see by. I stripped out of my uniform and hung it up. I toyed with the idea of putting on a shipsuit, but the weight of fatigue overwhelmed my desire to do anything but wash my face and go to bed.

As I crossed to my bunk, I did something I couldn't ever remember doing on board a ship. I stripped out of my ship tee and boxers, tossing them into the cleaner on the way by and slipped my naked body between the cool, crisp sheets. It felt decadent and luxurious, and as the smooth fabric warmed around me, I slid down the soft curve into sleep.

I woke as gently as I'd gone to sleep, surfacing from dream state to reality in a comfortable warm glow and rolling over to see the chrono on the bulkhead click over from 0522 to 0523. I weighed the hedonistic urge to savor the moment of sleepy comfort against a day's worth of possibilities, starting with one of Mr. Wyatt's breakfasts.

Breakfast won.

I crawled out of bed and padded naked into the head to do the needful.

The shower finished waking me and fresh clothing felt good on my skin. As I slipped into my boots, I looked around the sleeping cabin and realized just how sterile the environment was. The sunny yellow color really only made me look jaundiced in the light of the overhead and there was nothing that gave the place any kind of lived-in look. I snorted when I realized that I'd seen hotel rooms with more personality.

Crossing through the main cabin on my way down to breakfast, I realized that it wasn't any better. The glare from the orbital's skin did absolutely nothing for the yellow on the bulkhead, and even the richer color of the bare, accent wall looked muddy and uneven in the light. I eyed the spot above my desk where I still hadn't framed and mounted my master's license.

Mr. Wyatt's breakfast was as delightful as I'd hoped it might be, a lovely egg-bake with savory sausage and potatoes with a compote of fruit with a yogurty dressing on the the the side. Mess was brief and conversations subdued but companionable enough. If they gave me the occasional weighing glance, I didn't blame them. Ms. Thomas and Mr. Schubert excused themselves after the meal and I helped the chief and Mr. Wyatt clean up, while Mr. Pall got caught up on the OD logs.

As we finished up, the chief gave me one of her sapphire glances. "Any plans for the day, Skipper?"

"Yes, actually, I have several errands to run today." I hadn't really given it a lot of conscious thought, but my brain had apparently been hard at work while I'd been eating. I smiled at her. "I think it's time I decorated the cabin."

It must have come at her from off the plane of her mental ecliptic because her face went blank for a moment as she processed what I'd said. "Decorate the cabin? You thinking of hanging drapes?" Her tone was light and amused.

I considered that idea. "Drapes. Hm. I hadn't actually thought of that, but now that you mention it, I ought to do something there."

Her smile became more bemused than amused and she just arched one eyebrow. "I'll be interested to see what you do with the place, Skipper." She glanced sideways toward Mr. Wyatt who looked on with a certain amused smile of his own.

The more I thought about it, the more I realized that I liked the idea. "If you'll excuse me, I need to see a man about a horse." I gave them a little smile and headed off to the cabin to retrieve my license before heading down to the chandlery.

It was only a matter of a couple of ticks and I was checking out at the brow when another thought crossed my mind. "Mr. Ricks? Mr. Schubert said you'd managed to pick up some tapestries yesterday at the flea?"

"That's right, Skipper. I think some of them might be rugs

actually, but the lady was selling them at a bargain rate at the end of the day so she didn't have to pack them up and drag them away." He grinned. "We got a couple of dozen."

"May I see them, Mr. Ricks?"

He shrugged. "Of course, Skipper." He went to the locker and swung open the doors. He pulled a couple of totes from the shelves and pulled out some heavy hangings. They were in a variety of colors, leaning toward lush earth tones of brown, gold, green, and red. Some were highly textured and others showed bold tribal patterns.

"Mr. Ricks, these are exquisite."

"Thank you, Captain. I thought they'd make us a nice profit at Dree."

I grinned at him. "I don't think you're going to actually get all of them to Dree before they're sold, Mr. Ricks." I pulled four of them from the stack–a large one with a subtle pattern in shades of red, one of the middle sized ones with green and gold, and a pair of small, highly patterned pieces in shades of black and brown. "How much for those, Mr. Ricks?"

He looked startled. "You're buying them, Skipper?"

"Depends on the price, Mr. Ricks." I grinned at him.

He shrugged. "You can have them at cost, Skipper. If it weren't for you, we wouldn't have any of them."

"How much is that, Mr. Ricks?"

He gave me a price. "That was a good deal, Mr. Ricks. Nicely done." I pulled out my tablet and credited the co-op's account with the price he'd given me plus ten percent. "If you'd log these to my mass allotment and set them aside? I've some errands to run and I'll pick them up when I get back."

"Of course, Skipper." He nodded and started re-stowing things while I headed out of the lock and down to the chandlery.

Arranging for the frame was simple. They stocked several styles of frame and matting and even offered to do the mounting for a modest fee while I waited. I took them up on the offer and went in search of paint. I wasn't really sure what color I was looking for but with the images of the tapestries fresh in my mind I narrowed the choices down to a few neutral ones before settling on a base color of pale gray with blue overtones and two highly saturated accent colors–a rich, ruby red and midnight blue. I took the paint chips with me and stopped for the license before heading back to the ship. I wasn't about to buy the paint until I'd checked the colors against the tapestries, but I was pretty sure I had the winning combination in my hand.

When I got back aboard, Mr. Ricks had my tapestries rolled in a bundle for me. I hefted them under my arm and headed up the ladder. Chief Gerheart saw me from the mess deck and came out to help me wrestle the roll up to the cabin. She chuckled all the way up.

"What's so amusing, Chief?"

"When you said decorate the cabin, you really meant decorate the cabin, Skipper." She flashed a sapphire-tinged smile in my direction. "I had no idea you were this serious."

By then I had the cabin door open and we dropped the tapestries onto the bench under the port. "Just look at this place, Chief." I waved my arm around at the empty walls, and vacant shelves. "I've seen hotels that looked more lived in."

She shrugged and nodded her agreement. "Very true, Skipper, but you have had a few things to do since you came aboard."

I sighed and nodded, perhaps a bit ruefully. "Very true." I pulled the framed license out of the box and held it up to the bulkhead. "What do you think, Chief?"

She nodded. "Looks good."

I left the frame on the desk and pulled the bundle of tapestries open, draping the largest one over the table and leaving the smaller ones spread out on the bench. I pulled the paint chips out of my pocket and started holding them up to the tapestries and then the walls.

The Chief leaned against my desk and observed it all with small smile curving her lips. As she watched me, the amused look shifted to sadly sympathetic. "I'm sorry, Skipper. This has to be hard for you."

I didn't look at her. "Yeah. It's one of those things. Better late than never, and seriously overdue." I shrugged. "We try to fix what we can, heal where it's possible, and keep moving, though, right?" I turned to look at her.

She nodded shortly and sighed. "Yep. That pretty much sums it up. Sucks to live through, though."

I gave my own little shrug of agreement. "Well, yeah." I held up the dark blue chip to see what the wall with the port on it would look like. "What do you think? Dark blue around the port? The gray-blue on the rest of the walls?"

She came to look over my shoulder to see what I was seeing. "You're going to put that big red tapestry on the bulkhead by the door?"

"Yeah. The other three in the sleeping compartment. Small ones on either side of the rack and the bigger one on the wall beside the door."

She looked at the other chips in my hand and pulled the red one out, holding it up beside the blue. "It's your cabin, but if it were me? I'd put this red around the port. It balances the red you're gonna have over by the door and that blue gray is neutral enough that the red will stand up and frame the Deep Dark while we're underway."

"What about the blue?"

"Paint the sleeping room blue. Use the blue-gray as accent color in there on the wall above the head of your bunk. It'll help keep it from turning into a cave and make a nice foil for those two small tapestries."

I spent a half a tick picturing it in my mind's eye. "Yes. I like that. Thank you, Chief." I looked at her and she smiled back. "Would you like your stateroom painted?"

She seemed a bit startled by the idea. "I hadn't thought of it, Skipper." I watched her focus shift inward for a heartbeat as she considered it. "Lemme think about it and get back to you."

"Sure thing, Chief. Just let me know."

She turned and looked around the cabin once more before turning her gaze back on me. "I'll do that, Skipper." She smiled then and headed for the door. "Well, I better go check on the tankage. Have fun decorating."

The Cabin seemed a lot emptier with her out of it. I sighed before picking up my tablet and placing a call to DST's office. As luck would have it, Mr. Jameson and his paint crew were available to start work at 1400.

Chapter Forty-nine
Diurnia System: 2372-June-05

We got underway for Dree just before noon. I'd made the offer to paint staterooms and berthing areas to all the crew, but nobody took me up on it. I left the offer open and allocated funds to an accounting line in the ledger. The co-op had done well, and they were beginning to get their processes down. I noted that they'd already replaced the goods I'd bought from them.

Jen sent a note on the morning we got underway. It read, "I'm sorry."

Part of me wanted to know which part of it she was sorry for. The little animal part of me kept feeling betrayed, but there was a more rational part–perhaps a colder part–that wouldn't let me ignore the reality that my long absences and short, infrequent returns were as much a factor as anything. She always played second fiddle to the ship, and as much as the little animal kept screaming his rage, I had to admit to myself that we really had no life together and never had. We had a contract that should have been dissolved long since.

I sent back a reply. "Me, too."

As the tug pushed us out towards the Deep Dark, I felt the ache begin to subside. If there was no compass pointing back to Diurnia any more, there was also no string pulling harder with each day. I'd always believed that when the lock closed, it severed my connection to Diurnia and the people there. For stanyers I'd been very successful in compartmentalizing but for the first time in a long time, there was no compartment and I finally realized just how wrong I'd been.

"Any word on pirate activity in the area, Mr. Pall?"

He seemed a bit startled by the question and I realized we'd been riding along in near silence since Mr. Wyatt had brought us our lunches at noon. "Not in this quadrant, Skipper. We should be clear to the jump point."

"Excellent news, Mr. Pall. Thank you."

"You're welcome, Skipper."

I glanced at Ms. Thomas. I know she saw me look but she studiously kept her focus on the console in front of her.

I settled back in my chair and felt the ship beneath me. It felt good.

Around 1610 the tug gave us our final boost and turned us loose to coast to the safety limit where we'd be able to raise the sails. I looked up at the drop-down repeater and had to admire Mr. Pall's elegant plotting. We'd been working on the wind flow models ever since Jett. It was fairly well established that the winds above and below the plane of the ecliptic were more laminar–less disturbed by the passage of the system's planets, asteroids, and other assorted paraphernalia. Most astrogators tended to ignore that as being an insignificant difference at the scales we operated on. I wasn't so sure myself, and Mr. Pall and I had agreed to try sailing a little higher and picking courses that were diametrically opposed to the system's center of mass to try to gain the shortest route to the burleson limit as we could. A day or two made a big difference in our operating expenses and if we could carve off two or three on each trip it would mean better profits over the long haul.

I had to marvel over how much the technology had improved just since my days on the *Lois*. New field integrity work back in the '60s meant we could have sails that were substantially larger now, and sail correspondingly faster. The *Agamemnon* was actually rated at two metric kilotons higher than the *Lois*, but we could make the run out to the burleson limit a week or so faster. Of course, being a bulk hauler, the tare mass on the hull was a third of what the Lois's had been so some part of that gain was inherent in the ship itself. Still, it startled me to realize that I'd been at it long enough to actually recognize the improvements.

"Coming up on the safety limit, Captain."

"Thank you, Ms. Thomas. If you'd notify the chief engineer?"

"Done, Captain."

By 1730 we were well underway with all sails up and drawing nicely and I gave the command to secure from navigation stations. First section would have the watch for a few ticks, which gave Mr. Pall and Mr. Ricks a chance to freshen up before they took it for the evening. Mr. Hill and I would have the evening off to rest up before taking the midwatch. We were back on the merry-go-round again.

Dinner was a jovial affair with Mr. Wyatt going all out to put on a feast of roast fowl, curried potatoes, and a delightful goulash of mixed vegetables. He'd been working on his soup stocks and the practice showed in a delicate opening broth laced with a collection of savories and textures. For dessert, he produced a fresh fruit pie stuffed with apples, pears, and raisins.

The crew set to with a will and good humor. If I seemed a little more subdued than normal, they were gracious enough to grant me the space. After helping to clean up after, I begged off and headed to the cabin claiming the need to rest as an excuse. Truthfully, I did need to rest. The stay at Diurnia had drained me, but I was just as conscious that my emotional state bled over into the crew and I needed to minimize that to whatever degree I could.

As always when underway, the port across the bow drew me. In the subdued lighting, the dark red around the open expanse of armor glass set off the true black of the Deep Dark ahead of us, just as the chief had predicted. The paler bulkheads on either side seemed to recede in my peripheral vision leaving only the bright sparkles of distant suns splashed across the view.

I found myself smiling—not a big smile, but a real one. I crossed to the desk and switched on the lamp there rather than turning on the overheads. It was enough light to see what I needed to see and added some warmth. I sat for a moment and ran through the incoming message traffic, scanning the logs briefly. I'd give them more attention during the midwatch, but I took a moment to see if anything needed immediate action. I disposed of the routine matters almost as fast as I read them, marking the more complex for later. There wasn't that much that needed my attention and I sat back in my chair, surveying my small domain.

The master's license hung on the bulkhead above my desk and it looked quite fitting there. The large hanging beside the cabin door was a perfect foil to the open port behind me and I'd noticed that the room seemed quieter. I hadn't actually noticed the way sound had echoed until the addition of the tapestry had damped it. I swiveled the desk chair around so that I could look out at the stars once more. The light behind me reflected on the armor glass and I could see my own image in silhouette reflected faintly back at me—a dark outline looking out into the dark.

I took a deep breath and let it out slowly, sitting there and listening to the ship around me, listening to my heartbeats, listening to the air in the vents and the air in my lungs. After a few ticks, I swiveled back to shut off the light and let my bunk call me. The merry-go-round continued spinning and I needed to be ready for my next pass at the brass ring.

We were two days out of Diurnia when I finally got around to updating the contest standings between Mr. Hill and Mr. Wyatt. In gross terms, Mr. Wyatt was ahead of Mr. Hill by close to a kilo cred. That sounded like a lot, but the grand totals were in the two hundred and fifty kilo cred range so the difference really only represented a fraction of a percent. I was amused to note that I was actually in the lead with a total almost fifteen kilocreds higher. I scrolled back through the transactions and traced it to a healthy variance on that first can from Diurnia to Welliver. It had looked like a relatively minor cargo, but we delivered it ahead of schedule and were able to capitalize on a bonus for early delivery. It had been luck more than planning, but I made a mental note to share the finding with my cargo pickers.

In running the numbers, I noted that the last three runs had yielded returns almost an order of magnitude higher than average for the entire previous stanyer. The resulting shares were substantial and having their work recognized in a tangible way like that was probably one reason that the terrible trio didn't get into any trouble at all while we were in Diurnia. I thought they were really beginning to come to grips with the reality that they actually did have a stake in how things went. Of course, in fairness to them, the dust-up on Jett was really not their fault either.

I finished updating the figures just a few ticks before Mr. Pall was due to relieve the watch at noon.

"The official count has you only a kilocred behind, Mr. Hill."

"That's not bad, Skipper. I think I can make it up on this run to Dree."

I looked at the manifest again and nodded slowly. "I think you may be right, Mr. Hill. How will you feel about it if you lose?"

He grinned over at me. "You have so little faith in me, Skipper?"

I chuckled. "No, Mr. Hill. Actually I expect you'll win, but I'm also thinking it's going to be as much luck as anything." I shrugged. "The dice may roll against you."

He nodded at that. "True enough, Captain." He thought it over for a few ticks. "I think I'd like to work with Mr. Wyatt, actually."

"Really, Mr. Hill?"

He shrugged and looked into his helm display. "He's really an interesting guy. I never realized it before. And he's certainly been picking better cargoes since you came aboard, Skipper." He shook his head ruefully. "It's like he's a different man." He looked at me out of the corner of his eye. "You're not picking for him, are you, Captain?"

I chuckled. "No, Mr. Hill, but I don't blame you for asking.

"He never picked cans like this before, Skipper."

"No, Mr. Hill. The absolute truth is, he never picked cans before."

He looked over at me. "What do you mean, he never picked cans?"

"He thought he was supposed to get a dispatch from DST. He'd call them up and they'd pick the first shipment on the list and off you'd go."

"So, wait, Captain." He turned to look at me. "He'd never picked a can?"

I shook my head. "No, Mr. Hill. Like so many other things about this ship, he was a victim of a process that he didn't understand."

"You knew this when we placed the bet, Skipper?"

"That he'd never actually picked a cargo on his own? Yes, Mr. Hill."

"So you bet that he could out pick me and you had no idea if he could pick a cargo or not?"

I smiled at him. "Yes, Mr. Hill. That's true." I let him consider it for a moment. "I did have reason to believe that he had some considerable data management talent that he wasn't using, and I bet on that. Either way, I couldn't lose."

"How do you figure that, Skipper?"

"I told you in the beginning, Mr. Hill. Whatever happens with the bet, the ship wins by having better profits. I was reasonably certain you'd be an excellent cargo picker. If I was wrong about Mr. Wyatt, then you'd make up for his shortfalls. I was right about you. I was right about him. The share values on these last three trips have been higher than in the previous three stanyers." I shrugged again. "I don't call that losing."

He thought about that a bit before glancing in my direction. "You don't play poker, do you, Captain?"

I shook my head. "No, Mr. Hill."

He sighed. "Pity, Captain."

I chuckled and when Mr. Pall came to relieve the watch, gave him the figures to add to the open cargo display. I wanted the rest of the crew to see the standings as we counted down our last two runs.

The quarterly ratings exams came around again while we were only two weeks out of Diurnia. I'd briefed Mr. Pall on the duties of a training officer. They weren't that onerous and he was already handling the systems updates to keep the testing portfolios up to date. I walked him through the procedures and turned the task of administering the exam over to him.

Mr. Schubert was working through his advanced maths course and decided not to try for Ship Handler One again until after he'd finished that task. Mr. Hill was ready for Cargoman Two and Mr. Ricks surprised me by going for Messman–the full share rating in the Steward Division.

"Messman, Mr. Ricks?"

"Yes, Skipper. I've been helping out Mr. Wyatt in the galley on my off time, and I kinda like it. It pays the same as able spacer and it's a day job. No watch standing."

"That's true, Mr. Ricks. It's not a bad job."

He shrugged and smiled. "I don't know if anybody would hire me, but you never know. I have to say the idea of not standing watch is really appealing, even if I do have to get up early and peel vegetables. It beats brow watch."

"I have to grant you that, Mr. Ricks." I smiled at him. "You sure you want to go for Messman right out of the blocks? You could try the Attendant exam."

"No, Skipper, but thanks for asking. I've been studying for Messman, and it's really not too difficult. Mostly sanitation and food handling regulations on top of the normal ship stuff." He grinned. "Besides, if I fail it, I'm not out anything and I can try again next quarter. If I get it, then I've got a second rating to fall back on."

"I just wanted to make sure, Mr. Ricks. Check with Mr. Pall and work out the schedule with him, if you would?"

"Aye, aye, Skipper."

I'd arranged with Mr. Pall to use the extra console on the bridge to give the two exams. We had to do a little finagling to get the line-up correct, but it worked out well with Mr. Ricks taking his test during the last stan of morning watch while Mr. Hill and I had the duty, and Mr. Hill taking his exam right after lunch during the afternoon watch while Mr. Ricks and Mr. Pall had the duty. Administering the exam was no burden on the OD watch, but the key was making sure the person taking the test wasn't actually supposed to be standing a watch.

It worked out, and I was grateful to Mr. Pall for taking on the ancillary duty.

They both passed their exams and I wondered if, perhaps, we might be losing one or more of them to other ships when we got back to Diurnia. With the contest for cargo picking going on, I didn't think we'd lose any of them until the bet was won and lost, but opportunities sometimes knock at the window while you're watching the door.

After that the merry-go-round spun largely unnoticed by anybody aboard. We made a routine jump from Diurnia to Dree on the twenty-ninth of June and ran through a complete round of ships drills on our way into the well. Every day that passed, I felt better about the way things were going. My tai chi practice went well, and I found myself slipping back into the meditation in motion of the discipline.

I also loved the redecorated cabin more each time I returned to it and saw it anew. I only wished that I had either a conversational grouping or pads on the bench in front of the port. What I really found myself craving was a comfy chair. Maybe it was age, or maybe it was just too much sitting at the consoles, but I found myself sitting on my bunk with the pillows behind my back more often than not when I'd really like to be sitting in the cabin looking out the port. The most comfortable chair on the ship was the captain's chair on the bridge. I only ever sat in that when we went to navigation stations. It seemed a bit unfair.

The trip was uneventful until we picked up the inner markers on the eighteenth of July. We started getting hourly updates on cargo and economic conditions and, as in most Confederated planets, the market in cargoes was exceptionally lively. The competition for them was lively as well. The one hour delay meant that the ships docked had an advantage in terms of snagging the prime cargoes.

In spite of that I managed to grab a can of raw silicon heading back to Diurnia. Mr. Wyatt and Mr. Hill scrambled to try to outpick each other and all the tractors already at the station. The rest of the crew helped to keep an eye on the status board on the mess deck. Neither was able to grab a cargo before we tied up and got into the real-time loop at the orbital, but it was great fun to watch. Frustrating for them, no doubt, but they persisted in good humor.

We locked down at Dree early in the evening watch on July 22nd. Mr. Hill and Mr. Wyatt closeted themselves in Mr. Wyatt's stateroom and stayed there until nearly 2300. They emerged with smiles. We had our load for the trip back. Mr. Wyatt had locked on a midrange priority can of mixed building materials within ticks of its appearance on the boards. Mr. Hill snagged a can of bulk sulfur with a very attractive early delivery bonus. It looked very much like the contest was going to go down to the wire.

Breakfast the next morning was well attended and I didn't get a chance to speak quietly with Mr. Wyatt until we'd finished cleaning up and the others drifted off to sleep or ashore. "You seem pretty pleased with the contest, Avery."

"I am, Skipper. Mr. Hill is a formidable researcher and he has great instincts."

"You may lose this, you know."

He grinned. "Frankly, Skipper, I hope I do."

I must have looked surprised.

His grin broadened and gave his head a little shake. "Don't get me wrong. I'm gonna try to beat him, but dealing with stores isn't that big a deal. I don't really need an apprentice to handle that. We make a very good team picking cargoes, actually, and I suspect that he'd be happy to help, just for the fun of it." He gave a little shrug. "But if *he* wins, we all get a hot tub."

I laughed. "Excellent point, Avery. I hadn't considered that you might want a hot tub more than you needed an apprentice."

He chuckled briefly and then looked at me out of the corners of his eyes. "Did you really think I could beat him, Skipper?"

"You mean when I placed the bet?"

"Yes, Captain." He shuffled his feet a little and shifted his weight. "We had a little talk about the bet and how it started. I'm embarrassed to admit that I really had no idea how we picked cargoes. On the Saltzman Leviathans, it all came out of the central clearing house. They were monstrous ships and lining up the fleet to keep them moving with optimal loads took a team of cargo wranglers on each orbital."

I shrugged. "The Saltzman operation is also very centralized, Avery. You never worked cargo anywhere else?"

He shook his head. "Landed a berth there right out of Port Newmar and stayed until I made chief. They only ever hired family for the chief officer posts there. I had to leave or stay cargo first."

"How'd you get the *Agamemnon*?"

"Luck of the draw. I'm not sure what happened to my predecessor. Rumor was he gave up the berth and went to run a warehouse operation planetside on Breakall. I was on the *Jeremiah* at the time. One of the Saltzman cousins had just made first and was ready to move up, so they were happy to let me go. Guess I wasn't quite as ready as I thought."

"Still, you stayed here, in spite of Captain Delman's evaluations."

"It was an easy berth, if rather boring." He paused before going on. "You bet on me not knowing if I could pick cargoes?"

"Well, yeah. I had no idea if you could pick or not. In those first few days aboard, things were all up in the air for all of us. I don't know why Captain Delman ran the ship the way he did. I'm not going even try to second guess him. I had some very specific ideas about what I wanted to do when I came aboard and I just went about trying to get everything lined up to do them."

He looked at me curiously. "What was your main objective, Skipper? Improve the ship's reputation?"

I shook my head. "You can't improve reputation by focusing on reputation, Avery. You always earn it by your actions." I stopped to think for a couple of heartbeats. "I almost didn't take the berth because of the *Agamemnon's* reputation on the docks, but once I was here, my main goal was pretty simple. Make money."

He cocked his head to one side. "Isn't that rather cold, Skipper? Make money?"

"Maybe." I shrugged. "But it's why we're out here. It's why the ship exists. We're all out here because we make money. If we didn't make a living at it, we couldn't do it."

"So, why the bet, Skipper?"

"I confess that was a spur of the moment opportunity. Mr. Hill had some rather pointed comments to make about the ship's performance and I put him in the position of having to put up or shut up."

"You expected him to win, then?"

I shook my head. "Remember that first task I set you? The menus?"

He looked surprised but nodded. "Yeah. Why?"

"Avery, I'm pretty good with data, but I doubt that even I could have come up with that menu that fast or accurately. I had no idea if Mr. Hill could pick either, but I know I can. I've done it before and while I'm no expert at it, I'm not completely lost. By giving you both something to focus on, I figured I'd learn a lot about the both of you."

Mr. Wyatt smirked. "And make money along the way."

I shrugged again. "Well, I got to pick one can, so I was pretty sure we'd make some. That priority to Jett was probably a mistake." I grimaced. "I got greedy, but I learned a lesson." I looked over at him. "But I didn't really have anything to lose in making the bet, did I?"

He considered that. "I guess not, Skipper." He wasn't finished. I could see it in his face. "Then why all this?" He waved his hand at the mess deck. "You spent money to replace the table, added the screen. The co-op?"

"The table was cheap, Avery, and I needed to make a statement. We're all in the same boat–literally, as it happens. We're all one crew. Those two tiny tables were a problem because there wasn't room for all of us. Compared to the value I got for it, that table was a bargain." I looked over at the screen. "I didn't buy that. I would have, but the chief had it in parts storage. I'm not sure why, or how, but it's a nice unit and it has made a big difference."

He finished his clean-up and folded the side towel into the rack.

"Avery? Why don't you take the day off?"

He looked startled. "Really?"

"Why not? Take Gwen out to dinner or something. I can handle it and you haven't really had a full day off in months."

He looked around the galley and eyed the chrono on the bulkhead. "Let me fix lunch. Gwen won't be up until then anyway. If you'd handle dinner and breakfast mess, Skipper, that would give us a nice night out. We can't stay out too late. She's got the day watch in the morning, but I wouldn't mind sleeping in."

I grinned at him. "You drive a hard bargain, Mr. Wyatt, but you win."

He laughed. "Well, then, I need to make a run down to the oh-one deck and see about our replenishment order. They're supposed to have good fish here and I'd like to stock up on some while we have a chance."

"I'll go with you. I want to see about getting some cushions for that bench in the cabin." I slotted my cup into the cleaner. "Meet you at the lock in five ticks?"

"Sounds good, Skipper."

I scampered up to the cabin and did a rough measurement of the bench. I could have asked the chief for a tape measure but I figured that the unit was probably standard and the chandlery would have something that was, likewise, standard. I took the chance to visit the head and on my way back through, paused at the door from the sleeping cabin to survey. I squinted my eyes and tried to imagine what Fredi would do with the space. Fredi was always at home in the cabin on the *Tinker*. When she took over from Rossett, the cabin took on a new life. It was still very businesslike when it needed to be, but it was also her home, in a very real sense. We spent many afternoons and evenings having informal gatherings of her command staff in the cabin. I really missed those.

The ticks were ticking, so I gave up on the reverie and went to meet Mr. Wyatt at the lock.

We separated at the chandlery. He headed for the replenishment office and I headed back to fittings and furnishings. As I suspected, they had a variety of standard seat cushions and pillows with clever velcro tags on them. In a ship underway, it wasn't a terribly good idea to have things just lying around loose. On the other hand, low mass items like pillows and cushions didn't need a lot of persuasion to keep them in place. I suspected that if the ship took enough of a hit that the velcro wouldn't hold them in place, then we'd have much more serious problems than flying foam in a closed compartment.

I arranged with the staff to get the cushions upholstered in a rich blue fabric and have them delivered to the ship before we sailed. As I finished up, Mr. Wyatt joined me and motioned me over to the mess deck section. They had the twin to our mess deck table set up in the showroom.

"Look at the benches, Captain."

The long benches down each side of the table gave a lot of flexibility in seating by allowing people to sit as close or as far from each other as space and disposition allowed. I remembered similar designs in picnic tables at the parks on Neris and Port Newmar. What they didn't have was a back, or padding on the seats. For the stan or so we spent sitting there during mess, it wasn't an issue, but sitting for an extended time–like during a movie–was sometimes less than comfortable. The benches on display had a pad that ran the full length of each bench and seemed to be held on with spring clips. They weren't very thick, but Mr. Wyatt and I both gave them the butt test and the high density foam added just enough padding to take the hardness off the bench.

We grinned at each other and went in search of chandlery staff to get a set added to our replenishment order.

The staff member was happy to take our order and even offered several options for covers. We chose a nice green color with darker piping on the seams and a smooth, vinyl fabric that could be wiped down with a sponge.

Mr. Wyatt was grinning like a kid in a candy store as we headed out of the store through the furnishing department. We were almost out when a display beside the door caught my eye and I detoured to it without even thinking.

Mr. Wyatt observed me with a quizzical expression on his face as I stopped and looked at the conversational grouping consisting of a pair of two-seat sofas with a steel trimmed, inlaid wood table between. It took me back to Neris, to the apartment I'd grown up in with my mother. It was scaled down a bit. Ours had been full sized couches. These were a lot shorter, but they were nearly the same style. I sat on one and my body just relaxed into it. I had to stop myself from putting my feet on the edge of the table, something that others hadn't done judging from the faint scuff marks I saw there.

"Do you think this would look good in the cabin, Mr. Wyatt?"

He eyed it dubiously. "I don't know, Skipper. Where would you put it?"

I considered the question but realized I already knew the answer. "Pull the conference table and put it there. The only time I've ever used that table was when we had the crew of the *Voice* aboard. We use the mess deck for crew meetings." I shrugged. "And if we need to meet there, then this would be a lot more comfortable than those plastic chairs."

He took a seat across from me. I grinned when I saw him fight the urge to put his feet up as well. He looked around in appraisal and ran a hand across the seat beside him. "Nice." He looked over to me with a shrug. "Can we afford it?"

An info sheet was taped to the table and I leaned over to read the specs. I winced a little at the price but remembered that I'd be saving in rent by not paying for the crew quarters on Diurnia. "Let's go find that helpful staff fellow and see what we can do."

In the end, even with the disposition of the old fixtures, the hit to my wallet was less than I had paid for rent. Mr. Wyatt seemed surprised. "You're not charging the ship, Skipper? It's a fixture, after all."

I considered it. "No, Avery. If I charge the ship, then it comes out of the profits, which has an effect on crew shares. I'll pay for this myself." I grinned. "I rather expect I'll get my use out of it."

He looked dubious but wisely didn't argue.

CHAPTER FIFTY-ONE
DREE ORBITAL: 2372-JULY-24

It really doesn't pay to get too complacent. I'd learned that lesson when I was young and I relearned it every so often.

My new furniture had been delivered and after a few bad moments, the shipfitters had removed the old conference table and installed the new. Placement was critical because, once locked down, they couldn't be moved without significant application of cutting tools. In the end, I'd arranged it so that the sofas were perpendicular to the port, letting me lounge sideways, and stare out the wide port to my heart's content. It wasn't actually long enough to stretch out on, but it was certainly more comfortable than any other seat on the ship. The cushions for the bench had been delivered as well, and I spent a pleasant half stan laying them out and sticking them down before stretching out on them to see how they worked.

Ms. Thomas relieved the watch at 1800 and I spent a quiet evening at the local pub on Dree, enjoying the quiet ambiance, some shore food, and a single gin and tonic. While I was there, several shoals of spacers wafted in and out and I remembered old times and past occasions. In the end, it got too lonely for me, so I paid the tab and headed back to the ship. It felt strange, in a way. I'd always had shipmates to go ashore with, but I'd long known that the captain didn't go ashore with the crew. Sometimes, for a special event like a getting underway party, or some other occasion, but it wasn't one of those "Let's go grab a drink" relationships. I knew then why one often saw captains dining with captains and made a note to see who was in port when I got back to Diurnia.

In the meantime, I headed back to the ship and my bunk. I didn't go back on duty until 1800 and I looked forward to the last good chance for sleep before we got underway again.

Too bad I didn't get it.

At 0500 Ms. Thomas woke me. "Skipper?"

She stood in the door to the sleeping cabin. She hadn't turned on a light, but the reflected light from the orbital's outer skin lit the room behind her. I could see her outlined in the doorway.

"Yes, Ms. Thomas?" I blinked and tried to focus.

"Orbital Security is here. They'd like to speak with you about Mr. Pall."

"Give them a cup of coffee, Ms. Thomas. I'll be right down."

She disappeared from my door and I made a beeline for the head. Whatever it was, it couldn't be good news. My groggy brain caught up with the watch rotation and I realized that Mr. Pall was supposed to be relieving the watch in the next stan.

In less than five ticks I met them on the mess deck. The two Orbital Security officers were not sipping coffee but were standing, shifting their respective centers of gravity and looking around the mess deck. They turned when I entered and the taller of the two shook my hand. "I'm Officer Laura Church. This is my partner Officer Martha Holloway."

"Captain Ishmael Wang, Officers. You have one of mine?"

"We think so, Captain." Church nodded to Holloway who held up a tablet with the picture of a rather badly bruised face. "Is he yours?"

"It could be. Mr. William Pall, second mate." I stepped back from the image.

"We found him under a ladder in one of the stairwells about three stans ago. No ID. Civvies pretty much destroyed. He went right into the can when we got him to medical. They popped the lid a little while ago. No serious injuries, not counting the broken leg." They looked at each other. "And he seems to be a bit delusional, Captain."

"Pirates?"

They looked startled. "How did you know?"

"It's Mr. Pall."

"He was unconscious when we got him. He's still pretty loopy from the initial treatment. When they popped the lid, he was able to give his name and ship and we came over to check out his story."

"Is he in any criminal trouble, Officers?"

They shook their heads. "We just wanted to make sure he was who he said he was. You can go see him. He won't be leaving Medical for awhile."

"Ms. Thomas, it looks like you'll have the watch for a little longer."

"No problem, Skipper. I can sleep later."

"Save me some breakfast, Mr. Wyatt. I'll be back as soon as I can."

The officers escorted me to Medical. We went up to the main medical station on the five-deck, the one reserved for serious cases that the first aid station down on oh-one couldn't handle. I braced myself.

Two medicos intercepted us as we entered and the officers excused themselves. "Good luck, Captain. We've got to finish the reports on this, so we'll leave you here."

"Thank you, Officer Church, Officer Holloway."

They nodded and left and the medicos took over. They introduced themselves but I missed the names.

"He's pretty rough looking, Captain. Looks like he took quite a beating and then rolled down a ladder."

"Is he conscious?"

The looked at each other. "So, so, Captain. He's pretty heavily sedated but he comes to now and again and mumbles something about pirates before going back out."

"That's not that unusual for Mr. Pall."

They looked at each other again before stepping back and ushering me into a curtained cubicle with an autodoc pod in it. The bottom half was closed, covering him from the hips down, but his bare chest looked–not too surprisingly–like he'd been rolled down a flight of stairs. His face wasn't much better. One eye was swollen almost shut and his upper lip was about twice normal size. He appeared to be asleep.

I nodded. "Yes. That's him. William Pall. Second mate on the *Agamemnon*."

They nodded and one made an entry on a tablet. "Will you be in port long, Captain?"

"We were going to leave tomorrow. You tell me."

They looked at each other again. I was beginning to wonder if there were some kind of medical mind meld in action but the shorter one answered. "He won't be able to travel for at least two days. Probably three. By then he'll be able to move around on his own, the swelling should be gone, and some of the bruising will look pretty spectacular but not dangerous."

The other one added, "His left leg will be in a cast from mid thigh to toe. He won't be walking on it for at least three weeks, even with the quick-knit."

I took a deep breath and let it out slowly. "Will he be fit for duty?"

They looked at each other one more time before the taller one answered. "Light duty. Anything he can do sitting down."

"Well, his job involves a lot of sitting so that shouldn't be a problem." Another thought occurred to me. "Medications? Anything that will impair his judgement?"

They shrugged in unison. "For the next couple of days, I wouldn't let him operate any heavy equipment, Captain, but after that, nothing worse than an over the counter analgesic."

"*Agamemnon* is at dock twelve. We can delay a couple of days until you get him back to us. Let us know if he needs anything."

On the way back to the ship, I wondered what effect the cast would have on his ability to get up and down the ladders.

It was just past 0600 when I got back aboard and I was pleased to see Mr. Ricks on the brow. "Good morning, Mr. Ricks. Looks like you'll be standing watch with somebody else for a bit."

"How is he, Skipper?"

I gave a little shrug. "He was out cold when I saw him. He looks pretty bad, but the medics say he'll be back with us in two or three days."

"So we'll wait for him, sar?"

"It'll probably be faster than trying to hire a new second mate, Mr. Ricks."

"Would you do that, Skipper?"

"If he were going to be laid up for an extended period, we'd have to, Mr. Ricks. As it is, I think we'll be okay to give him a couple of days to get back aboard."

I went on into the mess deck where Mr. Wyatt had breakfast underway. I grabbed coffee and food as I gave the assembled company the same news.

As I settled at the table, I turned to Chief Gerheart and Mr. Wyatt. "Can you two flip a coin? Loser gets to be the second section OD for a couple of days?"

They looked at each other and spoke in unison. "I'll do it."

We all laughed. The chief said, "Engineering is ready to go. I don't really have that much to do at the moment, Avery. It's no hardship."

He shrugged. "Okay, Chief, but I don't mind."

"Thank you, both. Mr. Wyatt may get his chance at OD once we get underway."

He looked concerned at that. "Skipper?"

"He'll be ambulatory and aboard. I have no idea what kind of shape he'll be in. He may not be able to take a deck watch, but I don't want to sit here if he could be healing up on the way. Ms. Thomas and I can go watch-and-watch for a short time if we need to, but it would work a lot better if you could hold the bridge watch down."

"But I'm not qualified, Skipper," Mr. Wyatt said.

"You're a senior officer of the ship, Avery. Any boot third mate is qualified. I'm pretty sure you can hold down bridge watch for a few days." I realized that my fork was scraping plate and I stopped trying to eat the china. "We can split the galley duty up so you're not stuck doing both, and it may not be necessary. I'm just laying in contingency plans."

"What about me, Captain?" Chief Gerheart threw her hat into the ring.

"You want to do bridge watch, Chief?"

She shrugged. "I could in a pinch. I've got a full engineering console up there so I can keep track of the girls while we're underway. Only problem would be if I needed to leave the bridge to physically check something. It wouldn't be any worse than if it went wrong in the middle of the night when I'm asleep." She shrugged. "These systems are pretty reliable so long as you keep up with maintenance, and I do."

"That's a good point, Chief. Thanks. Let me get back to you on that. It's good to know we've got some options. Now, if we can just get him back aboard."

I slotted my dirty dishes in the cleaner while Chief Gerheart relieved Ms. Thomas of the watch. The ratings followed my lead and we left the three of them with their heads together. I smiled inwardly and did what any good captain should do.

I went to the cabin and wrote up the report while my command staff solved the problem of making it all work.

I managed to get the report done and review the overnight logs before lunch mess. There was still an issue with the delivery dates on the cans, but we'd learned a lesson and picked dates that were well out. The key would be the jump. We could make up the time if we got a good jump. I wasn't willing to shave the safety margins, but luck did fall in our favor occasionally. It behooved us to be ready to take advantage of it when it did.

Mr. Ricks joined us at lunch mess, but it was a reduced company as both Schubert and Hill had gone up to the flea market. With the extra days of trading, they made arrangements to keep their booth, and took advantage of the time to both sell and buy. Conversation was desultory but in spite of that, I had a feeling that my senior officers were hatching something. It was nothing I could put my finger on. Just the way they kept shooting little knowing glances at each other.

I didn't know if I should be concerned or relieved.

After we secured the galley, I went up to medical to check on Mr.

Pall. The medics nodded me through and I found him conscious if not exactly lucid.

"Hello, Mr. Pall. You seem a bit under the weather."

"Pirates, Skipper. They're everywhere."

"So it would seem, Mr. Pall." I refrained from asking how he felt. I had a pretty good idea. "Is there anything you need from the ship?"

"Pants, Skipper. They took my pants."

"Yes, Mr. Pall. They'll give them back when you're able to wear them again."

"Oh. Good."

"You rest, Mr. Pall. Get well. We're holding the ship for you so you need to heal quickly."

That seemed to get through to a part of him that might have been tracking better. "I wondered if you'd replace me, Captain."

"Who would handle pirate watch, Mr. Pall?"

"I've been training Mr. Ricks, Skipper. He could do it in a pinch."

I grinned at him. "I fear he lacks your insight and experience, Mr. Pall."

He smiled back but fell asleep again before replying.

The medico on duty smiled and nodded as I left. There wasn't anything we could do but wait. Given that I'd be up all night on the midwatch, I thought I'd just as soon wait in my bunk.

Chapter Fifty-two
Dree Orbital: 2372-July-26

Mr. Pall rejoined the ship just before dinner mess but when they brought him aboard, I realized we had some significant challenges yet. Three days in the auto-doc hadn't done much for him. He looked weak and pale. He had never been overly robust, but he looked downright frail in the chair they wheeled him aboard in.

The corpsman who brought him aboard also brought a portfolio of information, a bag of drugs, and some modules for our own autodoc. We could put him in there, if things took a turn for the worse. That was a sobering thought, but I wasn't too worried. The autodoc would keep him going for a long time if push came to shove, but that was a very remote possibility. Assuming we kept him from falling down the ladders.

He managed to sit up through the dinner mess, but there was never any question that he'd be taking a watch any time soon. By the time we'd finished eating, he looked pinched around the eyes and drawn about the mouth. The food probably helped but he was already at the end of his strength. I started to suggest that he go to his stateroom and sleep, but stopped.

"Well, we have a bit of an engineering challenge ahead of us, people." They looked at me and I nodded at Mr. Pall in his chair. "Any ideas how we get him up the ladder to his stateroom before he keels over?"

Mr. Pall rallied a bit. "I'm not quite ready to keel over yet, Skipper."

"I'm thinking we have a short window of opportunity, Mr. Pall, and that you need to be sleeping in your own bunk before you do."

I could see both Ms. Thomas and Chief Gerheart frowning in concentration but Mr. Wyatt was looking at the chair contemplating the wheels.

"Suggestions, anybody?"

Ms. Thomas shrugged. "He's not that heavy. I could probably carry him up."

Mr. Wyatt nodded in agreement. "You probably could, especially if a couple of us helped, but that seems a trifle..." He paused looking for the right word. "Awkward."

The Chief suggested, "Grav pallet?"

Mr. Wyatt shook his head. "Certainly has lift capacity, but a standard grav pallet wouldn't go up the ladder either. It won't tilt and it doesn't have enough deck clearance to lift up. They work well on flat decks but they're impossible on any incline over five percent."

"Grav trunk will." We looked at Mr. Pall.

"Are you suggesting you get in it, Mr. Pall?"

He laughed. "No, Captain, but I can stand up well enough to sit on it if it was beside the chair."

"Mr. Wyatt, do you know what a grav trunk is rated to lift?"

"Something on the order of two hundred kilos, Captain. That's more than enough for Mr. Pall here."

I looked around the mess deck. "Mine's full of kit. Anybody have an empty one handy?"

They all shook heads. "Mr. Wyatt? Would you nip down to the chandlery and buy one for the ship please. Charge the pooka's account and we'll let the co-op use it when we're done with Mr. Pall, here."

"Aye, aye, Captain." He darted off on his errand.

"In the meantime, Mr. Pall. How can we make you more comfortable?"

He took a deep breath and let it out slowly. "If I could just sit here for a bit, Captain?" He looked around. "It's been a rough couple of days and I'm really glad to be back aboard."

"Of course, Mr. Pall. Relax."

Chief Gerheart took a seat on the bench near to where he'd been rolled up to the table. "Do you remember who did it? How it happened?"

He shook his head. "It was all so fast. I was coming back from the bar. I'd had a few but I was still tracking. I walked out of the bar, made the turn into the passageway to head for the lift, and woke up in the autodoc." He looked a bit shaken. "It's the darnedest thing I've ever experienced." He raised a hand to his still bruised face. "I think I'm glad I don't remember this happening, but I feel so helpless. They could have done anything. I have no idea what. That whole time is just... gone."

She reached over and patted his shoulder. "The medical people looked you over pretty closely. The physical parts will heal up right enough." She smiled gently. "The rest, we'll just have to wait and see."

We made small talk for another quarter stan before Mr. Wyatt came back with a grav trunk in tow and we all trooped out to the foot of the ladder, wheeling Mr. Pall ahead of us with Mr. Wyatt bringing the trunk up behind. It took a couple of false starts and some finagling to get Mr. Pall onto the front of the grav trunk's lid. Mr. Wyatt lifted the trunk off the deck and started up the ladder with it. It tilted alarmingly, but Mr. Pall just leaned forward to keep his balance on the front edge. Ms. Thomas followed them up to push but it wasn't necessary. Whatever small field generators they'd built into the trunk did most of the work of lifting and all Mr. Wyatt had to do was slide him along.

"It's a little worse than on a level deck, but certainly no strain, Skipper."

I grinned. "Well just don't let him slide off or let go of the handle, Mr. Wyatt. One injured crew is enough and I'd just as soon not drop that on Ms. Thomas or have Mr. Pall crash into the deck."

They chuckled but in less than a tick it was over. I shouldered the empty chair–it was a lightweight affair of tubes and wheels and fabric without a lot of mass to it–and ran it up the ladder while they towed Mr. Pall to his stateroom.

Chief Gerheart followed us up and supervised with a warm smile. "Makes you wonder why they don't make these chairs with grav plates in them or something."

Mr. Wyatt had an answer. "I suspect it has to do with mobility, Chief. You can't push yourself on the grav trunk. Somebody has to drag you. The chair's been around for hundreds of stanyers and the design's good for what it is. There's never been enough incentive to change it."

In a matter of a tick or two, Mr. Pall was dosed up and tucked in. We left him with one of the ship-issue tablets in case he needed to call for help, then shut off the lights and closed the door. I suspected he might have been asleep before we left.

The three senior officers followed me to the cabin. When I stopped at the door to look at them, Ms. Thomas had a very satisfied grin on her face while the chief and Mr. Wyatt looked like they might burst from holding in whatever secret it was they wanted to spring on me.

I eyed them dubiously and then swung the door open. "You may as well come in and make yourselves comfortable while you tell me." I led them in and we settled on the couches–Ms. Thomas and Mr. Wyatt sitting cozily together on one while the chief took the far corner on mine.

I looked from one to the other. Nobody wanted to speak first. I turned to Ms. Thomas. "So, should I assume that you've had a busy day, Ms. Thomas?"

She shook her head. "Oh, just a routine day on watch, Skipper. You know how they can get." She pointed at Mr. Wyatt and then the chief. "These two, though, had a very interesting day."

I looked back and forth between the chief and Mr. Wyatt. "Well? One of you? Both of you? Somebody want to tell me what this is in service of?"

They nodded at each other and pulled out their tablets, flicked up a screen, and simultaneously turned them so I could see.

It took me a moment to figure out what I was looking at. They both showed personnel records. I frowned trying to compare the two. They were both so different until I got to the bottom of the screen. They both had identical notations. "Third mate?"

The Chief laughed delightedly and Mr. Wyatt chuckled.

"What's this all about?"

The Chief tucked her tablet back in the holster and grinned. "It was something you said the other day about any boot third was qualified to stand a bridge watch."

Mr. Wyatt chimed in. "So, we got our heads together and looked over the study guide for the third mate's license and decided to get one."

"But why?"

Mr. Wyatt shrugged. "I know it's your prerogative to assign duties as you see fit, Captain, but if you're serious about assigning us to bridge watch while underway, we thought we should have at least a fig leaf to cover us if something should go wrong."

"But you're both chief officers in your own divisions! Why would anybody complain?"

Ms. Thomas answered that question. "Nobody in the fleet would think twice, Skipper, but what about insurance? We've got a clearly incapacitated second mate. You're certainly qualified to do the comms and systems work, and we can split astrogation without anybody complaining, but the bridge watch should be an officer certified in Deck Division–if for no other reason than to make sure the insurers have no wiggle room to deny a claim. We're getting underway short-handed, and I certainly don't want to go watch-and-watch for the next two weeks while Mr. Pall gets his feet under him, do you?"

I thought about that and grimaced at the idea. "Not really, no."

They all nodded. They had me and I knew it. I just needed to let them tell me how badly and in which direction. "So, what's the plan?"

They nodded for Ms. Thomas to continue. "Mr. Ricks will swap with Mr. Schubert. These two boot thirds will take turns as OD on second section. Mr. Schubert is the best ship handler we have, and they'll be able to depend on him to keep things flying without much supervision. Mr. Ricks and I get along just fine and you and Mr. Hill can keep third section. They split the load and get some experience in the bargain. It certainly couldn't hurt to get cross trained."

I looked at my new third mates. "You two are okay with this?"

They shrugged and Mr. Wyatt grinned. "We thought of it, Skipper. Not like we're going to back out now."

The chief nodded her agreement. "It'll be fun for a bit. Break up the routine, see how the other half lives." Her light and playful tone turned a bit more serious. "Realistically, how long do you think Mr. Pall will need to recoup?"

I took a deep breath and let it out slowly while I considered. "He's pretty beaten up but the only thing they found really damaged was his leg. It's a clean break and the quick-knit was already stabilizing it when I visited him yesterday." I shook my head. "I'd say a couple of weeks at least. I'm hoping we have him on the bridge by the time we jump. That gives him a little more than three weeks to recover. That's on the outside. I suspect he'll be trying to crawl up to the bridge within a week."

We all shared a laugh at the thought.

I looked around at them. "Thanks. That was good thinking. I appreciate your initiative here, and I believe it's a much better solution than I would have come up with."

They beamed. Ms. Thomas rose and pulled Mr. Wyatt up from the sofa. "Come on, good lookin'. This is our last night in port and I wanna go dancin'."

He groaned in mock dismay but grinned as she pulled him to his feet.

The chief rose, too. "I better go see if anything's broken. See you in the morning, Skipper."

They paraded out and closed the door gently behind them. The glare from the orbital's skin was a bit bright and I pondered my decision not to get some kind of curtain for when we were in port. It was only a few days at a time, and I kept thinking it wasn't that bad.

I also pondered how I'd managed to get such a strange and wonderful crew.

They were correct, of course. I'd completely overlooked the insurance aspect. I shouldn't have. That was a mistake on my part. I didn't think that it would matter, but when there's insurance money at stake, the careful customer dots all the i's and crosses every t. They were also correct about it being little more than a fig leaf if something desperate actually happened while one of them was on watch.

I sighed, mostly in satisfaction. It was a nice cabin, and the couch was comfy. I got up and went to bed before I started thinking about how much I now wanted somebody to share that couch with. I had day watch in the morning and I could use a little extra sleep.

CHAPTER FIFTY-THREE
DIURNIA SYSTEM: 2372-SEPTEMBER-09

The tug caught us for our final approach to Diurnia just after lunch mess. The forty-three day run set no records but was free of incident. With Mr. Wyatt and the chief trading off on OD watch, Mr. Pall was able to rest and heal. For the first week, we only took him up and down the ladder for dinner mess so he could get out of his stateroom for a bit each day and the small movements seemed to help. By the end of that first week, he was able to move around in his cast relatively well and we only had to make sure he didn't try to go up or down the ladder without a spotter to make sure he didn't trip and fall. Within ten days he was standing watches again and the merry-go-round began to go around more naturally.

It felt odd going into Diurnia knowing that nobody really waited there for me. As I sat in the chair and watched the tug maneuver us into position, I felt none of the anticipation I normally felt as the ship got close to what had felt like home to me for so long. The sense that Diurnia was just another port was stronger than it had been on the way out. I hadn't realized just how much that compass of home had drawn me until it was gone.

With each passing moment, I couldn't help but think of Jen. This time it wasn't in anticipation of homecoming, but rather with sadness for having been so misguided in the first place. There was a reason that spacer didn't marry station. I knew it going in, but believed myself to be exempt. She probably knew it, too. The stanyers when I'd dread getting underway because of the inevitable fight pained me the most. That was a clue, a symptom of a problem that I should have recognized and dealt with. Instead I just chalked it up to her being unreasonable and continued down my own selfish path. With the wisdom of hindsight, I had to give her credit for fighting so long.

As we nudged in for final docking, I wondered if anybody would understand that I didn't ask for a divorce because of who she might be sleeping with, but rather that having my face rubbed in it like that just crystallized the reality that neither of us was getting what we needed from the relationship. It was a seven stanyer habit that needed to be broken. She'd just started ahead of me. I probed that wound several times but found it was already healing over. It was still tender, but it wasn't bleeding any more.

We latched on and I suppressed a sigh. It was quiet enough on the bridge and I didn't want to have to explain it.

"Secure from navigation stations, Ms. Thomas. Feel free to declare liberty when the Customs people have cleared us to leave the ship."

"Aye, aye, Captain."

It was just about 1700 when I got back to the cabin and ran through the docking protocols. The formal customs declarations had been filed long since. We just needed to go through the inspection routine. The *Agamemnon* was a known entity and they cleared us with a only a perfunctory look at the embargo locker and formal examination of manifest and crew.

A message from "A. Pacquette, Solicitor" showed up in my inbox. She requested that I contact her office when convenient. I did treat myself to a sigh then. It would have been nice if she'd said why. My paranoid side said, "Uh oh! There's a problem." My rational side said, "Don't borrow trouble." Luckily I had a practical side that got me into a fresh undress uniform and headed for the lock to go find out what Ms. A. Pacquette, Solicitor, wanted to see me about.

On the way off the ship, I stopped in the mess deck. I found Mr. Wyatt putting out a light dinner. Ms. Thomas sat in her spot at the table watching the ready cargo list while he prepared. She smiled when I came in. "Going ashore, Captain?"

"Yes, Ms. Thomas. I need to tie off some loose ends before they trip me. I'll miss dinner mess, I expect, Mr. Wyatt."

He grinned. "No problem, Skipper. I didn't make much. I think almost everybody will be ashore tonight except for the duty section."

"What about you two? Heading out after mess?"

Ms. Thomas shrugged. "We haven't really talked about it yet." She glanced at him coyly. "Perhaps we'll find something to do."

He caught the glance and I thought he colored a bit.

"Well, I've got watch in the morning, so if you'd like to sleep in, Mr. Wyatt and take the day off tomorrow? I can cover through the dinner mess tomorrow night. I'm hoping it'll be a quiet watch."

"Thanks, Skipper. I'll take you up on that."

Mr. Pall came onto the Mess Deck. His cast had peeled off after about three weeks. The small sensors embedded in it determined that his leg was strong enough on its own and had triggered a chemical change in the compound of the cast. The change allowed Mr. Pall to basically wash the cast off in the shower and, after a couple of weeks of climbing the ladders, was showing no outward signs of his ordeal.

"Heading out, Skipper?"

"Yes, Mr. Pall. I have to take care of some business. I should be back in two or three stans"

"Understood, Captain." He nodded and smiled at me before relieving Ms. Thomas.

I headed down to oh-one. Ms. Pacquette was with a client when I entered, but the staffer showed me a quiet waiting room with some comfy chairs. "She'll be only a few more moments, Captain. Please make yourself comfortable and let me know if you need anything?"

I thanked him and settled into the nearest lounger. I took the opportunity to check on the ready cargo list. We hadn't picked cans yet. The bet was over and we were waiting for the final tally to come in from DST on how much the latest shipment had grossed the ship. It would have an effect on our shares, but more important, it would determine the winner of the bet. So much had changed in the eight months since I'd made that bet with Mr. Hill. I recognized that the balance of luck was definitely on my side, even with the setbacks on the priority cargo and personal issues that had brought me to the lawyer's office to begin with.

The staffer returned after only a few ticks and escorted me to the inner sanctum.

Ms. Pacquette rose to shake my hand before settling back into her chair behind the desk. "Thank you for coming so soon after docking, Captain." She smiled.

"I have duty tomorrow. I thought it would be expedient to find out what you needed as soon as possible."

She nodded and accepted a packet of paperwork from her assistant with a smile and a nod of thanks. The assistant left us alone while Ms. Pacquette opened the package and started pulling out papers.

"As you expected, your ex-wife signed the papers, Captain. The divorce hearing was held on August 1st with no objections placed by her counsel. Your ex-wife took the settlement and made no counter-demands on her own behalf. Since you made none against her, the adjudication hearing was *pro forma* and the decree finalized on September 1st." At each step she held up a particular sheet or form. "As of that date your marriage was ended and you owed no legal obligations under the contract."

I took a deep breath and let it out. Hearing it all laid out like that–cut, dried, done–reminded me that while I might be mostly healed, it was still a sore subject. "The apartment?"

"The lease was terminated effective September first. We hired a moving company to pack up. Your ex-wife took the furnishings and household gear. Your clothing and assorted memorabilia were placed in storage." She pulled a key card out of the packet and added it to the pile.

It was on the tip of my tongue to ask where Jen was, but I'd forfeited the right to know that with the divorce.

"Do you have any other requirements for my firm, Captain Wang?"

"No, Ms. Pacquette. Am I overlooking something? From a legal standpoint, is there anything that you think I should be considering?"

"No, Captain. I think it's all over now, unless you find something in that storage locker that's a problem. You do have some recourse if there are things missing, but there's a limitation on how long you have to file a claim. I'd check that as soon as possible if I were you."

"Thank you, Ms. Pacquette. I'll do that. There shouldn't be too much there. Frankly, I doubt that there's much there that I want."

She nodded and gathered up the package of materials again, putting them all neatly back in the folder. "In that case, Captain, there's only the matter of your final billing. Would you like me to send you an invoice?"

"Do you have it ready?"

"One moment and I'll see." She went out into the outer office and returned with a tablet a few moments later. "We've just added this visit to the total, Captain." She handed me the tablet.

I scrolled down through the listings. It wasn't an inconsiderable list, but each item seemed proper and appropriate. The total at the bottom was rather hefty, but not as much as I'd given Jen as a settlement. I thumbed it for payment and handed it back to her. "If you'd forward an electronic copy of that showing payment, Ms. Pacquette? Thanks for your help."

She smiled and shook my hand. "My pleasure, Captain. Would that all my cases were as readily handled as this one." She handed me the packet of official papers and walked me to the door.

In the passageway outside the office, I looked down at the packet.

It seemed too thin and light to hold the end of a marriage. I snorted a short laugh. Given the history, thin and light probably was a good description after all.

The storage locker turned out to hold just a few boxes with "Ishmael–clothing" scrawled on the ends. I made arrangement with the storage company to have them delivered to the ship the next day and headed down to the chandlery. I needed to see a man about a hot tub. I was still waiting for the final numbers, but I was pretty sure how it was going to go.

By the time I got out of the chandlery, it was nearly 2100 and I was running on empty. When I got onto the lift, I punched the down button and set a course for Over Easy. When I pushed through the door, the place wasn't exactly packed but there was a good crowd. Customers filled almost all the booths and a good number of the tables. I dithered for a moment just inside the door and my luck held as a stool opened up at the counter. It wasn't my normal stool but it was better than nothing. I could have taken a table, but it wasn't the same.

The guy behind the counter looked familiar and his name tag read "Seth." I thought I'd seen him before but they all had a very similar look. He gave me the normal chin-up, reverse nod and I spieled off my standard order. He grinned, poured coffee, wrote it down and slipped it into the clip with a hearty "Order, Frank."

I sipped the coffee gratefully and scoped out the place. The crowd appeared largely sober. In spite of being an around-the-clock operation, most people still did their serious drinking later in the evening and into the early morning hours. It always struck me as odd, each time I observed it. As a land rat, it seemed normal to me, but as a spacer used to watch standing, I found it interesting that even watch standers tended to carouse on a day-worker schedule.

My food slid onto the counter in front of me and Seth warmed the coffee. The rest of the room faded away as I tucked in. It was delicious, filling, and gone in about four ticks. It never ceased to amaze me how quickly a plate of food could disappear. I was certain that some of it must melt into the air while I was chewing. I sighed in satisfaction and slid the plate back across the counter.

Seth gave a knowing smirk as he cleared away and offered another refill on the coffee. I nodded to accept it and he topped it off. "Anything else, Captain?"

I gave my head a little shake and he held the tab for me to pay. A quick stroke of the thumb and we were square. I sipped my coffee and looked around a bit more. This was not my usual seat and it gave me a different perspective on the room. Normally I sat on one end or the other so I could get a good look at the other patrons without appearing to gawk. The seat midway along the counter kept my back to the door, and most of the room. It gave me a good look into the kitchen though and I could see the back of Frank's head bobbing about back there as he shuffled food and plates, dealing out the orders like a blackjack dealer on a hot Saturday night. I wondered how long he'd been doing the job. There'd always been a Frank in the kitchen. Well, almost always. I knew there were other cooks and sometimes there were a couple of them on during the busiest times.

I drank off half the mug of coffee and pushed the remainder toward the back side of the counter. A new party of spacers came noisily through the door and I took that as my cue to leave. With a nod to Seth, I vacated the stool and headed back to the ship and my bunk.

Chapter Fifty-four
Diurnia Orbital: 2372-September-09

Mr. Hill and I relieved the watch at 0545 and I opened the breakfast mess at 0600. Mr. Pall and Mr. Schubert stayed around to eat. Even Chief Gerheart joined us, looking bright eyed and chipper compared to Mr. Pall's still rather pallid and rumpled appearance.

We were the only ones aboard and we shared a quiet meal before sending the midwatch off to sleep. Mr. Hill took his station at the brow and the chief helped me clear.

"Have you given any thought to the hot tub, Chief?"

She grinned. "Actually, I've had several thoughts, Captain, but I'm guessing you're not talking about those."

I chuckled a bit. "Actually, I was referring to the installation issues."

She shook her head. "No. Why? Are we going to have a hot tub?" She turned to look at the unchanged status numbers. "Did Mr. Hill win?"

I glanced at the entry and shook my head. "Not yet. The final numbers should be down today, and we need to get a cargo lined up for departure before tomorrow." I grinned. "I'm used to having the cans lined up and locked down by now. Maybe we should keep the arrangement going."

She considered that and gave a little shrug. "Maybe, but do you think he's going to win?"

I gave my head a little shake. "No, I don't think he will. Mr. Wyatt was in the lead on the preliminary numbers."

"Then why would I be thinking about installing a hot tub, Captain?" She looked at me out of the corner of her eye.

"I thought it was such a good idea, we oughta have one anyway."

Her face lit up and split in a grin. "I like the way you think,

Skipper."

"Thanks, Chief." Her approval felt better than I thought it should have, but I smiled back.

Just then my tablet bipped and I opened the message. "Well, I'll be."

"What is it, Captain?"

I held up the tablet so she could read it. "Mr. Hill won."

She frowned at the numbers and then looked up at the scores posted by the cargo list. She looked back and forth several times before laughing loudly. "By one cred?"

"One cred is as good as a million."

"Well, not if I'm getting paid share of it, Skipper. I'll take the million."

She made me laugh at that. "Good point, Chief, but for the bet? We didn't say he had to win by a particular margin." I shrugged. "You better go start prepping the area back there for a hot tub."

"We have a little while before we need to worry about that, don't we, Skipper?"

I looked at the chrono. "I'd guess about ten ticks, Chief."

She blinked in confusion. "How can that be?"

"Because I expect the chandlery crew to be up here about that time and looking to install a hot tub."

She finally caught up with me. "You already ordered it?"

"Last night." I shrugged. "Either way, it was a sure bet."

She frowned and snickered a little. "How do you figure that, Skipper?"

"Well, either Mr. Hill won," I held up my tablet, "and I pay off the bet by getting a hot tub for the crew. Or Mr. Wyatt won, and I get a hot tub for the crew." I made a show of considering it. "I don't see a down side to this, do you?"

She hesitated for just about four heartbeats. "If there is, I don't see it, Skipper. Let me go see what kind of shape the room is in and start some of the prep." With that she ambled out of the mess deck and I followed her out, heading for the lock.

"Mr. Hill, congratulations!"

He looked up as I approached. "Thank you, Captain. For what?"

"You beat Mr. Wyatt after five trips. Your picking beat his."

He blinked in disbelief. "How is that possible, Captain?"

I shrugged. "When the dust settled, your total was higher than his. By one credit."

He barked a laugh. "One? Over five picks I beat him by one miserable credit?"

I shrugged and held up my tablet so he could see the numbers.

"One credit, Mr. Hill. It's all you needed to win."

He shook his head. "I can't believe it." He leaned in to look at my tablet more closely, then he looked me in the eye. "You beat us both by ten kilocreds, Captain?"

I shrugged again. "I got lucky."

"We should be taking cargo picking lessons from you, sar!"

"We're all the same crew, Mr. Hill, and we were operating under artificial constraints."

He scratched his nose and glanced at me sideways. "So, we're getting the hot tub, Captain?"

I smiled. "Yes, Mr. Hill. You won the bet. We're getting the hot tub."

He beamed. "That's excellent, Captain. Do you think we'll have it before we get underway again?"

I made a show of considering the question. "I believe that can be arranged, Mr. Hill, yes."

The call buzzer broke into the conversation.

"That should be the delivery now."

He keyed the lock and we went out to meet the shipfitters. "Charlie! Good to see you again."

"Hello, Captain." He grinned back. "More remodeling?"

"Well, I need to pay off a bet with my crew. They delivered and now I need to."

He nodded. "I've got the equipment and I brought a couple of piping specialists today. Where do you want it?"

We led them into the ship and I took Charlie and his gang back to where the chief was pulling exercise equipment out of the workout room. I left them to the details and headed back to the mess deck. Mr. Hill called to me before I made the turn and I went out to the lock to see what he needed.

"Yes, Mr. Hill?"

"Captain? How did that crew get here so fast?"

"I'm not sure I follow, Mr. Hill."

"You haven't been keeping up with your lying practice, Skipper."

I shrugged apologetically. "I haven't had much cause to lately, Mr. Hill."

"You just got those final numbers on the bet, Skipper, but that crew showed up within a dozen ticks."

"True, Mr. Hill." I smiled at him. "And you find that odd?"

"Well, Skipper, it sort of implies that you must have ordered that hot tub sometime yesterday at the latest."

"Why, yes, I believe that's a valid assessment, Mr. Hill."

"Before you knew if I won or not."

"True again."

"And last night it looked like Mr. Wyatt was going to win it."

"Yes, Mr. Hill. It did. Your logical construction leads you to only one conclusion, I trust?"

"Yes, Captain. You were going to get the hot tub whether I won or not."

"I believe that would be a fair conclusion, Mr. Hill. Do you have a problem with that?"

He frowned. "Why, Captain?"

"I thought it sounded like a great idea, and win or lose, the ship has made more than enough profit to cover it. For the last couple of weeks I've been thinking how nice it would be to take a nice hot soak after watch."

"You don't expect me to actually be Mr. Wyatt's apprentice in return or anything do you, Captain?" He looked a little wary.

"No, Mr. Hill. A bet's a bet and this one is over and paid off. You're under no obligation."

That seemed to mollify him and he nodded. "Okay, then, Skipper. Thank you, and thanks for the chance to try to beat him."

"Thanks for laying the challenge out there. It's paid off handsomely for all of us, I think." I started to head to the galley but another thought struck me and I turned back to him. "Will you be taking your cargo rating and trying to find another berth, Mr. Hill?"

"I thought about it, Captain, but unless something drastically better comes along, I think I'd like to stay here and see what happens next."

"Thank you, Mr. Hill. I appreciate your candor." I went into the mess deck and poured a cup of coffee before settling at the table and pulling up the cargo lists. I didn't expect to spot anything but it passed the time before I needed to start on lunch.

The installation of the hot tub took most of the day, but by the time I started dealing with the dinner mess, Charlie and his crew were picking up their tools and policing the area. Chief Gerheart appeared at the entrance to the mess deck and grinned. "You might wanna check this out before they get all packed up, Skipper."

"Why? Is there something wrong with it?"

She shook her head. "Oh, no. It looks great to me."

I followed her back down to the workout room. The tub was not one of the larger models. Realistically, no more than a half dozen people needed to be able to use it at a time. More likely it would be a couple of us at once, maybe as many as four, but with watches underway and liberty while docked, it was plenty large enough for what I thought we needed. Roughly oblong with rounded corners, a molded cowling latched to a frame on the deck and concealed the plumbing works. The whole thing was a little more than a meter tall, extended from the bulkhead about two meters in one direction and three in the other. It was already about half full of water and was slowly filling as we watched.

Charlie came over to point out the main features. "You'll want to wait until it's full, Captain, and then you can start-up the heaters. I've left the full instructions with the chief there, but this should be a warm treat in the Deep Dark."

I nodded as I admired his work. "Thanks, Charlie. I'm looking forward to it myself."

He pointed out things like the safety lid that locked down to prevent sloppage, and the automatic cutoffs that prevented scalding the crew. He was grinning. "Wait'll you try the jets, Skipper."

I laughed. "I *have* been in a hot tub before, Charlie. I think I know what jets do."

He grinned knowingly. "All right then, Captain, but don't say I didn't tell ya."

He signaled his crew and they all trouped back to the lock while I got on with fixing dinner. I didn't expect too many people aboard, but I had a mind to make a nice beef roast with vegetables. The leftovers, if there were any, would make a good soup.

At 1700, Mr. Wyatt and Ms. Thomas came back aboard and by 1715, Mr. Ricks was aboard as well, bringing the co-op goods back to the ship with Mr. Schubert's help. I revised my estimate for dinner and added a few more vegetables to the pot. Mr. Wyatt joined me after changing out of his civvies.

"Nice day off, Mr. Wyatt?"

"Yes, Captain. Thank you. It was lovely." He had a dreamy smile on his face and I didn't pry. "Anything new here?"

"Mr. Hill won the bet." I glanced at him as I said it.

"Oh, excellent. I was hoping he would. I'd much rather have the hot tub than an assistant."

I chuckled. "Well, we have the hot tub."

He blinked at me. "Already?"

"Ship fitters left half a stan ago. The tub's filling now and should be up to temp by this time tomorrow."

He grinned. "You acted very fast!"

"I ordered it last night."

He looked surprised. "Did you think he'd win last night?"

I shook my head. "He won by one cred. The numbers came down around 0830."

He whistled appreciatively. "That's cutting it fine." He turned to peeling the extra carrots and we got the dinner mess underway in record time.

As it happened everybody but Mr. Pall was aboard for dinner and I hoped that he wouldn't be falling down any more ladders. At 1745, Ms. Thomas and Mr. Ricks relieved the watch and Mr. Hill joined us on the mess deck.

Mr. Wyatt greeted him warmly. "Congratulations, Mr. Hill."

"Thank you, sar." He nodded in acknowledgement. "Did the captain tell you what his total was?"

Mr. Wyatt turned to me. "Your total, Captain?"

"I did pretty well."

"Pretty well? He beat us by ten kilocreds, Mr. Wyatt."

Ms. Thomas, who was sitting at the table, laughed. "You've been hiding your light under a bushel, Captain!"

Mr. Wyatt raised his eyebrows. "Any special knowledge, Skipper? Tips for the working stiffs?"

I laughed. "No, Mr. Wyatt. Almost all of it was because of the early delivery bonus on that very first can. It was luck more than anything."

Mr. Wyatt mugged for Mr. Hill. "The captain says luck, Mr. Hill. I think he's holding out."

"Well, we need a shipment, don't we, Mr. Wyatt?" Mr. Hill was having fun. "Maybe we should get the captain to show us how it's done."

The level of joviality ran quite high and the chief joined us as the chrono clicked up towards 1800.

I looked over my shoulder from where I was draining vegetables just in time to see a three can cargo with a high priority hit the top of the free-cargo list on the repeater. "Mr. Hill? My hands are wet, would you check the delivery date on that priority?"

He turned to look and then dove for the keyboard to drill into the record. "November fifth, Skipper. Eight weeks."

"Mr. Wyatt, you're the cargo officer here and I'm up to my elbows in hot food. In your professional opinion, is that a cargo we should take?"

He was already sprinting for the cargo terminal and a tick later the cargo status changed to show we had a cargo bound for Breakall.

He was grinning broadly as he came back onto the mess deck. "Skipper? You're systems certified. Is there any way we can modify my tablet so it'll place an order?"

"See me after mess, Mr. Wyatt. I'll show you."

I'd wondered why he always went to the cargo terminal to place the orders, but I assumed it was for some personal reason. I chuckled to myself. That would probably not actually teach me, but it was certainly one more lesson in making assumptions.

Dinner mess went smoothly and everybody helped clean up after, except Mr. Ricks who went back to his watch station. By 1930, I'd shown Mr. Wyatt how to slave the cargo terminal to his tablet and headed to the cabin. I settled at my desk and filed the flight plan to Breakall with departure set for the thirteenth. That gave us a full four day port stay and, if the preliminary course projections were even close, we'd be in Breakall a week before the deadline on the cargo.

I clicked through the pending reports and by 2000 sat back in my chair. A feeling of "now what?" washed over me. I found it unsettling. I looked around the cabin and–with the exception of the glare from the port–I liked what I saw. I looked at the armor glass and wondered for the umpteenth time if I should do something about the light reflecting in from the side of the orbital. I decided for the umpteenth time that it wasn't worth the effort because we'd be under way soon. I'd have weeks of Deep Dark to look at.

There was also the unsettling feeling of being single. I tried to get a handle on that. For seven stanyers, I'd had a commitment that needed to be honored. That was gone and it felt like it had disappeared suddenly. Sure, I'd known it was going away for weeks, but the packet of papers in my grav trunk said it was over. The reality of it fell upon me and I wanted to feel jubilant. I wanted to feel freed. I wanted to feel *something*.

The cabin felt like home, but I needed to get out for awhile and stretch my legs. I wasn't really sure I wanted to be around people, but I also didn't want to spend the evening sitting there feeling sorry for myself. I headed for my civvies and an old ritual came back to me as I was washing up. I grinned as I clipped my fingernails.

Chapter Fifty-five
Diurnia Orbital: 2372-September-10

When I left the ship, I just followed my nose. I couldn't very well go down to the oh-two deck. That was where crews went. As a rule, one didn't see captains down there. I headed up to the civilian areas on seven and strolled around the orbital looking for someplace. I didn't really know what I was looking for and I was feeling a bit sorry for myself. It had been so long since I'd been single, I wasn't sure what I was supposed to do any more. Being a captain only made that worse. There were proprieties to observe that I hadn't had to deal with before.

The stroll felt good to legs that had been too long in a can. I made two full circuits of the seven deck without seeing anything that appealed to me. I was familiar with most of the restaurants and watering holes on seven but seldom frequented them. When I passed the ladder up to eight deck, I climbed up and made a circuit there as well. I recognized some of the places but certainly not all.

Eventually I settled on an upscale coffee boutique called Light City. The smell attracted me as much as anything and after nearly a stan of walking in circles, a cup of coffee and a sit down sounded like a good idea. Inside the place was outfitted with a collection of sofas and chairs, a few restaurant style tables, and a heavy wooden bar with about ten tall stools. The place wasn't crowded but it was far from empty and a low buzz of conversation wafted over a whirring, rattling sound coming from a glorious bronze and dark metal contraption against the far wall. It was roped off from casual approach, but held obvious pride of place.

I was drawn towards it and as I approached I could feel the heat on my face. A short, wiry man with a completely shaved head was opening some sort of lever and allowing the contents to pour

375

out into a rotating wire basket. When the cinnamon colored flow stopped, he reached back and flipped a couple of switches and a low-pitched motor sound died out as the heavier noise of the machine's mechanism faded. The basket was filled with toasted coffee beans. The aroma was almost overwhelming.

With his tasks complete, he turned to me with a grin. "Good evening, Captain. How may I help you?"

I could feel myself grinning. "I think I'd like a cup of coffee."

He laughed. "We might be able to find the odd cup or two. Do you have a preference?" He stepped out of the roped area and led me to the counter and I hitched a hip onto one of the empty stools.

"Well, I'm most familiar with Djartmo Arabasti in a medium roast but Sarabanda Dark isn't bad either."

He grinned happily. "You at least know the difference! I'm impressed. Most people can't tell espresso from press. How adventurous are you?" He had a twinkle in his eye.

"Relatively. That roast there smells wonderful. What's that?"

"One of the components of a house blend. That's an Arabasti base bean, shade grown on Grail. We roast that to a nice light city and blend it with a city roasted Zenovka Taratzu. We call it Moscow Morning."

I held out my hand. "Ishmael Wang. Nice to meet you."

He grinned, wiped his hand on his apron before returning the shake. "Steve Jacob. Nice to meet you, Captain. Now what can I show you?"

I spent a delicious stan talking coffee, sipping samples, and savoring a large cup of an appropriately named Evening Mug. The flavor was rich and fruity with an almost cinnamon aftertaste. The shop did a moderate walk-in business but Steve handled all the customers personally. Many of them appeared to be regulars who walked up to the counter, were greeted by name, and settled onto the various chairs and couches depending on their preference.

The tension I didn't realize I'd been carrying melted away as the level in the mug went down.

"I don't suppose you sell much in bulk, do you, Steve?"

He chuckled. "No. Vinnie there is my only roaster and I can only do twenty kilos at a time."

"Vinnie?"

He laughed. "Yep. It's a Vincenzo Victorex 900 roaster. It's almost an antique at this point. I call him Vinnie." He looked over at it fondly for a moment before continuing. "I package a few kilos for regulars but all the bulk stuff is custom order. I try not to have roasted beans laying around too long."

"Define too long."

"More than a couple days." He grinned. "I keep a few kilos bricked up, if you'd like to take some with you, but I can't handle starship quantities."

"What's your largest package?"

"I can do five kilo pails, but mostly I sell the two kilo bricks." He shrugged. "My coffee's expensive because it's custom roasted in small batches from special beans." He wasn't apologizing, just explaining.

In the end I bought a brick of the Evening Mug and another of the Moscow Morning. The four kilos of coffee cost a little more than a full pail of our Djartmo Arabasti, but it would make a nice break in the routine. He put them in a carry-sack for me. "They'll keep in that package for two or three weeks without any problem, Ishmael, but once you open them, try to use them up within a few days. The flavor will degrade pretty rapidly."

"At the rate we go through coffee, these won't last more than a few days." I thanked him, shouldered my load and headed back to the ship.

Riding down in the lift, it occurred to me that I hadn't really found what I had gone out looking for, but had found something else instead. Funny how that works so often. Serendipity strikes at odd moments and always when you're not looking. I chuckled to myself, realizing that if I'd been looking, then it wouldn't have been serendipity to begin with.

The lift opened onto the dock but the chill air reminded me of one other errand that I should run, so I punched the button for the oh-one deck and headed for the chandlery. I needed a bathing suit before heading back to the ship for the night and a well earned snooze.

My treacherous body clock overwhelmed me at 0600. It had been my intention to sleep in, but in the battle between brain and bladder, bladder won every time. Once moving, there was no going back so I bowed to the inevitable and headed for breakfast.

Most of the crew was present, including a rumpled and not very well rested Mr. Pall. I gave my bundle of coffee to Mr. Wyatt and suggested he tuck it away until we got underway. The breakfast mess went smoothly with Mr. Wyatt presiding over a waffle iron and the rest of us enjoying the fruits of his labor. The only odd spot in the proceeding was Mr. Ricks. There was something going on, judging from the looks he was exchanging with his fellow ratings.

As we cleared the breakfast away, I took the opportunity to speak to him quietly.

"Is there something you'd like to talk with me about, Mr. Ricks?"

He looked like a kid caught with his hand in the candy jar.

"Why do you ask, Captain?"

I eyed him and then pointedly looked at the other ratings. "They seem to think something's up."

He looked at the deck. "Skipper, there's an opening on the board for a messman."

"Which ship?"

"The *Paul Fischer* out of Martha's Haven. They're getting underway day after tomorrow."

"Did you apply, Mr. Ricks?"

"I'd like to, Captain, but they think I should stay."

"What's your reasoning, Mr. Ricks?"

He shrugged. "The shares have been great and the ship has really perked up since you've been aboard, Captain."

"But..?"

"But this watch stander thing is getting old. I feel like I'm off balance and exhausted all the time. I think I'd like to try working the mess deck. Day workers don't have it any easier, I know, and the mess deck on a big ship isn't exactly glamorous, but when the day's over, I can sleep."

"So? What's holding you back, Mr. Ricks. Those sound like excellent reasons."

"Well, you'll need to replace me, Skipper. Assuming I can even get the job to begin with."

"That's true of any of us, Mr. Ricks. Why don't you apply and see what happens. In the meantime, I'll contact the office and see if there's anybody waiting in the wings."

He looked up at me. "Really, Captain?"

I shrugged. "Look, Mr. Ricks. You've been a good shipmate and you're qualified to take this berth. You've got some good reasons for taking it and the only obstacle is actually getting it. You can't manage your career solely on the basis of what's good for the ship, but you have to look out for you, too. It's too cold out in the Deep Dark to do a job you don't like."

"But what if I get it and you have to replace me. You could be delayed for days."

I chuckled. "Look at the list of open berths for deck ratings, Mr. Ricks."

He blinked at me. "There aren't that many to look at, Skipper. A few Able Spacers and once in a while you'll see an Ordinary Spacer, but they don't last long."

"Why do you suppose that is, Mr. Ricks?"

"There aren't that many openings, sar?"

I shook my head. "There's usually a waiting list of people to fill them. You don't see them because they get filled too quickly.

Don't fret about it, Mr. Ricks. Follow your gut. If you want it, apply. If you apply, let me know so I can be prepared to replace you. That's all I ask."

He looked me square in the face. "Thanks, Captain. I'll apply as soon as we get the co-op set up this morning and I'll let you know what I hear."

"Thank you, Mr. Ricks, and good luck."

By the time we finished our little corner discussion, we'd attracted the attention of Mr. Wyatt and Ms. Thomas. They kept their distance but looked questioningly at me as Mr. Ricks smiled and hustled off the mess deck to help Mr. Hill set up the day's co-op activities.

Ms. Thomas nodded after him. "Trouble in paradise, Skipper?"

I shook my head. "The boys aren't happy with Mr. Ricks because he's thinking of leaving our merry band of travelers and taking up with another ship."

Mr. Wyatt looked surprised. "Whatever for, Captain?"

"He's got some good reasons, Avery. And I can't fault him for wanting to move on to something that he might like better."

Ms. Thomas nodded her agreement. "Yeah. Sometimes you just need a break. What's he going for, Skipper?"

"There's an open berth for a messman. He passed the test a while back. He's qualified, although he has no mess deck experience. He'll be okay on a larger vessel where he can be part of an established mess gang."

The answer seemed to answer their immediate needs so I excused myself and headed for the cabin to check in with DST. I needed to know if we had any crew on the wait list.

My inquiry returned in a matter of half a stan with a summons to meet Mr. Maloney for lunch.

CHAPTER FIFTY-SIX
DIURNIA ORBITAL: 2372-SEPTEMBER-10

Mr. Maloney met me for lunch at a place called "Sandy's Seafood" up on the seven deck. I'd heard of it, but never tried it before. The decor was what I think could be euphemistically called "rustic" with plastic table cloths patterned in red and white checks and large areas of "family seating" where people who didn't know each other could sit and pretend they were all part of an extended family. I never really understood that part from a patron's point of view. I did understand that it allowed the restaurant to put more seats per square meter and probably turned those seats over faster as people discovered they really didn't like sitting next to that crazy guy with the orange hair.

I was grateful to see that Mr. Maloney had taken a booth in the corner. Kurt was in the next booth where he could keep an eye on the room and the door. I nodded to him and he gave me a small smile and a nod as I approached and took my seat across from Mr. Maloney.

Mr. Maloney smiled and shook my hand, half rising to greet me, and with ceremony served, we settled down to menu perusal. The waitress–a perky young woman in a red gingham uniform and a name tag that said "Mary"–seemed disappointed that we ordered water, coffee, and two bowls of "Sandy's Signature Chowder."

"Ishmael, I've got to hand it to you." Mr. Maloney smiled at me. "I really felt bad about giving you the *Agamemnon*. For most people, that's a punishment berth. What in the world did you do over there?"

I gave him a run down of the issues with various crew members, standing orders, and the assumptions that many of them were working under. "I really didn't do that much, except take a look at why the ship wasn't making money and figure out ways to fix it."

He nodded slowly. "Your opinion of Delman?"

"No comment. He was the skipper for a long time and I don't want to second guess him."

Mr. Maloney snorted. "Do I need to worry about the *Tinker*?"

That was a fair question and I considered it, sipping my coffee to buy a little time. "He started with a good, competent crew. If he keeps them, they should help him. Inertia is a powerful force."

"What did you do with Wyatt? Your cargo performance has gone through the roof."

It was my turn to snort at that. "Check with your front office Cargo Dispatch people."

"We don't have any front office Cargo Dispatch people."

"That's who was picking his cargoes. He didn't know he could pick his own so he called the office and your clerks would pick for him. For the last five runs we've been having a little cargo picking contest. Winner after five runs gets a prize."

He perked up at that. "Contest? You and Wyatt?"

"Mr. Wyatt against Brandon Hill. I picked the third can just so they'd be on an even footing."

"Hill? You let Hill pick cargoes?"

I shrugged. "Kept him out of trouble on the docks, and he's got a keen eye for value."

"He's an Able Spacer. How could you let a rating pick cargo?"

I shrugged again. "It worked out. Why not? We could hardly have done any worse having him pick one can out of three than having your desk clerks around the sector picking the whole load." I eyed him and let that sink in for a few heartbeats. "And he won the bet."

Mr. Maloney blinked at me. "He outpicked Wyatt?"

I nodded.

"Well, I can't demote Wyatt any more than putting him on the *Agamemnon*." He sighed, and then realized what he'd just implied. He had the grace to look embarrassed. "Oh. Sorry."

"Why would you want to demote him? Mr. Hill outpicked him by exactly one credit after five cans and the ship itself has turned more profit in the last eight months than it has the last two stanyers combined."

Mr. Maloney frowned but nodded in agreement to cede the point.

The chowder arrived and we took a few ticks to savor the rich creamy broth with potatoes, onions, and several kinds of fish. It was liberally sprinkled with fresh ground pepper and a spattering of minced chives. It came with a basket of warm biscuits.

When the initial survey of the soup was completed, I glanced over to him. "So? Thanks for lunch, but I'm guessing there's more on your mind than catching up on old times?"

Behind me I heard Kurt snicker quietly from the next booth.

Mr. Maloney shot him an amused look before turning back to me. "Yes, well. The inquiry about the wait list."

"I thought it might be something like that."

"Who've you lost?" He frowned. "I didn't see any personnel actions on the files."

"Nobody yet." I shrugged. "We may not. Zack Ricks is going for a job on the *Paul Fischer* out of Martha's Haven."

Mr. Maloney looked blank for a tick. "I don't know that one."

"Mixed freight hauler. Eighty metric kilotons. Private owner."

"They need a spacer?"

I shook my head. "No. The opening is for a messman. Mr. Ricks qualified and is going for it."

Mr. Maloney looked surprised. "He's going for mess deck duty?"

"Is there something wrong with mess deck duty?"

He shrugged. "Not really. Just seems like a step down from Deck Division."

I stared at him. I think it wasn't really with the full respect he might have thought he deserved. "Deck Division needs to eat, just like the rest, and full share is full share."

Behind me Kurt coughed. It sounded to me like he was covering a laugh.

"I suppose." Mr. Maloney scraped the bottom of his bowl and reached for another biscuit while he considered. "How do you feel about losing him?"

"He's a good shipmate. He made a good morale officer and he'll be missed."

"You want me to scotch it for you?"

"Excuse me? Scotch what?"

He gave a small shrug and smile. "If I put a word in the captain's ear on this–what is it? *Paul Fischer?* He won't get the berth."

I worked to keep my face carefully neutral. "I've already written him a recommendation and sent it along to Captain Plested."

Mr. Maloney looked confused. "If he was such a good shipmate, why would you do that, Ishmael? Shouldn't you be trying to keep him?"

The sigh almost escaped but I think I covered it adequately by sipping my coffee. "No, sir. He earned the berth. I owe it to him to help him get the berth he wants."

He arched an eyebrow in my direction. "You realize you're going to have to break in a new crewman if he goes?"

I shrugged. "Of course. It's the nature of the business."

Mr. Maloney chewed the end of his biscuit and gave me a long look across the table.

"I assume you have somebody on the wait list, sir?"

He nodded slowly. "Several somebodies."

I could see him running through the list in his mind and I could only imagine what formula was being worked as he weighed what I'd told him against the list of spacers waiting for a berth. I waited him out, drinking my coffee.

"Stacie Arellone. Spacer Apprentice."

Kurt snorted.

I sipped my coffee once more and met his challenging stare from across the checked table cloth. "She's the worst of the bunch, huh? You don't have anybody worse?"

Mr. Maloney looked slightly offended that I'd commented. "She's next on the list. Been ashore the longest and can't seem to find a skipper who'll take her."

I shrugged. "Okay. If Mr. Ricks gets the berth, I'll let the office know and you can send her over."

"You might want to interview her first, Ishmael." His voice held a note of caution and something sounded suspiciously like amusement.

"I intend to, Mr. Maloney."

"No, you miss my point." The amusement bubbled up. "You'll need to get her out of the brig before we can send her over. You might want to interview her before you sign up to be responsible for her." He was grinning broadly.

"Brig? What's she in for?"

"Knifing a guy in a brawl."

"What's her side of it?"

He shrugged. "I have no idea. It's not the only time she's been in trouble. A real hard case."

"She's being held on station?"

He nodded. "Short term detention on the oh-eleven deck. I'm not sure how much longer her sentence is. She got 30 days."

From behind me, Kurt spoke quietly. "Ten more days."

"They'll let me take her instead of serving out her sentence?"

Mr. Maloney shrugged. "She wouldn't have served a day if she had had a ship. Judge wanted her off the orbital and needed a captain to release her to. Failing that?" He shrugged again. "She's in detention."

The sigh escaped before I could stop it.

Mr. Maloney grinned.

I didn't punch him and gave myself high marks for my self control.

"So? You still want to lose Ricks?"

I shook my head. "I never wanted to lose Mr. Ricks. What I want is the best for my people. Keeping him or not isn't the question."

He smirked. "Visit Arellone first. Then see what you think."

I nodded. "I'll do that. Thanks for the advice."

Mary returned to the table. "Can I interest you gentlemen in dessert today?"

Mr. Maloney smiled. "I'd love a slice of the apple pie, and a fresh coffee?"

She nodded and turned to me.

I shook my head. "No, thank you, Mary. I've got to get back to work."

I slipped out of the booth and nodded to Mr. Maloney. "Thanks for lunch, boss, and the enlightening conversation."

He acknowledged it with an airy wave of his hand while Mary retreated to fetch his dessert. "My pleasure, Ishmael." He grinned a little evilly. "Don't say I didn't warn you."

I nodded to him and turned to Kurt. "Nice to see you again, Kurt."

"You, too, Captain. Congratulations on turning that ship around."

"Thanks." I smiled and headed toward the door.

Outside in the passageway, I made sure the recommendation for Mr. Ricks had been delivered to the *Fischer* and then pulled Arellone's records up out of the DST office files. Her public profile was bad enough. Her private record was much worse. The ID photo showed a young woman with flashing dark eyes and brown hair. It didn't say much about her. ID photos are notoriously bad.

I headed for the lift.

The oh-eleven deck was all security. The doors opened and I stepped into a small anteroom. A security officer sat behind a tall podium. She was looking at me even as the lift doors opened. Her eyes flickered to my collar tabs as I approached and she smiled pleasantly enough.

"Good afternoon, Captain. Can I help you?"

I pulled out my ID tab and offered it to her. "Good afternoon, Officer. I'm here about one of the prisoners, Spacer Apprentice Stacie Arellone."

She took my tab and slotted it into the terminal on her podium. She consulted with something for a few heartbeats and nodded. "Are you related, Captain? Is she one of your crew?"

I shook my head. "Not related, and not part of my crew yet. She's next on the waiting list and I'm expecting an opening."

She eyed me over the top of her terminal. "And you're going to hire her?"

"I'm not sure. A lot will depend on whether she wants to be hired, and whether I can get her released in time to sail."

She tapped a few keys. "You'd have to file a request to get her released on your recognizance, Captain, but she's served over half her term." She shrugged. "When do you sail?"

"Probably within the next two days. It really depends on whether I have a crew." I smiled. "Is it possible to meet with Ms. Arellone?"

She pulled a badge out from under the podium that was already embossed with my picture and printed with some officialese culled from my ID tab. She handed it to me. "If you'd clip that to your collar, Captain, and go through that door?" She pointed to my right. "The duty officer there should be able to help you." She pulled my ID tab from the slot and put it in a drawer in her podium. "We'll hold this until you're ready to leave, Captain."

I nodded, clipped on the temporary badge, and went through the indicated door.

Within a few ticks I was seated at a table in an interview room while a security officer fetched Ms. Arellone. I noted the obvious security cameras in the corners of the room and assumed there were other, less obvious ones as well. The table itself was bolted to the deck, but I was amused to note that the chairs were not.

The door opened and the officer held it for a woman in a neon green jumpsuit with a large black "P" on the front. I recognized the eyes from the ID. Her hair had grown out a bit and her attitude was a hundred percent hardcase.

I stood as she entered and crossed to the chair on the far side of the table. The security officer closed the door and took up his station on the inside of it without comment.

Ms. Arellone pulled the chair out from the table and plonked herself down into it, leaning back and sneering at me across the scarred plastic surface.

I took my own seat and regarded her. The deep brown eyes had some fire left in them and her hair needed clipping. She had no visible piercings but there were holes in her lobes.

She arched an eyebrow at my scrutiny. "Getting a good look, Captain?"

"No tattoos, Ms. Arellone?"

"None visible."

I shrugged noncommittally. "So? What's a nice girl like you doing in a place like this?"

She barked a laugh. "You didn't see my rap sheet, Captain?"

"I saw it. I'm asking you, Ms. Arellone."

She backed down a little. Not much, but a little. "Then you know. It's pretty much all true."

"What parts aren't?"

"Courts don't like little girls who aren't nice. You wouldn't understand that, would you. Captain."

She bit off the last word as if it were a curse.

I considered that. "No, you're probably right. It's outside my experience. Never having been a girl nor arrested, I couldn't say. I'll take your report as evidence."

She seemed a little surprised by my response and I saw a flicker in her eyes before the shields closed back down. "So? What do you want from me, Captain? Your cabin boy leave you and you thinkin' of branchin' out?"

"Your record says you're rated as Able Spacer but were busted back to Apprentice."

"Four times, Captain." She said it almost proudly.

"One of mine may be going to another ship. I need a replacement. You want a job?"

She eyed me. "Maloney hate you or something?"

"My relationship with Mr. Maloney is not on the table, Ms. Arellone. Frankly, I think he's using you as a threat to keep me from letting my crewman go to another fleet."

She was surprised at that and let her guard down almost completely. "Usin' me as a threat?"

"If I let my crewman leave, he's going to assign you to my ship."

She laughed derisively. "What's your ship? *Agamemnon*?"

I grinned. "How'd you guess?"

She stopped laughing suddenly. "You're kiddin' me. *Agamemnon*? What happened to Captain Dorkman?" She pronounced it carefully as two full syllables.

"Captain Delman went to the *Tinker*. I was next in line for Captain. Mr. Maloney gave me the berth."

"Gads! He must hate you. Who's leavin'? Chooch finally grow a pair?"

"You know my crew?"

She shrugged. "The ratings are pretty well known on the docks. Penny ante junk mostly. Bar fights, and the odd blackmarket deal." Her eyes narrowed and she looked at me. "I haven't heard much from them for the last few months. You keep them confined to the ship or somethin'?"

I shook my head. "No, Ms. Arellone. We've been hauling freight."

She snickered. "That's what we're calling it these days?"

"That's what I've always called it, Ms. Arellone. I'm in the business to make money. I'm captain and I get the biggest share. It's also true that the more money I make, the more money the crew makes."

She threw back her head and brayed a raucous horse laugh. "And what princely sum did your crew make on your latest run, Captain Midas?"

"I believe full share on this last run was in excess of two kilocreds." I said it quietly and let it lay on the table for her to notice.

She stopped laughing but didn't look convinced. "You expect me to believe that?"

I shook my head. "No. I expect you to distrust it with every fiber of your being. You don't know me and you have no reason to trust me."

She leaned forward and slapped the table with an open palm. "Then why'd ya say it?"

"You asked. That's the answer. I have no reason to lie, but you have no reason to know that." I shrugged and looked at her. "So? If this berth opens up, are you interested? Or should I tell Mr. Maloney he needs to find another threat to hold over my head?"

She frowned at me. "You're serious."

"Yes, Ms. Arellone. I'm serious. I've already sent a letter of recommendation on behalf of my crewman and I intend to follow it up. He wants to get off the *Agamemnon*. He thinks this is a good move. I want to help him. That's all there is to it."

She leaned back and turned half sideways in her chair. She was regarding me like some kind of foreign life form and I just let her look. After a few ticks, she spoke. "What's in it for me?"

I waved a hand. "Well, you would have to give up your palatial apartment here and move into crew berthing."

She snickered.

"You would have to give up that lovely green jump suit as well. Then there's the endless watches."

"You really know how to show a girl a good time, Captain."

"I try, Ms. Arellone."

It slipped under her guard and she gave a short, and genuine, laugh.

"Are you in or out, Ms. Arellone?"

"Like I have a choice?"

"As I understand it, in a few more days, you'll be out from under this little rainbow and you can do what you want. Find another berth, maybe."

Her face screwed up in a bitter grimace. "Yeah. That'll happen, I'm sure."

I gave a half shrug. "I'm offering you a berth. Quarter share for now until you can take the exam again. After that, it's up to you."

"Up to Maloney, you mean?"

I thought about that for a few heartbeats. "Yes. He has some input into it. If you pass the exam, I'll put you back up as soon as DST authorizes it. I'm willing to go to bat for you. Got any other offers?"

She looked at me then, square in the face. "And what do I have to do to earn this spectacular largesse. Captain?"

"Stand your watch. Do your job. Pull your weight."

She arched one eyebrow. "That's it? No 'ancillary duties as required'? No, 'be a good girl and do what you're told'?"

I paused. "Well, there may be an ancillary duty or two, Ms. Arellone."

She barked a harsh, "Ha!"

"Mr. Ricks is Morale Officer. If he leaves, that will be open and I think that generally falls to the junior member of the crew. In the event that you're it, that would be your ancillary duty."

She all but guffawed. "Morale Officer? Me?"

"Who better to suggest ways to improve morale than the one person with the most to gain?"

I let her digest that for a full tick. Her expression went from contempt and surprise to serious contemplation.

"You're serious."

I nodded. "Yes, Ms. Arellone. I'm serious."

I let her stew for a half dozen heartbeats.

"So? You interested?"

She squinted her eyes and blew a long breath out of her nose before replying. "Yes, Captain. I'm interested. I think you're blowing smoke but I'm interested."

I nodded and reached across the table to offer my hand. The guard at the door flinched and I looked at him. "Problem?"

He eyed me and then her and shook his head.

She reached across and took my hand, shaking it briefly.

"Thank you, Ms. Arellone. I look forward to sailing with you."

She retreated behind her shields. "I bet you do."

I nodded at the guard and he opened the door and escorted the prisoner away.

She didn't look back.

The crew said good-bye to Mr. Ricks at breakfast. The real send-off had apparently happened the night before, judging from the blood-shot eyes and general level of energy among the three ratings. He was due to report at 0800 and we waved him out the lock at 0715 with plenty of time to spare.

I'd also made arrangements with the orbital's security staff to have Ms. Arellone released on my recognizance at 0730. They knew we were on a tight schedule and they were happy to see her leave. I only had to present myself, a copy of her employment contract, and sign a bond that I'd be responsible for her. They had her ready and waiting for me and the whole transaction was done in less than two ticks.

She wore rumpled jeans and a jersey top and carried a bundle of personal goods under her arm. We got onto the lift and I glanced over at her. "Do you have anything you need to do before we get underway? Close up an apartment? Pick up goods from storage? Anything like that, Ms. Arellone?"

She shrugged and didn't look at me. "Quarter share can't take much, Captain. I have a duffel in a locker on oh-one. The apartment was closed for me when I got sent down."

I punched the button for oh-one and we stopped to pick up her bag. She shouldered it easily and we headed out.

"You need any personal gear? Toothpaste? Anything? We're getting underway this afternoon. When we get back to the ship, you're pretty much stuck," I said.

She glared at me. "Am I under house arrest or something, Captain?"

I shook my head. "Nothing of the kind, Ms. Arellone. I'm just trying to make the transition as easy as possible. I'm serious about getting under way, and you won't have a chance to get anything once we get to the ship."

She hefted the bag on her shoulder. "I can't afford any more mass, Captain."

I sighed and led her into the chandlery. I bought an empty duffel bag. "You have a bathing suit in that bag?"

She looked at me like I'd grown a second head. "You getting pervy already, Captain?"

"We have a hot tub. You need a suit. Do you have one?"

"Hot tub? On the *Agamemnon*?"

"Yes, Ms. Arellone. Please focus. I'm supposed to be on watch. We need to move. Do you have a bathing suit in that bag?"

"No."

"Buy one." I pointed at the hygiene counter. "And anything else you'll need for an eight week voyage. Just do it fast, Ms. Arellone."

She was fast. I'll give her that. In four ticks flat she had what she needed on the counter and the clerk checking her out gave her the tab to thumb. She hesitated.

"Problems, Ms. Arellone?"

She looked down and turned a little toward me. "I–I can't afford this, Captain."

I looked at the bill. It was two digits. I thumbed it, pushed all the gear into the second duffel, zipped it and pointed to the door. "Go. We're late."

We hit the lock by 0800 and I left her with Mr. Hill to get checked in while I headed for the mess deck to take my watch back from Ms. Thomas. I found her and Mr. Wyatt sitting at the table with the cribbage board set up between them.

They looked up with smiles when I came around the corner. "Back so soon, Skipper?"

"Yes, Ms. Thomas. Thanks for covering the watch."

She shrugged. "No problem, Captain. Avery's trying to teach me how to play cribbage."

I grinned. "A lovely game. How's it going?"

Mr. Wyatt shook his head. "The problem is that I'm not sure I know how, Captain. We're just kinda fumbling around here."

"We'll have time to pick it up underway. Mr. Hill is quite a good player at this point."

Ms. Thomas nodded. "Well, how's our new crew?"

I shrugged. "She'll be okay, I think. Need to get her calmed down a little."

"Calmed down, Captain?" Mr. Wyatt raised an eyebrow.

"She's a bit tense, but I think she'll be okay once we get underway."

"Still going to put her on my watch, Skipper?"

I thought about it. "Yes, I think you two will hit it off."

"Captain!" Mr. Hill's voice echoed onto the mess deck. There was a note of urgency in it.

"Maybe you'd like to come meet her, Ms. Thomas?"

She arched an eyebrow but started to get up from the table while I headed for the lock.

I found a furious Ms. Arellone standing on the scales with her two duffels and Mr. Hill looking flummoxed. "Yes, Mr. Hill? Is there a problem?"

"She's over mass, Skipper." He paused for a heartbeat. "She's also armed. I saw her slip a knife into her boot."

Ms. Thomas and Mr. Wyatt came up behind me as I turned to Ms. Arellone. "That didn't take long, Ms. Arellone. I assume it was in your duffelbag?"

She had the grace to look abashed. "Yes, Captain."

"How much over is she, Mr. Hill?"

"Double, Captain. Not quite. Eighteen kilos."

"So she'd be good if she were full share, Mr. Hill?"

"Yes, sar."

"Thank you, Mr. Hill." I turned to Ms. Thomas. "Ms. Thomas, I'd like you to meet your new watch stander. Spacer Apprentice Stacie Arellone. Ms. Arellone? This is our first mate, Ms. Gwen Thomas. You'll be joining first section as soon as we get you aboard."

Ms. Thomas's lips twisted up at the corner in a bit of a smile. "Nice to meet you, Ms. Arellone."

Ms. Arellone appeared a bit off balance but nodded back. "Ms. Thomas."

"Ms. Thomas, why don't you take Ms. Arellone over there out of the way of the lock and help her sort out the essentials into one of the duffelbags and the extras into the other?" I looked at Mr. Wyatt and Mr. Hill. "Gentlemen? Why don't we get a cup of coffee and let the ladies have a little privacy while they adjust the luggage?"

Mr. Hill started to say something.

"I think Ms. Thomas can keep an eye on the lock for a few ticks, Mr. Hill."

"But she's armed, Captain."

"Who? Ms. Thomas? Surely not."

"No, sar, Arellone." He seemed a bit exasperated.

"Oh, yes. Thank you. Ms. Arellone–" and I placed special emphasis on the word miz "– is most assuredly armed and we are all alerted to that fact. I'm more than confident that Ms. Thomas is in no danger."

I looked at Ms. Thomas who smiled happily and shrugged. "No worries on my part, Captain."

I turned back to Mr. Hill. "See, Mr. Hill? No worries. Now, if you please?" I held a hand out pointing down the passage. "I need a cuppa and these ladies need a little room to work without being second guessed at each turn. Shall we?"

Mr. Wyatt led the way and I could hear Mr. Hill following me, but I didn't look back.

We took turns at the coffee pots and then arrayed ourselves around the mess deck. Mr. Wyatt resumed his seat at the table, while Mr. Hill and I leaned against the counters.

Mr. Wyatt looked amused. "What cat have you dragged home now, Skipper?"

I shrugged and sipped. "She was next on the wait list, Mr. Wyatt."

"She was in detention, Captain."

I wrinkled my nose dismissively. "A detail. Mr. Hill would have been in detention more than once if he hadn't had a ship to escape to." I arched an eyebrow in his direction. "True, Mr. Hill?"

He glanced at me before lowering his eyes to the mug in his hands. After a heartbeat he nodded. "Probably so, Skipper."

"So, now, she's one of us." I shrugged. "We get underway in a few stans and we'll see what happens when we get to Breakall. Six weeks in the can should let us know if we're going to be able to get along."

Mr. Wyatt looked surprised. "You'd put her ashore again, Captain?"

I made a show of considering it. "I'll put anybody ashore if I think they're a threat to the ship, Mr. Wyatt." I sipped to let that sink in. "But she's no danger to the ship."

I felt Mr. Hill stiffen. "You seem pretty certain, Captain."

"I am, Mr. Hill." I turned to look at him. "How long have you known her, Mr. Hill?"

He seemed startled and looked up at me, but then shrugged. "Couple stanyers, Skipper. Most of the tractor crews know each other. Same fleet, same runs, same ships. We cross paths more often than some."

"You have any personal issues? Does Mr. Schubert?"

He thought about it for a couple heartbeats before shaking his head. "No, Skipper. I don't and I don't think Chooch does." He sipped and I could tell he was still thinking. "She's got a reputation on the docks. Most people give her a wide berth. She's bounced around a lot." He glanced up at me before lowering his eyes again.

"Go on, Mr. Hill."

He took a short breath before replying. "The word is she's a bit quick with the knife. You don't want to get too close."

"Ah, I see." I took a quick swallow from the top of my mug. "That's why you're concerned about Ms. Thomas?"

He nodded but didn't speak.

"You ever own a cat, Mr. Hill?"

"A cat?" He shook his head. "No, sar."

"Me, either, Mr. Hill, but I have it on good authority that cats have claws. They tend to use them when they feel threatened." I turned my head in his direction just slightly. "Sometimes people don't heed the warnings and they get clawed."

He looked up with a frown. "What if there's no warning, Skipper?"

I smiled. "Well, that's a good point. And a good reason to give a cat a wide berth." I arched an eyebrow.

The point struck home and he nodded again.

I heard Ms. Thomas call from the lock. "Skipper? I think we're ready now."

I downed the tail of my coffee and slotted the dirty cup. Mr. Hill was ahead of me, taking his with him back to his watch.

Mr. Wyatt caught my eye. "You sure about this stray cat, Skipper?" He had a gentle smile on his face.

I stopped and thought for a heartbeat. "No, Avery. I'm not." I stopped to really think about it for another heartbeat and decided to let him in on the secret. "Mr. Maloney used her as a threat to get me to torpedo Mr. Ricks' chances. That didn't sit well with me."

He looked concerned. "So you're gonna bring her aboard to spite him, Skipper?"

I shook my head a little. "Yeah, I know it looks that way, but there's more here than meets the eye." I grinned and shrugged. "I don't know what. In a lot of ways we're all stray cats aboard this ship."

He gave a small laugh and raised his mug in salute. "Can't argue that, Skipper."

I gave him a little nod and headed out to the lock where Ms. Arellone stood on the scale with one duffelbag. Ms. Thomas stood beside her with the second. "Is she under the limit, Mr. Hill?"

He squinted at the screen. "By about 10 grams, Skipper."

I caught Ms. Thomas's eye and she nodded back.

"Okay, then, book her aboard, Mr. Hill." I turned to Ms. Arellone. "Are you still armed, Ms. Arellone?"

She looked at me somewhat sullenly. "No, Captain."

"Where are your weapons?"

Ms. Thomas held up the second duffel. "In here, Captain."

"Mr. Hill? Would you weigh in that second bag please?"

They did the weigh in and when the numbers were up, turned to me.

"Book it to Agamemnon, if you please, Mr. Hill."

He looked surprised, but Ms. Thomas didn't.

I turned to Ms. Arellone. "We'll store that in the embargo locker until such time as you re-earn your full share rating. You can have it back then."

She nodded warily. "Thank you, Captain." She wanted to ask something else.

"Yes? I hear a 'but' there, Ms. Arellone?"

"What about my blades?"

"Oh, yes! Thank you for reminding me." I turned to Ms. Thomas. "Would you get her weapons out of there, Ms. Thomas?"

She looked at me curiously. "Aye, aye, Captain."

She unzipped the bag and pulled out a pair of blades bound together with a spare belt.

"Ms. Arellone? Are those all the weapons in that bag?"

She started to say yes, but looked at me. "No, Captain."

"Would you help Ms. Thomas find them all, please?"

"Aye, aye, Captain." She didn't look pleased but she crossed to where Gwen had the bag open and pulled out a heavy belt with an ornate buckle. She held it up. "That's all that's in that bag, sar."

I pointed to the watch stander console. "If you'd put them on the desk, please?"

She did so and Ms. Thomas zipped up the bag in front of her.

"Now, would you get the weapons you've managed to put into this bag on the desk as well, Ms. Arellone?" I nudged the duffel that she'd been holding while at the scales.

Ms. Thomas shot me a look and Mr. Hill looked a bit smug. Ms. Arellone scowled but knelt beside the bag and pulled out a spare boot. She reached inside and retrieved a small sheathed blade.

I nodded to the desk and she placed it in the pile.

"Any more, Ms. Arellone?"

"No, Captain. That's all I managed to pack."

I nodded and indicated that she should zip up the duffel. We waited while she complied and stood.

Ms. Thomas was hiding a small smile behind her hand and Mr. Hill was looking at the pile of cutlery with some amount of awe.

"Now, if you'd put all your hold out weapons on the table as well, please, Ms. Arellone?"

She turned to me, surprise writ large in her eyes. "I don't–" she started to say, but clamped her jaw shut before she could finish the statement when I arched a brow. She sighed and pulled a small blade from her boot and slipped another from the back of her collar.

Ms. Thomas looked amused. Mr. Hill looked appalled.

"Is that all, Ms. Arellone?"

She scowled but she nodded. "Yes, Captain. That's all of my blades."

"Is that all of your weapons, Ms. Arellone?"

She sighed and pulled a slim pen shaped cylinder from the pocket of her pants, placing it on the desk. She patted her pockets and then looked at me. "That's all." She seemed smaller somehow.

I crossed to the desk and looked the pile over. Before reaching for anything I looked to her. "May I examine them, Ms. Arellone?"

She shrugged sullenly. "It's your ship, Captain."

I took that as permission and picked up the pen shaped object. It appeared to be a pen but made of solid metal. It massed more than it looked like it should have. I held it up in front of her. "Can you explain this?"

Her eyes focused on it. "Tactical defense device. The point isn't sharp but it hurts if you press it into somebody. The flat top works too if you just want to convince people to back off."

"Thank you, Ms. Arellone."

I turned back to the pile on the desk. The boot and collar blades were small, lightweight ceramics, meant to be concealed. The larger blades were the obvious ones, the ones you'd wear to scare people off. I placed the pen back on the desk and picked up the heavier blades and the belt which had been stowed in the extra duffel.

I turned to Ms. Arellone and held them up. "These, we'll store in the weapons locker for now." I handed them to Ms. Thomas. "If you'd take care of that and give her a receipt for them, please, Ms. Thomas?"

"Aye, aye, Captain."

They all looked at me expectantly. I scanned from one face to another. "Is there something else?"

Mr. Hill nodded at the remaining weapons on the desk. "What would you like us to do with these, Captain?"

"Oh, of course. Sorry." I turned to Ms. Arellone. "Thank you, Ms. Arellone? If you'd collect your gear and get into a shipsuit? We'll get your orientation underway. We have freight to haul and I want to get underway this afternoon."

Mr. Hill started to object. "But, Captain–"

I looked at him. "Yes, Mr. Hill?"

To her credit, Ms. Arellone didn't grab for the weaponry although I thought I saw her hands twitch.

"You're going to let her carry weapons aboard?"

I shrugged. "They're her weapons, Mr. Hill. They came in under her mass allotment. What is your point?"

He seemed non-plussed. "We don't carry weapons aboard, sar! It just isn't done."

I shrugged. "If you'll notice, Mr. Hill, Ms. Arellone is currently unarmed. So she claims and so I believe. Those are hers. I see no reason to prevent her from having them. I don't question what you have in your duffel bag, do I?"

"No, Captain, but I don't have knives in my bag!"

I shrugged again. "Probably just as well, Mr. Hill. Knives are a specialist tool. All weapons are. Like tools, they can do great harm to the wielder if not used properly. If you ask nicely, I suspect Ms. Arellone will help you learn." I turned to her. "I'm particularly interested in that pen-device, myself. Perhaps you'd give me a demonstration when we're underway, Ms. Arellone?"

She stared at me in disbelief but her mouth worked on auto-pilot. "Of course, Captain."

I stood back out of the way while she collected the bundle of weapons from the desk and I turned to Ms. Thomas. "If you'd show Ms. Arellone to crew berthing and help her get settled, Ms. Thomas?"

"I've served on tractors before, Captain."

I smiled at her. "Of course, you were on the *Paris* and the *Hector* as well, weren't you?" I nodded at Ms. Thomas. "She was on the *Hector* too."

Ms. Thomas took the opening and led her into the ship and around the corner to crew berthing, leaving Mr. Hill and me alone at the lock.

He was staring at me incredulously.

I snagged the spare duffel from the deck and looped the strap over my shoulder. "Yes, Mr. Hill?"

"Skipper? I can't believe you let her carry weapons onto the ship."

"Why, Mr. Hill? Do you feel threatened by them? Do you think she'll attack you in your sleep?"

"She might, sar!"

"To what end, Mr. Hill? Where will she run to? How would she escape?"

"She's not rational, Captain." He was losing steam in the face of my unwillingness to panic.

I looked down the passageway toward the ship. "On the contrary, Mr. Hill. She's perhaps the most rational member of the crew, barring Chief Gerheart."

His eyes almost bugged out of his head. "How can you say that, Captain?"

I looked back at him. "Well, I've spent the last eight months in very close proximity to you all and I have to say, I think the chief may be the most rational. Just personal judgment and I'm not an expert on rationality. The fact that I don't include myself on the roster of rationality should tell you something, Mr. Hill." I grinned at him.

"But you don't know her!" He pointed in the direction of crew berthing.

I sighed. "That's true, Mr. Hill. I don't know her, but she's one of us now. We take care of our own here, in case you've missed that."

He looked abashed at that, but not quite done. "We know that, Skipper, but does she?"

I gave a half nod to cede the point. "Granted, Mr. Hill, but we don't convince her by just telling her. We have to show her." I let that sink in for a heart beat. "Show her some respect and give her a chance to show some back, eh?"

"What if she doesn't, Captain?"

I took a deep breath and let it out before speaking. "It's a long walk home, Mr. Hill."

Chapter Fifty-eight
Diurnia System: 2372-September-13

Lunch was an all hands affair. The lock was secured for departure at 1000 and we gathered for what was turning into a traditional pre-departure meeting over the lunch mess. I was interested to see where Ms. Arellone would pick to sit. We were mostly all present when Mr. Wyatt opened the lunch mess and I led the parade through the serving line. Ms. Arellone had emerged from crew berthing in a clean shipsuit with her hair still slicked back from the showers. She hadn't been aboard a ship in a long time and the chestnut hair was growing out in an artless cap. She looked more like a spacer and less like a dockrat, even so.

I took my seat and was followed rapidly by Ms. Thomas, Mr. Pall, and the chief. Mr. Hill and Mr. Schubert took seats on my side of the table leaving Ms. Arellone standing with a tray full of food and measuring the situation with her eyes. I paid close attention to stirring my coffee and waited to see where she'd go. She surprised me by sitting halfway between the chief and the end of the table. I wasn't sure how to read that one. I would have bet on her taking the end of the bench opposite Mr. Hill.

With serving done, Mr. Wyatt took up a tray and joined us and I took the ceremonial first bite and when the initial round of savory was completed, started the pre-flight discussion by raising my coffee mug in salute to Ms. Arellone. "I'd like to formally welcome our newest crew member, Ms. Stacie Arellone."

The others at the table raised a glass or cup or mug, as appropriate, and echoed various words of welcome. They had no more idea than I did what to say. We were making it up as we went.

She looked a little flustered and colored a bit at all the attention but managed to smile slightly and nod back to the room at large.

I let her off the hook by proceeding to more mundane matters pertaining to our departure. "How're the girls doing, Chief?"

"They're warmed up and ready to go, Skipper." Her sapphire smile flashed from across the table.

"Any issues?"

"No, Skipper. Tanks are full and spares are loaded. Scrubber two has been refitted and scrubber one should be able to hold us almost to jump."

"Mr. Wyatt? Stores are adequate?"

"Yes, Skipper. Full up and ready to go. I've got some new recipes to try this run."

"The cans are locked down?"

"Since yesterday afternoon, Skipper."

"Mr. Pall? What news from astrogation? Any pirates?"

Mr. Pall surprised me then. I hadn't seen him much since getting underway from Dree. "Course is laid in, Captain. We've a good planetary alignment for the exit. Three weeks to jump, more or less."

I looked at him. He seemed subdued. He felt me looking at him and turned his head slightly to see. He shrugged into himself a bit and I didn't press.

Ms. Thomas noticed the exchange and cocked her head slightly when I turned to her. "Any concerns about the ship, Ms. Thomas?"

"None, Captain. We're ready to sail as soon as they can pull us out. Tug should be on station at 1430."

"Thank you, all, and I think we're ready to go."

Lunch devolved into quiet conversations and general horseplay. Mr. Schubert and Mr. Hill had their heads together over co-op business and soon drew Ms. Arellone into the conversation by explaining the co-op to her. The chief and Ms. Thomas did some talking around Mr. Wyatt and I ate quietly watching the lot of them. Mr. Pall did not join in the general joviality. In fact the longer we sat there, the more withdrawn he seemed.

After dessert he excused himself. "I'd like to check on the plot again. See you on the bridge."

All three of the officers across the table looked at me expectantly.

"We'll need box lunches for dinner, Mr. Wyatt. Do you have enough help?"

He looked around the table and nodded. "Yes, I think we can handle it, Skipper."

I grinned, stood, and bussed my tray. "In that case, I need to see a man about an eye patch. Ms. Thomas would you plan to call navigation stations at 1400?"

"Stations at 1400, aye, Skipper."

I followed in Mr. Pall's wake and got to the bridge as he was settling into his seat at the astrogation station. "All updates in place, Mr. Pall?"

"Yes, Skipper. Been up to date for a couple of days now. Nothing new has been posted since then."

I took a seat at the duty deck officer station and fired up the display. I spoke to him without peeking around the console. "So, how are you doing, Mr. Pall?"

"Fine, Captain."

I did lean out to look around the console at him then. "Really, Mr. Pall?"

He turned his head to look at me looking at him. He sighed. "No, Captain."

"Wanna talk about it?"

He glanced at the ladder and then back at me.

"We can go to the cabin if you'd prefer?"

He considered it. That worried me. He finally shook his head and shrugged. "It's okay."

I stood up from the watch stander's chair and crossed to sit across from him at the spare terminal there. "What's up, William?"

He closed his eyes and turned his head away from me a bit. "I can't stop thinking about the attack, sar."

I shrugged. "I'm not surprised, Mr. Pall. It was horrendous."

He sighed. "No, Captain. You don't understand. I don't remember a thing."

I let him see me thinking about that for a couple of heartbeats before I answered. "Is that a bad thing, William?"

"I have no idea what they did to me, Captain." He looked small and weak and scared.

"Well, we know they beat you up, smashed your tablet, rolled you down a ladder. Isn't that enough?" I said it gently.

He laughed a sad little laugh. "Oh, what we know is bad enough." He turned away and put his hands on his keyboard, facing his console as if he were looking at it. "What else did they do?"

"What are you afraid they did, William?"

He didn't answer for a long time. "Rape, Captain." He said it very softly.

"You're afraid they raped you, William?"

He shrugged without looking at me. "I don't know, Captain. I think I'd feel better knowing." He took a quavery breath and let it out. "Not knowing if I've been violated or not. I –"

"William?" I interrupted him and he turned to me. "William, whether you were raped or not, you were violated. Rape's never about sex. It's always about power. Somebody didn't like you for some reason. I doubt that we'll ever know why. They took your power and violated your will. You know that, already."

He looked like I'd hit him and I tried to smile encouragingly at him.

"Your body has mostly healed, but it'll be a while for the rest of it. Somehow, you've got to find a way to deal with it. It's not right. It's not fair. It's just what is."

He turned away to look at his computer and I stood and walked carefully off the bridge without looking back at him.

At the top of the ladder I stopped, but I didn't turn back. "You've got people who care about you here, Mr. Pall. Any time you need to talk, you can talk to any of us."

I headed down over the ladder and heard a muffled, "Thank you, Captain."

I found Chief Gerheart waiting outside the cabin. She pointed upwards with her chin. "Everything okay, Skipper?" The concern was evident in her face.

I sighed. "Pirates aren't so funny after you've been raped and pillaged, Chief."

She hung her head forward on her neck and uttered a most unladylike single word. She stood there for a moment and blew out her breath before looking up again. "Anything we can do?"

I shrugged. "You probably know better than I do."

She shot me a look.

"I think time and support are all we can offer. The rest has to come from him," I said.

Her look turned inward and a bit dark. After a couple of heartbeats she looked back at me. "Yeah." She sighed and headed down the ladder while I went to the cabin to make sure all the paperwork was filed for departure.

Ms. Thomas called the crew to navigation stations promptly at 1400 and for once I did the proper thing and let the crew assemble on the bridge before I joined them. The tug tied on promptly at 1430 and we cleared the orbital without mishap.

I admit I had a bad moment only after we pulled out, thinking of the several cubic meters of hot water sloshing in the workout room. It was all I could do to not rush down and see what damage had been caused. I mustered my self-control, reasoning that it was already too late and the pull out had been so gentle it hadn't disturbed the coffee in my mug.

We began the long push out to the safety limit by 1500 and Mr. Wyatt brought up water and coffee around 1600.

"How're things below, Mr. Wyatt?"

"Just fine, Captain. We're getting along swimmingly."

I looked at him sharply, remembering my earlier worries about the hot tub.

He seemed confused by the sudden attention. "No, really. It's going well, Skipper."

I smiled. "Sorry, Mr. Wyatt. I was hoping we hadn't spilled the hot tub."

He laughed. "Not to worry, Captain. We locked the lid down right before lunch mess. The chief showed me how and we double checked each other to make sure it was locked."

"Thank you, Mr. Wyatt. I'm reassured."

He grinned and headed back down the ladder.

Ms. Thomas was looking at me strangely. "Did you really think we'd sloshed the hot tub, Skipper?"

I had to laugh. "I think I was more concerned that it hadn't occurred to me until after it was too late, Ms. Thomas."

She nodded sympathetically. "That infallibility of captains is a terrible burden, isn't it, Skipper?"

"It seems to be, Ms. Thomas. Apparently it's a condition which I have not yet inherited with my mantle of command."

She smirked. "Don't sell yourself short, Captain."

I started to follow up with that when Mr. Pall reported. "The tug needs to drop us a bit early, Skipper. He's got an emergency call back."

"Problems at the orbital, Mr. Pall?"

"Sister tug has a thruster problem. They need to go help out." He consulted his screen. "He's giving us a bit of extra boost before he cuts us loose."

"Thank him for me, Mr. Pall."

"Done, Captain."

"Thank you, Mr. Pall."

We watched as the tug finished the boost and cast us off.

"What will that do to our course timings, Mr. Pall?"

"Running it now, Skipper. Looks like we'll be about half a stan later than we planned." He glanced at the chronometer. "We expected 1915 to the safety border. It'll be more like 1945."

"Ms. Thomas would you announce that to the ship, please?"

"Aye, aye, Captain."

She did and we settled down to doing a serious impersonation of an asteroid in flight.

At 1800, Mr. Wyatt and Ms. Arellone brought up the boxed lunches and some more coffee. She seemed to be at home on the bridge and was even smiling a little as she refreshed the coffee mugs for us while Mr. Wyatt distributed the boxes.

She headed down the ladder ahead of Mr. Wyatt and he looked

over his shoulder with a look that said, "So far, so good."

Ms. Thomas caught the look as well. "Well, our new addition seems to be adjusting."

Mr. Schubert gave a small snort.

"Comment, Mr. Schubert?"

He looked over at me with a shrug. "It's going to be interesting in berthing, Skipper."

"Why's that Mr. Schubert."

"We've been all guys for so long. She's not the only one who needs to adjust a bit, Skipper." He shrugged apologetically with a glance at Ms. Thomas. "No offense, Ms. Thomas."

"None taken, Mr. Schubert."

"It's a good and valid point, Mr. Schubert. Do you have any reservations?"

"I'm good, Captain. When I came aboard, I was the only rooster in the hen house as it were." He grimaced. "It wasn't as fun as you might think."

I chuckled sympathetically.

"I remember what that was like, Skipper." He looked over at me as if looking for permission to speak. I nodded encouragingly. "I've known Stacie for stanyers, off and on. She's okay. Arrogant piece of work, but she seems to know her stuff and she can handle herself on the dock."

"Mr. Hill seems to think she may murder you in your sleep."

He snorted. "He doesn't really, Skipper. He–" he started to say something and then realized where he was and thought better of it. "He's just adjusting."

Ms. Thomas coughed softly and I looked in her direction.

She shook her head slightly.

"Thank you for that insight, Mr. Schubert. Please keep me informed as the situation develops."

"Aye, aye, Captain."

We rode along almost in silence, finishing our boxed lunches, and admiring the stars. That was one of the things about getting underway, heading out while still fresh from the dock. The merry-go-round hadn't started to spin and there were fresh possibilities ahead in the Deep Dark. For the most part we were rested, and mostly healthy, if a little tattered in places. The grind of the mundane hadn't set in and we still found beauty outside the armor glass.

Soon enough we crossed the safety border and the chief fired up the sail and keel generators.

"Ship has way, Captain!" Ms. Thomas gave the report.

"Thank you, Ms. Thomas. Secure from navigation stations, and set normal watch." I looked at the chrono on the bulkhead. "First section has the duty."

"Aye, aye, Captain. Securing from navigation stations. First section has the watch."

It took another tick but Ms. Arellone came up over the ladder and crossed to the helm. She went through the change over protocols and took Mr. Schubert's seat while Ms. Thomas finished assuming the officer of the deck logs.

I led Mr. Pall and Mr. Schubert off the bridge, they went in separate directions to prepare to take the midwatch in just a few stans. I headed for the cabin.

A quick refresh in the head and I headed down to check out the hot tub. I couldn't shake the feeling that something was wrong and felt much better seeing that the safety lid was, in fact, latched down. While I was standing there, the chief came padding in wearing a terry cloth robe. She flashed one of her sapphire-studded smiles in my direction.

"Worried, Captain?"

I laughed. "Yes, I was. Thanks for looking out for this."

She laughed in return. "Trust me, Skipper. It was purely selfish." She released the latches on the cover and swung it up out of the way. "I've been waiting for three days to try this baby out and I wanted it hot and full!"

She climbed the short steps up to the decking and swished one bare foot in the water tentatively before punching the button that started the jets. They added an almost subsonic thrum to the already vibrating ship, but weren't really audible in themselves over the sound of the water itself.

She grinned at me, slipped the terry cloth off and let it pool on the deck beside the opening. She was wearing a modest one piece bathing suit in navy blue, but I only had a moment to admire it before she stepped quickly down into the tub, and submerged completely before coming back up, face first and letting the water stream back off her face. She lay back against one of the head rests and settled down for a soak. "Ahhhh." Her sigh of contentment carried clearly to me and stabbed at something I didn't dare feel.

I found myself back in the cabin without really remembering how I got there. The door closed behind me with a soft click and I leaned back against it. My heart pounded in my chest and air rasped in and out of my throat. I crossed to my desk and clicked on the light. I couldn't seem to think. I was having trouble breathing. I lowered myself into the chair and laid my forehead against the cool laminate of the desktop until I could get my breath back.

Slowly I pushed up and leaned back in my chair, letting my eyes rake across the room. My survey took me back around to look out the wide port and once more I could see the stars sparkling across the velvet night of the Deep Dark. The faint reflection of the room showed in the armor glass. I stood and crossed to stand closer, the shadow from my body creating a window in the reflection, a hole in the room where an empty man stood.

The chrono clicked over to 2320 and I became aware of the ship around me again. The spasm had passed and I was able to breathe almost normally. The familiar sounds of the ship wrapped me like a comfortable blanket. I sighed one last time and headed for my bunk.

The merry-go-round had started to spin once more. I needed to be back on my horse in the morning.

Nathan Lowell

The Golden Age of the Solar Clipper

Quarter Share

Half Share

Full Share

Double Share

Captains Share

Owners Share

South Coast

Tanyth Fairport Adventures

Ravenwood

Zypherias Call

The Hermit Of Lammas Wood

Awards

2011 Parsec Award Winner for Best Speculative Fiction
(Long Form) for *Owners Share*

2010 Parsec Award Winner for Best Speculative Fiction
(Long Form) for *Captains Share*

2009 Podiobooks Founders Choice Award for Captains Share

2009 Parsec Award Finalist for Best Speculative Fiction
(Long Form) for *Double Share*

2008 Podiobooks Founders Choice Award for *Double Share*

2008 Parsec Award Finalist for Best Speculative Fiction
(Long Form) for *Full Share*

2008 Parsec Award Finalist for Best Speculative Fiction
(Long Form) for *South Coast*

Nathan Lowell

Contact

Website: nathanlowell.com
Twitter: twitter.com/nlowell
Email: nathan.lowell@gmail.com

About The Author

Nathan Lowell first entered the literary world by podcasting his novels. The Golden Age of the Solar Clipper grew from his life-long fascination with space opera and his own experiences shipboard in the United States Coast Guard. Unlike most works which focus on a larger-than-life hero, Nathan centers on the people behind the scenes—ordinary men and women trying to make a living in the depths of interstellar space. In his novels, there are no bug-eyed monsters, or galactic space battles, instead he paints a richly vivid and realistic world where the hero uses hard work and his own innate talents to improve his station and the lives of those of his community.

Dr. Nathan Lowell holds a Ph.D. in Educational Technology with specializations in Distance Education and Instructional Design. He also holds an M.A. in Educational Technology and a BS in Business Administration. He grew up on the south coast of Maine and is strongly rooted in the maritime heritage of the sea-farer. He served in the USCG from 1970 to 1975, seeing duty aboard a cutter on hurricane patrol in the North Atlantic and at a communications station in Kodiak, Alaska. He currently lives on the plains east of the Rocky Mountains with his wife and two daughters.